AUGURY

AUGURY

S. E. Lister

First published in Great Britain in 2020

Old Street Publishing Ltd
Notaries House, Exeter EX1 1AJ

www.oldstreetpublishing.co.uk

ISBN 978-1-910400-94-4

10 9 8 7 6 5 4 3 2 1

A CIP catalogue record for this title is available from the British Library.

Printed and bound by PBTisk

*To Charissa B
and Jenny M
my heart and lungs.*

DRAMATIS PERSONAE

ADELFA - small daughter of Antonus and Junia

AEMILIA - acolyte; adopted daughter of The Augur

ANTONIA - adolescent daughter of Antonus and Junia

ANTONUS - brother of Emperor *Laonatus*, husband of Junia, father of Adelfa, Eryx and Antonia

ATHRAXUS - High Priest of the Dark Temple, father of Myloxenes

AUGUR, THE - prophetess at the Augur's Temple

CALIX - husband of Mersia, son-in-law of Lennes

CASSANDANE - wife of Emperor Laonatus

ERYX - small son of Antonus and Junia

FELIX - slave of Antonus and Junia

HESTIA - entertainer to the Emperor

JUNIA - wife of Antonus

LAEYLA - mother of Myloxenes

LAONATUS - the Emperor, brother of Antonus

LENNES - Court Steward

MANDANE - wife of Emperor Laonatus

MERSIA - daughter of Lennes, sister of Rufus, wife of Calix

MYLOXENES ('Mylo') - son of Athraxus and Laeyla, friend of Rufus

RUFUS - son of Lennes, brother of Mersia, friend of Myloxenes

SABA - acolyte; adopted daughter of The Augur

Religion comes from our pity for humans
They are too weak to live without divine protection.
Too weak to listen to the screeching noise of the turning of infernal
wheels.
Who among us would accept a universe in which there was not one voice
Of compassion, pity, understanding?
To be human is to be completely alien amid the galaxies.
Which is sufficient reason for erecting, together with others, the temples
of an unimaginable mercy.

Czeslaw Milosz

S ee what she sees, for the gods are close enough to breathe on us. Look there, in the easternmost corner. Three black birds, crossing the horizon from left to right.

The Augur lifts her gaze, her eyes level beneath the hood of her cloak. One palm raised, the other clasping her curved staff. The skies divided by her hand. A deep hush lies over the grove, near the top of the mountain, an afternoon's walk up from the city. The soles of her bare feet are thick. She has walked on them this way, so often up this very path, all of her six decades.

Her hand quarters the sky, anterior, posterior, left, right. The birds, they are forming against the dusk like lines of script upon a page. Three have become a rippling, undulating shoal. The Augur's face contracts. She is reading their dance.

"Starlings," says the woman, aloud. "What do you have for me?"

You might think her old, until you saw her close. She has lived many years, more perhaps than any other in that city below, but these years have not mastered her. Her features carved as though from the twisting roots of an olive tree, her skin paved with thick cracks like a crudely-made mosaic. She is not old, but ageless. Her back is barely bent, her arms and legs bound all around with muscles. She could lift a pitcher filled to its brim and not stumble. She might have been one of the moss-covered boulders from the mountainside, uncurled from its place, granted movement and life.

Watch with her, if there is any love of divine things in you. She is waiting to see whether there are any signs from the earth. Any alterations in the weather. A slight wind bends the cedars. Beyond the web of branches, far away in the clear air, the sea dances and glitters. There is a scent or a shimmer in the grove beyond the detection of the senses. It is this to which she attends, eyes still fixed upon the birds. Her expression is unmoved, but each leaf in the grove is shivering now upon its branch. The flock is spiralling downward in the sky.

The Augur lowers her palm. She turns to look over her shoulder at the city below. It has fallen under the shadow of the coming night.

Under the deep glow of sunset the arches look half-sunk, like bones laid to rest. Wisps of smoke between the rooftops, the glow of courtyard fires, lantern-lights. The city is set between the mountain and the sea, the harbour and low slums sprawling along the shore to the south. Her own temple is perched high upon a pale outcrop of rock on the north side. Along the high walls of the emperor's palace, gilt statues seem to bend and bow as darkness passes across them. The river that winds around the main square and down past the palace into the sea is coloured crimson in the dying light.

The Augur stands very still in the grove on the mountainside, watching the birds pulse and wheel above the city. And then... *oh, my innards*. She bends as though a hand has reached into her abdomen and clasped hold of her liver, the source of her life. The mountain beneath her feet moves, inhales, exhales with a tremble. The Augur listens to its breath. The horizon is streaked with eerie green. The birds wrap themselves around the dusk.

In pain, she lowers her body, lays hands on the ground. *Have you waited for this sign, Prophetess? Hoped for it?* More than fifty years ago she came to that harbour, a tiny child with tar on her bare feet, dirty face, wrists bound in ropes, destined for slavery in the Temple of Blood. Her body browned with bruises like a peach from the bottom of the basket. A little girl looking up from the water to the heights of the city, sun blazing from behind the mountain that morning. The glory of the city in the morning light, in the

4

eyes of the small child. Red and golden drapes hung between the colonnades, white sails catching the wind all around, palms and green fern fronds and sea-lilies, perfume of ladies who wore their hair in tumbling coils, the bright spray of fountains. Butchers, costers, slavers, creak and crash of boats putting down anchor. Small girl with bound hands and bare feet, never seen anything like this city. Never smelled anything like the smell of this city, its thousand mingled perfumes, its sewers and steaming bathhouses and rotting rubbish-heaps. Its incense and its earth.

Fifty years lived here as an alien and stranger. The tide of those years retreated now. What is it to her, this city? The bright glory of that first morning never quite vanished from memory, but scratched away, flaked away to show the crumbling stone beneath. In those years she has been crushed beneath the weight of this marble. She has crawled in gutters and washed clean in courtyard pools. She has eaten the fruit of this city's flourishing. She has held this place in her arms and cradled it close like the child she never felt move in her own womb, she has disciplined it in anger and chided and patiently taught. She has fed it from her table. She has shed tears for its waywardness when it was strong and grown and gone from her grasp.

You were not born here, Prophetess. No inheritance owed you, for a long time now no bonds to hold you here, save those you have chosen. The Augur kneels in the dirt on the mountain and holds her side, where sharp darts of pain come and go like labour pangs. The open ribcage of the city spread before her, entrails ripe for the reading. Cut open the lungs and liver. These organs are black and bloody and malformed. There is no mistaking it. A rumble in the earth deep below her palms, and she waits in stillness.

Have you waited for this? Wanted this? Cherished for a lifetime your bitter hatred of this city, even while you nursed it at your breast?

Words find her lips. "You have known nothing, rulers and

5

priests, save for the life of this city. It birthed and milk-fed and fattened you. But your time is ending." She speaks softly into the night. Not without triumph, not without sadness. "This is what is read in the flight of the starling flock. The life of this city will fly away like a bird."

She stands, gathering her cloak about her. A lone figure on the mountainside against the darkening sky. The weakness of her body passed, she turns her back and strides out of the grove, up between the rocks. A jade-coloured dragonfly hovers, zipping to and fro in the air, coming to land on a dogbane branch. The cicadas have begun to sing.

*

A mouth gapes in the side of the mountain. A crack from which darkness bleeds. The Augur stops at the opening, the strange wind from within catching at her robes. She removes her hood and steps down into the earth. The mouth whispers. It spits sulphur and ash. The darkness sighs and settles like a creature woken after long sleep.

As the sun sinks behind the blue ridge of the far mountains along the coast, blazing for a moment before it vanishes from view, she finds her footing. She dips her hands into the bowl of spring-water at the entrance. From the bowl of ash, paints a grey line across her forehead.

There are no lights, save for the fading shaft of twilight from outside. But the gaping space seems possessed of an unworldly luminescence. Hot bursts of air hiss up from within the rock, and with them a white crackle like lightning, fingers of jumping energy which wreath the Augur's ankles and staff as she takes her seat in the three-legged throne. Steam rises from cracks open onto the sacred substance of the unseen realm.

The smell of the place is overpowering. The Augur's head begins to tilt and her hands are outstretched. She breathes deeply and loudly, in time with the shuddering breaths of the earth. Her eyes roll up and back into her skull. The holy glow seems once again to suffuse her skin. It snaps about her fingertips. By its light, old bones and jars and withered laurel wreaths shiver, suspended from the cavern ceiling.

Suddenly she is thrown forward in her chair. A violent shudder, a hideous crack of the neck. Her body hangs there, limp and still, and it is no longer hers. Threads of dark vapour rise to envelop her. There is silence.

Then a hard clear voice speaks in the blackness. "*This*," it says. "*This from the Unknown God*."

SAVAGE

I

They are up to their elbows in blood.

Every year, at the summer's height, the same rites. Saba and Aemilia, one at each of the bull's horns as it brays and screams and thrashes out the last of its life on the temple steps. Saba has the knife, the novice-attendants have the ropes. Her last deep cut made in its throat, the young priestess stands back, wipes the knife with three strong strokes on a wet cloth. Hot breath steams from the beast's nose. Every burst of it a shock at the sudden pain dulling its world. Saba gestures to Aemilia to let go, and the novices pull the ropes taut, waiting for the weight of the bull to fall. Its pouring throat open wide the creature buckles and sways. On the white steps its blood flows down, a river into the city. The solstice sun sags with heat.

For a moment it looks as though the bull will go backwards, sinking onto its haunches like a tired dog. But just as the novices have adjusted the ropes, a final surge of life through its spine throws it sideways. The girls leap clear just in time, and the beast's weight shudders stone below, carrying it in a slide towards the steps. Saba imagines the body somersaulting head over hooves down fifty stone steps, legs flailing, to land in a gory heap in the street below. At the thought she yelps in laughter.

"*Hold!*" she cries to the novice-attendants and Aemilia, snatching at the nearest rope and digging in her heels to add her own strength. "Brace yourselves!"

The weight of them is just enough to arrest the monstrous body in its slide. The bull rests at last with its head and forelegs sprawled backwards down the top three steps, neck broken, long tongue gaping at the sky. Dark liquid lies splashed in patterned pools all around. Light-footed, Saba hops atop the corpse and balances there for a moment above the sunlit city, a haze of steam golden over the bath-house, the bright barrels of the spice-sellers in the square, the glitter of the sea beyond. She breathes in the hundred heady smells of the city. She bends and cuts a long deep slit in the bull's belly. Plunges an unhesitating hand through its innards, fingers searching expertly, gut, stomachs, bladder – and there. The liver, the source of its life. Saba wraps it in a cloth, still steaming, and sets it aside for the Augur.

Now: the peeling away of the hide. The attendants help saw off the legs, slice the still-heaving muscle from the rump, the shoulders, the neck. Meat cut and parcelled and carried away in preparation for the feast. Saba and Aemilia light fires all along the temple walls, and soon fat is dripping under every grate. Bones from the thighs and tail blacken and crumble. Smoke rises in the heat of the midsummer day from these burnt offerings to please the gods.

After the wild braying of the bull and the bustle of bodies all around the carcass, peace once more. Saba sprinkles oil at the place where the beast gave up its life. The low bell swings at the heart of the temple. With Aemilia she makes her way through the hall to the place where a crack in the rock of the mountain behind leads to a gorge, a waterfall plunging into a pool beneath. The rocks all around are soft with green moss. The water flows underground from here, emerging from a culvert far below in the city. The two young priestesses take off their sandals and balance across the slippery stones, crouching in the middle of the stream and bending low to wash their arms in its cool flow. Elbows to fingertips, until their skin is clean again.

10

At the front of the temple, the novices scrub the steps until this year's blood is part of the old stain, the deep shadow on the stone.

*

"Saba," says Aemilia, "what time was it when she left?"

"Before midday, I think."

"Why doesn't she leave earlier and come back before dark?"

"Don't you know," says Saba, "that the gods bend closer to the world at twilight? They like the smell of honeysuckle. And to peer in through chamber windows when mortals are undressing for bed."

"*Saba.*"

"It's true. That's why the Prophetess must go to the mountain at dusk."

"I don't remember our mother ever teaching us that."

They are climbing the winding stairs to their room above the walled part of the temple, eating raisin-cakes pilfered from the temple supply. The afternoon gone in bundling herbs for the altar and washing pots and boiling meat for the next day's feast. Their arms are aching. "The gods are at work in the divine realm in the morning and the afternoon," says Saba. "Just like us. They sleep in the midday heat. They come close to us in the cool part of the day, in the evening. You think they aren't curious about our lives? That they don't have desires, like us?"

"I never know when to believe you."

Saba grins, digs at her sister's waist with her elbow. "If you like we can stay awake tonight, 'Milia, and watch for them out of the window. Here, give me the rest of that cake! We'll save it for an offering."

"Now I know that you're teasing."

In their chamber they change out of their saffron robes, sit on their pallets, weary, clean. The little room is neatly swept and bare save for the two straw mats and a lamp beside the window. Moonlight falls upon the stone floor.

Aemilia, still worrying at the same thought, asks, "But you'll hear her when she gets back, won't you?"

"I always do."

"Even if you're asleep."

"She takes a torch from the gates to see her to her chamber." Saba kneads her mat beneath her knuckles and lies back. "The light in the courtyard wakes me." She turns onto her side to look at Aemilia, who is braiding her long wet hair. Sister, she thinks, dear sister, these solstice days have happened the same way every year since we came to the Augur's temple. Yet every year you find reason to be anxious.

They make strange sisters, the two of them. Aemilia's skin is white as milk, where Saba is darker than the wood of the walnut tree. Aemilia is plump and yellow-haired: Saba is sharpness and angles, her head shaved close to the scalp. They have shared this chamber since the day they first came to this city, long ago.

"Will you wake me too? When she comes back? Otherwise I'll have bad dreams."

"I'll wake you, 'Milia."

"Then I'll sleep again until morning."

Aemilia sits down on her pallet, but then immediately stands again, shuffling from the room to check the novices' chambers for a second time. Saba, fingers poised to snuff out the wick of the oil lamp, draws back with a smile. When Aemilia comes back in again, reassured, she climbs onto her mat and nods to Saba.

"Blessed until you rise, sister."

"Blessed until you rise."

In no time, Aemilia's breaths have grown long and heavy. Saba closes her eyes, but something holds her to wakefulness. *These solstice days have happened in the same way since we came to the temple, since we were frightened children led up those steps holding the hands of the Prophetess.* But seasons change. Children grow up, prophets grow old.

Saba started her bleed three years ago: she is not a child any more. The younger priestesses do what she tells them, and her mother the Augur will sometimes ask her advice on temple matters. Saba has noticed recently that when she is at the marketplace some people now dip their gaze or touch their foreheads at her approach, as they might for the Augur herself.

When they visit the temple, they want more than a simple blessing. They bring the concerns of their lives to her — and frequently, at the moment, the stories they've heard in the city. *Priestess, a baby was born in a house near the fish-market without eyes or a mouth, what does this mean? My neighbour told me a man jumped from the cliff into the sea with his wife and child in a sack, did the gods make him do that?*

Some of them tell her that the city has not always been this way, that it's one of those times which come around, trees offering poor fruit and crops wilting in the fields. But Saba isn't sure she believes them. It's the nature of people, so it seems to her, to think things are always getting worse. She assures them they've only ordinary suffering to fear, and they leave her presence consoled.

These first marks of authority sit well with Saba, who has long had an assuredness beyond her years. She has lived most of her life in the city, though she was not born here. Her people are somewhere far away in a country she is stubbornly certain she remembers. She was raised by the Augur, a parent of unpredictable wildness and wisdom, whose affections are prickly as thorns.

She sits up and rests her arms on the sill beside her sleeping-place. Breathes in the warm night air through the window. From here, the rooftops of the city, the courtyard fires, the street scraps and stray dogs and swine snuffling in the shadows. The calm sea and blazing stars. Smoke rises still from the temple pyres, and Saba breathes it in, prayers of the city ascending heavenward in ashes and in dust.

The invisible things in the world are all in balance. The age-old agreement with the powers at work behind the world is kept. Hold back calamity, prays the city, for we would not long survive it. Hold back the floods which overwhelm and the hail which falls upon our crops, hold back armies which sweep swift and deadly over land and waves toward us. Come in through our open doors, you gods, and chase the shadow from our hearths. Devour those most awful infections of our bodies, the rot of limbs and stomachs and old unhealed wounds; reach down your hands and spare us barren wives, unchaste daughters, weak sons. Spare us restless nights and empty bellies. Spare us from going unremembered to the ground.

So sleeps the city between the mountain and the sea. Saba leans over, and pinches out the lamp.

*

She wakes in darkness, and knows at once that the Augur has not yet returned from the mountain. She lies on her back, senses suddenly sharp.

And then the earth begins to move.

II

His leg is troubling him again.

He does not wake Junia, but slips out of bed and limps through the outer room into the courtyard. It is a clear night. The warm air is full of honeysuckle pollen. Antonus sits on a bench beside the rainwater-pool, and looks up at the stars.

There is the hare, the drowned man, the drawn sword. The weeping widow. He kneads the heels of his hands into his aching flesh. *Gods, send me relief, or I will be in a bad temper by morning.* The pain in its many degrees and qualities is companion to him, an enemy so constant that it is almost a friend. When it abates, sometimes for weeks or months at a time, he feels lost.

Once as a younger man, still wracked with bitter anger, he had visited the healing-houses in a city across the mountains. He had bathed in the warm water from their sacred springs, been prayed over by their priests and killed an unblemished calf. He had slept three nights in a secluded sanctuary, surrounded by the votive offerings of those who came before. *Ambyses, healed of a malignant ulceration. Ichemedes, healed of deafness. Coesa, healed in her barren womb after a vision of the mother-goddess.*

He had limped away on the fourth day still leaning on his staff. But he had dreamed. Which gods or god he had seen, or what form they had taken in these dreams, he cannot say. What they had declared over him, what covenant they had made with him, seems always just beyond his recollection. Some faint impression of the deep sadness and delight he had felt dwells with him still, all these years later. For a covenant has been made, he is sure of this: and the pain is part of it, and the blessing, too.

Antonus is in his fortieth year, his close-cut brown beard liberally patched with grey. He has led a life coloured by peculiar blessings, and he knows this now, after the passing of his long bitterness. He is inclined to think that generosity from the heavens is best not questioned, or boasted of, or even acknowledged aloud. It is better looked at sideways. Happiness is a bird of rare beauty which flies to the house unbidden, which nests in dusty corners above the eaves. Which might take wing again just as soon, if you are too curious, if you are so crude as to take it in your hands and pluck out its feathers.

Antonus yawns widely. His daughter Adelfa's white cat, sat on the opposite sill, does likewise. "Tomorrow," he tells the cat, "I have to climb the temple steps. A hundred stone steps, and then sit beside my brother for a whole evening." The animal curls its tattered tail and narrows its eyes. "You wouldn't care to go in my place, would you?"

As though in attendance to a call that Antonus cannot hear, the cat suddenly turns its head, frozen to the spot. Then it leaps from the sill, claws scrabbling, and bolts across the courtyard into the undergrowth. Antonus laughs. "Come back! I was joking." Overhead, he spies a flock of birds flying fast from the mountain towards the sea. A breeze blows through the honeysuckle and troubles the surface of the pool.

Antonus turns to look in the direction from which the birds have come, the jagged mountain towering high above the city. Before he quite knows what is happening he finds that he has dropped his walking stick, both hands gripping the edge of the bench, water lurching over the sides of the pool and stones rattling across the courtyard. A deep noise like thunder in the earth. For a moment it feels as though the city is about to slide free of its foundations and crumble into the sea.

The cataclysm is over in seconds. The night is still again. Antonus clings to his seat with whitened hands, breath held. He hears Junia stir on the bed in the inner chamber, but she does not call out. Neither do their children cry, nor does the slave Felix come stumbling in with a lamp and a look of bafflement. Slowly, he loosens his grip. Wonders whether he might, in passing, have taken leave of his senses.

He scrabbles for his stick with unsteady hands, his ears still ringing. Rises, the constellations seeming to wheel overhead.

*

"Your trouble again?" she asks. Her back to him, she reaches behind to place a hand upon his thigh. Junia is still half asleep.

"You weren't woken?"

"I heard you get up. I didn't hear you come back."

He has been restless for hours, open-eyed to see the sun climb over the city and spill its light into their chamber. The swallows are noisy in the nest above the window. Antonus sits up and looks at his wife's back, wondering whether he ought to wait until she is risen, until her mind is keener. "Not by me. I meant..."

Outside the window, his vineyard, his wheat field, his little olive grove. Fruit trees planted five summers ago. Green and gold beneath the rising solstice sun. The last few harvests have not been the best, but this has hardly discomforted them. Junia rubs her hand sympathetically against his thigh. "I'll send Felix down for opium. But the markets will be busy today."

"It's not so bad. Not enough for opium."

He is no stranger to the midnight hour. To the tricks that darkness can play. The quiet of his home in the light of morning, and already he begins to doubt.

"Rest," she says, indistinctly. "You have to climb the steps."

He lies down again beside her. Adelfa's cat pads light-footed past the doorway.

*

Midday, and the boy Myloxenes comes striding up through the grove, clouds of pollen all about him. Antonus's children have met him on the path, Antonia and Adelfa swinging one upon each arm, their chattering voices vying for his ear. Little Eryx catches up before they reach the house and is lifted onto Mylo's shoulders.

"Sound the trumpets," says Felix, the house-slave, shelling peas with Antonus in the doorway. "Our celebrated scholar is here."

"And look! He's brought me a brace of new servants."

The two men shade their eyes and watch the approaching party. "Strong, I am sure," says Felix. "And small enough to sweep in all the nooks and crannies that I'm too old to reach. The youngest could scrub inside the latrine."

Eryx is laughing, fists buried in Mylo's curly hair. "I *shan't!*"

"Then I shall sell you on again," says Antonus, splitting open a pod with a deft flick of his knife, "and purchase a monkey for the task instead."

"You shan't, you *shan't!*"

"Here…" Myloxenes has shaken the girls, and lifts Eryx down with care. The child is gone again at once, short legs pumping as he chases a stray chicken across the yard. "Solstice blessings on your household."

"And upon you, Master Mylo."

"It's a hot day in the city."

Antonia is tugging at Antonus's robe. "Father. *Father.*"

Felix points his shelling-knife at Myloxenes. "You've been in the library all night, I can see it, and not had breakfast."

The boy passes a hand over his ink-stained tunic. He has grown taller lately, and it's possible to make out the shadow of his first beard. "I wouldn't have eaten at my father's, either. He keeps nothing in his kitchens."

"*Father.*" Antonia's pleas are persistent. "Mylo says there will be fire-eaters in the city tonight. And a troupe of dancing pygmies. And cherry tarts. And lotus cakes."

"And a tiger on a chain," adds Adelfa.

Antonus looks at the two of them, matched like kittens in a litter. His dark-haired daughters. Antonia who is always blowing in stormy weather, Adelfa who slipped into the world already content with it. "If you want your mother to take you later, you'll have to ask her. And Felix to go with you."

"Felix will come," says Antonia at once, imperious. The old slave smiles, shrugs, throws a handful of peas into the bucket. Both girls clatter inside, calling for their mother.

"I'm sorry," says Mylo. "I thought they'd like to hear."

"If you go with the children, I can keep company with a very large jug of wine instead," says Felix.

The boy scratches at his tunic again. "I thought I'd go with you, actually, Antonus."

"To the temple?" Antonus pauses in his work. Watching Mylo shift hesitantly from foot to foot, he withholds his dismissal – that it might not be permitted, that it will be dull, that the boy's father will be there. He lays down his knife and reaches for his stick. "Here, let's go inside."

"I asked my father," says Myloxenes at once, when they have entered the shade of the courtyard. "A few days ago." Antonus moves across to lean against the wall, away from the noise of the children in the inner room and of Felix whistling outside. Mylo follows him at a short distance, touching a finger to the shrine of the household gods.

"Is that so? And what did he say?"

"He said that he couldn't see why the rites would hold any particular interest for me. I told him that I'm interested in the Augur's Temple for the sake of my work, since it's the oldest in the city, and I want to hear this Augur speak before she dies. She's been well-regarded in her time."

He is too young to be so serious, in Antonus's eyes. He is a little thin, still, too; but at least he has a healthier look about him than he once did, browner, broader in the chest. He has learnt to smile more easily. He speaks before he is spoken to, liberally fills his plate at mealtimes. And now at least his seriousness has character, has blood and passion in it.

"And did he give you permission?" asks Antonus. If a youth

would rather sit among dusty temple rituals than dance around the solstice fires, let it be because the strange and the old things of the world light a fire in him.

Myloxenes picks a honeysuckle flower and turns it between his fingertips. "He asked, have I been with a prostitute recently or killed any man or been near a corpse or house of sickness? And I told him, no sir. He asked, have I eaten the flesh of any unfit beast or been with a woman during her monthly bleed? And I said, no sir, I've not done anything else to make me unclean. I promised to sit with the least important men and not to speak to anyone of standing, or do anything to disgrace him." As he speaks, he plucks the yellow petals of the flower one at a time. "My father said, that since Antonus the Cripple attends these rites every year and is now no doubt too lame to climb the temple steps, I must be asking on his behalf, so that I could come as his walking-stick."

"Is that right?"

"That's right, sir."

They share a slanted smile. Mylo lifts what remains of the honeysuckle bloom to his lips, and drinks the sweetness inside.

*

Evening, and Junia helps her husband into his fresh-washed feasting-robes. Fixes a band of myrtle leaves about his brow, because of the blood from which he comes. He lowers his head and lets her fix the wreath in place, her careful fingers in his hair. They are quiet, since he is thinking about the climb, the hours ahead in the temple.

"Gone too grey, I suppose," Antonus says.

"You were never handsome, in any case."

Junia herself is formidable, tall with strong features and a mass of thick hair. Licking a thumb, she smooths back stray hair from his forehead, adjusts the sash at his shoulder. She has been weaving all day, her rows of dyed cloth hung drying from the roof outside.

"I wish you wouldn't go," she says.

"Mylo will help me. I can rest tomorrow."

"That's not what I meant."

Through the chamber doorway, over her shoulder, Antonus sees Antonia chasing Eryx around the table with a wooden sword in her hand.

"He likes you out of sight the whole year. And then to command you up there, where it's hardest for you to go, simply because he can. You know that he likes you to sit next to him so that they can all compare his strength to yours?"

"I know."

In the other room, Felix has intervened and set Eryx up on the table beyond his sister's reach. Myloxenes knocks at the wall and enters through the hanging. As ever he is sheepish in finery, tugging at the long sleeves of his tunic, scratching his neck where his cloak is fastened.

"Now there," says Junia, "is a handsome man."

He flushes and squirms. Antonus rises with Junia's help, and kisses her lightly. "Don't waste worry on us. This fine fellow and I will be back before midnight."

III

"As you can see," mutters Antonus, "the table is arranged, so. Your father will be seated to the left of the Augur, at the head, with the Emperor to the right. I should think you'll be with the scholars and younger men of the council, near the foot."

Myloxenes nods. The table is laid out all along the long hall, heavy with platters of juniper-roasted beef, with cakes and barley-bread. Incense-holders are suspended above the fireplace, filling the air with spiralling smoke. The magistrates, priests of the Dark

21

Temple, nobles and men of the council stand clustered about in fine linens and silks, gold about their necks and wrists, their eyes painted in the Emperor's style. The Augur's saffron-clad attendants dart among the crowd with pitchers. Mylo turns eagerly to look about him, but the old woman herself is nowhere to be seen.

"When does she speak?" he asks Antonus. "Before the meal, or afterwards?"

"Usually when the feast itself is over. She's wise enough to know that men don't listen when their stomachs are empty."

"Do you think they'd let me come back another time, and talk to the attendants here? The scholars at the library can hardly tell me anything about this temple, and it seems to me that any history of the city should devote a chapter at least…"

"Anyone can come here at any time, Mylo, and consult the priestesses. Your father may not like it, but there are people who still find comfort in this place."

The midsummer feast is the last vestige of it now, but not so long ago the Augur's Temple was the most important place in the city. In some households there was no decision that would be taken without speaking to the priestesses – which contractor should build the new roof, when to slaughter the prize pig, which tutor to hire for the children. The will and wisdom of the heavens have been divined here for centuries. There are other ways to make offerings to the gods, but this, so tradition has it, is where they speak.

When Antonus was a boy his father, the last Emperor, would send food and gifts to the priestesses, and his mother would come here weekly to make her offerings. The Prophetess herself had been given the seat of honour at every palace feast. He'd been too young at the time to understand what happened behind the closed doors of the council chambers, but he knew that the old woman (she'd seemed old, even then) had often been a guest there. She must have had his father's ear.

It wasn't just that the Augur's Temple had held more influence – he remembers there being *more* temples when he was young. He doesn't walk about in the city very much these days, but he is sure that there was once a shrine on every corner, places dedicated to this cult or that minor deity. At some point in the last thirty years, while he was looking the other way, the Dark Temple reared its head and swallowed them all.

Now the feast only happens here because the Emperor still has a fondness for it, and the city's most powerful men attend to show their fondness for the Emperor. Antonus pours half his cup into Mylo's, and drinks with a careful eye cast over the rim, taking in each new arrival, each man's movements about the hall. He is waiting for his brother, and for Athraxus. He wants to keep his wits, as much as one might, at a feast. "Look at Lennes the Steward," he says, turning slightly so that he is addressing the wall, the movements of his mouth hidden from the room. "The man looks quite ill. He hasn't spoken to a soul."

"Will Rufus take over his post do you think, if he's taken sick?"

"Perhaps. That could be to your advantage. And pay attention to that boy Andis, your father's favoured priest. He carries himself well these days."

"Fat from plenty of offerings."

"That brooch looks costly."

"They say that the wife of Hiramen the Magistrate buys him expensive gifts, in return for some, ah, personal services..."

Antonus looks sideways at his companion, who is already flushed and bright-eyed. Part of him finds pride in the thought that Myloxenes might be sharp enough to flourish, after all, in such company. Part of him wants to steer the younger man out of the hall before he is hurt or corrupted, through the temple gates, all the way back to the villa above the quiet vineyard.

Mylo takes his shoulder. "Come on, you're in pain. Let's sit on that step."

"I'll sit. You'll find companions of your own age, and have a better night for it."

From a bench at the side of the hall, Antonus has a wider view of the gathering. He knows that he is watched, too; sideways glances, mutterings. This is the only day of the year when he puts himself on public view in this way. They are assessing whether there is more grey in his beard, with whom he has chosen to speak, whether he has been leaning more heavily on his staff. Years ago it infuriated him, to be meat for their curiosity, but now their talk passes him by.

He checks that the wreath his wife placed upon his hair is still in place. Let them see me however they wish to. The cripple who would have been Emperor.

He is fascinated by the ebb and flow of talk, the patterns in the shape of the crowd. The old councillor who defects from one conversation as it ceases to hold his interest, sidles up to another. The three nobles who have had each others' arms for an hour, whispering close in each others' ears. Antonus imagines they are the congested organs through which the blood of the city passes, stomach, liver, brain. Was it like this in his father's day, these men yawning comfortably in palace chambers, fattening their own interests over oysters and wine, every new decree forever deferred while the city settles into listless discomfort?

Nearer the edges of the hall hover the men less certain of their position, the up-and-coming politicians who have yet to grow their first beards, the philosophers whose thinking has lately fallen out of fashion. None of these men has the slightest interest in the Augur or the religion of her temple: they were never educated as to its history or importance, never brought here by their mothers and sternly told to respect the Prophetess. But as long as the Emperor still feasts here, they will follow.

Antonus takes one of the priestesses by the arm as she passes.

24

"Tell me, is your mistress here? I haven't yet seen her."

"She's resting. She will be here soon. Will you take more wine? It is the kind we make here at the temple."

"No, thank you."

The girl has moved along, and a voice from beside Antonus says, "The Augur's feast without the Augur. An omen we can interpret without her help."

He turns. Lennes the Steward has joined him on the bench. He has always been mournful-looking, long of body and face, sinking now into old age with glum resignation. He has spent a lifetime shuffling papers and counting coins. He is the dullest man Antonus knows. Tonight he is unusually animated, eyes bulging as they dart about the room, wiping a profusion of sweat from his forehead with his sleeve.

Antonus wonders whether the steward has a fever. He makes to shift a few inches sideways on the bench, but Lennes has fixed him with a morose stare. "A man might be going about his business, might he not, he might be living quietly, when it is suddenly revealed to him that he is living in ill-favoured times."

"Perhaps you've been working too hard, Lennes."

He can see the unhealthy whites of the Steward's eyes. "A man might be disposed to quiet living. It won't save him. He must speak, or perish with silence."

At that moment, the High Priest of the Dark Temple comes striding in between the pillars, tall and imposing; accompanied not by the Emperor, but by the three heavyset dogs he likes to keep close at his heels. Night has fallen. At Athraxus's entrance the whole of the large company quietens. The dogs lay themselves down before the hearth, eyes glowing like dull coals.

There is a breathless hesitation about the room. The gaze of the crowd passes over the Emperor's chair, the Augur's.

"Well?" Athraxus demands. He addresses the dark-skinned girl who has paused across from him, carrying a pitcher half the size of her own body.

"The Prophetess is resting," she says, in a clear voice which carries through the hall. "She will come and she will speak, when she is ready."

"Then we will feast without her," says Athraxus. He makes no mention of the other empty seat. Antonus thinks that he sees a look pass between this girl and the High Priest of the Dark Temple, a weighing, a measuring.

If the Prophetess has not appeared and spoken before the night is ended, thinks Antonus, her influence in this city will be diminished beyond repair. This might be the last year we feast here. The pain in his leg is already intensifying, burning up his patience. In this mood he can barely bring himself to care about temples or prophecies, or whatever it was that Athraxus whispered in the Emperor's ear to keep him away.

The hesitant silence gives way to murmurs. Still, nobody approaches the table. Athraxus rolls up his sleeves and takes his appointed place, and suddenly there is a rush, a scramble to join him. Nobody wishes to be seen holding back. Antonus waits until the way is clear before limping to the seat allotted to him, leaning on his stick.

"Will you speak a blessing over us?" Athraxus asks the young priestess. She puts down the pitcher and makes her way to the fire. She raises a hand and says, in the same carrying voice, *"Consume, oh men, the beast that bled to supplicate the gods. Through the one who is appointed to it, know their will. For they are close enough to breathe on us."*

*

The gap at the end of the table draws every eye. Those surrounding eat quietly, while at the other end of the hall talk has begun to spring up. Clemon son of Clemnes, the ambitious young courtier with whom Myloxenes had been speaking before Athraxus arrived, leans over to engage him once again. He wears a brooch in the shape of a diving hawk, and the predatory look of a man who smells gain in every encounter.

"What does he mean by it?"

"Who?"

"The Emperor! What does he mean by not coming tonight? You must ask your father, you must tell me what he says."

"There's no point trying to cultivate Mylo," says Rufus, Lennes' redheaded son, reaching across to dip his bread in a bowl of sauce. "He's useless. He doesn't even live in his father's house."

"Is that so? Then he might not know that Theagenes the Elder is sleeping with his mother."

"I knew that," says Mylo.

"You know which one he is? Here, I'll point him out." Reluctantly, Mylo follows Clemon's gesture, and brings himself to look on the latest man to cuckold his father. Theagenes is around fifty and has the look of a soldier gone to seed, the expensive cloth of his robe stretched across his stomach, gold glinting on his wrists and brow. He is laughing heartily at something his neighbour has just said, slapping the table and unsettling his wine cup.

"Mylo knows that his mother is a whore," says Rufus son of Lennes. "You can't shock him."

"A very obliging whore, since she doesn't charge. I wonder if any magistrate would grant her a license, or whether—"

"Councillor," says Mylo. "Another time, the regulation of whores. Tonight, tell me about the great work you've done to meet the concerns of the people."

"The concerns of the people are dice games and fornication," says Clemon.

Mylo feels his cheeks glowing with the warmth of the room.

"Then you," he says, "are a man of the people indeed."

Behind him, someone lets out a laugh. He turns and glimpses the dark-skinned priestess as she leans over to fill Rufus's wine cup, the flash of her grin.

"See, Myloxenes, you've got the wits to amuse this foreigner! I wonder whether you aren't wasted among your books and scrolls." Clemon swills his wine around his cup. "I've got half a mind to recommend you for the council, since I'm sure it would annoy you..."

Mylo watches the priestess make her way along the table, the huge wine-jug borne skilfully in her arms, as though it is barely any burden. For a moment his attention goes with her, and he feels buoyant: but then she is gone from sight, and the mood fades.

The feast at the Augur's Temple is not so dignified an occasion as he has always imagined it. It is as though these men have dragged the dust and the coarse noise of the city into the temple with them, and there is nobody to oversee them with an eye of restraint, to make sure that they have washed their feet. The Augur's seat is still empty. She is an old woman, he hears it whispered, weak and fading. The temple itself, from what he can see of it, is in need of repairs. The priestess's saffron robes are patched and frayed.

He feels a tug of disappointment at the ordinariness of this space, the hall which smells of goats and straw and soot. He has never set foot inside this temple before, has always looked up at its pale stones from the city below, or, as a small boy, waited at its gates for his father. In the courts of the Emperor he's seen indolence, crass disregard for tradition or virtue; on the streets of the city, ignorance, stench, superstition. He realises that he has long been imagining the Augur's Temple as the one place set above this tide of decay. A place where the ancient fire still burns, a place where the priestesses have no need to eat or sleep or defecate but drift about their sacred business, in tune with voices from the heavens.

Eighteen years ago Myloxenes came from his mother's womb wide-eyed into the world, and ever since it has wounded him with disappointments. But he *believes* still, somehow, and does not quite know what it is that he believes in. Only that he thinks sometimes he glimpses another city, among the city, beyond or beneath the city. His best answer is that this is the city which once was, and so he buries himself in dusty scrolls and searches for it.

Quietly, beneath the rising din of drunken talk, in the smoke belching from the fireplace, he wonders whether he has been wrong about the nature of the world. He has always imagined that, though the rivers of the city are thick with filth, they flowed first from a pure spring.

*

It is hot close to the fire, where Saba has stationed herself to keep an eye upon the High Priest Athraxus. She can feel her face glowing uncomfortably. Three times already that night she has sent priestesses to check for the Augur's return. There is no sign of her: not in her quarters, not in the sanctuary, not in the city square below. Is she still up on the mountain? She has never failed to come back by morning before, let alone missed a moment of the feast.

Nobody else has said a word about the shaking of the earth, but Saba knows she didn't dream it. An event like this is certain to be a sign of one kind or another. She has heard of such things happening, though never before in this city. What it might portend is beyond her – she will have to ask the Augur.

Saba has told the novices in the sternest terms what they must and must not say. She has hidden her own rising panic to quell theirs, and sent them to work at their tasks: sweeping the courtyards and the inner rooms, lighting the braziers and the oil-lamps, scrubbing and setting the long table here in the hall. Now that their guests are here the priestesses valiantly continue as normal, bringing in jars of wine and platters of spiced fruits, heaps of knotted bread, though they feel themselves closely scrutinised.

Stay calm, Saba. Arrange your face. The worst thing you can do in front of all these people is betray your consternation.

Athraxus is speaking with one of the magistrates. They all look the same to Saba: she cannot recall the man's name. They all have the same thick necks, red-patched cheeks, thinning hair, the same air of bloated satisfaction.

She catches Athraxus's eye for a moment over the table, and wonders about the night's other glaring absence. *What did you say to the Emperor? What proof are you trying to make of your power over him?*

The temple in the city below where this priest presides is an ancient one, and it has waxed and waned, as all temples do, even during his lifetime. This is according to the Augur: for as long as Saba can remember, Athraxus has been on the climb. She cannot understand why. His cult seems dour and ugly to her, built not around the promise of access to the gods, but the very opposite. Certain people must be beguiled by the idea that truth is silent on every question that matters.

And perhaps the Emperor is one of them. The balance is tipping, says his empty chair, says the hard glitter of Athraxus's look. The Dark Temple rises. The Augur's Temple falls. This is the way of things.

And then she feels the growling of the High Priest's dogs rising from the floor.

Her eye falls upon Lennes. The Steward, seated a few places down from Athraxus, is looking paler by the moment. He has barely touched a morsel of food. As Saba watches, he rises to his feet, as though he is about to make his exit from the hall. But he does not move. He sways a little on the spot. Only those seated nearest to him have noticed. In the rest of the hall the feast continues, and

Saba is aware of each of the priestesses, her saffron-robed sisters, busying about with their pitchers and platters.

Your mother is not here, Saba, and so they are all in your care. This handful of young girls has no defence in the city except the authority of this temple. *Protect us*, she prays silently. *Gods of rock and river and cedar grove.Whatever passes here tonight, may we be in your favour.*

"The gods have spoken!" cries Lennes. His voice cuts through the hall like a cold blade. "They have made themselves known to me!"

A stir and a rustle of astonishment through the suddenly quiet company. The ink-fingered, the coin-grubbing Steward, who has never called the attention of a room in his lifelong career. The words, their high strained tone, unnaturally drawn from him.

"It has been revealed to me… that we are living in ill-favoured times!"

Lennes is clasping the table to stay upright. Already Saba can sense Athraxus's wrath.The tense turn of his body, a rumble in his throat.

"Last night, the gods sent me a dream. In the dream I stood on the mountain, at the mouth of the cave which is forbidden to all but the Augur. I heard a voice telling me to go in, but I was too afraid. Then I saw that the cave was a mouth, with teeth and lips and a tongue.The voice was coming from the cave. It told me to be attentive to the signs. Then a great worm came out from the mouth, from between the lips of the mouth, and it crawled down the side of the mountain to the city.The worm began to eat into the heart of the city, and the voice said, *what is rotten will be devoured*."

Saba feels a shock resonate deep within her ribcage. She is aware of Aemilia creeping to her side. Lennes' red-haired son is leaning forward at the foot of the lower table, incredulous. Athraxus is on his feet too, now.

"Then a dark bird came climbing from the mouth. Its wings were wide and when it took to the air its shadow covered the city, and the worm that was eating the city. The bird flew towards the sun and its shadow covered the sun. The voice from the mouth said, *what shines will be extinguished.*" Lennes is visibly shaking now. Droplets of sweat run down his face. "Then there came from the mouth a starred lizard, a salamander. Its eyes were coal and its breath was fire. The lizard crawled from the mouth and down the mountain towards the city. Its body was aflame, and it carried the flames into the city. The voice said to me, *what is decaying must burn.*"

A ripple passes through the hall. The face of every man turned towards Lennes. Knives still held poised above plates, morsels of food hanging, forgotten. Impossible, in that moment, to tell whether these men are ready to leap up and tear out his throat for the insult to their city, or to throw back their heads and laugh.

Saba steels herself for the uproar. Her mind is racing so fast, following the currents which are now carrying the room, that is does not occur to her to try and stop what is unfolding.

"The gods made this known to you." The voice of Athraxus sinks through the company like the stone around a condemned man's ankles. Lennes turns his bulging eyes.

"Yes."

"To you alone, this vision was granted. To the High Priest of the Balanced Books." There are a few nervous snickers of laughter from the lower end of the table. The hall seems about to turn, to tip over into mirth. Lennes destined for an anecdote to be chuckled over in the baths and the rooms behind the council chamber, mad Lennes, too many nights burning candles into the small hours and toiling over columns of figures.

"You blaspheme," says Athraxus.

The low growling of his dogs. The oppressive heat of the fire. Guards step forward from out of the shadows, but in two strides the priest himself has crossed to where Lennes stands. A quick violent movement and the steward lands flat on his back with a jarring crack and a groan. Athraxus is crawling astride him, pinning down his limbs.

"What do you say? Your words blaspheme the Dark Temple! Your words blaspheme the Emperor himself!"

Lennes can only splutter, the breath choked from him. A ringing silence has fallen across the hall. The priestesses stand frozen. Men turn their gaze away. Saba starts forward, but a trembling Aemilia grabs at her elbow.

"Do you have any more words for us?" hisses Athraxus. *"You must speak, oh great prophet! We must hear you!* Any further messages from the gods which you have to spit up?"

And then with no warning Athraxus has forced his fingers into the man's mouth, hooking them beneath his lip and forcing it upwards until Lennes begins to scream in incoherent panic. He vomits and it dribbles down his chin, mingling with the blood which begins to flow as Athraxus's fingertips reach the roots of his teeth.

"The city is eager for more of your wisdom! Won't you speak, man? Why won't you speak?"

"Enough," says a low voice. "Leave him alone."

Saba turns sharply to see the man known as Antonus the Cripple, seated a little way down from the head of the table. He is greying, stooped, unimpressive. He has not spoken loudly, or risen from his seat, but Athraxus glances around nonetheless. The steward's shrieking protests have sprayed blood across the priest's face. His dogs are barking.

The men along the length of the table and the priestesses are looking at Antonus now, too. He looks at his hand, and appearing to notice its tremor, lays his table-knife carefully down. Saba holds her breath. All she knows about this man is that he was to have been Emperor, once, and now hides himself away, disfigured and disgraced.

33

Antonus fumbles below the table for his walking-stick, and positions it to take his weight as he stands. "Athraxus. If the man has offended, let him defend himself. And remember what ground we're standing on."

Athraxus withdraws his hand from the steward's mouth. He dips his head stiffly. "I'm sure your brother would thank you for honouring the Augur's Temple."

"We give honour to the Emperor's chosen officials, too, don't we?"

"Until they turn and bite our heels." Athraxus rises, and Lennes crumples to the floor. From the foot of the table, the Steward's son creeps towards him. "You do not understand this man's true meaning. I would not expect you to. Only those who serve this city would be grieved to hear it so insulted."

Fingers dripping with gore, he beckons. His guards come forward at once. Lennes is lifted by the arms, pulled from the grasp of his son, who seems too shocked to protest. The Steward is dragged groaning from the hall.

Athraxus wipes his hands upon his robes. This gesture is a signal, and is obeyed in an instant. Talk springs up hastily. The priestesses take up their wine jars and platters of cakes. Lennes' son retreats back to his seat.

The room seems to spin, the night beyond the pillars a blur of blackness and firelight. The muffled sound of festivities in the city below, pipes and singing and a hundred different pounding drumbeats. The sparks of bonfires.

Antonus the Cripple raises his fingers to his forehead, perhaps wondering what in all the world he has just done. In sympathy, and in curiosity, Saba steps forward to fill his empty wine-cup. He holds up a hand to stay her.

IV

Junia does not keep hold of her daughters' hands. They run ahead
of her on the path down into the city. They do not glance back,
and she is glad. They have not yet learnt to be afraid in the world.

She lifts a shawl over her thick dark hair. "Antonia!" she calls.
"Adelfa! Wait when you reach the colonnade!"

By the light of torches and bonfires she sees them swarming
below, the dancers and the drunkards and the maskers and
pickpockets, the slaves given their freedom for the night. In
moments like this the city seems repellent to her, crawling like an
anthill.

"I'll take him," she says to the slave Felix, who has her son on his
shoulders. "Go. Drink with your friends."

Felix, who was purchased and given as a gift to her husband on
the day they were married, who has been at her side for eighteen
years, looks at her and does not reply. Though his hair is silver now
he is never above mischief. "What should we get you to eat?" he
asks Eryx. "How many cakes can you fit in your mouth?"

"Five," says the child decisively.

"Only five? I could eat seven, at least."

"*Mama!*" yells Antonia, from down the hill. "*Mama, I can see boats!*"

Lanterns hanging from their white sails, out on the dark water.
A shoal of stars reflected in the ocean. Junia runs her fingertips
through the long scented grass which is brushing against her thighs.
Felix swings her son down to the ground and now her children are
running, all three, away from her on the path into the city.

*

The night belongs to the Dark Temple. Before they join the revels
the people of the city bring their offerings there. Blood flows in

the gutters from out of this temple. Feverish, the people press in around the entrance, crying for the priests' attention, waving their coins. Those who cannot find their way to the front of the crowd, whose offerings are not received before the sun comes up, will not have their prayers heard for the coming year. Cripples wail at the roadside and beg passers-by to make offerings on their behalf.

The city was full of temples once. Children learnt to lay offerings on twenty different altars. *Ask the gods for what you desire in the coming year. No, don't tell me. In secret.* Gods of earth and of air, gods of river-bend and mountainside, gods of hearth and sea-voyage. Now everybody is heading for the same little side-street, for that squat building with its faceless guardians of stone, where for one night they might pay their way to an audience.

Junia doesn't pay much attention to changing fashions in the city, but the rise of the Dark Temple has been hard to ignore. The wealthy women who buy her weaving are beguiled by Athraxus's teaching, by the idea of sacred mysteries shrouded in shadow. Their husbands buy membership to temple societies where they are initiated through a series of elaborately structured grades, until they can boast knowledge of unspeakable things. These men mark their bodies in private and greet one another in public through arcane signs.

The common people, excluded from such secrets, revere them all the more. They jostle for a place in the temple's shadow, as plants jostle for sunlight. Its gods can hardly be heard or known or reached, and so must be more important than the grubby clay idols that occupy household shrines — those earth-smelling deities low enough to meddle in everyday affairs.

Junia sees the sense in not asking too many questions of the gods, or expecting answers. And tonight, the only time of the year when the temple accepts petitions, she doesn't mind spending a few coins for her children's sake. On the way there the twins are lost in a sea of legs, weaving between the revellers, catching bursts of heat from nearby bonfires. Delicious smells waft from every direction, roasting chestnuts and catfish on a hot grill, burnt sugar and honeyed wine. They are giddy, as though the drunkenness of the crowd has passed to them. Adelfa glances over her shoulder every now and then, reassured by the sight of Eryx bobbing high on Felix's back, not far behind. She waves to her brother, who unclasps his small fist in greeting.

In the packed street outside the Dark Temple, Felix buys the children each a pigeon. Bodies jostle as people compete to approach the nearest priest, shouting and waving their gold. The priest is dressed in wine-red. His face is covered. With a knife in his hand he deftly splits the throats of proffered birds, bends their heads back, sprinkles the blood. The air is thick with a red haze.

"Now take this coin," says Felix to Antonia and Adelfa, "and pay him for his service. Call for him until you get his attention. Hold your brother's hand."

Antonia pushes her way forcefully through the crowd, dragging Adelfa and Eryx behind her. When at last they reach the priest Antonia seizes the sleeve of his robe and presses the coin into his palm. Above the cloth that covers his mouth she glimpses the man's eyes, the madness of their huge black pupils. He has spent the day breathing the smoke of offerings in an underground chamber. Cutting into his flesh to bleed on the altars. In the mind of Antonia, in the mind of the city, the depths of the Dark Temple writhe with things unformed and unseen. With shapes dimly familiar from the depths of ancient memory. Since nobody has seen inside the sanctuary of that temple, it has its own life in every imagination. The temple takes its hold this way.

The priest takes the birds by the legs, one at a time. He bends back their heads and splits the skin of their throats. With the tips of his fingers he flicks blood over the three children, who close their eyes and plead with the gods in secret.

It's easy, what to ask for. Eryx wants a horse, a wooden one, with wheels. Adelfa prays, *take my father's pain away. Let it end.* Antonia clenches both of her fists and moves her lips silently. Prays with all the power of her will, *for Mylo, who I will marry. Who I must marry.*

*

The arches and colonnades of the old city wall have been garlanded with lily-wreathes, with drapes of blue and gold. On the bathhouse steps a troupe of players are enacting the tale of how the solstice revels came to be. This, Antonia and Adelfa have heard many times from Felix, who spins them stories as their bedside lamp is sputtering through the last of its oil. He is not so tidy a weaver as their mother. His stories are made with threads of memory and fancy and his own invention, patterns copied from older cloths, colours from the far countries where he has been. The twins do not trust a single thing he tells them, and they believe every word.

There was once a city, so Felix says, which incurred the anger of the gods. They determined to send rain from the waters above the firmament, fountains from the waters below the earth, gushing with a great and terrible roar through the city to wash its people and its wickedness away. But the youngest of the gods, the god of the river-reeds, was infatuated with a mortal man. He told this mortal lover what was coming, and instructed him to take apart the timbers of his house to build a raft.

But what will I do? Asked the mortal lover, what shall I tell the people of the city when they ask me why I am pulling down the timbers of my home? Tell them, said the river-reed god, that you are under a curse. Tell them that you are building a boat to sail away from the city, and that when you are gone a flood of blessings will pour down upon them. Tell them that on the night of the year's longest day they should dance and play songs and ask the gods for whatever their hearts desire, and that very night there will be wine and fish and grain raining down upon them from the heavens.

And so it was, that the people were found feasting when the flood came.

*

Later, when the music in the city has grown louder and more riotous, when the bonfires burn higher and the dancers divest themselves of their clothes, Junia sits alone beneath the stars. She perches on the wall behind the villa. At her back, the mountain stands huge and silent. Her eyes are drawn across the fires of the city to the Augur's Temple, alone upon its outcrop of rock.

Her fingertips touch the strings of her lyre, barely drawing a sound. She hums the beginnings of a tune in the back of her throat. Streaks of cloud hang across the moon, then lift, casting silver across the sea.

She is so absorbed that she hardly notices Felix join her. He picks up the tune she has started and puts in a rhythm, drumming his fingers on his leg.

"Are they asleep?" she asks, after a while.

"Not yet. They want to see their father."

She strums the chord she has been looking for with more confidence. "There. *Hymn to the God in the Hurricane.*"

"*The arm of the god is strong,*" he sings. "*With the strength of his hands the god may lift ships from the seas.*"

"*The breath of the god...* what is it?"

"*The breath of the god stirs high waves...*"

"Oh, yes." She plucks a few more chords and then silences them, restless. "They ought to be back by now."

"It's not midnight yet. Perhaps they got caught up in the crowds."

Junia lays down her instrument and draws her shawl around her shoulders. She looks at Felix, who is pouring himself a cup of wine.

He raises her a toast.

"Solstice blessings, Mistress Junia."

"And upon you."

"By next year, I'll be gone," he says. The lines around his eyes crease as he grins. "You'll see."

She laughs. "Gone on the seas. Back to your life of adventure."

"I'll take you with me, if you like. Away from that tyrant and his household."

"You're a hero."

He passes her the bottle and she drinks straight from it, the strong wine spreading warmth through her body. It washes away what remains of the night's fears. The streets of the city have never seemed hers to walk, not since she was a child, before her world changed. But here on the hill above the vineyard, these are her safe acres. She can breathe.

"If you can't love the place where you were born," says Felix, "then you're freer than most."

"It's the city which has no love for me."

Felix raises his cup again. "To being free. To being a foreigner, in a land whose dust won't stick to your feet."

Junia's dyed cloths flap noisily in a sudden gust of wind. She rises to her feet and goes to take them down, folding them and draping them over her shoulder.

The noise of her lyre, played a little less skilfully than by her own, more sober hand, drifts in through the dark archway. "*And on midsummer's night, the eyes of the gods are straying... to a window by lamplight...*"

"Felix."

"*...and a maiden undressing...*"

"The whole city doesn't need singing to sleep."

*

40

On their way back through the city Antonus leans upon Mylo's shoulder, gritting his teeth. His leg feels as though it is on fire, and for the moment he can think of nothing else. Out of long habit his body hunches over and twists around to compensate for his uneven gait. He knows that he must look monstrous, a grimaced thing.

Through the chaos of the dancers and the quickening music around the bonfires, through the darkness and the ashes. "Nearly there," breathes Mylo. "Nearly home." They stop to catch their breath beside the colonnade. Antonus presses his hands against the old wall and bites his tongue to keep from howling like a dog.

They lurch together along the uneven path through the fields and the vineyard. They do not have a lantern, but the moon is bright and firelight from the city has cast a red glow on the low clouds. Antonus knows that Mylo is trying to conceal his exhaustion, the younger man's breath heavy and strained. They do not speak to one another until at last they reach the villa, and Antonus sinks down onto the bench beside the pool with a low groan.

"Are you alright? I'll wake Junia."

He holds up a hand. "Don't. I just need to sit for a while."

"You're so pale…"

"Don't *fuss*, Mylo." He regrets snapping at once, and gestures for the boy to sit down next to him. He presses into the knotted muscle of his leg and as the cloud of pain slowly clears, becomes aware that Mylo is bursting to speak again. "What is it?"

"What are we going to do?" he blurts out. "What will happen to Lennes? Should we go and petition my father for him in the morning?"

Antonus looks at Mylo's expectant, moonlit face, and feels too tired to offer more than perfunctory comfort. "Lennes is still a man of the Emperor's council. He'll be freed in the morning to nurse his bruises, and think better of believing his own madness."

"But Rufus says that—"

"Rufus will have a hard night of it. If the time has come, he will do very well as steward. It's happened before, sons taking over while fathers are still living."

"That's a sign of a disordered world." Mylo still looks unhappy. Antonus thinks of Athraxus, the sudden viciousness of his descent upon Lennes, the blood dripping from his fingertips. He knows that Mylo is thinking of these things too.

He remembers the first time he ever saw Athraxus's son at close quarters, kicking his heels in the outer chamber of the council rooms, waiting with nothing to entertain him while his father sat in on the day's interminable meeting. Timid eyes set deep in a too-earnest face, in hollows like bruises. Antonus had moved closer, watching the child from behind a pillar, finding in himself the overwhelming urge to step out and greet him like an old friend. And what to say? I've long pitied you from afar?

He'd had no children of his own, then, and supposed he never would. This grief hung sharp and silent between him and Junia, a twisted bramble. It had been soon after his sojourn in the healing-houses. Newly alive to the small and the weak things of the world, softened to the presence of suffering, he had limped over to the bench, and sat down.

At that time the boy had startled when you entered a room and flinched when you addressed him. Both of them so often consigned to waiting in the empty echoing hall – Mylo for his father, Antonus at the beck and call of his brother – yet it had taken months to get a word out of him. The trick in the end had been Felix's fig-cakes, wrapped in a cloth, placed on the bench between them without comment. It was the same way you might go about taming a wild deer, coaxing it little by little out of the shadows.

Nobody it seemed had thought to feed the boy properly in his father's house. Before long the parcels of cake became entire meals packed in baskets, fresh-baked bread and goat's milk, olives and grapes and boiled eggs. Antonus had never seen a child eat so seriously, one mouthful at a time, forehead furrowed as though tackling a mathematical problem.

If he's always waiting about and nobody cares where he is, why don't you just bring him back here at supper-time? Junia had asked. *Saves us packing a basket.* When he told her about the boy, it was the first time he saw her react in curiosity to anything — saw a spark in her beyond blank-eyed obedience. It was her idea. Cloths to dye and a harvest to bring in, last year's wine to take to market, a cow to slaughter and preserve; what was one more mouth to feed?

No children in their household and they found themselves longing for him. Caught each other looking at him, saw each other, at last.

Such a small thing, then. A man at the tiller of a boat might touch the wheel so lightly, and alter its whole course.

"You'll stay here tonight?" asks Antonus, more gently.

Mylo nods. "Do you think," he begins, "I mean to say, the dreams of Lennes—"

At that moment Junia emerges from the inner chamber, shawl wrapped about her shoulders. She halts mid-step as the two of them turn to look at her, and touches her fingertips to the shrine of the household gods. "You're so late, I fell asleep. What happened? Did the Augur decide to keep making prophecies until sunrise?"

"The Augur wasn't there," says Mylo immediately.

Antonus catches his wife's eye. He gives a small shake of the head: *we'll talk. Not in front of the boy.*

"We've had a strange night," he says aloud. "And now I am too tired to talk about it. Help me, will you?"

Moths flap about the lamps in the courtyard, cicadas chirping in the nearby trees. Adelfa's cat has curled up and fallen asleep in the roof-gutter. In the inner chamber Antonus sinks onto the bed, stretching out his leg with a groan. He motions Junia to sit beside him. She is holding a marrowbone pipe which she lights from the flame of the bedside lamp. She sits and holds the pipe to his mouth. He inhales deeply, rich smoke filling his lungs. A warm pressure in his head, which Junia has cupped in her hand and now lays back upon the pillow. The pain in his leg melts away and the room dissolves in a gentle haze.

The children's sleeping breaths are three soft separate rhythms, at odds with one another. Felix can be heard snoring from his quarters. All the night-time noises of the villa, the little creaks and groans of its timbers and the breeze upon the vineyards beyond.

On the edge of consciousness he sees Junia inhale from the pipe before lying back on the bed beside him. The smell of her long thick hair, the pungency of the dyes she uses in her weaving and the musk of wood-smoke, the sweat of her day's work. His favourite scent. He leans over and kisses her neck below her hair.

They lie this way for a while, quiet. In the cloud that engulfs them, Junia moves her hand beneath his tunic and rests it on his thigh. Her fingers, long-practised, make circular motions along the crooked, knotted muscles. He breathes. Her hand strays sideways and warmth spreads through his blood. But then suddenly, as though he has seen a watcher stood in the doorway, he is uneasy.

Antonus sits up. The quick movement makes his head spin. He has the sense of trying to reach through his drowsiness, through the comfortable fog of the herb into the thing that is wrong.

"We had a strange night," he says, thickly. "There was some trouble."

"Trouble? With your brother?"

"He wasn't there. I think he was persuaded not to come."

"Trouble for us?"

She is looking sharply up at him in the dark. He considers. "I don't think so. No. But there will be changes in the city. The Augur's Temple is descendant."

Junia lays her head down again. "That's been true for years."

"Athraxus pulled a man's teeth out with his fingers."

She does not seem to have heard him. She yawns, turning over, and murmurs into the pillow. "Changes come. Let the dogs in the city fight over bones, for all we care."

V

A noise startles her, and Saba sits bolt upright. She hadn't meant to sleep at all, sitting vigil on narrow stone staircase outside the Augur's chamber – but her lamp has gone out and she is sore from leaning against the wall. Rubbing her neck, she hears it again, somebody knocking at the bars of the gate outside across the courtyard.

Wondering what she might have slept through, she jumps up and pushes open the chamber door. The moonlit room is empty. Loose leaves of parchment are strewn across the floor. Saba stands for a moment in the doorway, hearing her own heart beat harder. She feels a shadow pass over her, as though a flock of birds has winged overhead. Saba, who barely has it in her nature to worry or to fear.

She strikes a spark and lights her lamp again before descending to the courtyard, cloak carried behind her in the wind which has risen in the warm night. Saba's quick bare feet, certain of their place on the uneven stones. She recognises one of the voices beyond the gate and calls out his name, a hand shielding her flickering flame.

"Athraxus!"

The High Priest of the other temple raises his own torch to see who answers to him, and his guards each mutter their respect, touching their fingertips to their foreheads. Athraxus is flushed, tip of his tongue dampening dry lips, hair slick with sweat. "Open the gate, won't you? Before my patience runs out."

"Your business can't be too important to wait until morning."

He stands fully head and shoulders higher than her. Though advancing in years now, his eyes miss nothing, and there is savagery still in his hands. The angles of his face are steep and shifting by torchlight. He smells of dust gathered over decades, of dead and rotting things.

"Child," says the High Priest Athraxus. "Fear me more in your speech." His eyes are the same dark colour as her own, but without warmth, like dead embers. He stares past her into the courtyard, as though the Augur might be concealed there. "Well?" he demands, "Where is she? We need to talk."

Saba does not need to ask who he means. "What do you want from her?"

"We've been questioning Lennes since sundown, and he won't tell. But I know she put him up to it. That's all she has left now, this pathetic sort of trouble. I'll hear it from her own mouth."

Trying to halt the High Priest in his tracks is rarely any use – he is too potent a force. A lie won't hold him long. Saba sees a chance to direct him towards a useful purpose. "You won't find the Augur here. She never came back from the mountain. I was about to go and search for her, but if I find her and she's hurt, I won't be able to carry her back. "

Athraxus looks at her suspiciously, then turns to his guards. "What time is it?"

"The fourth hour past midnight," says one of the men.

"Maybe she fled," Athraxus muses aloud. "Insulted this city one last time and left it forever. Good riddance to her."

"I wouldn't speak like that in front of your master the Emperor. We both know he's not ready to lose her yet." Saba is gambling on being right. "What if she dies up there, and he hears that you refused to help her?"

Athraxus reacts at once, turning on her with irritation. "Where

46

was the Emperor tonight if she is so precious to him?" he snaps. But nevertheless he lifts his eyes, reluctant, to the mountain.

Saba holds her lamp steady, waiting, until the priest's thoughts have gained pace and drawn level with her own. His lip lifts. "You women, in your wisdom, to let her go up there alone! By now you should be wiping up her piss and feeding her porridge from a spoon. You should be tucking her in her bed and praying she passes in the night."

"Fear her more," says Saba quietly, "in your speech."

A pack of dogs sets off barking in the dark street far below. The guards yell and fling stones down the steps. The missiles skitter and thud, and the barking renews, fiercer than before.

Athraxus wipes sweat from his forehead with the sleeve of his robe. "If we will go, it must be now, before the sun rises. If she has fallen over a rock and broken her head open, I want to know before dawn. We can burn her up with the rest of the dead flesh on the pyre." His tongue, like Saba's, is looser in the night hours. She knows that his thoughts are flying now, spinning off in far directions, and he is looking at her with new and sharp attention.

She is sixteen years in the world. She knows every stone in the Augur's temple. There are those who quake and scrape before him, this man who leads the dark at his heels like a whipped and snarling dog. This man with blackened blood beneath his fingernails. The priestess stands unafraid before his gaze.

*

"Maybe she has met with a wild animal, or the climb up here defeated her old heart," Athraxus mutters under his breath. "Or maybe the gods have struck her down at last for her presumptuousness." His lantern swings from side to side as he tries to finds a sure footing on the steep path. Its shadow sweeps across the grasses and amongst the clusters of rock-roses which have grown up between boulders.

Saba, ten paces ahead and impatient, can hear his every word. The guards bring up the rear, grumbling. Her lamp is extinguished now but the moon is high and round and bright, pouring down silver light upon the mountainside and the rooftops of the city below. *Keep up, old man, keep up.*

"There are wolves in these woods," says one of the guards. "And bears, I heard. But we're marching on up by moonlight."

"Does this girl even know the way?"

"She knows the way," says Saba, beneath her breath. The night on the mountain is sweet to her senses. Cicadas are singing. An overpowering fragrance of wild lilac, of iris and marjoram. In the branches of a thin pine tree she glimpses an owl, white and silent, watching the human party ascend the path. For a moment Saba meets the bird's dark-glass gaze.

"Have we marched here to find an old woman?" Athraxus calls over his shoulder to his guards. "Or to complain like one?"

The two men split and take their lamps into the high grasses on either side of the path. She is aware of Athraxus picking up his pace, scrabbling up a steep stretch of stone so that he might draw level with her. As a beam of lamplight crosses the pine branches the owl takes flight, letting out an echoing cry. The priest comes to Saba's side and walks there a while, his breath heavy. She pulls the hood of her robe lower over her face, and waits.

"If it is the time," says Athraxus.

They climb further in silence. Saba feels a fluttering across her chest, as though the owl had beat its wings there.

"If it is indeed the time. She has chosen you. Hasn't she?"

Saba nods. She cannot remember when she first understood that she was to succeed the Augur. There was no single moment when they first spoke of it openly between them. No ritual, no ceremony of commissioning. Perhaps it was clear to the Augur from the beginning, when she excelled at every lesson, dived fearlessly into the business of making oracles. And it has been clear to Saba too: since she heard the story of how there first came to be an Augur in the city, and felt her heart grow warm.

She can sense him looking sideways at her. Athraxus, his words are a treacherous current. In an instant he will snatch your feet from beneath you, pull you into his depths.

"The favour she enjoys." He has lowered his voice to a whisper, though the guards are far behind and there is no-one to hear them but the mountain. "It's just for her. It is not for the Augur's Temple. Not any more. Do you understand?"

"I understand that the Emperor still favours her."

"He knew her from a boy. His sentiments do him credit. But he's growing wiser."

"You mean, you're bringing him under your thumb."

He ignores her. "There is no faith in your temple among the people, no favour in the palace. When she passes, the age of the prophets in this city will pass too."

"So this is what you really came to tell her," says Saba. "This is what you're desperate for all of us to know. That it's not the fashion now, for a god to speak."

Still beside her, he takes her wrist in a hard grip. "Her successor," he breathes in her ear, "would do well to pay attention." Savagery enough in his hands to snap her arm between finger and thumb, if he wished. "I will be kind. Your temple will stand. You may go about your business. Sacrifice your animals and burn your incenses and have your rituals behind your walls. Serve the little old grandmothers and the unwashed beggars who still come to you, until they die off. But as to the rest of them, the hearts of the city, the purses of the city. They are already with me."

Her quick tongue, her silver tongue finds nothing in reply. Saba squirms but he does not let go. So high does he stand above her, he might lift her by the skin of the neck like a rabbit.

"So, little Augur. This is the future that I see. You will not make declarations down into the city about the voices heard in dreams. You will not bewitch the people or the palace with fanciful talk. Wouldn't it be best for us, we two who sit in the highest seats of the two temples, to agree with each other?"

Saba ceases her struggle. She lets her arm fall limp in his grip, darting her eyes sideways. "I don't sit there yet."

Shadows loom above. They have reached the grove near the top of the mountain. A breeze like cool breath stirs the branches of the cedars, and Saba feels a shudder run through the High Priest's body. Something in the air has changed. He lets go of her arm. They stand for a moment, priest and priestess, silent before the tall trees.

He leads the way in. The moonlight is thin and bluish here, dappled on the dusty ground. There are footprints, marks where the Augur's sandals trod. There, the imprint of her staff. Saba moves on ahead towards the edge of the grove, where the trees frame the city and the sea below. It is here where the Augur would have watched the dusk flight of the birds, marked their movements.

"*Prophetess,*" calls Saba softly. "*Where are you?*"

"Prophetess!" calls Athraxus. He lifts a branch from the ground and parts the undergrowth. A cloud of pale moths rises and flutters about his head. His voice is muted in the grove, swallowed by the heavy air. Saba watches him. The strangeness of that place, of the hour. Step with care, High Priest. For the veil is thin here, between this world and the next.

The moon above the sea. Athraxus approaches the edge of the grove, peers over the cliff to the rocks below. The huge round hanging moon beyond the branches. He stares into its light, the night at his back, and raises the hood of his robe.

The guards come cautiously into the trees. "No sight of her, master. Not a sign."

"Could she have gone down another way?"

"There is no second way down the mountain," says Saba.

"Then curse her," says Athraxus from the shadow of his hood, "and we'll return to our beds." His discomfort in the grove is like his discomfort at the gate of the Augur's Temple. These trees will not bend at his word, will not shower down their secrets when he shakes them. He does not know how to hold himself, in a scene not subject to his will.

"Will you go, then?" asks Saba.

"Will you stay here? She's lost in the night, over the cliff perhaps, into the sea. The Emperor will hear that I did my part. We'll see whether the morning washes her in."

"Or finds her very much alive."

She cannot see his face. His voice is full of scorn. "The sun has set upon your Augur. Begin your weeping now, child, and weep yourself dry before the morning."

*

But we are not yet finished here, High Priest of the Dark Temple. Man of that temple, so ill at ease in the night on the mountain. There is yet another place where she might be. Leave the guards to wait beside the grove, as they will not wish to draw too near. Hold your cloak close about you. And take off your sandals.

Vapour rises from the crack in the earth. In the shadow of his hood, she sees the High Priest's face curl in disgust at the smell of it. Hot steam and rank sulphur. He covers his mouth, he who dwells among bones in the Temple of Blood. The blackness within the earth is absolute. It is a living, breathing being.

Saba reaches out a hand on either side to steady herself against the rocks. It is as though the smoke has coiled in winding ropes about her ribcage, and is pulling at her now, drawing her in, drawing her down. She gulps the night air. The blackness in the earth beats in her chest, heavier than her own heart. She looks at the High Priest, his look in return a flash of naked fear.

A rumble within. Sightless and alone now Saba feels her way along the wall of rock, dips fingertips in the bowl of spring-water, the bowl of ash. Draws line with shaking hand across her forehead. Prayer wordless on her lips, descends to the underworld.

VI

The sun rising from over the plain beyond the city wall, fingers of rose-coloured light across the rooftops, a solitary ship going out from the harbour with breeze in its sails. Daylight has reached the cobblestones, and the roads around the square already bustle with tradesmen setting their stalls. Cloths shaken out, carts unloaded, baskets overflowing with fish and flowers and fruit. Slaves sweeping the pavements, chasing dogs away with clattering pans. Old men taking the early sun, chattering women climbing the bathhouse steps.

At the temple Aemilia whispers words in the goats' silken ears, which she rubs between finger and thumb. She becomes preoccupied at the pen, feeding them old bread, singing softly. The same songs will be the last thing they hear when the time comes for her to cover their eyes and slice their throats with a sharp blade. She likes to think that it comforts them.

"It will be quick. It will be quiet. *Like sleep with henbane and with poppy, like sleep without dreaming, going down to the dark place.* Don't fear, beautiful ones. I will be with you."

They trust her, the dumb beasts. Her hands smell of hay. There is a weed which grows on the windy slopes of the mountain, which she makes into a brew to slow their senses. Under its influence they are unsuspecting of the knife she carries, the ropes which bind their legs. She is known at the temple, Aemilia, for her soundless sacrifices. Not for her oracles, which are never better than they were when she was first coaxed to make them, as a small child. She peers only dimly through the smoke. She forgets all but snatches of the voices heard in dreams. This does not distress her. It must be fearful, she thinks, to see through to the marrow of things.

She has never matched the sharpness of Saba, who came to the temple at the same time as her and sat through the same lessons, who took great strides ahead of her from the beginning. She is content to do the bidding of those who see further. Since Saba will always be at her side, making up for what she lacks, there is no need for envy. In any case, how to envy someone who has always seemed a part of her own self?

She is not made, Aemilia, for times that will be written of in history books. Rather, for slow, forgotten, ordinary hours. For mending robes in the courtyard shade, for the well-trodden confines of comfortable rooms. For the world as it is already known.

*

Saba leads Athraxus and his guards towards the temple steps by alleyways where their passing will go unnoticed. The priest's men are tired from bearing their burden and full of bitter complaint, but Saba's feet dart across the stones as though over hot coals. The whole way down the mountain she has barely torn her eyes from the Augur's ashen face. She knows that the Prophetess lives because she bent close in that terrible cave until faint breath moistened her cheek. She had taken the Augur's cold hands in her own and felt a shock like lightning jolt through her skin. *I'll never know what passed here, but she lives. Oh thank the gods, she lives!*

Saba had shouted herself hoarse before any of the men were

willing to descend down there after her, to help drag the Augur out. She hates the way they are carrying the old woman now, like a sack of grain, one holding her legs and two others heaving at the head and shoulders. She lolls between them and Athraxus does not once tell them to take care. The priest's mouth is twisted sourly. He has had a disappointing night.

Though he has not lifted a finger to help bear the Augur, the night's climb and long descent have nonetheless taken their toll on him, his face flushed red as his robe and his steps not quite steady. Daylight shows up the grey in his hair and the hollows of his cheeks.

The Augur may yet outlive him, thinks Saba, with a surge of triumph. My mother. She will still be climbing the mountain when he is laid low in his grave.

"I know what you are doing." He does not quite have enough breath for his usual snarl. "Trying to lead us by the back ways. As though they don't already scorn her in the city. They can see frailty at a mile."

"You'd best keep out of their sight, then."

His cheeks colour deeper. "Is she still alive?" he asks his guards, loudly. "Or have the cobbles shaken it out of her?"

One of the men holds the back of his hand to the Augur's mouth. "She's breathing," he says.

They have neared the steps, in full view now of the square, and Athraxus turns like the tide. His form is changed, his spine straightening. "You're done here," he says to his guards. "Go back to my temple. Lay her down. I will carry her."

The men look up at the tall flight of steps rising above them, and then disbelievingly back at their master. The task has been hard enough with two of them, moving downhill. Saba catches ambition rolling from Athraxus with the stench of his sweat. She sees at once what he is doing, and hopes it will burst his old heart.

"Lay her down," she echoes. The guards do not need telling again. They roll the Augur onto the ground and then stagger backwards, bled dry by their labour. "Will you take her up again, then?" Saba demands of the High Priest. Perhaps it would have been to the Augur's good, to let the men carry her the rest of the way, but something else is unfolding now. The twist in Athraxus's mouth becomes a sneer.

He kneels with a sweep of his robe. Though his knees buckle for a moment and his face contorts, he rises again with the Augur in his arms. His eyes bore into Saba's all the while. He must have made a deal with the gods in the blackened bowels of that temple of his, she thinks: he must have bound up an unblemished white calf and cut its throat upon their altar. Perhaps he promised them the blood of his firstborn son in return for the unnatural strength they have granted, so late in his life.

And so with the rising of the sun upon the summer solstice, the High Priest of the Dark Temple bears the unconscious Prophetess up the hundred stone steps above the city. He makes no sound, not even a grunt of effort; and the priestess beside him holds her breath half the way, in terror for her mistress, in fury at his arrogance. At the sight of his profane hands gripping the Augur's body.

Looking up she sees smoke rising from the temple kitchens, where the novices are beginning to portion out the meat from yesterday's sacrifice. Some of them will be kneading dough, chopping herbs and onions. The roasting-fire lit and the room already hot. They do not yet know that the Augur is not in her bed.

"*There is a golden flower grows,*" sings the voice of the girl Cassia, "*by the stream where my sister was drowned... and a sturdy yew where my father lay down...*"

"Sisters!" calls Saba. "Sisters! Help us!"

Athraxus breaks his silence to laugh at her plea. Someone is pulling open the gate, squinting down at them into the sunlight. Aemilia lets out a cry. Saba rushes to meet her, stretching out a hand.

"*Sister*." Her own voice sounds distant to her, soft and urgent. "No distress, not now. She's alive. Help us bring her inside."

They shift the heavy gate between them so that Athraxus can stagger through. As though woken from a trance Saba moves close to his side, taking the weight of the Augur's legs, almost trying to pull her away from his grasp. Aemilia dances on tiptoes a little distance away, trying to get a glimpse of the old woman's face.

"Is she breathing? Can she speak?"

"Take me to her chamber." Athraxus's arms convulse and grip tightly.

By now the novices have heard the commotion and come running to the courtyard, gasping and exclaiming at the sight of their mother borne like a trussed goat. They will not approach the High Priest either, parting in a hurry as he passes between them. Aemilia leads the way past the walled part of the temple and then – strange, too strange that Athraxus's feet should tread here – up the tower staircase and into the narrow passage which leads up to the Augur's quarters. Athraxus grunts and curses beneath his burden, Saba forced now to fall behind him.

"The steps are steep there! Her legs are slipping, be careful… now lay her down gently…"

They stand, the three of them, and look upon the Prophetess. Prone, dumb, as they have never known her before. Mouth open, eyes moving beneath closed lids. Athraxus lowers his hood and wipes his forehead with his sleeve. Triumph, hunger flashing for a moment across his face. As though after bearing her body all of this way up to the temple, he might lick his lips and devour it. Saba turns on him at once, fierce and foolish in her exhaustion. "*This man*, he would rather she was dead and drowned. He couldn't imagine anything worse than to climb the mountain for her and find her living!"

Aemilia's lips form Saba's name, but in her terror no voice emerges. Athraxus does not strike out. He stands breathing heavily. The oddness of his presence in the Augur's chamber seems to grow more pressing by the moment.

"Now go." Saba tilts her chin upwards. "This is not your temple."

Athraxus moves away without hesitation, no doubt keen to get back to his prisoner. In the doorway he turns and fixes Saba with a hunter's look.

Says, "If it is the time. Think on it."

*

They kneel at her bedside. Aemilia wipes the dust from the old woman's face and hands with a cool cloth. Saba, bent forward and battling sleep, has hold of the hand which hangs limply from the bed. Their duties go neglected and they are silent, attendant to her long slow breaths.

"Do you remember?" whispers Aemilia.

Saba is with her at once. Years ago in their filth in the bottom of that boat as it bobbed in the harbour of the strange city. Wrists rubbed raw by the ropes that tied them. The two of them blinking up at the tall figure who stood silhouetted against the sky. Waves sloshing against the shore, bright light in their eyes. "She came to us like a heavenly being."

And it had seemed that way: this woman unlike anything they had seen before, the knotted muscles of her arms, the magnificent arch of her nose. She had hardly looked like a woman to them, or a man, or indeed anything human. She dwelled alone in a towering temple of stone, and communed with unseen gods.

"She bought back our lives for us," recalls Aemilia. As young children they had often asked their mother to tell them this story, until it became so familiar they could recite it like a prayer. *What did you think when you saw us, Mother? That I had never seen two creatures so pitiful, or so in need of a bath. And what did you pay to take us away? You cost me eight gold coins apiece. More than a jar of fine perfume, more than an unblemished calf.*

The breathing of the Augur, in, out. Close-to, the cracked plaster of her skin.

"*Saba,*" whispers Aemilia. "*Saba. What happened?*"

Saba is staring straight ahead. She thinks of Athraxus and her stomach twists. "He sent his guards away at the bottom of the steps. So that he could carry her up here himself. Like the head of a conquering army."

"On the mountain, Saba."

She looks around. Aemilia hands her the cloth, which she regards with some surprise. She raises it to her ash-smeared forehead, suddenly remembering the stain there. "On the mountain..."

"You didn't wake me."

"No. Athraxus came to see her in the night, and I persuaded him to come up there with me. We went to the cedar grove, but there was no trace. He wishes she'd been eaten by wild beasts. Fallen off the cliff and washed to the shore in the morning. He would have gone back to his bed and slept more soundly for it." She wants to spit on the ground to rid her mouth of its bitter taste. "I told him, that there's another place on the mountain where the Augur goes. I told him I wouldn't leave the mountain until we had searched for her there."

Saba's hands have steadied. She gives Aemilia the cloth, now dirtied with ash. Aemilia turns it over, aghast. "You went down to that place?"

"I was thinking how she might have been overcome by the presence of the gods. Isn't she mortal as any of us? And after all it

58

can't be forbidden for me, not completely, since I'll be seeking the gods there myself one day."

Aemilia gapes, and it seems she is on the verge of asking, *what did you see? What was there to see below the world?* But she holds back, and Saba is glad. She does not want to recall the sulphur and the shadows, the terrible earth-deep shudder of divinity close at hand.

The Augur stirs on her bed, murmuring. They both sit up sharply. "Mother." Saba takes both of the old woman's hands in hers. "Mother, what is it?"

With whispers and with careful fingertips they unwrap her head-cloth, loosen the cloak fastened at her throat. Her thin hair falls about her shoulders. The bulk of her body looks sturdy as a deep-rooted tree. She will wake, she will be herself again.

"Shall I fetch her some food?"

"Yes, 'Milia, and a fresh robe. She will wake soon."

VII

When Myloxenes unlocks the door to his rooms at the library, he finds Rufus already inside, sprawled on the bed and reading from his manuscript.

"I'm sure your research is very thorough, but it's a little dry. I wanted to know more about the mad Emperor Filestes and his fifty-seven concubines."

"How did you get in?"

Rufus points at the small, high window. "I really wish you wouldn't lock the door. Were you at the villa? It's nearly midday and I've been waiting here since sunrise." He sits up. He looks tired and dishevelled, still wearing the previous night's robes.

"Yes. Sorry. What happened?" Mylo takes the manuscript from Rufus's hands and carefully collects the scattered leaves of parchment from the bed and floor. He lays the half-finished book upon the desk.

"I'll tell you, I haven't so much as shut my eyes. I spent half the night hammering on the door of the Dark Temple like a fool until somebody told me they'd taken him to the council chamber, since his offence was against the Emperor as well as the gods. Then on the way there I thought I had better go and wake Mersia in case Calix might hold more sway with the council than I do, but it turned out that he was already awake and with the council, and Mersia was furious with me for wasting time. She says that she saw Father yesterday afternoon and thought he looked unwell and told him to stay in bed, and now she thinks I ought to have stopped him from speaking at all since I was there and apparently I could have prevented all of this if I'd only thought fast enough. Of course if *she'd* been born a man our family would be dining at the Emperor's table every night. Don't I wish it had been that way around?"

Throughout this Rufus's feet are tapping impatiently against the floor. He is squinting up at Mylo through bloodshot eyes. "So anyway, by the time I made it to the council chamber they'd taken him back to the temple, and as far as I can tell they still have him there. I can't get a useful word out of anybody. Calix says that your father is salivating to have a public flogging at the very least. I need you to come with me, Mylo, I need you to come with me and talk very calmly and reasonably with him until he relents."

Mylo hesitates. It is true that he had thought to go to his father and petition for Lennes, but he had imagined going with Antonus at his side, not Rufus. Antonus could have done most of the talking; he commands at least some of the respect due to his years and his blood. "Antonus said they were sure to have freed your father by now."

"I assure you they haven't. Are you going to help me or not?"

"I thought that I was useless to you in these matters." He is teasing, but an irritable glance tells him that Rufus is hardly in the mood. It is a little strange between them these days. They were lovers for a short time the previous summer. It seems entirely sensible to Mylo to have ended it: such attachments are for boys, and they are both now of marriageable age.

"You can tell your father that mine is a senile dolt. Say that he's served this city so long and so faithfully that the hard work has scrambled his brain."

"Is that true?" Mylo asks before he can stop himself. He wills Rufus to say, yes, it is true. The dreams of Lennes are nothing more than a tired old man's confusion.

With discomfort, he sees a frown cross his friend's face. In all the chaos of the previous night, it seems that Rufus has not yet stopped to give this consideration. "You know," he says slowly, "I don't think it is. A dullard, yes, even more so in his old age. But still quite in possession of his senses, until now. Never given to invention or fancy. He fears the Emperor and the gods."

"Then what do you make of it? That he stood in front of that whole assembly and came out with something so extraordinary?"

Rufus shakes his head like a cat shaking water from its whiskers. "I don't know, Mylo. I hardly care. Let's get him out of their grasp, and worry about the rest of this madness later."

*

Myloxenes hates to enter even the outer courts of the Dark Temple. Deeper within, he knows, the blackness in that place has legs. It creeps down his neck and beneath his tunic, in against his skin. In the courtyard lie piles of bones from sacrifices which are not burned but left to rot. On the suffocating air the smell of stale entrails and centuries-old secrecy, the dust from the heavy curtains which conceal the sanctuary. It is the smell which since earliest childhood he has associated with his father.

The shrine-prostitutes who are kept in the temple sanctuary

have no faces. They cannot have faces, since there is no light in that place. They have bodies, which are there for the use of the men who come to the temple to seek union with the gods. Such a union, the temple teaches, can be sought but never found: in darkness, in unknowing, in fear and pain. That is what the rite means, and how it was born.

Guides lead men to their beds. When Myloxenes was thirteen his father first brought him to the temple, and handed him over to a guide. He is seized sometimes by the paralysing memory of these visits, which ceased when he was sixteen and left his father's home for good. The way the dead air of that place swallows daylight. The weight of Athraxus's hand pressing the back of his neck. The way the women did not weep.

The Temple of Blood, as it is also known, squats half-hidden in a narrow street near the heart of the city. Its stones were cut from pale mountain rock long ago, but have since been blackened by soot and grease and ash. Around the entrance sellers jostle for position, waving braces of doves, calling the prices of their goats and prayer-scrolls and carved votive statues, rattling bags of coins. Though the crowd is crammed dense and loud into the street, the sanctuary entrance itself is tiny, a square doorway barely high enough for a man to walk through. On either side of this doorway stand two stone gods, one male, one female. Both are naked. Their bodies are contorted as though caught in spasms of pain. Both hide their faces in their hands.

Mylo follows Rufus, who is elbowing his way persistently through the crowd, heading for the side of the temple and the entrance into the outer courts. When the guard only stares at them, his huge body blocking the way in, Rufus empties an entire purse of coins into his hand.

After the noise and bustle outside, the courtyard seems eerily quiet. A few rats scurry through the dust and a red-robed priest sits upon a wall, eating a lump of fatty meat and licking his fingers. Rufus kicks a stone in his direction. "You! Did you see where they took the Steward?"

The priest, a boy of no more than eleven, shrugs. "Not mine to know," he says. "Can't claim certainty."

"I'll stuff that down your throat, you cocky little——"

Mylo touches Rufus on the shoulder, and points. Shadows are moving in a chamber at the far end of the courtyard. They cross it quickly, and as they draw closer hear a series of dull thuds and a grunt of pain. Rufus winces, stops on the spot. He turns to Mylo, pale. *"Will you go in?"* he whispers.

Mylo feels the familiar wave of nausea wash over him. He looks back across the courtyard. Dust blows through piles of bones and the priest is picking gristle from between his teeth. It must be done quickly, he resolves, or not at all. He ducks inside.

The chamber is low and long, the far wall stacked with sacks of grain. Two slit windows permit only meagre light. Green mould has taken hold at the root of the wall where the grain sacks have split. In the centre of the room Lennes has been bound with ropes to a chair. Three temple guards stand over him. His face is florid with bruises, blooming purple along his jawline, eyes swollen and closed to slits. One of his arms hangs bloodied at an odd angle. He has been stripped to his undergarment.

"This is not your business, boy." Athraxus is leaning against the stack of wine-barrels at the side of the room, supervising the proceedings. He looks, Mylo thinks, half-wild: for some reason there are briers caught on his cloak, sweat and ash-stains mingled on his face. His dogs are sat at his feet, and at once, their dark bodies begin rumbling in warning.

Mylo feels his tongue grow thick and heavy. "This man," he manages to say. "He's addled. His children say so. He doesn't know his own mind."

"Couldn't your cripple limp here himself, if he cares for this man's life?" Athraxus raises two fingers of his right hand. A guard brings a wooden club down forcefully on Lennes' collarbone, and the Steward howls with pain. His thinning hair falls forward across his face as he bends forward, trying fruitlessly to break free of his bonds. His ribcage heaves. "Well, whatever Antonus hoped to achieve by sending you here, it's no use. Nothing will dissuade our Steward from continuing in his blasphemy."

Lennes spits blood out of his mouth. "The gods have spoken," he says, indistinctly. Mylo sees that more of his teeth are missing. "The gods have made themselves known——" One of the other guards strikes him across the face.

"Antonus didn't send me," says Mylo. He can't meet his father's gaze, that look of naked contempt which never fails to strip him of his courage. But he doesn't want to look at the disfigured Steward either. He stares fixedly at a space of wall over Athraxus's shoulder. "I came — we came — of our own accord." He is aware of Rufus creeping in at his shoulder, and of his own voice cracking feebly. "This man has... he's been a faithful servant of the city..."

"He'll be whipped in the market square, unless he swallows his words by sundown."

"The market square?" Mylo manages to say. "He's a councillor, Father, well-respected... with silver in his beard..."

"The Emperor will allow it," says Athraxus.

"The law for blasphemy is one night," says one of the guards. "Not a night and a day."

Athraxus straightens, taking a step towards the centre of the room. "There it is, then." He is looming over Lennes now, just as he did at the feast. He seizes a handful of beard-hair, and pulls. *What are the names of the gods?*

"*Their names are not ours to utter*," say the temple guards, in unison.

64

Lennes rocks back and forth. Splinters of his shattered collarbone are protruding through his skin.

"*Shall we see the faces of the gods?*"

"*Their faces are hidden from us.*"

"*Shall we hear the voices of the gods?*"

Lennes' swollen eyes roll in his head. He stammers, "Only say – what I have heard. No – use. Must speak or perish, must—"

His eyes widen suddenly, and his voice fades away. He has seen Rufus.

Mylo is aware of his friend moving out of the doorway. Rufus is even paler than before, round-eyed as a child, apparently unable to look away. The sight of his son seems to extinguish Lennes' guttering resolve. He swallows the end of his sentence and the two stare at one another.

The moment tightens. Mylo sees Athraxus shift slightly, a sated expression flickering across his face. The kill is already made. When Lennes' son-in-law Calix stumbles suddenly into the room, breathless and waving a roll of parchment, Athraxus barely reacts.

"I have it!" cries Calix, bending to catch his breath, hands on his knees. A big man, he is sweating profusely. "You can let him go! Here..." He waves the scroll in Athraxus' direction, and it unfurls. "The name and trading address of a very ... *disreputable* ... apothecary ... and his assistant, who just an hour ago confessed to selling this man a draught cut with herbs for inducing visions..."

Athraxus takes the scroll, and Mylo catches a flicker of movement in the fingers of Calix's right hand, a sign made just within the High Priest's vision. "At his request?"

"Without his knowledge, sir! He drank it as a sleeping-draught, and against his will took a preparation of vervain, earth-almond and fox's blood, over which forbidden prayers and chants had been sung."

"And was it the intention of these apothecaries to disrupt the order of this city?"

"It was, sir! To create the semblance of a divine vision by trickery, so that they could mislead the gullible and discredit the authority of this temple."

Mylo sees a glitter in his father's eye, a moment of pleasure. Athraxus enjoys a game well-played. He examines the scroll before carefully rolling it up again. Lennes' head is slumped now on his chest, a thread of blood hanging from the corner of his mouth. He seems beyond hearing or caring. The guards, standing over the limp body in the chair, look to Athraxus for their instructions.

"This seems to be in order," says the High Priest. "Untie him."

*

It is Calix who takes the weight of the all-but-unconscious Steward, pulling the man's arm over his own shoulders and dragging him bodily along the narrow street, away from the temple. Mylo and Rufus follow close at his heels, trying to ignore as best they can the jeers and shouted questions of the surrounding crowd, who press closer to get a better look. This man of the Emperor's council, silver in his beard, bleeding onto the dung-strewn dirt.

"Hey, Steward's boy!" calls one of the sellers. "What did he do, try to abolish the temple tax?"

"I'll abolish you and your chance at progeny," snarls Rufus, but Mylo pulls him away, letting the burly form of Calix cut a path through the crowd ahead of them. Still fuming, Rufus brushes Mylo off and pushes ahead to catch up with his brother-in-law.

"You're not nearly clever enough to have concocted such a story. I detect Mersia's work."

"I never claimed credit," grunts Calix.

"Where is she, then? Waiting for you to drag in her prize, like a good dog?"

"That's the size of it."

"And she couldn't have birthed her scheme a few hours earlier, and saved me the run-around? Seeing as she *always* knows best?"

Out on the main street, they fall into step. The city square is strewn with debris and not yet empty of solstice revellers. Some are insensible, slumped against walls or over wine-caskets, while others are still dancing, half-naked and smeared in ash. Their low fires have yet to burn out, and around their feet, dogs are fighting over the carcass of a sacrificed goat. Mylo catches the gaze of one of the nearby dancers, and quickly looks away. The man's eyes are wild and black. He moves closer to Calix and takes the Steward's other arm.

Calix and Mersia's home is tucked away behind a busy trading street, reached through a passage leading between the shop-fronts. Awkwardly, the three of them manoeuvre Lennes through the passage, the sound of hurried footsteps greeting them as they emerge into the high, round atrium.

"There you are! Don't manhandle him!" Mersia looks a great deal like her brother, the same snub, upturned nose and freckled skin. Despite the hour she looks ready to attend a night's feasting at the palace, her hair piled atop her head in an extravagant, fashionable style. Like Rufus she is fond of expensive silks, and she made a shrewd marriage so that she might afford more of them. Gold glitters on her ears, fingers and wrists as she rushes forward and seizes Lennes by the shoulders. She recoils at the sight of his face.

"Oh, he's getting blood on my floor..." Slaves come darting into the room, and Mersia waves her hands at them impatiently. "My father is hurt. Carry him to the inner rooms, gently, gently now! And fetch a physician. And a cloth."

Relieved of his burden, Calix wipes distastefully at the bloodstains on his tunic. Mylo watches the slaves carry Lennes away. Rufus, meanwhile, has rounded on his sister.

"So *very* gracious of you to get off your day-bed and help us out, Mers, I know how you need your beauty sleep."

"I've been up all night, as you well know, you ungrateful little—"

"I'm going to the baths," announces Calix. They both ignore him, and he stomps away.

"Oh yes, I'm sure you must have had an awful time of it on your reclining couch, while I was tearing down the door of the Dark Temple for him!"

"You shouldn't have needed to," yells Mersia, "if you hadn't allowed him to make a fool of himself in public! By all the gods, brother!"

"You think that's all this is? That he had too much wine and spoke out of turn? You weren't there, you didn't hear him!"

"He's right," Mylo intervenes, before Mersia can start shouting again. His ears are ringing and he feels as though someone has poured syrup into his brains. He wants nothing more than to crawl into his bed, but there is still business to be done here, if Lennes is to be kept safe from Athraxus.

The lady of the house folds her arms and turns her unimpressed gaze upon him. "And I suppose we have *your* father to thank for this whole adventure, Myloxenes."

Rufus rolls his eyes and turns away, irritated, but Mylo stands his ground. "This isn't going to disappear overnight. Your father thinks he's had a divine vision of the city being destroyed. He wouldn't be convinced otherwise, not even by the temple guards and their clubs. There were lots of witnesses to what he said, it'll be all over the city already."

The horror of this dawns visibly on Mersia. She clasps her hands to her breast. "I'll make some visits," she mutters, to herself. "I'll throw a dinner. A party."

"I hope our reputation will mend that easily," says Rufus darkly.

"What I meant was," persists Mylo, "you'll have to keep a close watch on him, because Athraxus certainly will. Maybe don't let him resume his council post. Encourage him to take a quiet retirement. At least keep him out of the public eye until he's seen sense, won't you?"

"I can't *baby* him." Mersia adjusts the bracelets on her wrists. "I have things to do."

"Then have somebody do it for you."

"How long for?"

The household is starting to come awake around them. Slaves are carrying plates of fresh fruit and sweetbreads into the sunny courtyard. Mersia's little daughter, Calica, spies Rufus from across the atrium and comes running across the colourful tiles with a squeal of delight. Her uncle sweeps her up into his arms, still frowning as he turns to Mylo. "How long do you think your father will hold a grudge?"

He looks at the three of them, the same bright hair, the same childish, expectant look, and gives a tired laugh. "Until the mountains fall."

*

The two apothecaries named by Mersia are taken that afternoon from their place of business and whipped until bloody and then hung from the tall trees next to the city boundary. In the hot sun they attract a small crowd, who mill around eating grilled fish from a nearby stall. The talk is good humoured for the most part, jokes about the mad Steward, rumours about the concoction he supposedly ingested. There is some admiration for the audacity of the dead men, scorn for the sight of their naked bodies, their dangling legs and ridiculous exposed private parts. Flies land on their open wounds, their mouths and eyes. Nobody chases away the hungry dogs which are already skulking nearby.

Mylo and Rufus, passing by to see that the thing has been done, pause and look on. The smaller of the hanging men looks as though he might have died before being strung up; his back is black with bruises and the rope has been forced around his neck at an odd angle. The other is swollen grotesquely in the face, tongue sticking out between his puffy lips.

Rufus exhales in relief, brightening as he turns away.

"Well. There's that dealt with, at least. You hungry?"

VIII

In the dead of night, in the stone silence of the temple, Saba remembers first coming to this city. Long ago in the belly of the boat from the country where she was sold as a slave. Her wrists and ankles tied, sitting in her own filth. The sound of that other slave-child weeping for countless days and nights until her eyes were dry and her stomach sick. Saba had reached for her hand in the darkness. Wrapped firm arms around her through the night and listened to her whimpering. Poor scraps. Poor flea-bitten bundles, little war-spoils.

"Saba. Are you awake?'

"What is it, 'Milia?"

"The dreams of Lennes." Saba turns over. Aemilia's anxious face stares back at her in the dimness. "Do you think that the gods might really send dreams to a man like that?"

Saba has been running this question through her wakeful mind. She does not reply. It is far-fetched, it is unlikely, that any vision should come to the city unmediated by priest or priestess. Let alone a vision of the kind that the Steward described. In this age the gods are not known to move among the people. Why send a word such as this to a man such as that?

And yet. Attend, Saba, to the trembling of the earth beneath

70

you. To the quiet rustling of the leaves in the cedar grove. To the whispers in the blackness of the cavern in the rocks. Once every thousand lifetimes the gods begin a new work. Her mother the Augur has raised her to pause and listen in any place where divine breath might breathe.

"It's not impossible," she says.

Aemilia is quiet for a long time. "If even the smallest part of it is true," she says at last, "it would mean great trouble for the city. Saba? Wouldn't it?"

"I suppose it would."

She imagines the stars raining down from the firmament. She imagines the face of the moon turned red as blood. Far away, on the mountain, a wolf begins to wail.

"Saba," says Aemilia very quietly. "Do you remember holding on to me? You didn't know my name yet, but you held my hand."

"Yes, sister. We had different names, then."

Something must have formed in your heart over the course of that voyage, Saba. You know you wept, too, endless silent tears into Aemilia's matted hair. But you do not remember being afraid. Though one world was gone, you knew somehow that the world was not ended. Your hands gripped tightly. Life beat on in you, a seam of stubborn joy which had no place being there. It surfaces in you still.

Tonight she knows that Aemilia needs to travel back into the familiar story of who they are. She needs to nudge the foundation-stones back into place, to know that the world's borders and boundaries are restored.

"And our mother came for us, do you remember that? They were going to sell us to the Dark Temple. She purchased our lives for us. Eight gold coins each."

"Yes, 'Milia. I remember. She gave us new names."

You, small one, are Saba. Pale-haired girl, Aemilia. Who are Saba and

71

Aemilia twelve years on, fed on this city's bread, the first tongues they spoke forgotten? They do not look like the natives here, who are olive-skinned and brown-eyed. In the land where Aemilia was born, ten months' sailing to the north, the sun shines at midnight and women slip on sleek new skins to go swimming under the water. Their hair is pale as the snows which fall in winter, their eyes like chipped ice. They look like people whose colour has been washed away by the waves.

Ten months' riding to the south, Saba's people sing to the stars above the desert plain. It was hot there, hotter than the city at midsummer. She has a memory of sand scorching the soles of her feet. Sitting on a round mat woven with patterns like sunbursts. The crisp-sweet smell of roots frying in a pan. Saba lies awake sometimes and turns over these pictures hungrily in her mind, as though picking the last meat from a bone. Once the recollections of her senses were vividly painted, but she has long since handled them too much, and they have lost their sheen. When she enters into them now they are memories of memories, wishfully remade.

One thing alone she still recalls with bruising clarity: the day she was taken. The long clouds of the rain season hung in the sky. There had been a hunt. Her mother and her mother's mother wore the claws of slain lionesses about their necks. Saba knows that they live, these mothers, because when she listens for it she can still hear the howling they lifted to the heavens as she was torn from their grip.

That day she screamed in answer over many miles until her throat was raw. She scratched her captors' hands until they trussed her like a rabbit and bundled her onto the back of a horse. Little Saba, that fearless child. She spat out the food she was given, and tore her hair. She was not quietly made their captive.

She thinks she can remember, in her first weeks and months in this city, missing home with a savage and unhealing ache that she was far too young to comprehend. And she longs for that place still, though with a vaguer kind of pain. *Home* now, that first home, is somewhere she has built for herself, held safe within the walls of her heart, hardly a real place of solid earth.

All her years in the city she has used a sharpened blade to cut her hair close to her head. She has prayed to her mothers, who live, and vowed in her heart: my hair shall not grow again until I am returned to them. For the first time in a long while Saba remembers that this promise was once more than symbol and ritual.

"There will be prayers. Won't there, Saba?" asks Aemilia, still preoccupied. "If there's any truth in it. We'll beg the gods for mercy. We'll fast. We'll make offerings. Our mother, she'll tell us all what to do."

"We can only wait," says Saba, "and take care of her, and pay close attention to the signs."

Aemilia's voice has dropped to barely a whisper. "Saba. When do you think that you'll be made Augur?"

She does not answer. Impossibilities are taking form in her mind. What will there be, if this temple is gone? This city? Already she can feel her heart righting itself like a ship upon storm-stirred water. Your heart, Saba; it is so reckless in its courage.

Slowly, she speaks to the darkness.

"We were not born here, Aemilia. We grew up under foreign stars. We grew up under our captors' constellations, far from home."

IX

Why did the gods create us?
   This secret is hidden in darkness.
What do the gods desire of us?

73

It is not ours to know.
What are the names of the gods?
Their names are not ours to utter.
Shall we see the faces of the gods?
Their faces are hidden from us.
Shall we hear the voices of the gods?
They do not speak for our hearing.
Are we pleasing to the gods? Are our lives pleasing to them?
It is blasphemous to claim certainty.
We might come with supplication and with prayer.
We might surrender offerings to the flames.
We might spill blood, and hope for mercy.

The man under the ground walks with slow steps. His feet are bare. In the crook of each arm he holds a bundle. He stares glassy-eyed into the darkness, moving through a dream.

The tunnel stretches onward and downward ahead of him, like the throat of a giant. Though it is unlit, he knows the way. He is wearing a long robe which sweeps the ground behind him.

A brightness appears and he continues in his walk towards it, unhurried. The firelight illuminates him as he draws closer. His eyes are large and golden as a hawk's, ringed with dark paint. On his face, an expression of bliss.

There are ripples in the air. The shape of the tunnel distorts in a wave of heat. Still he walks on. The paint around his eyes begins to melt, turning to black tears. He bows his head against the roaring onslaught of the heat. He rounds a corner.

The bundles in his arms begin to stir and cry. *Shhh,* he murmurs, *shhh. No need to fret.* His eyes close. His lips begin to move in silent supplication.

The furnace blazes ahead.

ARCADIAN

I

The Augur taught Saba the virtue of preparation: and now, she likes to think, she is prepared. Waking, she lies still for moment on her straw pallet, securing a plan in her mind. The most important thing is that the Augur is cared for. But it must also be seen to that the younger priestesses are kept from seeing her in such a weakened condition, or from spreading rumours amongst themselves about the events of the night before. Any visitors to the temple must know that all continues here as normal. There will be gossip in the streets, but better that it be about Lennes, not the Prophetess who collapsed in the cave on the mountain and was absent from her own feast.

Saba feels as though she has grown shrewder overnight. She has understood for a long time the place this temple has in the city, and now she sees the intricacy, the delicacy of that balance. A set of scales upon which the Augur is the decisive counter. The love that a ruler or a people have for their religion, perhaps it has never been so much a matter of the heart, but one of power.

The favour she enjoys, Athraxus had warned, *it's for her. It's not for the temple.* Over the course of a long lifetime the Augur has sent her roots out into the city, and now she holds its crumbling stones together. She is the last place the city can look for communion with the gods. Lift the old woman away, and what are we left with?

A lesser heart might have trembled. I must hold it all in place, resolves Saba, I must tend to all of this until she is strong again. What I haven't yet learned of her ways, I'll have to guess at or invent for myself.

When the grain delivery arrives before midday, she makes for the kitchens to call on the priestesses for help. But on her way she is shocked to see the Augur herself striding down from the tower, hair tied under a clean cloth, sleeves rolled up. She looks brisk, bright, the wrinkled skin of her face fresh-scrubbed. Saba swallows her astonishment. "My mother, I didn't know you were awake..."

"Since before dawn. Did you think you'd spend another day sponging my forehead, Saba?"

This woman is an ancient olive tree, and no storm may uproot her. Together they approach the heap of grain-sacks and the men beside the gate, who are waiting to be paid. The men are grumbling amongst themselves about the long climb in the heat, but fall quiet as the two priestesses draw near. Saba thinks that they seem warier than usual, their eyes darting sideways as coins are handed over. They hurry away without pausing to pass the time of day or to share tales of their solstice excesses. Has the story of what happened at the feast already spread?

They haul the sacks one by one inside the gate and into the store-room. The Augur has regained her strength: her thick, sinewy arms are strong enough to lift two at a time. Saba, half her mistress's size, works in determined silence until the job is done and they take a minute's rest in the cool of the store. The Augur pulls a small knife from inside her robes and slashes the side of one of the bags. She takes a handful of grain and places several kernels, raw, between her teeth.

Saba wipes the back of her hand across her sweating forehead. "What are you doing?"

The knife is proffered to her. "We ought to test all of them. Don't eat too many. Check for a bitter taste."

"You think—"

"I think that we can't be certain any more about our lives in this city."

Saba's hand tightens around the handle of the knife. She cuts the side of the nearest sack. Places a pinch of kernels between her teeth, tastes them, spits them out. They do this together until all of the sacks have been checked. Saba glances frequently over her shoulder at the doorway, afraid that Aemilia or one of the others will find them in this macabre activity, and ask for an explanation.

Her mind is racing. "Do you think that Athraxus would dare to do this? We went together to find you on the mountain, and he spoke to me. He said that we – that I – wouldn't have any power or protection, if you were gone."

"He tried to scare you." The Augur is looking at her with level eyes.

"He said that he wouldn't destroy us, though. That he'd let this temple stand."

"Since when do wolves keep to their word?"

It is so comforting to have the Augur here present and alert that Saba cannot find it in herself to fear Athraxus today. She finds a grin curling the edges of her mouth. "You should have seen him in the cedar grove. So uncomfortable, stamping around as though he was trying to scare birds out of the bushes. I think the gods must have been laughing."

"I'm sure they were. A man like that, in such a place. They should have spoken out in their most thunderous voices, and given him the shock of his life."

"Did they speak to you, Mother?" Saba asks, before she can stop herself.

They look at one another. The Augur's eyes are grey like heavy clouds. "I watched the starlings fly," she says quietly. "I went into the cavern. The air was very close there, and I felt faint. I am well again now, as you see."

It is unlike the Augur to hold back anything of importance from Saba. They both know it. Saba looks into her mistress's face, and sees mystery, and comfort, and danger.

"The gods didn't say anything important, I suppose," she says, lightly.

A shadow passes across the Augur's features. The younger priestesses complain, sometimes, that her face is impossible to divine; that one might as well seek feeling from an old cloth or a rock in the road. She has, they say, only one expression – a deeply furrowed frown. We do not know, they say, whether we have met with her approval. Can you tell us, Saba? We can't tell whether her peering into the smoke and the entrails has brought her joy or trepidation or simply left her irritable and bored.

Saba loves the Augur's face. The sun-beaten, rough-hewn features, the large hooked nose. Saba sees the power which resides in those harsh lines, the piercing wisdom of the deep-set eyes. She remembers her first glimpse of that face, peering down into the stall where they had been flung with the animals, in the chaos of the harbour, that morning long ago.

The Augur had been alone at that time, all of her priestesses lately put to death on the orders of the Emperor. Saba has always told Aemilia, the gods showed us to her in a dream. The gods led her down to the harbour that day. She went for oysters, and instead she found us, curled up filthy in our chains among the sheep and the goats.

The Augur had been the first person to shave Saba's head, cutting away the rank tangles of hair with the blade of a knife. Her hands firm and calloused but not rough. Aemilia's hair had been cut off too, their smarting heads doused with vinegar and terebinth to kill the lice. The Augur gave them two straw mats but they slept together, clinging to one another. For some months there had only been the three of them at the temple, their footsteps sounding too loud in the empty halls and passageways. Not so much as a common language between them. Each nursing, in secret, the fresh wound of her losses.

Words had reached them. The Augur spoke stories at their bedside until they began to understand, until they tried the new tongue for themselves. She stood over them like the mountain, and they were safe in her shadow. This was how they anchored themselves to their present life, the three of them, reaching for it like a rock in the ocean. Dough was kneaded, floors swept, and they learned each other's daily rhythms. They began to breathe again.

The others had come, sent from homes in the city that could not feed them: clever Liva, bold and curious as a blackbird. Cassia, good-natured, vain of her pretty face and voice. Blunt, contrary Eris – and then the little ones, filling the rooms of the temple with chatter and argument and laughter. Saba and Aemilia had gathered these arrivals in as their mother had gathered them, proud to be first among the priestesses. Though hardly so much greater in age or experience, the two knew they held an honoured place. Daughters born from barrenness, chosen by the Augur's own hand.

All of this is close to Saba's heart as she regards her mistress now. A shaft of sunlight is shining through the doorway of the storeroom. Cassia can be heard singing in the kitchens, and the goats are bleating. Dust dances in the bright morning.

"Is Lennes the Steward old and mad?" she asks.

"What do you think, Saba?"

"I don't know. No. I can't entirely believe it. Mother, I felt the earth shake."

She expects the Augur to respond to this last with an explanation – or at least with interest. But she only wipes the grain-dust from her hands, moving towards the door. Saba catches up with her, and they emerge together into the daylight. Above them, the stained white stones of their temple. Below, the smoky, uneven sprawl of the city.

Saba turns to her mistress. It is an old riddle: but today it feels urgent. "How can there be two temples in the city, when one temple says, *the gods do not speak*, and the other says, *the gods have spoken?*"

"You know it's not that simple."

"You're not going anywhere, are you?"

"No, Saba. I'm not."

*

They sit, ten or eleven of the younger girls, cross-legged in the temple hall. In front of each of them, Saba has set light to some small quantity of sage. The smoke does not rise above their heads, as it might in more ordinary times, but lingers in a dull cloud all about them. Saba knows what sort of sign this is, but none of the girls seem to have noticed it.

"Saba, do we have to do this much longer?" complains Eris, tall for her eleven years, ever impatient.

"My knees are hurting," pipes up Amone, the youngest.

"I wanted to see if there were ripe peaches at the market."

They sigh and squirm and protest that nothing is revealed, that on such a hot day they would rather be dipping their feet in the river. Before the events of the solstice Saba would have let them go, would have assumed that there was time.

"Watch the curling of the leaves. The direction of the flames. Pay attention to these patterns."

They shuffle and grumble. Saba feels an unfamiliar heaviness in her heart. The meaning of these lessons, of the priestess's lives, is changed. They have no idea of it, but now they are like the watchmen who would once stand upon the city wall, scanning the horizon for an approaching army. If there is any sign from the gods of things to come, surely it will be sighted first in the Augur's Temple. Best that the watchers are alert and awake.

They are so young. But then Saba herself was only seven years old when the Augur first killed a calf in front of her and laid out its body, legs splayed, innards glistening. *Here, hold the liver. Don't be afraid. You smell like that on the inside too, child. It's just how living things are.* She had been instantly fascinated. Each warm organ weighing heavy in her palm. These hidden mysteries, wrapped in flesh, now hers for the taking if she had the wit to interpret them.

Today in the cloud of sage she sees the city hung as though by a thread before her. She hears again the sneering voice of Athraxus. *If it is the time...*

For a long time now, the fact that she will one day be called Prophetess has sat with Saba as certain but not immediate, far in the hazy future. After all, it won't happen until the present Augur passes on – which is like saying, until the oceans dry up.

"Sister," blurts out one of the girls. "Saba."

"We've been wondering..."

"The old Steward, can you interpret what he said for us?" Even sensible Liva, the oldest of them, cannot quell her curiosity. "The worm, the bird, the salamander, what's it all about?"

"Do you think it's really a message from the gods?"

There is trouble under every rock today. Saba resists pointing out to her pupils that Lennes has already offered interpretation, along with his prophecy. *What is rotten will be devoured, what shines will be extinguished, what is decaying must burn.* The last thing she wants is to have them dwelling on these words.

"That's for the Augur to worry about. Now, how will you see into hidden things if you can't keep quiet for an hour?"

They are obedient, and in the silence which follows Saba wonders that they trust her so much. Those priestesses who came before me and Aemilia, she thinks, they must have trusted the Augur. But when the Emperor's favour turned she could not protect them.

Laonatus ordered those murders, and yet Saba knows that the Augur still counsels him, gets up when he calls for her in the night, listens to his questions and complaints. This used to confuse her — wouldn't a bold prophet name his evils to his face, refuse to serve him until he repented? As she gets older she begins to understand. For a woman who is nobody to wield the smallest influence over an Emperor, the slightest chance of guiding him, she must ride on a tiger's back.

I was so angry, Saba, raging, but there was nothing I could do. It changed me. Being that helpless made me wiser, in the end. The Augur is slower these days, so she says, both to conclusion and to action. There is little in this realm or the next that can be answered at once. In her youth she used to charge headlong into each day and its encounters, head bent low like a bull's, braced to throw all opposition from her path. Now she pauses in uncertainties. Walks with one foot on either side of the divide, lets the words of gods and hearts of men be revealed in whatever time they will. *This much, Saba, even the Dark Temple understands: truth is no cheap thing.* Saba had been ten when the Augur first told her about the murdered priestesses who came before. She thinks of them now, those girls thrown into the ground, and grows sober. The nature of the power that we hold, it is so elusive. It is there for all to see and then it is nothing, in an instant melted away, like land formed by haze at the horizon on a hot day.

*

In the heart of the Augur's temple there is a fire which burns without ceasing. It was set alight by the city's first forefathers, and has blazed ever since. It was set alight by those ancients themselves, shuffling from their tallow-stained caves, holding forth torches to light their way out of the savage age. It was set alight by the god from the cloud-wrapped mountain, stepping downward in that green dawn, bearing furs to cover the shame of men.

When Saba was too young to understand the tale, the Augur told her how the two temples came to be. How there came a time among the ancients when it no longer seemed enough for each man to speak for his own life. How they began to hand themselves over, a piece at a time, to men among them who kept the truth inside their tents. Who said that they possessed holy knowledge. Who promised the people that for a price they too might be permitted to glimpse the brightness which breathes behind all things.

According to these men, there were things forbidden. Things fearful. Things before which the people must cover their eyes. Narrow paths that must not be strayed from. Power before which all must tremble. Their tales spun in finest thread that space where no sandalled foot might tread, that space called sacred.

These men came to own the secrets of the people's hearts. They claimed they had the power to transform into birds or foxes or bears; the power of flight, to bring the weather at their will. They called out to the homing flock of the people's hearts, and all flew to them. They held out welcoming hands. They whispered: *The gods are displeased. The gods do not walk in the world as they once did. You thirst, but there is no drinking freely. What you seek is far away.*

This absence will find you when you are alone, lying in the dark of your bed. You will crave consolation the way a man crossing the desert craves water. Any cost, to dip your hands, to drink even a drop from the fountain of life. So enter our doorway, and take a knife. Cut into your own flesh.

It was always dark inside their tents. Mysteries whispered of in rooms whose doors were closed. *The knowledge of the heartbeat of your life, so say the gods, is not for you. No more than this can be known.*

So unconsoled and unguided, the people appointed a listener.

Did they appoint her, that first in the lineage? Perhaps not. Perhaps she simply came one day to the public square and began to speak. None can recall. A woman, barely more than a child, born far from the comforts of the palace or the blessings of the temple. She was nobody. She said: *I can hear.*

No strength, no name, no sons. A channel. A vessel. She spoke softly and was still heard, because her words were not her own. She said, *it is granted to me, to be the mouthpiece of the gods.* The words she spoke carried their own weight. And the city listened

*

Saba closes her eyes to picture the first Augur. This woman stands in the grove between the cedar trees at the thin time in the year when the sun hangs longest and highest in the sky. The birds spell out mysteries for her.

The priests and the rulers, they barely notice her. When they notice her, it is with trepidation first, with anger, with mockery, with puzzlement. Since the city listens, and the people of the city outnumber them, they do not yet cover her mouth. Among themselves, they whisper of her. They watch. They wait. She is one solitary voice, after all. She is barely a small stone in the city's balance.

This woman climbs and makes her home above the city. Folds her cloak about her, looks out over the rooftops. Lights a fire there in the space between the rocks, to warm her hands.

II

"Mother?" Aemilia, bearing barley-bread and cheese and grapes and a cup of goat's milk, knocks on the door to the Augur's chamber. "There's food here, if you want it, or I could come back..."

"No, I am hungry."

"Or I could make you some mild food, some porridge…"

"Here, child, come in."

Aemilia pushes open the door and enters with undue caution, peering inside, unsure of what she will find there. Her distress at seeing her mistress so feeble the day before has not yet faded. She is relieved to find the Prophetess cross-legged upon the floor, straight as a sapling, poring over her scrolls as though nothing out of the ordinary has happened.

"Saba said you looked better."

"She's right. Bring that over here."

Aemilia sets the food down upon the floor beside the Augur, who stretches to grasp at it, a thick chunk of bread in her fist. "Come, sit. Eat with me."

Aemilia sits obediently and picks at the fruit, darting glances at her mistress.

"I have recovered," says the Augur more gently, looking up at her. "I promise. You have been worrying."

Aemilia nods.

"Nearly fifty years now I've sought the gods for this city, and hardly had a day's sickness. Do you think many people live so long, dove?"

"I don't know."

"It is a blessing, a sign of special favour. It means the gods still have more for me to do."

"Oh." Aemilia is not sure that she would want divine favour of this kind. She would rather live an unexceptional span, and escape the gods' notice.

She does not ask what happened at the grove on the mountain. Neither does she ask about the feast. Any disruption of the usual order is worrisome to Aemilia, whose imagination is at once too large and too limited: she fears small calamities without knowing how small they are. The idea of any greater cataclysm is quite beyond her grasp. They eat together, and when they are finished she makes to get up and leave, but the Augur stays her.

The old woman reaches out to bind again the white cloth that holds Aemilia's hair. She tightens the corners and tucks in strands which have strayed from the coiled braid.

"Can you see what kind of future awaits you?" she asks.

"*Me*, Mother?"

"Even you. Dear child, from now on the theatre can have no spectators. All of us are players. You live in this city, don't you?"

Much of what the Augur says is mysterious to Aemilia, and always has been. This has never troubled her before: Saba has been there to explain, when she wants it, and often she does not. Even when her mind cannot keep pace, her heart has always known to grow calm in the old woman's presence.

But now she finds herself backing deliberately away from the Augur's meaning, as though from a precarious ledge. "Mother, I should go. They need my help in the kitchens."

"They will have to do without you tonight. Aemilia. Listen to me." Reluctantly, she meets her mother's eyes. The Augur's expression is grave. "There is a man who comes to the solstice feast every year. He is known as Antonus the Cripple. He usually sits to the left of his brother the Emperor. He walks with a staff. Do you know him?"

"I- I think so."

"I have heard that he spoke, last night, in defence of the Steward."

Aemilia shudders at the memory. She glances away, towards the floor. She does not want to relive the terror and confusion of the solstice feast.

"I have a message for this man. But I can't go to him myself, or send for him. Athraxus is watching."

"Shall I fetch Saba?"

"No, child. I want her to serve in the sanctuary tonight. This is a job for you." With this the Augur rises to her feet, and holds out a hand to help Aemilia up. The leaves of paper scattered about them rustle and whisper. "It must be done quietly, by cover of darkness. He lives in a villa in the fields beyond the colonnade."

"Through the city? In the dark? Can I take Cassia with me?"

"No, my child, nobody else must know about this. Not even Saba. After sundown tonight, take a lantern, and go quickly."

Aemilia has never been alone in the city before, let alone by night. The thought all but paralyses her. But she learned obedience, as well as love, in her years at the Augur's feet. "I'll do it, Mother. What is the message?"

*

At dusk in the city, the pigs come out to feed. They stick their snouts in the gutters at the roadside and devour rotten cabbage leaves, broken eggs, burnt bread, mixed in with mud and excrement and straw. They grow to a great size. Aemilia catches the red flashes of their eyes between the houses as she hurries past, hears their greedy grunts and snuffles.

There are still men in the square, packing away the market and haggling over the last scraps. Women get attacked near here sometimes, the rumours say. Aemilia holds her cloak tightly and hurries, her footsteps echoing on the cobbles. Beneath her breath she repeats every auspicious word she can remember. *Every deity with ears, let them not see me. Sun and stars and rain and earth...*

With the Augur's message burning on her tongue it seems to Aemilia that a shadow has shifted across the warmth and brightness in her world, as the body of the moon will on occasion move in the heavens to hide the sun.

Through streets with clogged gutters and lopsided shop-fronts.

A donkey dozes tethered to a post. Behind doorways and beyond the lit windows of a tavern, music and laughter. This face of the city is strange to her. Sometimes she goes to the market with Saba or the riverbank with the other girls, set apart by their saffron robes. People often stare at them, but she has never thought to stare back. The temple is all of her world.

Aemilia passes the crumbling watchtower which is a part of the old city wall. Torch-flames burn bright along the colonnade. An owl cries suddenly from a crack in the stones and she whips around, heart fluttering. The shadows of her lamp are thrown around her in every direction, dancing like wood-spirits. She flees with flapping sandals and runs for the green slopes which lie at the foot of the mountain, until the only noise is the wind among the vines, the sigh of the sea far below.

Breathless, she proceeds more slowly. A few shepherd's dwellings here, too ramshackle to be the home of the Emperor's brother. After she has walked for a while the villa comes into sight as the Augur described it, a smallish red-roofed place, resting against the slope as though it has rolled there like a forgotten marble. Instead of proceeding to the gate Aemilia sinks towards the shadowy ground beneath the olive trees. Lamplight plays upon their leaves. It is peaceful here.

A white cat comes padding curiously towards her from the direction of the house, diverted from its night-time hunt. Aemilia rubs its forehead with her fingertips. She notices that her hands are shaking and damp with sweat. She wipes them on her robes.

"Pretty thing," she whispers. "Will you come with me? I'm supposed to go and wake your master."

The cat arches and purrs, butting its head against her ankles. It follows Aemilia as she slips in through the gate, taps tentatively at the wooden door-frame. There is no answer until she tries knocking more insistently, which brings the sound of footsteps.

The doors are opened by a man whose outer robe has been flung about him in a hurry. Though his long hair is silver and his face lined, he has not lost the striking looks he must have had in his youth. His eyes are sea-green. Around his neck, on a leather cord, the yellowed tooth of some long-dead creature.

"Are you Antonus the C-cripple?" stammers Aemilia.

The man laughs. "Can't you see I'm standing on both legs? No, child, I'm his house-slave."

"Oh." She loses her words. The handsome slave regards her with benign puzzlement.

"A funny time to come calling. Whose messenger are you? Or are you lost?"

"A messenger of the Augur," she whispers. "I'm a priestess of her temple."

She cannot read his expression. He looks past her into the night, then back over his shoulder into the darkened house. Evidently deciding that no harm can come of it, he beckons her inside. "What's your business?" he asks.

"Her message – my mistress's message – it's only for him."

The slave seems a little amused by the seriousness of her manner. "Alright, priestess. Wait here. I'll go and fetch him."

Antonus, woken from a light sleep into a cloud of night-time pain, hardly understands what Felix is saying to him. Irritable, since the respite of sleep is not easily come by, he allows himself to be chivvied from his bedchamber and into the outer room. He sees a plump girl in priestess's robes. She is a foreigner, her skin, hair and brows so pale as to be almost white.

"Greetings, priestess," he says hoarsely. "And every blessing on the temple where you serve. You won't think it's disrespectful if I sit?"

She stares at him, shakes her head, and then continues to gaze around the room as though she has never crossed the threshold of any home in the city before. He lights an oil-lamp upon the table, shifts Eryx's wooden sword and Felix's lyre out of the way, and sinks down onto the nearest stool.

He gestures for the priestess to sit also, but she does not. Aemilia has caught a glimpse through a nearby doorway of three small figures covered by a blanket. She is visited by a pang low in her stomach, some smoke-blurred snatch of memory. She wants to wrap this place around her back like a cloak. In another life she once slept in a bed between numerous brothers, their dirty feet against her shins, melted snow dripping about the low coals in the hearth.

Antonus watches her shuffle and stare. He makes a gesture to Felix, who gives him a quizzical look before leaving the room.

"I'm sorry to get you out of bed," says the priestess.

"It's nothing. I'm accustomed to waking often." Antonus indicates his leg. "What does the Augur have to say to me?" he asks.

Aemilia tries to summon a courage she has never possessed. Maybe she has seen this man at the temple before, but there is nothing memorable about his mild face and manner. His nose is bent, as is his back. He looks like a tree felled by a storm that kept on growing in a broken shape.

She wishes that Saba was beside her, or better, here in her stead. Saba would have stood boldly and declared the Augur's words. *Come on, 'Milia. Like tying up a goat and sticking in the knife. You're good at that.*

Aemilia swallows. When she speaks her voice does not resonate like a prophet's but drops and trembles. "The Augur my mother asked me to tell you, you should believe what has been foreseen in the dreams of Lennes. The same was revealed to her at the grove on the mountain. This age, this age in this city…" She stumbles over the memorised syllables. "This age is coming to an end. The

Augur says, sow no crops and put aside no grain. Drink the wine you have been storing in your cellar."

The oil lamp on the table casts a flickering light across the face of Antonus the Cripple. He says nothing. His expression is impassive.

"She says, you haven't escaped her attention these twenty years. Now at this time you have a choice. She says you can gather up your household, and any who you love, and leave before the trouble comes."

"She means this for *me?*" This seems to be the point which causes him incredulity. "What am I to her?" Aemilia squirms in discomfort. He actually laughs. "Tell me, are you really her messenger? It's a poor piece of folly, if not."

Aemilia closes her eyes to concentrate on the last portion of the Augur's message. She has some sense of the danger she brings into being, merely by carrying these words to his ears. "You have a choice. Gods may be appeased. You were to be Emperor, once. The Augur says, think on it again."

There is a long moment of quiet. The lamp sputters and spits, and the white cat comes slinking in from outside to wind itself around Aemilia's ankles.

"What is your name, child?" Antonus asks.

"Aemilia, my master."

"How old are you, Aemilia?"

"Fifteen or sixteen summers. I can't be sure."

"I have two daughters, just a little younger than you. I have a small son. I'm to flee from this city — to go where? With my children, and my wife, and my old slave, and my useless leg? Hasn't the Augur included this in her message?"

Aemilia shakes her head.

"And she won't speak with me herself?"

"She says that Athraxus is watching. She told me to come here in secret."

Antonus is about to raise his voice in anger – how little you seem to know, priestess, of what you come here to trouble me with in the dead of night! – but something holds him back. He sees that she is trembling. A jolt to his bones, and the second part of the Augur's message breaks over him like a sudden madness. *Think on it again.*

In that moment twenty years and more fall away from him and he is a young man again. No pain, no grey hairs or deep lines beneath his eyes, legs that will carry him at a run along the sunlit seashore. The swagger of expectation. You were born, were you not Antonus, to the highest things. To the cool alabaster chambers of the palace, its white pillars and gold inlays. Music and perfume. Born to lift your hand and see servants rush to your bidding, councilmen bow to your instruction, armies hang on your command.

Antonus is so taken by this flash of memory that he forgets, for a moment, where he is. Returning to the darkened villa and the plump, nervous priestess is a crushing disappointment. His heart is hammering, and he is shocked at himself. He had not known that his former life still holds such a place in him.

"You must stay," he says curtly, to the priestess Aemilia. "It's not safe for you to go back to your temple in the dark. We have a bed which we keep for a friend who isn't here tonight. Stay until first light, and leave before my children are awake."

"What should I tell my mistress?" whispers Aemilia.

"Tell her that she should know better than to send young girls alone into this city in the darkness." He stands, with difficulty. Reaches for a way to collect his spiralling thoughts. "Tell her that she has stolen my sleep tonight. And for some nights to come."

There is an old widow in the sanctuary, wrinkled and purse-lipped. Saba guesses that it has probably taken her since sundown to shuffle her way up the steps. They crouch now on the floor before the altar while sage burns between them.

The woman chews methodically on a strip of spruce-bark and says very little. She has not asked questions or made requests, and Saba senses that her visit is not a purposeful one. It is often like this, with the passing generation. Neither their future fortune nor present choices seem urgent to them, but they have the habit of sitting for a while at an altar. The crowds outside the other temple are too rough and too loud. The priests there rattle their pockets until they are given gold.

When the bundle of green stems has blackened and crumbled Saba reaches a thumb into the still-hot ash and then traces a line across the old woman's forehead. The tortoise lips move to mouth the blessing along with her. *Receive, for they are close enough to breathe on us.*

Saba sweeps and trims the lamps and waits for the next supplicant. A man comes whose only hand is wrapped in ragged bandages and whose face is hidden beneath his hood. He carries with him the smell of rotting flesh. For him she splits the belly of a hare and parses the entrails, looking for any hopeful sign. But the liver is small and of a dull colour, the creature's blood pooling unevenly upon the altar.

"You shouldn't spend your gold on a visit to the healing-houses across the mountains," she tells him. "It will not go well for you."

"Are you certain?" His voice is muffled. She supposes that his mouth is bandaged too.

"As certain as anyone can be."

"And will you pray to the gods on my behalf?

"If it would comfort you."

"My father didn't fear them. And I'm not allowed into the Blood Temple to make atonement. I think this is the source of my suffering."

Some nights at the temple it seems that there is nothing more common than suffering. The people eat it like bread. The explanations for this, Saba learned long ago at the Augur's feet, are numerous and filled with mystery. The priests of the Dark Temple sweat at their underground altars and spill droplets of their own blood, so as to pre-empt any punishment. The world is full of deep pitfalls. Curses passed between generations, a god offended by an offhand word, a balance in nature disrupted or disturbed. *All we can do*, the Augur says, *is ask, and hope, and wait. Do not harm, but heal us. Have mercy, you gods, and put what is disordered into wholeness again.*

A young fisherman tells her a story that is circulating in the lower city, about a girl who suffocated her own mother while she was sleeping. He says that he has heard night-birds singing in the daytime, seen no white butterflies this year of the kind which always flock in the sea-grass beside the cliffs. A woman whose womb is barren brings two bags of grain and a jar of oil, and a sack of ram's lungs, for burning. Saba is growing tired now, and fights to keep her eyes open as the sanctuary fills with smoke once again, the woman hunched muttering over the lump of meat on the fire. Saba's eyes are drawn to the moon which is rising over the city. Between the pillars of the temple the smoke coils away into the starry heavens. *Hear my plea, hear my plea.*

Such a distance, it seems tonight, that smoke must travel. Momentarily she feels in accord with the younger priestesses, who complain of the gods just as they complain of the Augur: that they do not spell out their will clearly enough. *When we say that they are close it is not because we always feel them here, not because they are much in the habit of reaching down.* And now they are angry. Saba realises that she does not doubt it. And not just this: that she is angry too.

She hardly sees the flames burn low and the barren woman leave the sanctuary, her intercession made. Saba looks down at her own hands, which are clenched into fists. Stars move around her in their night-time course. In the temple overlooking the city, with the breeze blowing in from between the pillars, the life that she has known seems to have been consumed too on the altar.

Hope has always been her gift: and anger does not feel like a denial of hope, but a part of it. *I am sorry, mothers of mine. I made a promise long ago, and have done nothing to see it brought to fullness. Twelve years I have eaten the bread of this city. Twelve years gone from your side. How easily I forget.*

*

Myloxenes falls asleep among his books again and wakes stiff-necked, the last man in the library. The wick of his lamp is smoking, extinguished hours ago. Groggy, he gathers his things and makes towards his rooms, footsteps echoing on the flagstones. A shaft of moonlight from a high window illuminates the shelves which tower either side of him. Many of the scrolls kept here have been untouched for centuries. On the lower shelves reside manuscripts concerning subjects which have become fashionable under the Emperor Laonatus: astronomy, anatomy, the speculations of certain philosophers, the lore of the Dark Temple. Mylo, who often commandeers a long ladder to reach the histories near the ceiling, knows that there was a time when ships from across the known world would bring works here to be copied and studied. Little is added to the collections now.

On the pillars are carved the likenesses of the wise men who once walked the city. Beyond the reading room he passes through the meeting-chamber where scholars gather to debate – or more accurately, to drink wine until they are red in the face and shout at one another. *One cup is for pleasure*, Felix says, *another for courage, another for sleep. Then after that, it's outspokenness, hubris, insults, punches, breaking the furniture, madness and finally unconsciousness. Philosophers are no better than pirates in that regard. I've taken wine with both.*

According to Felix, the oldest thing that survives in the city is the fire in the heart of the Augur's Temple. *Before there was fire, there was water. When the gods made the world they divided the water to make space for the earth and the sky. They wrestled chaos into the deep. The sweat of the gods after the battle watered the earth, and grass and trees sprung up. The first day dawned in a green light. As to the making of man...*

Sometimes Mylo imagines how this city, how every city came to be. How men first built high walls to keep out wolves, how they dug deep channels to tame the rivers and enrich the earth for their crops. Something called them to lay down their bows and hunting-spears, to instead grow grain and gather it in, pile it in storehouses, fatten their cattle. To put down their own roots.

They would have learned to press reed-pulp into flat sheets and crush beetle-shells for ink. A discovery as momentous as fire, that the cut nib of a quill could give substance to sound, to things which could now be passed on to those not yet born. Mylo imagines that there would have been music in such a city. Craftsmen who summoned beauty from panels of oiled cedar-wood, from mounted gems and molten silver, from blocks of stone.

The people of such a place composed the world into order as the gods once composed space amid the waters. Their sundials and wax tapers measured out the hours between dawn and nightfall. Their charts divided seasons into months, weeks, days. Perhaps this order shone like a light to them in the wide wild world. Perhaps they did not feel small and afraid, as he so often does, encamped in their stone dwellings beneath the canopy of ancient stars.

Mylo crosses the courtyard and fumbles with his key, emptying his armful of scrolls onto his desk and rearranging them carefully into piles before collapsing on the bed. He realises that he has spilt oil from the lamp onto his robes, and divests himself impatiently of his outer clothing. It is a hot night, and the dark little chamber is far too close after the vastness of the reading room. Lying on his back, he twists his head around to look out of the window behind him. That moon. He can feel its light on his skin like cool water.

Here in his own bed, sleep does not come. He thinks about Rufus, and about Lennes, whose bruises must be turning black by now. He hopes that Mersia has the sense to keep her father from solid food, and from the prying eyes of priests and councilmen. Mylo presses his thumbs into his eyes, which are tense and strained from the night's reading. He cannot share Rufus's casual conviction that the worst of their trouble is over. The first time I am permitted to attend the feast at the Augur's Temple, he thinks, and it turns to this catastrophe. The anger of gods or the madness of men. Both, perhaps. How can anybody rest in this city tonight?

He rises very suddenly and wraps himself in a thin cloak, his feet carrying him from the library and towards that swollen moon. It is not safe to walk alone in the city after darkness, let alone to do what he has in mind. But Myloxenes knows only one way to quiet his own relentless thoughts.

*

The ocean takes him in its arms. He sinks back into the black water, hears the roar of waves crashing over his head. The dirt and sweat of the long day is washed away. He surfaces and pushes back his drenched hair from his face, drifting out from the shore. The moon hangs overhead. The city is behind him, a little way up the cliff. There is nothing to see all the way out to the horizon except for the silver reflections of stars upon the water. A breeze makes the skin of his shoulders prickle.

As a young boy he used to fantasise about disappearing this way, slipping into the depths and never coming up again.

His father had first flung him in the water when he was very small, during the brief time when Athraxus tried to make something of him. He'd choked and cried and flailed his arms, but because nobody came to help him he'd learnt to stay afloat. Encouraged by this flicker of a man's spirit, his father had put a wooden sword in his hand. He flinches at the memory: few men of such high standing would have taken their own sons to the training-yard, would have worked under the midday sun to correct footing and grip, would have worn out their own voices in discipline. It was soon obvious that he had little aptitude for it, nor for running, boxing, oratory, or the other things Athraxus put him to. He had been five years old.

He remembers – or thinks he remembers – a certain keen look in his father's face that faded each time he failed at something new. He has not seen this look for many years, or anything resembling it. It had been replaced first by confusion, then indifference.

It was Antonus who had given him old scrolls and taken him to the library – had sent him tumbling headfirst into history, into a realm of fascination and delight. These days he calls himself a scholar but he feels more like a hunter, searching for tracks in a quiet paper forest. That other city. It eludes him just as it captivates, and within its walls are housed his secret and his painful hopes.

Mylo dips his head under the cool water. Things become clearer to him, here. The nature of the place he is searching for. Let me go back to the time when these statues and stones were newly carved, this gold untarnished, these streets filled with songs. There must have been a time when we were wiser, better known to ourselves. When each created thing had its place and the universe hummed like the strummed strings of a lyre.

Perhaps the gods dwelt more closely with us, then. Perhaps they took shade in our gardens and accepted our offerings with their own hands. We saw their faces, and our converse with them was full and free.

*

In the midst of Saba's reverie, smoke clears. There is somebody in the sanctuary with her. Caught in her own thoughts, she did not notice him arrive. He is sat, quiet and attentive, on the other side of the embers.

She lowers the hood of her saffron robe, the better to look at him.

"Is the hour too late?" he asks.

She indicates the altar-lamp, the wick almost burned to its base.

"I'm sorry. I had a notion..." He makes to stand and leave, but she gestures, and he sits again. His hair, she notices, is wet, and a smell of sea-salt hangs on him. He is wearing a cloak wrapped around his damp tunic. "I had a notion that there might still be a priestess on duty."

"I was just about to douse the lamp."

"I'm glad that you're still here. I wanted to ask you something. I mean, to ask something of the temple."

Myloxenes recognises her, the small strong priestess from the feast. The one who laughed when he insulted Clemon son of Clemnes. Her eyes are bright and shrewd.

"Did you bring anything to burn?"

He shakes his head sheepishly. He did not pause long enough to examine the impulse which brought him up here. The thing that he really wants to know now feels foolish, and he diverts.

"I'm working on a history," he says. "The story of this city, from ancient times. I'm told that this temple has been here since the beginning, but I've searched all of the scrolls in the library, and there's so little written about it."

He feels that she is weighing him. There is such a sharp intelligence in her look that he fears she sees the most childish part of him, and finds him ridiculous. She says, "Our history has never been kept that way. Everything which matters is passed down from one Prophetess to the next."

"Are you — do you have that kind of knowledge? It would be good to speak to someone."

"It's late for that, my master."

"I meant, I could come again, at a better time, to talk with you. Or with the Augur herself, if you think she would..."

"Do you often wash in the sea?" asks the priestess. "By moonlight?" He feels himself flush. But she is grinning at him. "I'll ask her for you, scholar, if you like. I don't think it'll be the kind of history you like to read in your books, though."

He remembers his disappointment at the earthbound smell of the temple hall, on the night of the solstice, and feels a pang of desperation. He doesn't even know what it is that he wants to hear. The lamp on the altar is flickering. He tries to feel it, the power in this place, the presence of that long lineage who have faithfully spoken for the gods. He ventures, "Is it true that there's a fire in the temple which has never been extinguished, since the beginning?"

"Only because generations of girls like me got shouted at when it burned too low. And got splinters in their fingers gathering firewood on the mountain."

Mylo is not sure whether he is supposed to laugh. Her eyes are glittering. Flustered, he blurts out without meaning to, "I was at the feast."

"I remember you. You were rude to your friend."

"Clemon isn't my friend." Mylo draws an unsteady breath. It is cooler up here than in the city below, and he realises that he is shivering in his damp clothes. "I heard Lennes the Steward speak.

I saw what happened to him. I can't get it out of my mind. Is that foolish?"

No laughter, now. The priestess's expressive brows have contracted. "No, man of this city," she says, quietly. "I don't think it is."

He wants to ask her what the Augur has said, what the talk is in the temple. She raises her eyes to meet his, and he hardly needs to. The heap of ashes between them glows and crumbles.

Slowly, as though he has requested that she do so, the priestess dips her thumb in the ash and leans forward to trace a firm line across his forehead. He closes his eyes and feels her breath on his face. "*Receive. For they are close enough to breathe on us.*"

*

With that the altar-lamp sputters its last and the sanctuary falls into shadow. Saba can tell that the young man is still troubled. There is a strange, deep pause, and as though frightened by it he quickly stands, gathering his cloak about him. His hands fumble the fastenings, and he pauses as he makes to leave between the pillars. Turns back to her. He is her own age, older, but something about him makes her think of a very small child. He asks, "Is it true that you hear the gods?"

Oh, that question. Saba has spent so many nights here in the sanctuary listening to the troubles of the people. She has spoken blessing and intercession, burned flesh and herbs on their behalf. She hears, more clearly than any other she knows — as clearly, perhaps, as the Augur herself. But still there is doubt. *We do not hear enough to be sure of the gods' truth or their pity. To turn back the change which once came into the world.*

"What is your name, scholar?" she asks. "So that I can take your request to the Augur."

"I am Myloxenes, the only son of Athraxus."

101

It is his last question which stays with her; the turn of his head, the widening of his eyes. *Is it true that you hear the gods?* She imagines, briefly, growing up in the shadow of the Dark Temple. In its stench and secrecy, in its darkness and doubt. She has always known, now she thinks of it, that the High Priest Athraxus has a wife and a son. Why has she never paused to pity them before?

Saba lingers in the sanctuary that night far longer than she needs to, sweeping up the ashes, topping up the oil in the lamps along the wall. She feels her skin prickle, sees in her mind's eye an image of Athraxus, squatting over the city like an alligator over its eggs. And before him another such priest, before him another, right back to the time before memory.

Burn this city, she beseeches the gods, in her self-righting heart. Burn it, if you will, and burn these men with it. Let the worm devour and the starred lizard set it all aflame. I myself will be long-gone.

When she finally returns to the room in the tower, ready to sleep, the morning sun nearly at the horizon; it is to find Aemilia's bed empty.

IV

"Are you going to the market today?" Antonus asks his wife, as they finish their breakfast of fresh peaches together on the front step of the villa. Behind them, Junia's bright woven cloths hang against the backdrop of the mountain.

"Yes. Renna's coming, and I'll take the girls. I should go and see that they're ready."

Her hand brushes his shoulder as she heads inside, and he thinks, *happiness is a bird of rare beauty, happiness is . . .*

He watches Junia's friend Renna roll up in her donkey-cart, dust rising beneath its wheels. Watches his wife and daughters carry out rolls of cloth by the armful, waves to them as they pile onto the back of the cart and lurch away into the city. When Felix finds him some while later he is still sitting in the same place, staring absently into the distance.

"She's gone, then?"

"Renna came early. I think they've got a lot to sell."

"I meant the priestess."

Antonus looks up at Felix, who is leaning against the doorway. "Were you eavesdropping last night? I'll have your ears cut off."

"Oh be merciful, my master!"

Felix does not offer any opinion on the priestess Aemilia, and Antonus wonders whether he is reserving judgement. It is not the slave's way to be much moved by rumours. He would rather amuse himself in watching others lose their heads.

Antonus stands with the aid of the door-frame, and finds Felix looking at him with a curious expression, weighing him anew. They have lived under the same roof for eighteen years. Felix has never been contemptuous of him, not even in those early days, contemptuous of the young, thwarted, bitter, disfigured master. But neither has he ever looked at him this way, as though his authority might be something other than a fluke of the universe.

"Felix. Send a messenger to the palace, will you? Or better, go yourself. Tonight I will see my brother."

*

He waits until dusk, since he wants to see Laonatus alone, not surrounded by slaves and advisers and wives and sons. The soldiers at the palace know Antonus by sight, and let him through, two of them leaving their posts to flank him as he makes his slow way towards the Emperor's private quarters, through vaulted hallways high enough to fit the whole of the Augur's Temple within them, between towering alabaster columns, along corridors whose intricate patterned tiles and gold-enriched frescoes shimmer in the torchlight.

They pass the feasting-hall, which is an indoor garden, a waterfall spilling from the far wall into a pool surrounded by ferns. Fat bunches of grapes burst from vines, colourful birds preening amid the leaves. A few of the Emperor's retinue are still reclining there, drinking iced wine from goblets and laughing amongst themselves. There are six or so small boys loose about the place, hardly kept in order by their attendant slaves, chasing each other between the couches and splashing their hands in the pool.

Laonatus's reception-room is empty, as are his observatory and private library. The guards at the doorway to his bedchamber point Antonus and his escort underground, down the series of spiralling staircases which lead into the bowels of the building. There is a space in the foundations, at the centre of the catacombs below the city, where hot springs bubble up in the red earth. The tiled chamber is thick with bay-scented steam. Two slaves, sweating through their loincloths, crouch low to the ground on the edge of the largest pool, bearing jars of oil. The naked figure of the Emperor Laonatus is submerged in the water.

Antonus has long known his brother to be an uncommonly beautiful man. Here he is a god in his realm. He looks, if possible, yet younger and more vital than when Antonus last saw him, a year before. Catching sight of Antonus, his painted eyes widen in pleasure. He floats to the edge of the pool as Antonus limps over, breathless and unsteady from the effort of the stairs.

"Brother!" calls Laonatus. His voice echoes from the damp walls. "What a delightful surprise!"

No surprise though, brother, since I sent notice of my coming.

And I have little doubt that you chose this for our meeting-place. Considered the details of your appearance, the angle from which I would see you. Considered the supple strength of your body moving effortlessly through the water, the whole of it displayed as an edict.

Laonatus rests his elbows on the side of the pool, raising his torso, wiping his wet face with his hands. "You may go," he says to the guards. The slaves remain where they are, crouched in complete stillness, except for their legs, which are beginning to tremble. Antonus moves between the pools. He finds a spot against the wall opposite his brother where he can lean, wedging his body against an outcrop in the rock. They regard one another, searching out what the last year has wrought.

"How many sons, now?" asks Antonus.

"Six that survive," says Laonatus, with relish. "And I'll put another in Cassandane this year."

"Won't she and Mandane soon be too old to bear you any more?"

"I'll get another three or so wives." He shakes his sodden hair back from his face. "You can have Mandane and Cassandane, if you wish," he adds generously. "Once I am done with them."

"I am such a dull man, that I'm satisfied by the first wife you gave me."

"They are curious creatures. Aren't they, brother? You could spend a lifetime studying them and die in ignorance. The gods made them of different clay."

"Have you come to this conclusion by yourself?"

"I have it of my philosophers. The madness in the nature of women comes from the closed mouth of the womb, which blocks the flow of blood to her other organs. It benefits them when we unblock this mouth through frequent intercourse. You have daughters, don't you, Antonus? Marry them young, so that pregnancy will cure them."

Droplets of sweat trickle down Antonus's face. His tunic is damp against his body. He wonders whether the visit of the priestess Aemilia has lit a fever in him. His heart is pounding again, and he is struggling to attend to his brother's words. He thinks of Lennes the Steward, the sickness in his eyes before he rose to speak. Could it be, Antonus, that you now wear that same look?

"It *is* good to see you," says Laonatus. His head rests upon his arms, his gaze upon Antonus. "I was afraid we might not meet this year."

"I thought we would meet at midsummer. As we always have."

The Emperor's eyes rove away. "I had other more pressing engagements," he says, of his empty seat at the Augur's feast.

"Did Athraxus persuade you to it?" asks Antonus, quietly. He doesn't know quite how the High Priest has wormed his way so close in recent years, but his handiwork is plain to see.

Laonatus shrugs. "I am advised by the wisest men. Such has been their thinking lately."

He signals the slaves, who are upon their feet at once and hurrying to spread cloths across a raised stone table beside the wall. The Emperor rises from the pool and stands for a moment before Antonus, water streaming from his naked form. When he has laid himself upon the table to be oiled, Antonus is obliged to move in order to continue conversing with him. He perches somewhat precariously on the edge of a clay vase. The slaves pour scented oil into their palms and massage it across the Emperor's shoulders, back, buttocks, legs.

"I wouldn't expect you to know about the winds that stir the high places of this city." Laonatus stretches out his bronzed limbs. "It's for me to have my ear attuned. I hear, and see, and judge with wisdom. It's for me to say which food is for the eating and which for the fire. If there is an instrument in my hand which has served its purpose, it's for me to lay it down."

"In your place," says Antonus, "I wouldn't have the courage to break so boldly with what has gone before."

Laonatus turns and smiles. Firelight fills his large golden eyes. "Then let's be thankful that the gods decreed this place to be my own."

He truly believes it, thinks Antonus. This is the gift of Laonatus, to believe each word from his own tongue as though it were a proclamation from the highest temple. Even if this word turns one way in the morning and another at night, Laonatus is faithful to his religion.

The slaves use curved shells to scrape away the oil, beginning at his shoulder-blades. The Emperor's skin flushes pink. Laonatus lays his head down into his arms again, yawning. "You'll have a good harvest this year," he says, muffled. "We have been favoured with the finest summer in memory. You must send a slave with some of your wine. It pleases me, now and then, to taste provincial things."

His exposed body transforms itself for a moment, before Antonus's eyes. Is this body so different, in the end, from those other bodies which go to hang beside the city boundary? Is it so very different from Antonus's own body, bent and failed and fragile with pain? Antonus imagines a blade tracing a line across that throat, or thrust into the back, between the shoulders. Hands dropping a cup and clasping at the belly. Would that be best then, poison? He would not even have to do it himself.

*

Emperors die before their time. Stomach complaints or violent encounters on quiet roads or upon the swords of their own soldiers, or smothered in their beds. No cause to mourn them for long; empires and centuries are formed by such actions, as the seashore by waves. Antonus and Laonatus's father, Arcturus, in the same fire that consumed the old palace and killed their sleeping sisters and left Antonus for dead. By the time the cry went up that he would live, Laonatus, a boy of eleven, had already been made Emperor.

No use raging. Don't you see, Laonatus's wide beatific eyes say to him each time they meet, don't you understand? Just waves on sand. What hand held the torch to the bedclothes, it does not matter. Just the distant rumbling of rocks below the ocean's depths, shifting the shape of the world. Gods rolling their dice.

He was a hungry child, Laonatus, and he has eaten well these twenty years. His seat in the council chambers is made of gold. When there are games – and there were often games, in times past – he is carried through the streets in his own chariot. Men who defile his altars and statues are flogged until they cannot stand or cry out any longer. There is always feasting in the palace, even when famine in the streets. Any man who might be called rival, save Antonus himself, found guilty of some crime deserving exile or death.

In the first years of his rule Laonatus sent out warships to the seas, toppled towns and tribes to his command, carried home ivory and pearls, spices and silks and slaves, gemstones and oils and wines. Now the new palace creaks with lavish furnishings, the old soldiers are fat, and go sailing no more. The tribes return to their ways and the tributes trickle out. The priests of the Dark Temple have the Emperor's ear, and whatever gold is not poured into Laonatus's own favourite projects finds its way to their coffers.

Antonus, who might you have been in his place? The question carries so much grief that he has rarely allowed himself to consider it. Now, the long bridge of the last two decades seems to have shortened to a mere few paces. The agony is fresh with him – and why? Because the Augur sent a message which he is not sure he either understands or believes. In the mere act of speaking, she has placed everything that was lost within his reach once again.

No, Antonus — not lost. Stolen. He feels his fists clench, and tastes bile. *Oh man who would have been Emperor, oh Arcturus's heir, how long you have slept!* Didn't the earth convulse, as though trying to wake you? As though the rocks themselves are at last shaking off this injustice?

You surely would have been strong, and just, and wise. You would have brought down blessing upon this city and its people, and not hoarded it for yourself. You would have been remembered for many ages to come.

*

This madness burns all the hotter as Antonus climbs the steps out of the cavern, and is escorted back through the palace, out of its doors, to be left alone between the pillars in the night.

But just as suddenly as it has threatened to consume him, the fever breaks. Weakness fills his body, and he grabs at the nearest pillar, gasping for breath. He is so exhausted that he might have just run up the mountain and back down again.

The night is scented with mingled spices from the nearby palace kitchens. Ginger and cloves and cardamom. Antonus gulps the cool air in a desperate thirst. Junia is probably waiting for him back at the villa, washing the day's dust from her feet, combing through the tangles in her hair with her fingertips. The children will be sleeping in their bed. He imagines limping up the hill, along the path across the fields and along the olive grove, through the shadowed vineyard. The red roof-tiles of his home, speckled with green moss, a lantern hanging from the door-frame.

In the obscuring vapour of the cavern below the palace, he became something other than himself. The wild possibilities which unfurled before him there dissolve now like a dream.

What would you do? Pay some ruffian to slice your brother's throat? No. You were taken out from the flow of history long ago.

And besides: he loves you, Antonus. That, you have never had reason to doubt.

He leans his head against the pillar, and weeps.

V

"This is everything that she said."

"Just this. That we should believe the dreams Lennes declared at the Augur's feast. That this age in the city is ending. That the anger of the gods could be turned away if I supplanted my brother as Emperor."

Antonus is seated upon the edge of the bed, a hot cloth applied to his leg, while Junia paces the room in her shawl and undergarments. Felix's snores have fallen quiet; the only sound is the cicadas from the mountain and the breeze in the vineyard. The spitting of the lamp.

"There was some trouble. That's what you told me. The Augur's Temple is descendant."

"I didn't think the rest was worth telling."

She laughs, and Antonus laughs too. For a moment nothing is wrong.

"You thought that you felt the ground shake. Then the Augur told you to stake your claim on the Emperor's seat. And you didn't think I'd want to hear."

"I don't know what to think."

"You've never been interested in the Augur's temple," she says.

It is true. He only visits for the midsummer feast, preferring to keep his gods tucked secretively into household alcoves, soot-stained beside offerings of oil and coins. Gods of the healing-houses and the god of the harvest, gods of dreamless sleep and of the vineyard. They do not have their own dedicated temples or public shrines any more.

Junia, whose deities are those of childbirth and weaving and music, goes to see the Augur's priestesses twice or three times a year. Antonus does not know what she prays for there. She returns, sometimes, with a strange hard look about her, and does not speak to him for hours.

"You set some store by the Prophetess," he says. "I know you do. Or at least you have done, in the past."

"Many women do."

Junia's arms are folded across her chest. He waits, fighting the urge to lie back upon the bed and close his eyes. The day has been so very long. He waits for his wife to say something which will slow the uneasy racing of his heart, which will put the disorder of his mind to rest.

She stops her pacing and fixes him with an uncomfortably piercing look. "Did you see your brother today to decide if you have the stomach for it? For this... reversal of your fortunes?"

He does not reply.

"What's the outcome of your enquiry?"

Antonus rubs the bridge of his nose between his fingers. "Don't ask me that. Tell me what you think."

Junia pauses for what feels like a painfully long while. Then she moves to the dresser and sits on the stool there, peers at herself in the silvered glass as she braids her thick hair, ties the end with yarn. The process takes some time, and as the minutes pass the wick of the lamp sputters. Shadows scale the wall.

"You know," Junia says, to the mirror, "I think she's a little in love with him."

"What? Who?"

"Antonia." From her tone, this might have been the only topic of their night's talk. "I think she's a little in love with Mylo. Don't you

111

see it? I've been thinking it for months. It won't be long now before both girls bleed, and we should start thinking about husbands. I know Athraxus hates you, but would he really object to connecting himself with Laonatus's family?"

"No – no, I don't suppose..."

Junia turns, and her smile guides him like a shepherd's crook, away from the path of danger. Back to what is real, and present, and good. To the life they have salvaged together from the dust.

"It's sentimental of me, I know, but it would be such a joy to bring him into this household as our son. Truly our son. He would care for her so faithfully. I might talk to him about it, if you're willing."

Antonus nods, touched, nonplussed. His wife gets up and carries the darkening lamp over to the bedside. Then she kneels on the floor beside his feet, lays a hand upon his knee. Her eyes search his face, and he understands her.

"I sold enough of my work today to see us through until winter," she confides. "Some hangings. And the embroidered robes are selling well. Renna has a friend who might be interested in becoming my patron. A councillor's wife, a wealthy woman. We could buy Eryx the best sort of schooling. Perhaps extend the villa, build rooms for Mylo and Antonia, once they're married, and for their children, some day..."

Antonus says nothing. She takes his hand and turns it over, kisses the palm. "Old man," she says, with a warm curl of the mouth. She kisses the other hand, and he closes his fingers around hers. He feels relief bathe him, a sense of slipping back towards slumber.

*

Junia leaves her loom for a while the next afternoon and takes a walk through the sun-beaten vineyard, examining the ripening fruit and pruning some of the dead branches with a small knife. Her thoughts stray then to money for dowries. To Antonia and Adelfa being given to good men, to young men who they have met, and agreed to. To wedding days filled with feasting and laughter and dancing.

From here, unbidden and unwelcome, the memory of her own wedding. It had come soon after her childhood was ended by two men in an alleyway beside the market square, who afterwards paid her father five gold pieces and a jar of oil for their misdeed.

She had not been told who she was to marry, though the rumour reached her, through the flurry in her father's household, that it had been arranged by the Emperor himself. After the parade through the streets from her father's house, she had glimpsed the shape of her new husband through the thin fabric of her veil. His bent silhouette, like the cyclops from the old story. She remembers the taste of terror and disgust upon her tongue.

Through the ceremony and the feasting that followed, shortened to a mere day, she had kept her veil across her face and her eyes downcast. The guests were few. Though she mouthed the words required of her, no sound came out. *I leave my old life buried. I have fled worse and found better.* No morsel of food passed her lips. Her heart panicking like a captured bird, time lurching forward towards the night and the dark of the bedchamber. Fourteen years old, already she had known too much of men.

As it turned out, the cripple who was her husband did not hurt her. He did not raise his hand to her, and in the bed they shared seemed humiliated by what was required of him. He would not look at her, or speak a word to her unless it was necessary. They dwelt side by side in separate realms.

The slave Felix would say, *I will escape this city.* He told her that he had been both a slave and a free man many times before, in other cities, in other lands. *I will escape this household before the moon wanes. Will you come with me, Mistress Junia?* A knowing grin, fingertips fondling the tooth worn around his neck. *Come with me, and be my bride instead.*

But he did not leave, and she would not have gone with him. The city was all that she had ever known. The men from the market square trailed her through her dreams. She began to go now and then to the Augur's Temple, and pray that these men would choke in their sleep or drown in the ocean or be trampled underfoot by wild horses.

Seven years of her young life were sunk and lost as she sat unmoving beside the window in the villa on the mountain slopes. Several times she marked the signs her stepmother had told her to watch for, and knew herself to be with child. But each time the pains came far too soon and she bled out. Junia wrapped the tiny bodies, barely bodies, in strips of cloth and buried them at the edge of the cornfield. She told nobody. She supposed she must have been damaged in some lasting way, on the inside.

*

How did it change, Junia? Was it your heart that moved first, or his? They were locked together outside the life of the city which had no place for them, exiled by the families on whom they brought shame.

How did he change to your eyes, this husband of yours? It began, surely, before you felt Antonia and Adelfa move in your womb. Before they clung there together, growing stubbornly into being. Some softening, some shift in the weather. It must have been when the lost boy first came to eat at your table, huge eyes taking you in, small hands reaching fearfully for bread. You'd had nowhere to put your love, the love you'd been burying under the field, until then: and you learned that after everything there was still love in you.

He moved you both, and so you moved towards each other. A new thing breathed into being, miraculous as the creation of the world.

It amazes her. She fought for it fiercely then, that life, and she fights for it still. Daily she breaks a path through whatever thorns and thistles have grown to block Antonus from her view. She burns with pride for Mylo, grown strong and tall. She dreams for her daughters, and her son. She has set store by the Augur, in her day — but present goodness is more real to her now than past pain. To be enraged by the cruelties visited upon us, she has lately told herself, is like taking the wolf to task for hunting. Cruelty is woven into the nature of things. If you have by some blessed chance escaped it then run, run, and do not look back.

She begins to wend her way back along the vineyard path towards the villa. She catches sight of Mylo and Rufus coming up through the fields, two youths bathed in sunlight and laughing together, as though they have strolled out of some Arcadian age.

VI

The first story Saba remembers hearing is from the Augur. For some reason it has come back to her in recent days, that tale she was first told as a child at the temple, after she had mastered the new language. Unlike Aemilia she never sat quietly during the Augur's lessons. Cross-legged and fidgeting, scratching beneath her saffron robe, bursting with curious questions.

"Once," said the Augur, "we dwelt in gardens. There was a great garden that the gods had planted, stretching from the seashore to the edge of the world beyond the mountains in the west. There were three rivers that ran through this garden, and gemstones beneath the earth. In the garden grew palms and fruit trees and cedars."

"What kind of fruit, Mother?"

"Peaches, Saba, and dates, and figs, and sweet berries. There were lilies in the water and trailing green vines. There were animals in the garden; shoals of fish swam through the rivers, and birds came into the trees to nest. And the gods lived there among us."

"What did they look like?"

"They looked much like men and women, but taller and more beautiful. When we tell of this," said the Augur, "we ache, and barely know why. We tell these tales differently each time, since the memories passed down to us are always in retreat. We can follow the flame back, if we are so entranced by shadows. We can chase after it into the far-gone past, into the mouth of the dark.

"In the garden, the gods gave men their names. They asked of the gods why they had been created, and the gods answered, to dwell here in the world. To make shelters for yourselves, to gather and to eat and drink. For companionship and for desire. To labour until you tire, and then to rest. To bring offerings to us, your gods, and know our blessing in return. For songs and wine, for the warmth in your bodies and the sweetness from the earth. To plant more gardens.

"So men made shelters out of vines and branches, and lit fires among these shelters when night came. They learnt to sing. Their women danced barefoot in the ashes. In daily converse with the gods they spoke of matters small and great, of this rainstorm and that row of seedlings, of the first forging of the stars."

*

She does not remember the stories told to her by her first mothers, or their kindnesses. This thought preoccupies her as she goes with Aemilia into the city before the heat of midday to buy more livestock. It has never been possible for the two of them to leave the temple without feeling their foreignness, without drawing remarks and ill-disguised glances: they are strangers even after twelve years here. Their skin betrays them. But if I was to go back, thinks Saba, if I was to walk into the place where I was born, would I be a stranger there too?

No, it will not do to imagine it that way. Along my journey, thinks Saba, as I'm returning to them, I will invent new stories to replace the ones that I have lost. And then I will plant myself back into that land and flourish there, like a great spreading tree.

Aemilia interrupts her reverie. "Have you seen our mother yet this morning, Saba?"

"I took her barley-bread and cheese. She seems as strong as she's ever been." She has not yet asked Aemilia about her absence from their chamber the previous morning. There does not seem to have been time. "I hope you're not worrying about her, 'Milia."

"Has she said anything more?" Aemilia asks in an unsteady voice, as they enter the market square. "About the dreams of Lennes? You said we ought to pay attention to the signs."

Saba touches her arm, alert to the bustling crowd about them. "Let's not talk about that here."

Flies buzz around their heads, and Saba dances sideways to avoid treading in a heap of dung. Nearby a blind man bangs a drum and wails for coins. A butcher hacks at a mutton carcass. Sure enough, amid the noise and busyness, Saba is aware that they are drawing more attention even than usual. Heads turn as they pass and whispers spring up like weeds. There is no-one here who has not heard some account of what happened in the temple hall at midsummer.

The goats they have come to purchase are being held in a pen near the bathhouse. Saba lets Aemilia examine them, running her hands along their flanks and legs, checking their teeth, talking soothingly to them all the while. In such moments Aemilia looks almost tranquil: the only thing she excels at more than caring for these creatures is killing them. Saba considers her sister's round pale face, solemn in concentration, and wonders what has passed through her mind in these few days. It is hard to know sometimes whether Aemilia is storing up fears in private, or simply failing to grasp the flow of events.

Saba knows that Aemilia is not as dull as some think her. She only needs more time than most, a touch of encouragement. Saba's strength is matched to Aemilia's weakness in this way.

"How are they? How many do we buy?"

"This one has a deformed hind leg. I think we can take the others."

Only unblemished beasts can be sacrificed at the temple. They hand over a bag of coins and lead their purchases away, roped together in a loose train. Before taking them up the steps to the temple they stop off at the riverbank, letting the goats tread into the reeds and drink the cool water. Saba and Aemilia take off their sandals and sit on the bank, dipping their feet. Palm branches stir and a boat drifts downriver towards the palace. There is a particular kind of light in the city on days like today, in the late part of the summer, when the sun takes on a rust-gold hue which is reflected from the sea. Time seems to contract, and Saba remembers playing here as a child, released from temple duties and the Augur's watchful eye. She and Aemilia would hitch up their robes and splash waist-deep into the water.

We gave our hours and our energies to the temple, even then. We felt ourselves more than slaves and prisoners here, though isn't that what we were? Somehow the Augur made us feel otherwise. Since the first day she walked into the temple Saba has felt keenly her place in a long lineage. Known in her bones what the city needs from her, known that she has strength enough to give it. And Aemilia? Aemilia has simply followed where it is safest, where there is lamplight and warmth.

A yellow dragonfly hovers beside them, and a frog puffs out its throat in a cluster of bull-rushes. In this lazy quiet Saba wants Aemilia to ask her again about Lennes, but she does not. Saba knows that she needs to shield the younger priestesses at this time from too much knowledge – but Aemilia is different. She has always told Aemilia everything that is in her thoughts, and has known herself to be loved, if not always understood. It is strange today with so much weighing heavy on her mind that they say nothing to one another.

Is all of this a part of the power of Lennes' words? To set loose a longing for other lives long left behind; to bind the tongues of beloved sisters in each other's presence?

*

Saba sits with the priestesses at their letters, the hall quiet except for the scratching of their quills on parchment, the occasional rebellious whisper. The girls know how to form the simplest symbols, tracing them out over and over again, tongues bitten in concentration. Not one of them, had they not been taken in by the temple, would ever have learnt such a thing.

Would you, Saba, in that other life? She does not know how they live, those people who gave birth to her, or who she might be among them. She cannot imagine what it might have meant, to have a different name. It will have to be wordless, she thinks, our reunion. When I run into the arms of the mothers who birthed me, we will have only our arms, our smiles, our tears.

The Augur often takes her rest in the shade of the courtyard in the afternoon. Saba finds her seated there on a three-legged stool, stitching up a hole in her spare robe with great concentration. Chickens scratch around her feet.

"Mother! I'll get one of the girls to do that."

"I can still see, Saba. I can still hold a needle."

"They ought to learn how to do these things properly."

"And you'll teach them, I don't doubt, when I'm gone."

There it is, without ceremony. They have never been in the habit of speaking about it, not even in private, about the closing of the book of the Augur's long life. The world has already changed so much. Saba looks away, towards the sunlit city, and feels a sudden prickling in her eyes.

"Mourn me at the proper time, Saba, and not before."

"Yes, Mother." She wipes a few hot tears away with the back of her hand. She thinks of five decades, longer, spent within the temple's walls, and is suddenly shocked. She has always been curious about everything except the Augur's own history: the old woman seems so monolithic, so complete, as though she was not born but sprung out of the crack in the mountain fully formed. *But isn't she mortal as any of us?* The Augur must have had people too, once. She was born of a mother, lay in a crib and cried, took first steps on fat unsteady legs.

Saba searches and finds she carries faint images, impressions of the Augur's former life. Maybe this story was murmured over her and Aemilia in the night when they were barely old enough to understand. Or maybe, thinks Saba, I made up a story for myself about my new mother. A myth befitting someone of such stature.

Has she imagined that the Prophetess, too, came to the city against her own will – served at first as one of those pitiful girls, one of those blind and silent prostitutes in the heart of the dark temple? There were rusted chains that crumbled in the night; an endless crawl through the filth of a sewer, naked in thick stench and blackness. And then, by the first light of dawn, hands raised trembling to the cold waters of a fountain.

The former Augur might have found her by the roadside in rags, living on scraps the pigs passed over, and brought her to the temple.

She might have wanted something else for herself, though it is not likely. Most girls who come to be priestesses must fervently praise the gods for the upturn in their fortunes.

Whether or not this tale is wholly true, thinks Saba, it's likely that the Augur came here like me with lice and ignorance and rags. And look what she has become. Look what she spun with the thin thread the gods granted her. She has shaped the fortunes of this city more than anyone else living.

And so become bound to it. Saba's feet shift, restless and the Augur reaches out to touch her arm. "My daughter, has the sanctuary been swept?"

"Yes, and the lamps have been filled. The girls are still at their lessons."

"Well done. It's important at a time like this for us to go about our business as we always have. To keep order in this temple. You understand that, don't you? What it is that we are, in such a time."

Saba nods resolutely. "I think so. The people will look to us first."

The Augur laughs. "You credit them with so much wisdom! Some will turn to us. Those who have nowhere else to place their trust. It has always been this way. But in the end, it's not for prophets to grasp on to power. We must seek and speak truth, wherever it leads us."

Every line of the old woman's face is so dearly known to Saba. Is it possible, she wonders, that the Augur knows the gods so deeply as this? That when she comes to read the auspices it is like sitting down among friends? Like reaching out to hold familiar hands, like comfort at a mother's feet.

Saba thinks of Myloxenes, son of Athraxus. The longing of his heart ringing across the city for her hearing, a note like an altar bell, tentatively struck. "The High Priest's son came here last night," she says. "He wants to see you."

"Is that so?"

"He's a scholar. He says that he wants to know the history of this temple."

Lines crease around the Augur's eyes. "Athraxus's boy. This might be the strangest auspice of them all. Yes, Saba, send him a message, and tell him he's welcome here. But first, sit with me a while. The sun is too hot this afternoon."

Saba sits down in the shade at her mistress's feet. The chickens are pecking at a patch of grain beneath the wall. Across the courtyard between the pillars of the temple hall, the priestesses bend their heads over their parchments. Today, since there are no rituals to perform, their head-cloths are those they have chosen themselves: pale blue, and orange, and moss-green. Saba traces her fingers through the dust. After a while she asks, "What about consolation, Mother? Are we here to offer that, too?"

The Augur lays down her needle, and considers Saba crookedly. Says, "That has always been your gift."

*

You understand, don't you, what the Augurs are here for? What we have always been here for. Because a change came into the world and now the people hardly know what they thirst for. Their bodies are dry in their exile in the city they call home. The bells at their altars are stifled. No breath stirs the heavy air of the temples they have built.

In this age the breath seems to withdraw yet further from the world, too faint to sense even in the thin places, where once it stirred the leaves.

Here is what happened in the garden. At the edge of the trees dwelt the god of the under-life, in the shadows, beneath the dripping palm leaves. He would not come near to the fires. Nor did he converse with men, who did not bring him offerings. He watched his divine brothers and sisters laden with gifts, heard the songs composed to their glory. Envy stirred in his heart.

He saw a woman alone one day washing her hair in the river, and swam to her in the form of a water-lizard. His eyes were yellow and his spines wound above the surface of the water. His tongue tasted her scent. *Forgive me, he said, I have never seen a creature of your kind before! Will you tell me, what is it that you are?*

I am a woman, she said. *I am made by the gods.*

And from what are you made?

From dust, from breath and blood.

If that is so, he said, *then why were you made?*

To dwell in the world, she said, *to eat and drink, to labour and rest. To plant and harvest, to share the warmth of a bed. To be blessed.*

Is this all? said the shadow-god.

A ripple passed across the waters. Widened and spread.

Such a small portion, this seems. Tell me, where might I see the towers you have built? Where might I see the forests you have laid low in this ambition, the beasts which submit to your command?

No such towers, no such beasts. All our life is in this garden.

Our life? said the shadow-god, in a voice of surprise. *Then you do not set a guard against your neighbour at the wall of your shelter? You do not keep your belongings for your own hands, in case the gods run out of blessings?*

The woman stared at her troubled reflection. Her fingers trailed upon the surface.

And tell me, what lands are yours? What wealth in gemstones?

None, whispered the woman.

You lack, said the shadow-god, *you lack.*

The woman knelt upon the bank of the river and felt a change creep into her heart, inexorable and deep.

Tell me, said the shadow-god, *where are your clothes? Why do you go about like this, in your shame?*

The woman looked down at her body in dawning horror. The colours in the garden changed. Her feet carried her back to the shelters, crying, *News! News!*

They fled the garden in a storm, those first people, with their burdens on their backs and a great wind tearing at the branches of the trees. Brown clouds tumbled through the spinning air. Raindrops pounded the dust. They shielded their faces from the wind and rain, and did not look back.

Trudged across a wide plain, their feet wrapped in skins. Orange disk of the sun rising, dropping, rising again, and the landscape looked the same on all sides. At last the mountains loomed. They found hawks' eggs in crannies in the rocks. They climbed high until they could see from the giddy mountaintop the lie of the land ahead. In the bronze light the world looked bold and endless. They pointed to the places where they would build shelters.

Outside the garden those first men found the ground dry, the nights colder. A hesitancy in their hearts which came when they woke at daybreak. The old answers already half-forgotten. In their place, restlessness. The words of the shadow-god burned in them. *Such a small portion, this seems.*

So they flung the blades of their axes into the white rock of the mountain, and began to build.

Those towers! There has never been a city like that first city. Towers that soared to touch the clouds. The stars could have flown in to roost in the tops of those towers. The first people sang and danced in celebration, since they had made this place for their own beyond the garden. They said to one another, now we have approached glory for ourselves. Here in the city we will be sated with all the world's riches. We will drink the cup of life to its dregs.

But the gods saw what the first people had done, and were displeased. *They have slighted us*, the gods said. *So let them bargain, let them beg for what once was freely given.* They closed the way into the garden, so that even if men one day remembered the first place they had dwelt and wished to return, they would not find it again.

The gods placed a curse upon the city. They said, *these men have made a dwelling for themselves, but they will never truly dwell there. Even when their bodies rest, their hearts will wander. They will live two lives, and barely live at all.*

VII

"Mersia's having one of her parties," Rufus tells Myloxenes, as they make their way back into the city after sundown. "Tomorrow night. You will come, won't you? Otherwise I'll have to endure Calix's tedious prattle about his inheritance woes and she'll try to marry me off to one of her dreadful friends."

"You should, you know."

"What?"

"Marry one of her dreadful friends. It might keep you out of trouble."

Rufus pauses to take a drink from a nearby fountain, kneeling on the stone brim and cupping a hand below the spout. He splashes a few droplets across his face, then dries himself on his tunic. "You'll be married soon," he says, in a deliberately casual tone, "if the look on Junia's face is anything to go by."

Mylo scratches his ear sheepishly.

"While we were eating. She was watching you with the look of a woman who intends to procure a son-in-law. I suppose it's what you want, too? They're still a little young, the daughters, but I daresay they won't be ugly. You'll have your pick of the two. I hope you can tell them apart."

Mylo looks away, smiling a little. "I can."

"Well, there you go. It's all but settled." They have arrived at the archway which leads through to Lennes's household, a low square villa in the wealthy district across the river from the palace. Unlike most of the buildings around it, Mylo knows, the Steward's home is not lavishly decorated on the inside, but plain and frugal. Since the death of his wife and the marriage of his daughter Lennes keeps only five or so servants and rarely serves meat, to his son's disgust. Though the sun has just gone down, the lamps are doused in the doorway.

Mylo wonders whether the Steward is at home; whether he is sleeping, or back at his work, or staring into his cold fireplace, still bloody and bruised. It has only been three days since the old man spoke out at the Augur's feast, and was beaten by Athraxus's temple guards. Is it possible already to talk of such ordinary things, to plan for the coming years as though nothing has changed?

Rufus leans against the arch, arms folded, a white climbing-rose in bloom all about him. He is watching Mylo's face very closely. The night is balmy, on the air a scent of pollen and rosemary. An elegant crescent moon slung like a hammock between the constellations. "Hardly a reputable family," he says. "Despite their blood connection. But you've always been unsophisticated about those sorts of things."

"Don't tease me. I owe them so much."

*

Mylo hears the noise from the party before he has even entered the passageway. He is dressed in the same cotton robe he wore to the Augur's feast; Junia made it for him, hemmed it with a red border and embroidered the sleeves with gold thread. Though his father is one of the wealthiest men in the city, this is the only fine garment he owns. For tonight he has added a brooch at the shoulder, and wears a few of Rufus's rings.

"You're late," the house-steward informs him as he enters

the atrium. The long-suffering man is slumped on a stool, legs stretched out in front of him. "They've already finished the first two courses."

"Hello Haran. Who's here?" A raucous burst of laughter from the banquet hall. Mylo can smell grilled sausages and plum syrup and peppered eggs, some kind of roasted fowl and a strong whiff of mingled perfumes.

"Everyone, master, and his wife. And his brothers and sisters too."

Mylo rolls his sleeves distractedly up and down again. "I suppose I'd better go in."

"Don't eat the lampreys, master. They've been too heavily spiced." Haran takes pride, Mylo knows, in the kitchen that he runs. It pains him to have food prepared to Calix's liking.

Upon entering the hall Mylo is taken aback for a moment by the uproarious cheering which greets him. Even by Mersia's standards the party is a large one: guests recline on every couch, some on cushions upon the floor, others arrayed in groups around the wine-jars. Some of these guests are oddly dressed in dark rough cloth instead of their best robes, ash smeared upon their faces. At least thirty lamps are suspended from the ceiling in elaborate hangers, their smoke scented with rose oil. Assaulted by a wall of noise, Mylo is barely able to take any of this in.

"Look who's here!"

"The High Priest's boy!"

"Just who we need at this fateful hour."

"Fetch your father, get him to sacrifice on our behalf!"

More gales of laughter, and the hostess herself comes sweeping up to greet him in a cloud of perfume. Mersia is wearing a gown of thin, expensive yellow linen which clashes with her hair, and through which her breasts are clearly visible. Her cheeks and lips are brightly rouged, huge gold earrings brushing her shoulders, decorative pins set among her curls. She takes Mylo by the arm and kisses him twice on each cheek. "Why aren't you in sackcloth and ashes?"

"What?"

She laughs, and the guests laugh too, many of them cheering loudly again and raising their cups. "Didn't Rufus tell you? It's the end of the world."

The group of young councillors reclining nearby begin to thump the table. Calix, a red sash stretched across his broad chest and a wreath of dying poppies on his head, climbs up onto the tabletop to wave his arms. Wine sloshes from his cup. "Quiet now! Quiet! It's time for the centrepiece!"

A burst of music, and Mylo realises that there are lute players and drummers clustered in the corner. A procession of slaves moves awkwardly into the room, bearing a long and heavy tray. When they set it down upon the main table he sees some kind of four-legged creature composed of sculpted, basted meats. Its fiery eyes are orange plums, its claws red radishes. Its back is covered in stars carved from orange-skins. It is the salamander from Lennes's dream.

"Let what is delicious be devoured!" cries Calix, and the whole room erupts in laughter. Mersia's laugh is tuneful and affected. She steers Mylo further into the room, as the guests descend upon Haran's magnificent centrepiece with knives and greasy fingers. The musicians are playing again, and yet more slaves have come parading through the door with heaped platters of oysters and cups of mountain snow. Mylo scans the room for Rufus but can't see him. Mersia forces him down onto a couch between Clemon – his rumour-hungry neighbour from the Augur's feast – and Clemon's half-sister, Filesta, who smirks at him flirtatiously. He notices that Mersia's two children are still awake, running between the tables and helping themselves, unheeded, to the spoils of the feast.

"So are you ready for the end, Myloxenes?" asks Filesta. "Have you drunk all of the wine in your cellar and made peace with your gods?"

"Oh for the wine from the High Priest's cellar!" says Clemon. "That's all this party is missing."

Filesta's hand strays to Mylo's knee. "If you've any other appetites to feed before the city burns…"

He takes several cups of wine to endure the next hour or so of their company, during which time Clemon, undeterred by their exchange at the Augur's temple, continues to interrogate him on the subject of Athraxus. They are joined by Calix and two court philosophers, who argue loudly and incoherently about the relation between the movements of the planets and the migrations of certain fish shoals. When the desserts are brought out Mylo manages to extricate himself and casts about again for Rufus, his senses now considerably foggier. One of the women has brought a small monkey on a gold chain, and a crowd has gathered round her to feed it grapes and figs. He sees Mersia break away from this group and slip out through a side door, and makes to follow her, only to be accosted by a cluster of men from the Emperor's retinue.

"We'd welcome some news from your father's household."

"Is it true that the old priest Justus is out of favour?"

"We'd heard that there are plans to honour our divine Emperor's dedication day with a magnificent feast at the new moon…"

They all look identical, a flock of tall storks. Their eyes are painted with kohl and dark powder, the style of their robes modelled after the Emperor's love for deep blue silks and trailing sleeves. Myloxenes grew up on the edges of Laonatus's court and their manner is all too familiar to him; their narrow gaze, the well-fed ease with which they carry themselves. He was poked and prodded by such men in his cradle. Before he can form a reply the music changes and a troupe of dancers come leaping into the hall with streamers and tambourines, men and women alike all naked except for their loincloths. The guests roar their approval, and Mylo spots Mersia's little son Rex dozing off beneath one of the tables, cheeks flushed bright pink, a half-eaten honey cake still clasped in his fist.

*

The passageway leading from the hall into the dark courtyard is cool and quiet. Mylo carries Rex through into Calix and Mersia's private quarters, the boy's head lolling onto his shoulder. Since he doesn't know this part of the house he is hoping to encounter Haran or one of the other slaves, but it seems that the whole household is occupied with the party. Poking his head into a few of the chambers he finds one which has a comfortable-looking couch, and lowers Rex onto it, slipping a cushion under his head.

He hesitates in the doorway, reluctant to go back into the hall but also unsure whether he ought to leave. He is uneasy. Then he hears the sound of footsteps, and to his surprise sees Lennes shuffling down the passage, muttering to himself. Mersia is on her father's heels, and has drawn level with him and taken him forcefully by the arm when she catches sight of Mylo.

"What are you doing out here?" she snaps.

The old man is dressed only in a stained tunic, no sandals, his hair in disarray. He looks shrunken, as though he has not eaten in days, and his many bruises have turned purple and yellow. His right arm is bandaged across his chest and there is a deep, swollen cut on his forehead. He peers at Mylo in the dimness, and then raises his free hand to point at him. "You are still young," he says clearly. "You have strong legs."

Mylo looks into his eyes, and feels his heart lurch.

"It's not your business." Mersia makes to pull Lennes away, but the Steward is fixed on Mylo now, his mournful countenance registering flickers of alarm.

"You can still run, boy. There's time."

"Father. I told you, your chamber is ready. You need to sleep."

"Wait, wait, I am addressing this boy."

"He's still here?" asks Mylo in an undertone. "Has he been back to his own house yet?"

"You're the one who told me to keep an eye on him!" Once more Mersia attempts, unsuccessfully, to steer Lennes back in the other direction.

"Has he seen a doctor? Mersia..."

"Of course he has. I am his dutiful child."

"Mersia, what is this?" The noise of the party is audible from across the courtyard. Lennes breaks free from his daughter's grip and wanders away again, still muttering. "You've made it a joke. You've made him a joke."

She rounds on Mylo, no trace of her earlier laughter in her face now. "I did what I had to do. I saved face for our family. Don't act like such an innocent."

He takes a step back, cowed. Mersia fixes a few pins which have come loose in her hair, and her hands continue to fuss, fiddling with the sash at her waist. "What has he been saying?" Mylo asks.

"Oh, the same, the same. The gods have spoken, the worm in the heart of the city, he must speak or perish with silence. And so on. He won't talk about anything else. The doctor gave him aloe for his injuries and extract of poppy to calm him, but it hasn't helped. He won't drink, he won't eat. He must be in pain."

"They won't heed the Prophetess!" Lennes has circled around again and now comes shuffling back towards them. "Look to her, look to her... And soon it will be too late..."

"Have you thought of taking him to the Augur's Temple?"

Mersia's laugh this time is harsher, bare of pretence. "So he can start more trouble, you mean? No, he stays in this house until he's fit to be out in public, and my brother and I will just have to keep taking it in turns to watch him…"

"That's where Rufus has been all night."

"I sent him back to the hall, he's about somewhere." Mersia lays hands on her father's arm, and he calms at last, allowing her to walk him the first few steps back towards his chamber. She casts a look over her shoulder. "I know I'm short with you," she adds, offhandedly. "But I like you, Myloxenes. You've always been good for him."

*

The party has spread now into the rooms adjoining the banquet hall, its atmosphere no longer loud and boisterous but strange, woozy. Most of the food has been demolished but the slaves are still bringing out more wine, the thick, blood-coloured kind, barely diluted. Few of the guests are on their feet. Those without couches or cushions are slumped in alcoves, sprawled across one another. Mylo squeezes past Clemon's philosopher friend, who is vomiting into an empty oyster dish. The musicians are strumming something low with a hypnotic rhythm. The monkey has broken loose from its chain and is clinging to one of the lamp-hangers, surveying the chaos beneath.

In a small enclosed chamber on the other side of the drapes a fire has been lit, hot stones arrayed within it. The silhouetted figures huddled against the glow are casting hemp seeds onto the stones, where they hiss and smoke, giving off a heady vapour which permeates the room. The dark space seems filled with elated whispers and sighs, with bodies intertwined. In the drapery Calix can be glimpsed with one of the dancers, his hairy hands crawling across her bare breasts.

Someone touches Mylo's shoulder, and he turns. There is Rufus in vivid green silk. He looks sad and worried. They look at one another for a moment and then Rufus moves a hand into Mylo's hair, leans close to kiss his mouth.

Mylo neither returns nor resists, and when they have broken apart says gently, "Ru..."

"It's the end of the world."

VIII

Snow is falling. Aemilia tilts back her head and opens her mouth. A white flake falls upon her tongue and dissolves there. All around her the sky is alight with wild colour. The tip of her nose stings in the cold. Curtains of green and rose-pink sway between the stars. She is aware of a wide quiet hugeness, a hush.

A rumble. A shadow with sails moving across the frozen ocean. The sky falls dark. There are her father and mother, coming towards her from over the hill, and they are burning. They are waving to her, catching the snow in their outstretched hands. Black smoke is rising from the fields and the circle of huts in the distance. There are her little brothers and her sisters, engulfed in halos of flame, running and laughing. Do they not know that their bodies are on fire? She tries to call out to them, but she has no voice.

Aemilia's mother is in front of her now, but the features of her face are all wrong. They will not form together into any remembered shape. Her face is charred coal and cinders. She reaches out a hand which is wreathed in flame. *Daughter,* she says, *won't you go inside and knead the dough?*

Hands seize Aemilia from behind. Arms lock tightly across her chest. She does not struggle. The arms close around her and she folds herself into a smaller shape, until those arms are all the world and she is nowhere.

*

Saba finds her with the goats, sitting on a bale of straw beside the gate to the pen and feeding pieces of oatcake to the jostling animals. "Here you are. That's four mornings now, you haven't been in your bed. Is this where you've been coming?"

Aemilia has not known what to say to Saba since her visit to the house of Antonus. The Augur told her to keep the errand secret, and she does not know how to keep secrets from Saba. Easier not to speak with her at all; but already that is taking its toll. Aemilia feels sick with worry. She wants to take Saba by the hand and tell her everything. "Bad dreams, sister," she mutters.

"I'll make you a medicine with vervain."

"Not the kind they say Lennes had."

"No, sister, not that kind." Saba leans on the gate and reaches over to scratch the nearest goat on the top of the head. Aemilia catches her looking sideways, and knows that the silence between them has not gone unnoticed. Saba's expression is determined — she is searching for a way in.

"You asked me at the market yesterday about Lennes' dreams."

"Maybe I shouldn't have. You understand more than I do, Saba. Maybe it's not my place to know."

"No, I'm glad you did. I've been wanting to talk to you." There is a light shining in Saba's eyes. "Aemilia," she says. "Have you considered, if it's true. Nobody believes it yet, but we…" She drops her voice. "We weren't born here. We can be wiser."

"What do you mean?" whispers Aemilia.

"If it is the time. If we walked out through the city gate, who would call us back? The Prophetess? I think she'd send us on our way with blessings and bags of bread. She might even come with us."

Change seems to churn somewhere deep under the rocks of the

134

earth, and Aemilia clings to her hay-bale, praying to every deity with ears. *Oh please, let me keep the life I know. Let the ground hold beneath me. Don't let her leave.*

Saba touches her on the arm. "I'm not saying let's do it now, not yet. Not until we're more certain about the will of the gods over this city. But let's be ready."

"Saba..."

"Don't you agree with me?"That shining face altered in the space of an instant. She has sharp edges, Saba, like the broken pieces of a pot. Pick her up carefully. Do not hold her too tightly in your hand. She will slice through your skin.

"It's not that. You always know better. But isn't our duty..."

"To this city? They brought us here as slaves with chains around our hands, don't you remember? They stole us from our homes. They would have sent us to rot in Athraxus's pit of a temple."

"It's not that. Saba. I couldn't."

Saba takes a step back. The goats, in the absence of further tidbits, shuffle away into their stall. When she speaks again, there is a harsh edge to her voice. "Do you never think of them? The home you left behind? Don't you want to go back to them?"

She has forgotten, Aemilia realises. Since they clung together in the belly of that terrible boat, since they first climbed hand-in-hand up the many steps to the Augur's Temple, their lives have been so closely twinned. But there were two worlds before that, and one of them is in ashes. She sees it dawn on Saba's face seconds later, a silent apology.

Do you never think of them? And she wants to answer, sister, that home comes to me in dreams which leave me shivering and grief-sick. I see the pointed trees white under the snow. I see clouds of many colours billowing across the frozen sky. I do not see the faces of those who loved me, only the faintest shapes of them, because they are gone and lost to all memory.

Saba does not go to supervise the novices in the kitchen, as she is supposed to. Instead she makes her way through the temple hall and climbs through the crack in the rock of the mountain, up to the hidden shrine beneath the water.

It is another bright day, and the needle stream cascading down the mountainside glitters in the sunlight. Saba removes her sandals. Cool green moss cushions her feet. She walks ankle-deep into the water and bends to dip her hands below the surface, feeling with her fingertips the symbols cut into the rock. They cannot be read now, since the language is lost, but sometimes she thinks the contours speak to her. This, perhaps, a hare or rabbit. This a sheaf of wheat. These the swollen curves of a budding flower. The first Augur must have cut them here, or her acolytes. Saba imagines that they were giddy with it, the form of freedom they had found. To make a mark, to bring something to birth that was not a son, that would endure longer than a bloodline.

With each rising of the sun Saba thanks the gods that she will never marry: that she need never wait in fear for some hard-handed stranger to come to her bed, or feel her dread swell along with her belly as childbirth draws near. Mercy of mercies. To marry is to die.

To be chaste is to stand outside of the body, loose from the curse of this anatomy, from the disappointment of the midwife who holds up the bloodied newborn by the ankle and declares, *girl-child*. When the womb is closed, so the physicians say, the mouth might open. Wed to the temple, set aside, a priestess is nobody, belongs to nobody. She might exist and flourish apart from the structures of men, in the cracks between their edifices, like a rock-rose on the mountain.

Saba stands in the flow of the stream, the shrine beneath the soles of her feet. Most of her life she has known herself this way, as the girl who serves in the temple, who will one day be Augur. True, she has kept herself sworn to her mothers in that other land. But she does not know what gods they worship.

She does not remember a temple. It was not a city, that place, not nearly as large. A village of baked ochre dwellings, fields of leafy green shoots growing higher than her head, spreading trees, a lake where wild horses bent to drink. Is that right, Saba? Or is this a story you have told yourself? Were there cattle with huge horns, and bright yellow finches, and flat round breads eaten with red stew? She has lost track, over the years, of what is remembered and what is her own invention.

The life she had seen laid out for her here at the Augur's temple is washing away. What might form in its place she cannot yet imagine, but Saba does not dwell upon uncertainties. The thought of walking halfway across the world to a place hardly recalled does not daunt her. She does not doubt that she can find her way back.

Aemilia will be persuaded, before the end comes. They will watch for the signs, wait for a word from the Augur, and then they will take another journey together. Saba will take her sister by the hand and assure her, *your home is with me. My people will be your people. Why perish here in a city not your own?*

It is good to be watchful. Saba watches for the cloaked figure ascending the steps to the temple at sundown. She wonders whether he has been swimming in the ocean again, whether his tunic is damp and his hair stiff with sea-salt. She waits at a distance until he has purified himself in the tall jar of spring-water at the entrance to the sanctuary. He dips his hands with reverent care, does not look around to see her in the shadows of the courtyard. When he has ducked in through the archway she draws nearer, crouching next to the jar, her back against the stone wall. She hears the crackle of a struck flint as the Augur lights the altar-lamp.

137

"I brought a calf's liver," says Myloxenes, son of Athraxus. A pause as the meat is portioned, and Saba smells it cast onto the fire. "I'm not here for a sacrifice. But I wanted to be respectful."

"They say that you're here to ask me scholar's questions."

"If you'll let me."

"You are the High Priest's boy," says the Augur. It is not an answer, or an accusation. Athraxus seems present in the quiet which follows. Saba imagines him stood in the darkening archway, a sneer curling his mouth, the heavy bodies of his dogs rumbling at his feet.

There is a tremor in Myloxenes' voice. "Will you tell him I've been here?"

"I am not in the business of telling Athraxus anything."

"I don't think he would much like it."

"No, indeed. But I see you, boy. Your mother is not your mother and your father is not your father."

A pause. Then Myloxenes lets out a surprised laugh. "It's true! What you see, it's true. I am the child of no fewer than five parents."

"And they say that the Augur's sight has weakened."

Saba inches closer to the archway. By the light of the altar-fire she can see the broad-shouldered shape of the Augur, who is crouching on the step, leaning forward towards the boy Myloxenes. He is stood in the middle of the shadowy space, his back to Saba. He looks slight and vulnerable.

"Tell me about your history," says the Augur.

"I've been working on it for four years or so. It's not much, but I've been trying to fill in the spaces that other accounts don't concern themselves with. Emperors with short reigns, and so on. And the time before that, before the Emperors. Is it true that this temple is the oldest in the city?"

"The building, yes, but only because others have fallen. This wasn't the first temple built in the city, and our teachings weren't the first."

"Oh. But the religion of this temple, you think it's the oldest religion. Perhaps the true religion."

"Nothing here is complete. We would not claim that. We wait, and we hope for what is to come."

"But do you think… do you think the wisdom of the Augurs is the oldest wisdom? The line of the Augurs is long, isn't it?"

"Son of Athraxus," says the Augur. "You have not come here to learn about history. You are looking for something pure and untouched. You are hoping to hear words from the mouths of the gods themselves."

Saba feels a tug in her stomach. Suddenly she is aware of her presence as an interloper. She leans back towards the wall again, wrapping her arms around her knees, while the altar-fire cracks and spits into the silence.

"All my life," says Myloxenes, at last, "there's so much I've felt uncertain of. There are times when the world seems to be full of loud disorder. It pains me that the gods are gone so far from us. And I worry that I'm too weak to overcome what I lack, not with sacrifices every day for a lifetime."

"Ah," says the Augur, and Saba thinks she hears something tender in the old woman's voice. "The lie from the garden."

"Prophetess, are there any that love me?"

"Don't you know, boy?" says the Augur. "Don't you know?"

IX

She comes late to the palace, hooded and cloaked, and is nodded through the main gateway by the guards. Only the Augur might enter the palace this way, unquestioned, unaccompanied after nightfall: but they are hostile, nonetheless. More so, now. Something has altered since the last time the Emperor called for her, months ago, long before the summer solstice.

There are slaves busy about the halls and the passageways, sweeping the stones, beating rugs and hangings, dousing lamps and pouring in fresh oil. They are quiet about their business, heads lowered. But they turn to watch the Augur as she passes. Deeper inside the palace it grows darker and quieter, her footsteps echoing between the columns. Somewhere a child is crying. Through a whispering curtain in a side-room crammed with rich furnishings are Mandane and Cassandane, one reclining on a couch and the other seated at her feet, whispering together. They look up at the Augur, who pauses in her path, but the women only blink blankly and draw their veils up over their mouths. They are not kept for their conversation, the Emperor's wives.

At the entrance to Laonatus's private quarters, the guards have just released a diminutive figure through the door. The Emperor's favourite entertainer, the dwarf known as Little Laonatus, stops in the passageway to lift off her encumbering headdress and outer robe. Her face, as usual, has been made up to look like the Emperor's own. She looks spent, but her expression brightens when she catches sight of the Augur.

"Prophetess! He's been so eager to see you."

"How will I find him?"

"Fretful. He isn't sleeping. He's sent for me every night this week, and won't be quieted with riddles or poems or songs. He wants you."

"I'm sure you've done your best."

"Oh, I'm sure I have. When he's out of sorts the whole palace is under a cloud. *The sun-god frowns, the grasses wither.* Like in the old verse." Her dark eyes glance in the direction of the guards before flicking back to the Augur. She lowers her voice. "It's his dedication feast soon and I know they're already tearing their hair out in the kitchens. He keeps changing his mind about the courses. *I will have the sea-urchins first. No, the braised hare, the lamb's head. And—*" Her voice drops even further. "I'm dreading the occasion. Is it all true, Prophetess? What they're saying about the feast at your temple?"

"So I am told," says the Augur. "I was taken ill, and not present."

"I keep hearing things. I'm worried that somebody will say something which displeases him, or make a joke in poor taste and get on Athraxus's bad side. You will be there, won't you?"

"I have not yet been asked," says the Augur. "I should think, no. You say that you hear things. Among them, surely, that I am falling out of favour."

*

The Emperor Laonatus is on his bed, resting against a mountain of embroidered cushions, his blue night-robe spread about him. On the tables and shelves around the large chamber, countless scrolls, curious brass and silver instruments, maps weighed down with stones, tapers and coloured lanterns, pots of perfumes and cosmetics. The remnants of the entertainer's time with him – her lyre and flute, a ladder to reach his shelves – have been left in a corner. In a cage suspended from the ceiling a long black-spotted lizard and a white crested bird are at an uneasy truce.

Laonatus sighs at the Augur's appearance, waving her in with a languid hand. "I have been thinking," he says, by way of greeting.

So many nights over the last twenty years have begun this way. Because the Emperor has time for thinking. He savours the kind of puzzles which have no solutions. He worries about the dim corners of knowledge; about the mysterious migratory destinations of sacred birds; the pages in his father's annals where records have been poorly kept, the nature and habits of the giant-men who are said to live in the arid country far over the mountains. Just as his bedside lamp is burning dry, Laonatus will rise and upend some dusty case of charts, then call for more lamps so that he can spend the small hours examining them. He will decide on a whim that he wishes to hear a particular word in a language spoken only by that trader who sells brass pots in the lower city market.

His chamber-slaves and closest attendants must learn all kinds of unblinking patience. They can all run in their sleep the route across the square and up the steps to the Augur's temple.

"I have been thinking," says Laonatus, "about something that Athraxus said to me. He told me that all the forms in this world are shadows or copies of brighter things. He said that somewhere there is another realm where nothing is dimmed or hidden, and that it's for us as the great men and priests of the city to turn our faces towards it. Only we can bear this acquaintance with greatness. And when we return to tell what we have seen, the people won't understand our wisdom." His large eyes are filling with emotion. "We'll have attained such heights, and the people only want their bread and their dice-games, their dim empty forms. Isn't that a beautiful and a terrible thought?"

"You are an eloquent poet, my lord Emperor, of the people's tragedy."

"A man must see into the higher things, to rule. But I won't deny that it is a burden to me." He means it; his shoulders slope, for a moment, beneath this burden. He reaches for the goblet of iced wine at his bedside, and drinks deeply. "It's the daily labour of Athraxus and the priests at his temple, to battle and bargain for his entrance into this place, on behalf of those who can never enter. Athraxus says that your temple makes light of these matters."

He is looking at her, all of a sudden, his gaze clear and coldly enquiring.

"I sent for you days ago."

"You know that I was taken ill, at the solstice."

"I have been quite unhappy. I have been unable to sleep. I have needed you."

"I am sorry, my lord Emperor. But I am with you now."

"There was a time, if I sent for you, you would have come within the hour."

"Yes, my lord Emperor. But you were so young, then."

"I am still young," he says.

They sit together in silence, for a while. They observe one another. Twenty years ago, she had visited the new child-Emperor after presiding over his father's burial. They had hung bells together from his chamber doorway to ward away his bad dreams. He had been afraid of other things, too; of the shadows cast by his bedside lamp, of lightning storms, of inauspicious omens. He fears all of these things, still.

"Athraxus says it would be wise if you didn't attend my dedication feast. He says that there was a skirmish of some sort at your temple at the solstice. He thinks your presence might disrupt the festivities."

"I've always been at your service, to summon or to send away as you see fit."

Laonatus picks an orange from a bowl of fruit upon his pillows and peels it. "Athraxus thinks that you've grown too old to carry out your duties," he says carelessly.

"Is that so? And what do you think?"

"I'm not sure." He puts a segment of orange into his mouth. "You have always looked old to me." He smiles. "Do you remember, when I decided to build a hundred new warships? You talked me down to twenty. You said the omens favoured a smaller fleet. Then there was the year you helped me choose all of my new magistrates. You said the gods had indicated particular men to you, in the flight of the starling flock."

"We have been blessed by their guidance."

"And I've been blessed by yours. There was a time, wasn't there, when I wouldn't have so much as chosen which sandals to wear without consulting your wisdom first." He eats another piece of orange, chews it slowly. "You were mother to the formation of my mind."

"You are generous. But your mind and your will have always been entirely your own, my lord Emperor."

"That's what Athraxus says. He thinks I ought to be weaned from a woman's counsel by now." Laonatus entertains the passing thought. "Do you remember," he says, "when you read the omens for that battle in the mountain pass, across the plain? Two hundred of my men slaughtered? That was the only time your sight has failed me."

"Yes, my lord Emperor. You said that it was not my sight that failed, but that my priestesses couldn't have been chaste. You had them all stoned outside the city wall. Their bodies were burned there."

"Oh yes," says Laonatus, with the pity of one hearing of a landslide or ruinous storm in a far-off place. "That was a terrible thing."

It is long past midnight. The many lamps on the Emperor's table and shelves are burning low. He flinches as a wick drops into a flame and its shadow rears and writhes on the far side of the ceiling. He draws his robe more closely about himself. He reaches into the fruit bowl again but seems to lose his appetite even as he does so, gazing out into the room.

"I have been thinking," he says fretfully, "about the appetite of the shadow-god. One hears accounts. One is advised, by the wisest of men. But whether there are enough sacrifices, to be certain..."

Night breathes around them. The Augur lays a hand upon her stiff lower back, and settles down again onto her stool. She will not leave this post until dawn. Because after all, is this not the blessing and the curse of every mother? To carry and raise up her son for the day that he no longer needs her?

X

Each festival must put the feasting of the last to shame. *Tonight,* boasts the Emperor, *each man's portion will be worth what a labourer in the city might earn in a year. Tonight you will taste delicacies that kings in other nations might sell their firstborn sons for. My lords, my counsellors and generals, my priests and diviners, philosophers, courtiers and courtesans, scholars and soothsayers, magicians, musicians, acrobats, dancers, players. My little fool. Feast with me. Such a feast has never before been seen in all of the known world.*

He is robed in blue and gold, this Emperor, glittering jewels upon his hands, crowned with a circlet of bronze. He is an exquisite work of the gods. There is divine light in his eyes. Look at what he has built for himself. A waterfall cascades through pools rich with greenery and filled with floating white lilies. Peacocks step between the sprouting ferns. Artisans have given their best years to the carvings upon the walls, depicting the exploits of this Emperor and of his forefathers, extending even to the far corners and high places of the hall where they will never be seen.

There have been Emperors as far back as anyone can remember. Before them men must press their foreheads to the dust. Shoulder the best of their grain and their meat and pass it upwards, into the hands of these rulers, these gods. Cities are bound together this way, by the blood spilt in temples and the sweat spilt in fields. Some nights, if the people are fortunate, the music and the perfume from the halls of their rulers will come drifting on the air into the city.

The Emperor upon his silk-cushioned stone seat and beside him that priest who leans so often to take him by the shoulder and whisper in his ear. Long and lean, this priest, as though he might slip through half-closed doors, as though he might be the Emperor's own narrow shadow. Robed in deep red. The latest in that lineage, which is older even than the lineage of rulers. Since the time before memory such men have whispered from behind seats of power.

Here comes the flowing wine, the platters groaning beneath the weight of their riches, the cornucopias bursting with ripe fruit, the dancers wearing bells about their ankles and wrists, the singers accompanied with lyres and drums, the troupe of players, the little fool with a familiar tale. Neither stories nor songs can much be heard over the din of the Emperor's guests, who devour his feast like locusts, who are drunk and red-faced with wine and laughter and the heat of the room.

This hall is the heart of the world and the Emperor's stone seat is its throne. There is nothing outside of these walls and none of the guests will ever leave. They will feast here for a thousand years, gorging themselves, their mouths always open, always chewing, another cup of wine forced between their red-stained lips. Slaves will bring in fresh platters of food without ever clearing out the old, leaving mountains of soft peaches and grapes and oranges to moulder there upon the table, leaving dogs to tear at rotten carcasses and squabble over bones. The sun in the sky will grow old and sink down swollen and scarlet over the rooftops of the palace while the guests of the Emperor still feast.

Who would notice, in the midst of such a feast, a red silk hanging flutter out of place as a tremor shakes loose a chunk of plaster from the eastern wall behind the Emperor's seat. Who would notice the set of symbols revealed there on the stone within the wall, just higher than the level of a man's head, paint still shining wet beneath the lamps. Another piece of plaster falls away with a scattering of dust. Nobody sees except for the fool, who points over the Emperor's shoulder and cries out in puzzlement, though her voice is too small to be heard. And then the priest, who leaps from his seat for a better look.

The Emperor turns. He pales, one arm raised as though to

shield him from the sight. A stray breeze carries the fallen hanging down from the dais and across the hall, undulating like a tongue of fire. The Emperor cries out and people begin to turn, a clatter and splash as they set down their cups.

Just paint upon stone. But that look. The look upon the Emperor's face.

*

He stands like a marble statue. Wine drips in a stream to the floor. Hush falls across the whole gathering as more heads turn, laughter and conversation dying. Slaves, sweating through their tunics, stare and tremble. The symbols shine white upon the dark stone. The room turns like a whirlwind with the Emperor's terrible silence at its heart, gathering up cries of distress and confusion, spinning faster and faster until the whole hall is in a panicked uproar.

It is the priest who comes to his senses first, who bellows for calm and for the Emperor's most learned scholars. Those not already present are swiftly sent for by messenger. For hours they confer in a huddle beneath the strange script, but though they are versed in many languages they cannot read it.

The guests disperse as the night wears on, subdued even in their drunkenness, whispering to one another. Rumours scatter like seeds. *Behind the plaster, on the stone, but the paint fresh and new. Were they hidden there by some trickery, or miracle? Did your eyes, did my eyes see them appear? Did the whole assembly see a hand manifest itself from the air and write, slowly, deliberately, before it vanished again?*

The Emperor paces the length of the hall, now petulant, now angry, now trembling with fear. He has not yet said a word. Next his philosophers are summoned, then the magicians and diviners, but none can puzzle it out.

At last, when only the priest and the fool and a handful of old nobles remain, the tables and floor strewn with debris and half-eaten food, the Emperor speaks. *It is time to send for the Prophetess.*

Ought it to take her so long? Hours pass, it seems, before she presents herself at the palace. She is entirely calm, leaning on her staff, her sharp little eyes darting from right to left as she stands before the script upon the wall. The Emperor is pacing again. The priest waits in stillness and silence. The Prophetess raises a hand to trace the outline of the lettering. Then, after only a few minutes, she turns.

It is the old language of the priestesses, she says. *The symbols used when they first built the temple. Many hundreds of years out of use. Only a memory of it remains.*

But can you read it? cries the Emperor.

I can. She does not bow her head, or so much as lower her eyes.

What does it mean? begs the fool, who has forgotten her place. The priest, agitated, hisses through his teeth. The Emperor stops on the spot. The fool finds the calm gaze of the Prophetess upon her. The old woman speaks to her as though the two of them are alone with this secret.

It means that the destruction of this city will come both from within and without.

CONSUMMATION

I

He lets Rufus share his bed, for old times' sake, and wakes before dawn full of panic. He casts off the bedclothes, fighting for breath, and feels for the wild beat of his heart. The room is spinning. He plants the soles of his feet upon the cool stone floor and waits for his senses to return.

Two days after he went there, he can still smell the smoke from the temple sanctuary. Mylo rubs his face with his hands and tries to recover what the Augur said to him: the way that her words undid him, and bound him back together. A glimpse of something bright and holy.

In the darkness he feels Rufus's arm encircle his ribcage. "What's wrong?"

His first urge is to fight free. "Nothing. Go back to sleep."

"Did you have a bad dream?" This enquiry has a fearful edge. In Rufus's world, now, a dream might strike a man down from out of nowhere, like lightning from a clear sky.

Mylo shakes his head. Rufus kisses his neck, but then moves back, reticent. When Mylo's silence does not break, he leans against the wall with a heavy sigh. "I can't spend another night in his house, Mylo. It's killing me. Everything's so dark there. The slaves all tiptoe about like they're shut inside a tomb. It'll only be worse, if he comes home."

"Can't you stay at Mersia's?"

"That's even more unbearable. She makes me watch him while she's out getting her hair curled and other nonsense. Every word out of his mouth is plague and perishing. And he's like a child. We have to cut his food into little pieces, he pisses himself. Calix is a lump, he won't do anything." Rufus pummels the pillow with his fists. "I wish Mother was here."

That was it: a breath of something in the house, a shutter broken open. He remembers Rufus and Mersia's mother, Minah, a clever, sharp-faced foreigner who has been dead for five years. There ought to be someone in every household who takes care to let in the daylight.

"Ru," he says faintly. Shadows encroach about the bed. The comfort of the Augur's Temple already feels lost to him. "Lennes is only the beginning of it. I can't see the way ahead. I don't know what the gods want from us."

"You think too much."

Now that his heartbeat has slowed, Mylo realises that he wants to be alone. Rufus is restless, twitching his legs and muttering under his breath. Their closeness tonight is not a comfort – in fact it is barely a distraction. He ought to have known better. At this moment Rufus is too much, and not enough.

Uncomfortable, he lies down and tries to find his place again. The tightness in his chest has hardly eased, and Mylo knows that he is awaiting the dawn with dread. There can only be more ill news, a darker sun. The bounds of the city feel as narrow tonight as the bounds of his bed.

*

Wanting to check on Lennes, he persuades Rufus that they ought to take breakfast with Mersia. Arriving, though, they find the household oddly quiet. There is nobody in the atrium to greet them. A slave scuttles past as though trying to evade notice. Rufus's niece Calica, cross-legged on the floor near the doorway, moves her dolls around with studied attention. He touches the top of her head. "Little bird, what's going on?"

"Rex wanted to play catch with me. He went outside."

"Where's Mama?"

She points in the direction of the inner room, without looking up from her game. "They were loud," she says, "but now they're quiet."

Rufus rolls his eyes at Mylo and proceeds inside, throwing back the drape without concern for his sister's privacy. "Here, you two! You can hold today's little spat until after breakfast."

They have interrupted Calix and Mersia in the act of hissing viciously at each other across the room. Mersia immediately folds her arms, sullen, her many bracelets jangling loudly. Calix is attired, peculiarly, in his feasting-robes. He seems flushed and overwrought.

Rufus looks his brother-in-law up and down. "Did you drink too much at the Emperor's feast and go home with that whore again?"

"Get him *out*," huffs Calix.

"No, I'm glad he's here." Mersia seizes her brother by the elbow. "Rufus, my husband wants us to tie up our ailing father and cast him onto the altar of the Dark Temple, for the dogs to eat."

Calix looks ready to strike her in his frustration. "I'm the head of this household. I've seen the way the wind's blowing. I won't have him under my roof any longer."

Mylo feels a shiver at the back of his neck, as though a cold hand has touched him there. "Calix, you can't mean that. He's as good as blood to you."

"Of course you're here too, sticking your nose in! You're not welcome in this house any more either, not so long as you hang around with Antonus the Cripple. He's a friend to Lennes and to the Augur, everybody saw that at midsummer, and no doubt he'll be next to get locked up!"

"Did something happen…?"

"The Prophetess is out of favour, for good this time. She tried to pull off a trick at the Emperor's expense, and finally got her comeuppance. Athraxus is going to ruin her."

Mylo feels sick to his stomach. "Is she, are her priestesses- "

"She's imprisoned. Oh, her temple's still standing, but we'll see how long it lasts without her! See how long *she* lasts in the hands of the High Priest! So I don't want you coming to this house again, and I want – *him* – out."

"I already dealt with it!" hisses Mersia. "Nobody thinks we're on his side!"

Rufus squares up to Calix, a housecat spitting at a bull. "Do you think you're going to get knocked back down the ladder, is that it? After you've forked out so much money getting cosy with the High Priest and the Emperor, dancing naked in the catacombs or whatever it is that you all do, flashing your secret handshakes…"

Mylo recalls the small gesture that Calix made to Athraxus in the courtyard room, the sign – he now realises – of a Dark Temple cult.

"How dare you mock what you don't understand."

"You're a toad, do you know that? I said it before she married you."

"And you're a wastrel. If you don't get out of here now, and take the old man with you, I'll see to it that he's handed back to the authorities." Mylo has rarely seen Calix exert his will so forcefully, especially not in opposition to Mersia. Whatever happened at the Emperor's feast and whatever is shifting in the balance of the city, he has been emboldened by it. "There will be no traitors under this roof. I am a man of the council. I will not let my standing with the Emperor be compromised by anyone."

*

"Where are you taking him, my masters?" The house-steward Haran waylays them as they pass through the atrium, Lennes supported between them. The old man is as weak now as he was on the morning they brought him here, but he has lost so much weight that he is easier to carry.

"Away, Haran. The master of this household——" Rufus spits on the ground – "won't have him any more. So much for a son's loyalty. That lump isn't family, he never was."

"We'll take him back to his own house," Mylo tells Haran. "He has people in his service who will care for him."

"It's a wicked thing, for a daughter to refuse hospitality to her father," says Haran, who is wringing his hands. He seems too carried away by emotion to be watching his words.

"Believe me, she doesn't do it willingly," snaps Rufus.

"No, I mean..." The slave makes a gesture Mylo hasn't seen in a long time, touching his chest and bowing his head towards the place in the wall where once there must have been a household shrine. "Oh, pardon me my masters. It's a sign of a disordered world. There have been so many, haven't there? That's what people are saying. Since midsummer I've been fearing for myself, for my children."

Lennes, whose eyes have been closed, opens them briefly. The wound above his bandaged arm is festering. His gaze moves from Haran to Rufus, and his mouth begins to move, though no words emerge. Rufus's face crumples.

"You'd best be careful who you say that to, these days," Mylo warns Haran in a low voice. His own heart is lurching fearfully.

"Pardon me," Haran says again. "I overhear too much. Before he goes, do you think he would bless me?"

"What do you mean?"

Haran glances over his shoulder. "Some in the city have been calling him a prophet."

Rufus lets out an involuntary, despairing laugh. Lennes, however, recovers enough strength in the moment to lean forward, attentive. Haran takes hold of the old man's hand, and in the sunlight which pours in through the high windows of the atrium, lays it to rest upon his own head.

II

The ninth morning after midsummer finds Antonus scattering grain in the yard at the front of the villa, watching the birds scratch about in the dust, when he sees a small figure coming up through the grove. His impression is of a child, a figure hardly as high as his hip. He is imagining some girl even younger than the priestess Aemilia, sent from the temple. His heart sinks to his stomach. What message from the Augur, now?

"Antonus?" the figure calls out from the dappled shade of the vines below. "Antonus, is that you?"

The voice is faintly familiar. And as she comes up the path between the fruit trees towards the house, he recognises her at last: it is Hestia, the little entertainer from the palace. They had been children together, many years ago.

She looks much as he remembers her, though more stooped, more lined about the eyes. He notices a flash of peacock blue beneath her cloak, the expensive clothes she is concealing. If she is here on behalf of his brother it would be strange to go about it so secretly. "Antonus," she says in a low voice, "you have hardly changed."

This is untrue: she cannot have seen him since he was crippled, since the fire that marred his face and broke his body. She must be remembering him as a youth, as her master, perhaps demanding another song after the evening's meal or laughing at a friend's lewd remark. He stood on both legs, then, on the cusp of inheriting the city. "Can I... can I fetch you something? A cup of wine?"

"It's good of you, but no." Hestia is still looking closely at Antonus. "I've always listened for news of you. I know you have daughters, and a son. I never even glimpsed you at the palace. I suppose you don't go there very often."

"Are you here on the Emperor's business?" he asks carefully.

"The Emperor doesn't know I'm here," says Hestia. She looks over her shoulder, then draws a deep breath, tightening the clasp of her cloak. Her small face is a mask, but he can see her fear and her urgency. "I know I should wait for you to invite me, but could we go inside...?"

"Of course." He ushers her through the archway and towards the inner room, calling for his wife, who appears with dye-stained hands. At the sight of Hestia she pauses, puzzled, wiping her palms on her apron. "This is my wife, Junia. This is Hestia, known as Little Laonatus, a servant to the Emperor. Hestia, please sit..."

Without a word, Junia leaves the room, returning with a jug of wine and with Felix at her heels. He lurks in the doorway, attentive, and Hestia asks, "Is your slave trustworthy?"

"He is."

"Here it is, then, since I can't stay long. They say that you spoke up for Lennes the Steward at the Augur's feast. There was another feast last night, at the palace. You've probably heard what happened, it's already spreading..."

"We are quiet, here," says Antonus. "News from the city can take days to reach us."

The children are playing in the courtyard. Their squeals over a rowdy game of dice punctuate Hestia's tale; she talks quickly and purposefully. Perched at the table in the inner room, she leaves the proffered cup of wine untouched. Antonus leans against the wall close by.

"I couldn't think where else to go, who else to go to. I can't speak openly at court. And when I heard that you showed sympathy to Lennes, I thought, maybe the older brother has grown wise. Perhaps we should look to Antonus now. So there it is, I'm in your hands. You can have me arrested as a traitor, like the Augur, if you want."

"*From within and without*," Felix repeats, when Hestia finally falls quiet. "These were her words."

"They're still ringing in my ears."

"So whether she somehow wrote that script, or merely interpreted it," says Antonus, "She openly prophesied our destruction," He hears finality in his own voice and knows then that he believes it, that he has believed it since Aemilia came. Perhaps even since Lennes spoke out at the solstice feast. He has kept this hidden from himself.

Where did it come from, his belief? Perhaps the very first sign, the tremor in the earth, began to shake it loose from inside him. Something must compel a man to choose which temple he worships in, to heed one prophet and dismiss another — especially when belief comes at some great cost. He only knows that he feels a life in these recent auspices beyond human power. They have a taste to them which reminds him of the fire which nearly killed him, of his nights in the healing-houses and the dreams he dreamed there.

He turns to his wife, who still seems ready to fight. Her brows are set fiercely. Gods in your all-seeing power, remake your plans for our world: Junia disapproves.

"This is court politics," she says. "This is temple business. It must be."

Hestia does not hesitate to contradict her. "Court politics were my mother's milk. And I've never known anything like this."

"Junia," says Felix inexplicably, from the edge of the room. "To being free, to being a foreigner. Remember?"

"I suppose that my brother has already been persuaded not to believe her," says Antonus.

"Athraxus told him it was trickery," says Hestia. "That it wouldn't have been difficult to create an illusion in the dim light, the way magicians do, what with the guests having drunk so much wine. But believe me, no prophet who wants influence speaks destruction over her city. No prophet who wants to live."

That must be a part of it, thinks Antonus. Of discerning truth. Those birds scattered in the sky, whether they fly with the prevailing wind, or in some more dangerous direction.

"And will they let her live?" asks Felix.

"She's been imprisoned. I've heard they are holding her at the House of the Magistrates."

"I wish we could speak with her directly." Antonus steadies himself against the wall. His body feels as burdensome as ever, but his mind is racing. *From within and without . . .* what might it mean? She didn't say any more than this?"

"No more than what I've told you. Nothing about how or when all this might happen." Hestia finally reaches for the cup of wine, and swallows half of it in one gulp. "Antonus, I don't think that we have very long. I'm afraid, for my life and for the city. I know we haven't spoken in years, but I don't think we have time for you to distrust me." She leans forward, urgent now. "You and I, we know Laonatus. He'll be persuaded to view this as an insult to his pride. He'll carry on as before, won't make any supplication to the gods. If anybody believes and tries to leave the city, he'll stop them. He will captain this ship straight into the storm."

It is on the tip of Antonus's tongue to tell her about the visit of Aemilia — that the Augur has already sounded him out. A glance at Felix is enough to know that he is thinking the same. Antonus hesitates.

"Is this slave trustworthy?" Felix asks.

Hestia holds up her hands. "The Augur would speak for me if she was here, I promise. You know that Laonatus would use somebody less absurd, if he was trying to entrap you. And besides..." She gestures to herself, a wry little plea. "I've been dancing for him like his favourite trained monkey since we were both children. Do you think I bear him much love?"

*

Antonus lights a stick of incense in the shrine of the household gods, dusts the heads of the bronze statues with his sleeve. He kneels and waits there a while, scented smoke drifting up and away over his head. No sound of thunder, no trembling in the ground. The gods do not speak. He feels a deep pang of frustration which passes into anger and then into something like grief. It is a strange thing to be a man on earth, subject to the forces which move oceans and empires, glimpsing their purpose so falteringly. For the first time he truly understands why it is widows and slaves, the poor and the sick, who most often frequent the Augur's temple. They more than any must long to hear the gods bridge the gap between the heavens and this dirt.

Shake again, rocks, and make me certain. Give me another sign before I commit my life to this perilous course. The divine realm asks what is unreasonable. For faith and sacrifice when only silence answers.

As he limps outside again Antonus takes in the breadth of his world, the peach trees, the vineyard and the olive grove, the white cat upon the wall and the children who are running to meet him. Let all of this go, now. The children running through the high corn with spider's webs in their hair, with woven dormouse-nests and brittle bird-skulls held out in their palms, offered up like precious votives. All part of what is destined for destruction.

It took you by surprise, he reminds himself, this measure of happiness which you have been granted. It grew out of barren ground.

You remember how Junia stood stiff and motionless below her veil through your wedding, like a trapped creature, and how later that night when you lifted it and saw her unclothed she looked at you as though you were her jailer, and pierced you to the heart.

How through the course of the years, in awkwardness and humiliation and then finally in fragile hope, some quiet alliance was woven between you. In the most ordinary moments; in the sound of her singing to herself as she washed in the morning. In the peace which came to fill the home each evening as the sun went down outside, in the first night she did not flinch away as you climbed into bed beside her.

How by the time she lay exhausted on her child-bed with a tiny bloodied girl at each breast, when the midwives outside the door were already muttering together of two girls, two worthless mouths to feed, misfortune upon misfortune for that most unfortunate of households, the cripple and the ruined woman, you got down on your knees beside her and met her questioning gaze and smiled to let her know that all was well.

When he climbs into bed that night she is already asleep, or so he thinks, her face turned towards the wall. She has hardly spoken a word to him since Hestia left them. He wonders how he can possibly convey to her the distance he has travelled that day, the weight of what he now knows he must do. She has already made her feelings clear to him. But he cannot find the courage for this without her.

"Felix is right," she says, suddenly. "I think I had forgotten, again. I'm still a foreigner here."

She is still facing away from him. He touches her waist. "What do you mean? You were born in the city."

"But I was made an exile. I knew this city was rotten, all these years. I smelled it. The smell of dying. I thought that if I didn't look back, I could escape it. I let myself forget. It's been possible to forget, in this life with you. "

Still not certain that he understands, he lies down against her back. Runs his palms over her shoulders.

"There was a time," she says, "I'd pray at the Augur's temple because I wanted destruction. I wanted blood. I believed the Prophetess saw what nobody else did, that she saw this city with clear eyes."

Cicadas chirp in the trees on the mountainside. The distant sounds of the city. He feels beneath her skin the heat of an anger which is more potent than his own. Her voice drops almost to a whisper.

"Time was, I would have burned all of this to the ground myself."

III

On the stone floor of the Augur's empty quarters, Saba sits cross-legged, burning a bundle of sage. She is trying to concentrate on the shapes formed by the rising silver smoke, but her whole body is squirming with impatience. She draws a series of deep breaths and imagines the Augur's voice, as she has heard it countless times, scolding her in her ear. *Keep still, and work upon the task. Whatever business your mind has elsewhere, it can wait.*

But the business my mind has today, Mother, is you. How they would not let you return here to fetch a spare cloak, or to gather up your scrolls. How we still do not know exactly what it was you did or said to anger them; how we did not even know your whereabouts until the rumour of it reached us through the crier in the marketplace: how the magistrates' guards would not let us into the rooms where you are being held, so that we might bring you food and talk with you. Can this matter wait, my mother? Can this be consigned to tomorrow?

The sage-smoke coils opaquely. In frustration Saba tears the cloth from her head and uses it to smother the smouldering leaves. The idea of having to wait and watch, which is the entire essence of augury, feels suddenly unbearable. How can she read the signs while she is so unquiet with indignation? How can she walk from this city and this life while the Augur is held prisoner here? How can she march into the magistrates' house when she is barely one small stone in the city's balance; when she knows, beyond a doubt, that it is Athraxus who is truly responsible?

I will claw his eyes out, she thinks. That priest. If I see him...

She finds Aemilia sitting on the steps at the bottom of the tower, staring out at the afternoon sky. The day is hot and close. There are feverish patches of colour in Aemilia's cheeks, and as Saba follows her gaze she sees a flock of starlings swooping low over the colonnades, rising again, looping and gliding through the air above the city. Aemilia seems entranced. The birds form a tight cloud and then disperse.

"What do you see?" asks Saba softly.

Aemilia does not turn. "They flew from the left to the right. Change, alteration. Then downward, then up again. Power lost and gained. That pattern repeated, three times. Then the flock divided. Discord."

She has been weeping, thinks Saba, looking sideways at Aemilia's face. She has not slept. She does not sound like herself.

"You said we should wait for the signs. And here it is. They've taken her away." Aemilia looks over her shoulder at last. "Are you going to leave now?"

Saba feels a guilty swoop in her stomach. She crouches beside Aemilia, reaches out to grasp her hand and finds it cool, limp. "How can you think that?"

"You said that you were getting ready."

"Oh, Aemilia." Saba is shocked that Aemilia could so readily believe this of her. Different as they are, she has never before felt so deeply misjudged. "I shouldn't have said that to you. Not yet, anyway. I shouldn't have told you any of it. Please don't worry. That isn't for today."

Aemilia lets out a slow sigh, turning again to watch the starlings. "Saba." Her voice is flat, almost trance-like. "She believed that Lennes told the truth. I didn't tell you. She sent me to see Antonus the Cripple."

"What?" At the sharp exclamation Aemilia flinches away, withdrawing her hand. Saba grabs her shoulder but Aemilia will not be hurried. She falls quiet for what feels like an age.

"You were serving in the sanctuary," she says, eventually. "She told me to go secretly, when it was dark. I went to the villa above the olive grove, at the foot of the mountain, and spoke with him. The villa with the red roof and the lantern outside. I gave him the message."

"...and then what, 'Milia? What message?"

"That he should leave the city. Or if he chose to, he could maybe appease the gods if he sat on the Emperor's seat in his brother's place."

"Our mother told you this?" asks Saba, astonished.

"Yes. I wasn't supposed to tell anyone, not even you. But I think now..."

A wave of emotion breaks over Saba, who draws back, rising to her feet. She walks a little way out into the courtyard. She is aware of her own breath coming quick and shallow. To hear for certain that the Augur believes in the dreams of Lennes, has already acted upon it in spite of the danger, this ought to be the news which changes everything. But somehow in Saba's heart the smaller facts loom larger: that Aemilia was trusted with this instead of her. That

162

Aemilia has not shared this with her until now.

It would have been nothing for the Augur to send Aemilia to the sanctuary that night, and Saba instead upon such crucial business. Saba knows herself to be braver: the journey through the city would have been nothing to her. More importantly, she can speak. It is not a matter of false pride but simply of fact, that she has a voice which can still a room. Aemilia holds nobody's attention. She stutters and stumbles.

Confused, oddly angry both with her sister and the absent Augur, Saba tries to compose herself. She turns, and walks back towards the tower steps. "What did he say, this man Antonus?"

Aemilia does not seem to have noticed Saba's distress. She is still staring out at the sky. "I don't think he believed me."

"Then we must go to him again, and see that he does."

*

The air of the temple is thick with rumours and with barely suppressed fear. Saba scolds three of the girls whom she catches whispering to one another when they are supposed to be sweeping the sanctuary, but later she calls all of the novices together. They huddle in a corner of the hall, near the fire which has burned since the first in the long line of the Augurs lit it there.

The time for shielding them is now passed. The Augur's imprisonment changes everything, With twenty pairs of expectant eyes upon her, Saba crouches on the step beside the pyre, and speaks plainly.

"Before any of us came to this temple there were other priestesses here, like us. And one day they fell into the Emperor's bad graces. You all know what happened. He had them stoned outside the city wall and threw their bodies into a pit with the traitors and the criminals."

There is a ripple of distress, glances exchanged. "Are you trying to reassure us?" asks Eris, aghast.

"I am trying to warn you." Saba looks around at them all, trying to meet every girl's frightened gaze. Amone has begun to cry: Cassia pulls her close. "Our protector is gone, and now we can't be certain of anything."

"What do they want with her?" Liva's horrified hands are at her face.

"When will they let her go?"

"Will they hurt her?"

"Will they come for us too?" whispers Cassia.

"I don't know," says Saba. Their stricken faces tug at her heart. "I'm sorry. I wish I could tell you more."

"Then what should we do?" Eris demands.

"Be ready." Saba knows she must speak to them not as defenceless children subject to whatever violence is visited upon their bodies, but as priestesses of the Augur's Temple, blessed with the power to see, to act. "For now, I think this temple is still the safest place for us. But that could change by tomorrow. Whatever possessions you have, wrap them in a cloth and keep it next to your pillow. Go to sleep at night with your cloak and sandals on. We'll take it in turns to keep a watch on our walls. The first sign of trouble, and we're gone. Through the city gate if we can do it secretly, or if not, up through the shrine-beneath-the-water and over the mountain."

Their eyes widen as they listen to her. Amone, the youngest, is no older than seven. Some of them were born in the city to families who could not feed another daughter; others, like Saba and Aemilia, came here in the galleys of ships or bound to the saddles of their captors. Saba thinks of Aemilia now, with an uncomfortable pang, and makes no appeal to these girls to remember their families or homelands. Most will recall nothing, and even for those who do, there is nothing to return to.

So what will you do with them, Saba? Alone you can scramble over the mountain rocks nimble as a goat, hide out in caves, drink from streams and live on a handful of berries. You are certain that you can follow the course of the sun and stars, follow the direction of the wind which blows from your red-dust country, until you find yourself beneath a familiar sky. But you cannot do these things with children trailing in your footsteps, thirsty, weary, crying because there is no such home at the end of their road. Even with Aemilia's help you cannot care for these children in the wilderness. Even if you could lead them to another city, what sanctuary would await there? For a girl-child without protection, belonging to no father or husband who will revenge her, every kind of danger awaits.

When night falls Saba takes the first watch at the wall herself. She paces the length of the temple courtyard. Alone with her thoughts in the darkness the notion comes to her that warning the priestesses is no more use than shouting into a thundercloud. Can anything truly be done, to prepare for what might be coming?

But Saba is not familiar with despair. She does not know the smell of it. She presses on, oblivious, in its shadow.

She is crouched low against the wall and resting her head against a pillow of moss, eyes closed, when she hears a sound. She barely has time to scramble to her feet when there is a pounding at the temple gate. Saba hoists herself up the uneven faces of the stones to peer over the top of the wall, seeing a familiar figure there in the pool of torchlight. His ascent of the steps must have been quick and quiet.

"You never seem to sleep," says Athraxus.

There is something different about him, something altered since he last left the temple. He carries himself like the sleekest wolf in the pack. She takes the measure of him. He has come alone, without his guards or his dogs; he cannot be here for any savagery. Not yet. He has come by cover of night; he cannot quite be confident that his interference at the Augur's Temple will meet with the Emperor's approval. From this she might deduce that the Augur still lives, and lives unharmed. But the High Priest has the blood-scent in his nose. He has his prey in sight, and will run her to the ground.

Saba leans over the top of the wall to look Athraxus in the eye. "He's not entirely yours yet, is he? The Emperor? That must drive you mad."

"I am going to hang up that old woman outside the city wall," says Athraxus. "I will strip her naked before the jeering crowd. Then I am going to come here and cut off your tongue with my eating-blade. Yours first. And then the tongues of all of your little priestesses. I tell you, I'll do it with my own hand. Then I will have red coals put to your eyes. Then I will have you chained and led in procession through the streets, ashes upon your heads, to serve the men who come to my temple. Your bodies will endure perhaps a few years before you die there in the darkness."

Saba recognises her own terror only as fury, running hot through her blood. If it were not for the gate between them she would already have flung herself at him, a whirlwind of fingers and teeth. It would do no good, but it might relieve for a moment the blazing hatred in her chest. "What do you want?" she demands. "You've taken our mother away from us already. What more can you want here, if you're not allowed to destroy us?"

"I have come for her scrolls."

She makes no move to open the gate. "So that you can twist the words of her prophecies and turn the Emperor against her?"

Shadows lick into the hollows of his eyes. "All your little priestesses must be asleep in their beds. Do you want them to wake up safely in the morning?"

It is in desperation that she lets him in and leads him across

166

the courtyard, up the twisting staircase to the tower. Past the doorways where Aemilia and the other priestesses lie sleeping. If she can only pacify him for long enough to keep the others alive, some way might be found to free the Augur. And then there is this man Antonus...

The thought of a possible ally in the city gives her courage. She stands over Athraxus as he rummages through the Augur's hundreds of papers, making a chaos of her chamber. It feels like a violation. What would the Augur do, here? Match him move for move, Saba, that's what. Be a thorn in his sandal. She draws closer to his shoulder. "You might turn the Emperor's head for a while," she says. "But you'll never have his love. Not the way my mistress did."

He looks back at her. "And tell me what that love has bought her, in the end?"

As she fights to find a reply, he makes a dismissive sound with his tongue. "You are a liar," he says. "You have all been liars, since the beginning. Whoring yourselves for a taste of power."

"And now you're here to light her funeral pyre," she says contemptuously.

Athraxus surveys the Augur's chamber. "Too long," he incants, "there have been two temples. Too long, two voices. Too long you've had two mouths in need of stopping. The first mouth, which you use so often and so unwisely in my presence, I'd have sewn shut. But I suppose that must wait for another day.

"As for the second... it ought to have been sewn when you were a child. My priests, they have a knife and a needle for that." Saba feels a frisson of shock. This is a matter of the Dark Temple, this is not spoken of. Athraxus's lip has twisted. "Do you know why your mouths need stopping? Because you have the appetites of beasts. All of you. Everything our hands have built, your appetites might tear down. Your licentious hunger would devour the civilised world, and throw it all into disorder. Since the beginning we've tried to tame you. To no avail."

The hatred in his voice seems to draw all warmth from the night air. In his presence tonight even Saba feels her certainty waver. Imagine, Saba. Imagine if the world was not the green and living place you always thought it, but instead a mere rock in a dark ocean. Swallowed by the chaos of the waves.

"Suppose that the Augur really is mistaken, or lying," she throws at him. "Suppose this city stands for centuries to come. How long do you think your temple will be in favour? One generation, maybe? Two, before some new philosophy comes along? There has always been an Augur in this city."

"And there has always been a temple filled with darkness, and an altar for the blood-sacrifice, and a priesthood that owns the secrets of men's hearts."

As the red-robed priest rises to his feet he towers over her, clutching a bundle of scrolls in each hand. The rest are trampled beneath his feet. A smile, empty as a cavern, widens his mouth. "Don't you know, child? We have been here since the beginning."

IV

Marinating in the tepid pool at the baths, Mylo is aware of something different about the atmosphere there. The place is just as crowded as usual – that gang of old counsellors who take the same corner of the pool at the same time every afternoon, sombre as toads in a pond; the youths splashing about and showing off for one another; the pot-bellied traders and preening athletes; the perfumed nobles surrounded by their retinues of slaves. But the talk is not the usual gossip of men idling away their leisure time.

He has already heard, by means of eavesdropping, three different accounts of what happened at the Emperor's feast. Other bathers are less subtle in their curiosity, muscling in to offer an opinion or demand details. The tales diverge on small points — whether the lobster tarts or the ram's testicles were served first, how many jars of wine had been poured out before the evening was interrupted, how many philosophers were consulted, whether it was Laonatus or Athraxus who at last sent for the Augur. They agree, however, on the substance of what occurred.

"I've never seen or heard of such a ridiculous thing. The whole court in uproar because an old woman contrived to write some words on a wall. The screaming and the shock! You'd think one of their number had been murdered in front of them!"

"You went quite pale yourself, Altecus, if I recall."

"I'll be paying for an extra sacrifice tonight, just in case," says the magistrate Estebus. "I've heard one too many odd stories flying about the city recently. There were people in the hall all day, how could anyone have hidden that writing behind the plaster? If this really was an omen I want protection for my household."

"Oh, nonsense!" This last from a burly man lowering his bulk into the water. Mylo recognises him, and for a moment cannot think why. "Would you start wailing and tearing your hair if your grandmother said she'd seen a snake fall off the roof? That's just what they want, these two-penny prophets, to cause an uproar. I pay my tax to the Dark Temple, as is good and proper…"

"Is that what you call it?" interrupts one of the others. Jeers, lewd gestures, and Mylo recognises the burly man as the old soldier Theagenes, his mother's lover.

"…as is good and proper, and the gods bless me for it. I've nothing to fear. The common people, who cannot pay and so can never hope to please the gods, go running to the Augur to feel better about themselves. It seems so quaint to me that our emperors have ever listened to these women! High time the tradition died, I say."

"You think you will be saved, then," says Mylo, from the corner of the pool.

He would not normally address a man so many years his senior, or indeed get drawn into any sort of quarrel with strangers at the baths. Perhaps it is the temperature of the room, but he feels fevered. Several of the men surrounding Theagenes turn around to get a look at him. The old soldier's eyes have narrowed, and Mylo knows that he too is now wracking his memory.

"Here, I know you. You're the absent son." Theagenes smirks, scratching his belly. "I'd heard you were a strange one."

"When it comes. You think the gods will spare you."

"Everybody! We've got ourselves a follower of the prophetess!" Laughter. Mylo is aware that the slaves around the edges of the pool have fallen still, listening. "Does your father know about this, boy?"

"I read history. Even if it doesn't come now, it'll come, in the end. Cities don't stand forever."

Theagenes' eyes have narrowed. "That's close to blasphemy."

Aware that he has been reckless, Mylo makes to get out of the pool. A slave gives him a linen cloth which he ties around his waist, hands shaking. "Then you can tell my mother she gave birth to a son who hates his emperor and his gods."

"I won't be telling your mother anything, boy. I'm done with her. A man can only discharge into the same rag so many times before he wants a clean one." Theagenes makes an exaggerated gesture in case any have missed his meaning, occasioning more laughter.

Mylo has heard men talk about his mother this way since before he was old enough to understand it. Today he is too anxious and preoccupied to have any response. He has already given them enough to gossip about. As he turns to leave, Theagenes calls after him.

"She says you never come to see her. It grieves her. You make her weep."

*

The old soldier was right about one thing: it has been too long. Though Mylo knows that Athraxus will not be there, his chest grows tighter as he makes his way past the palace to his father's house that afternoon. He does not go there any more, if he can help it.

Since Athraxus's duties at the temple often keep him there day and night, the High Priest's own home, though filled with costly things, is not kept in good order. The wall outside is overgrown with creepers and the unswept path covered in dead leaves. Mylo steps carefully past the two huge dogs which are sleeping chained to the wall. A slave in the doorway lets him through with a silent nod and a glare of recognition, but there is nobody else in sight. The passageway inside is dark, dust settled atop the decorative busts and vases which are set in alcoves along the walls. The marble fountain in the courtyard is dry. If he had not known the place to be inhabited, he might have thought it a ruin.

The house of Athraxus has not changed very much since Myloxenes was a child. He does not like to remember the years he spent alone within the confines of these walls. They keep no chamber for him here any more: but sometimes he has a strange feeling that a part of him remains here still, a small, meek, silent boy, keeping to the shadows.

The slaves outside his mother's rooms do not greet him. He smells Laeyla in her chamber before he even passes through the drapes. That overpowering, sweat-drenched stench of florid perfume, weeks too old, soaked into ample flesh. When he was a child Mylo used to be terrified of his mother, as much as he was of his father. Now he cannot think of her without an almost unbearable tenderness.

"Myloxenes? Is that you?"

In his mother's chamber, it is always dusk. Several lamps and a small fire are burning unnecessarily. Though the sun blazes outside he can hardly make out the shape of her in the reddish dimness. The stale air can barely have stirred in months. He hears her heaving herself from her pillows, and feels his way across to the bed so that he can bend and kiss her upon the cheek.

"Hello Mother. I'm sorry it's been so long."

"No, no." Her skin is dewy with sweat and smudged rouge. As his eyes become accustomed to the low light he can see her smiling up at him. "No, you're so good come and see me. My boy."

Her night-robe exposes much of her shoulders and breasts. The curls which he has inherited are spread in a tangle across the pillows. He sits upon the edge of the bed and lets her lay a moist palm against his face.

He wonders how long it has been since she last went outside, but does not ask. He has few memories of his mother which are not from this room. Her breath smells of wine. "Tell me news," she murmurs.

It is hard to know where to begin. "Something happened, Mother. At the Augur's Temple, at the solstice. Lennes the Steward, he—"

"Not that sort of news, Mylo. News about you. Who have you been spending your time with?"

He swallows his momentary incredulity. How is it possible to still be surprised by someone who remains unchanged, year on year? "Just Rufus, Mother. As usual. And most nights I eat at the house of Antonus."

"Antonus, Antonus, always this man Antonus. I don't think he is anybody at court."

"They are kind to me, Mother. Him and his wife."

"You must have an eye on your future." She is smiling, stroking his cheek. "So gifted, my boy, oh, since you were little! You don't need to worry. You don't need to waste yourself in obscurity. You are going to be somebody in this city, I've always known it."

The familiar dull, bruising shame. He turns his face away from her, but she does not notice.

"What parties have you been to? Is there a young woman who's caught your eye?"

"There was a party at Calix and Mersia's. I think half the city was there."

"Mersia is a pretty girl. What did she wear?"

"She wore yellow linen. They served oysters and roast pork."

"Oysters. You might have brought me some oysters."

"I'm sorry, Mother."

"The best oysters I ever tasted were the ones my father's slaves would bring back from the harbour market in the evening. The freshest catch." She smiles dreamily. "Served with wine sauce. Was there music, Mylo? I would have loved to hear music."

"There must have been twenty musicians, and dancers too."

"I am sure you wore finery. I am sure no man there looked more handsome. Come on, tell me, is there a girl?" She squeezes his hand conspiratorially. "I want my son married by next year."

He thinks of trying to explain to her: about the daughters of Antonus, his debt of gratitude. But she knows too little of his life to understand. She herself was married at fourteen, a beauty then, fat and guileless and glowing with health. The shock of that marriage, Mylo sometimes thinks, must have been like dying. He understands that now. There is only love and pity for her in his heart.

They are quiet together. After a while her wheezing breath tells him that she has fallen into a doze. He folds her hand between his and bends over to kiss it. Her eyes flicker below their lids, and he hopes that she is dreaming of oysters, and music, and dancing.

"I'll come for you, mother," he says aloud. "Before we're

destroyed, I'll lead you out of here. I'll take you somewhere safe. Don't be afraid."

*

He is so fragile from the encounter that he collides headlong with his father on his way out of the house. Athraxus is clearly in a great hurry, carrying his bundled cloak and a heap of papers which scatter across the path. Before they have exchanged a word Mylo is crawling in the dirt to retrieve the papers, Athraxus brushing himself down indignantly.

"Here…"Without meeting his father's eye, Mylo hands him the rolls of parchment and then quickly steps back.

"A rare sighting! You bestow your presence upon the house that raised you."

"I came to see Mother. I'm leaving."

"Have you been weeping into her lap?"

At the sound of their master's voice the dogs have awakened, snapping and yelping, pulling impatiently against their chains. Strings of drool hang from between their teeth. Mylo flinches instinctively and knows that his father has seen him do so. The corner of Athraxus's mouth curls.

"I didn't think you would be here," mutters Mylo.

"You have heard, I'm sure, that the Emperor's council has apprehended that brazen old woman who calls herself the Augur. *Old language of the priestesses,* indeed. She is going to be questioned. I have work to do."

"Then I'll leave you."

As Mylo turns to leave his father's hand seizes his upper arm. For a moment Athraxus only holds on and says nothing, dragging Mylo around to look at him, his grip tightening painfully. Mylo digs his heels into the dust but is no match for his father's strength.

The dogs are snarling now and scrabbling at the ground.

"I told you. Didn't I, boy? A long time ago. You live with a lame man, you'll start to limp." Athraxus gives him a forceful shake. "Time to reconsider the company you keep. The winds in this city are changing. Not that they've ever blown in that man's favour."

No reply forms in Mylo's throat. He keeps his face turned away. Athraxus's long fingernails draw blood.

"There might have been a time when Antonus the Cripple was protected by the kindness and mercy of the Emperor. But that time is ending. Don't true friends always reveal themselves? The Augur has been a false friend to this city for decades. The Emperor is finally starting to see her as she is. A witch who would have him suckle poison from her teat."

"What will you do to her?"

"She'll get what is due to a false prophet. And in the ripeness of time, so will anyone who aligns themselves with her."

Athraxus lets go without warning, and Mylo stumbles, landing on his hands and knees in the dirt once again. His father lets out a disgusted laugh.

"Even the day you were born, you were such a feeble, mewling thing. I said to myself, is this from my own flesh? Thank the gods your mother has bedded so many." He turns to head back towards the house. "I comfort myself that you could be a bastard."

*

Mylo has no appetite that night, though Junia and Felix have prepared just the sort of simple food he likes; rye bread, cheese, fruit, salt fish. While the twins squabble and Eryx rolls stones for the cat under the table, he stares at the moon rising over the mountain. He imagines trying to lead his mother up some narrow path between the rocks, towards... Where? He made her a hollow

175

promise. For those without a city, for an old woman gone from the walls of her husband's house, there is no sanctuary.

Antonus looks between Mylo's untouched food and his distant expression. "What kind of talk have you heard?"

"All kinds. Everybody's talking."

"You heard about the Emperor's feast?" asks Antonus, quietly. Junia turns her head.

"Is this what we do?" Mylo blurts out. He hears anger in his own voice, which cracks and rises in volume. "We bathe and eat and drink and go about our business and then one day the sky falls down?"

"Careful how you speak," says Junia. "The gods listen, you know." Felix has turned around now, too. Antonia and Adelfa, sensing a matter of weight, have stopped arguing to listen.

The fear and frustration which he smothered in his father's presence, in his mother's chamber, now spills over. "If the gods are already against us, why does it matter how I speak? I don't understand why we aren't already in sackcloth and ashes, begging for their mercy. Or why we aren't baking loaves for the road and fleeing to the mountains."

"If you imagine that our household laughs at prophecies," says Junia sharply, "you're wrong."

"I think it's time that the children were in bed," interjects Antonus. Felix responds at once, sweeping Eryx from his seat and then dangling him upside-down by the ankles. The boy's delighted squeals continue all the way inside.

"I'm not a child," protests Antonia fiercely. "What does that mean, loaves for the road?" Junia rises too and shepherds the girls towards the doorway, Antonia staring back over her shoulder with a scowl.

Antonus pours Mylo a cup of wine and they sit together in silence for a while, the cicadas growing louder around them. Mylo's hands toy absently with the cup. In the peaceful evening it all feels unreal. The surface of their lives remains as yet untroubled, despite the cataclysm unfolding beneath.

"I saw my mother today," he says at last. "My father, too."

"Where? You went to see them?"

"I went to see her. I wasn't expecting him to be there."

Antonus is watching his face. "How did you find her?"

"The same as always. I should go more often. I should bring her gifts."

"She knows that you care about her."

"But I don't do enough. I forget her for weeks at a time. I don't think she ever sees daylight." Antonus makes to take hold of his shoulder, but Mylo flinches away, as he might have done in years gone by.

"What about Athraxus?" Antonus asks.

"He's crowing over his prisoner. Do you think they'll really be able to hold her?"

"There won't be rioting in the streets, if that's what you mean. She's not popular enough, these days. As for my brother, who can predict? He's always relied on her, but that may mean nothing to him, in the end. He grants himself the power to alter the truth of any history, including his own."

Mylo picks up his cup and takes a deep drink, for courage. "I believe the Augur," he says. Antonus kneads the heel of his hand into his leg. The stars are beginning to show themselves overhead. "Lennes, too. I believe it all. Maybe I'm gullible and foolish. There's something in the air. I'm afraid of what's coming."

"Mylo," says Antonus. "I believe it too."

*

As Myloxenes turns to him, wide-eyed, as Antonus prepares

himself to relate the trembling of the earth and the visits of Aemilia and of Hestia and the Augur's message and what all of this means, he feels a moment of cold dread.

This boy. You felt it in the first moment that you met, and you feel it again now. Not in the fire, not in your dream at the healing-houses, or even your marriage to Junia. But in this boy, the consummation of your fate.

V

"What we really need," says Mylo, "is to talk with the Augur."

He is awake with Antonus, Junia and Felix, whispering by lamplight in the villa's small courtyard. They are all hoarse from the lateness of the hour and their long, circular conversation. Every word spoken seems to lead them deeper into a twisted thicket of uncertainties.

"We'd never get close," says Antonus. "She's at the House of the Magistrates. Athraxus will have a guard on her, night and day."

Junia is pacing back and forth. The edge of her long shawl ripples in her wake. "What about that priestess?" she asks. "The girl who came here?"

Felix shakes his head. "She was hardly more than a child."

"She was a messenger," says Antonus. "Young, yes, and afraid, but the Augur must have trusted her. She could be a gifted prophetess herself, for all we know."

"But she's not their leader," says Mylo, and hears his heart sound a note like an altar bell. "Remember at the feast? That girl who said the blessing. She's the one who had authority." He remembers the firm pressure of her thumb smearing ash across his forehead. The ashes crumbling between them. *The gods are close enough to breathe on us.*

"If they're the closest thing we have to the Augur, we need to speak with both of them," says Junia decisively. "And with the Emperor's servant, Hestia. And with Lennes. All together. Perhaps between us we can summon enough light to see the way ahead."

Silence. The same thought drifting between them: such a gathering could rightly be called a conspiracy.

Mylo looks between Antonus and Junia, half-expecting the idea to die as it is delivered into the world. But he can see in their expressions that it is drawing breath, growing stronger. He had not known, until that moment, that any plan made in opposition to the will of Athraxus stood a chance of life.

"We need to be certain that our faith isn't misplaced before we take actions that can't be reversed," Junia says.

Felix presses his hands to his chest. "Speak even less plainly than that, won't you, mistress? My old heart might fail."

*

It's Felix who is tasked with getting a message to Hestia. He oversees the delivery of three jars of their wine to the palace kitchens, as per the Emperor's own request, waiting patiently while they are sampled in front of him. He is detained by one of the bakers, a sometime drinking companion, and they talk of this and that while the noise and bustle of the kitchens goes on around them. As he takes his leave, sent on his way with an armful of bread and cakes and an earful of palace gossip, Felix adds as an afterthought, "Can someone tell that little jester we have more of our wine for her own personal store, as well? She can have it tonight if she sends payment."

Mylo, in his quest for the ear of Lennes the Steward, is less successful. He raises the subject with Rufus while they are sat playing draughts in a patch of sun on the bathhouse steps, and is met with a look of scepticism. "You know what sort of state he's in. I can tell you, he hasn't improved. There's no sense to be got out of him."

Mylo glances surreptitiously over his shoulder and takes the measure of the scene around them. Men coming out of the bathhouse, flushed and shining with sweat, in animated conversation with their companions. Children racing up and down the steps with a scrawny dog in tow, yapping and jumping at their ankles. An old man whistling to a cage of song-thrushes. A fried-fish vendor striding about, calling his wares. A group of women, baskets on their hips, gossiping on their way to the marketplace. Everybody about their business, as though nothing is amiss.

"We're gathering some people together," he says, carefully. He moves one of his counters to advance upon one of Rufus's. "Tonight, at Antonus's house. It's your father who started all this. He ought to be there."

Rufus, too, casts a look about him, though with less subtlety. He bends his head. "People?"

"Priestesses. A servant from the palace." Mylo is barely moving his mouth now. Rufus pretends to be deeply absorbed in the positions of his counters. "It's to do with the Augur. I can't say here."

"I understand." Rufus pushes one of his pieces, but it is a bad move. He is clearly distracted. "I know why you'd want Lennes there, Mylo. But I'm telling you, I'm not even sure he'd make it up the hill. He's said his piece, and it's done for him. He's finished."

Watching his friend's face, Mylo does not reach for his counter, but instead slowly withdraws his hands from the board. Rufus rubs the corners of his eyes rather violently, and then says, "I'll come."

"Are you sure?" Without saying more than he ought to in this public place, Mylo wants to impress upon Rufus the seriousness of this decision.

"Yes. I'll speak for him. I've heard more of his ranting than anybody."

"I mean…"

"I know what you mean. It's sweet of you to try and warn me. But I'm a coward. I'd rather not think about it too hard, if this is the place where it's too late to turn back."

*

A red-sky evening, the sun half sunk into the sea. Saba keeps her watch at the temple wall. The knife which she uses to shave her head, she has tucked inside her tunic, wrapped around with a cloth. This blunt little blade, if she were to draw it, the temple's last line of defence. She wonders how many small wounds a man like Athraxus might sustain, and still live.

But it is not Athraxus outside the gate tonight. Peering over the wall from her vantage point she sees the resemblance now: the son's eyes, too, are dark and deep-set. He has the same long nose and slanted cheekbones. For a moment the two men merge in her mind, and she feels a surge of disgust.

He draws closer, and her confusion melts like fog. Behind him, a hood over his distinctive hair, is a young man she recognises as the Steward's son. Saba remembers him running to his father as the Steward choked and bled onto the stone at the solstice feast. She climbs down to open the gate.

Myloxenes son of Athraxus bows his head in greeting. He is alive with nervous energy, his eyes darting eagerly across her face. "Blessings on your temple."

"And upon you, son of Athraxus."

Though he does not at once state his purpose, she knows already that he has not come to kneel beside the altar. He has taken on a decisiveness and an urgency since they last met. "I'm sorry for what happened to your mistress. Have you heard from her at all?"

Saba shakes her head. "We're forbidden from seeing her. Your

181

father was here last night. He took her scrolls."

The Steward's son hisses through his teeth. "He didn't waste any time."

"Did he threaten you?" asks Myloxenes, with concern.

"Of course." What else would Athraxus do?

"I'm sorry," says Myloxenes again, as though she might hold him responsible. "This is Rufus, son of Lennes. We've come on behalf of Antonus the Cripple."

Saba's heart gathers speed, sings to her, *see, see? There are allies in the city. Always a reason to hope.* "I know sbout him."

"There's another priestess here, a girl called Aemilia. Can you be spared tonight, both of you?"

"It's my turn to keep watch. The younger girls are in bed."

"It'll be a matter of a few hours."

Saba looks over her shoulder at the Augur's Temple, the white stones glowing rose-pink and golden beneath the sunset. Her chance to save the priestesses and the Augur lies not with the useless knife in her hand, but with this man Antonus. She has been itching for days to take action: if anything, she knows herself to be too eager.

"Wait here. I'll fetch Aemilia."

*

The house of Antonus is set above an olive grove and a vineyard against the foot of the mountain. Somebody has hung lanterns on poles along the path outside, lighting the way. For us, Saba realises, smiling to herself. For their guests.

They are led through an archway into a small courtyard and then to the inner room, where the last light from the evening sky outside falls through the stone arches. A row of cloths, dyed in yellows and rich purples, blows in the breeze. The mountain looms silent and black overhead.

Myloxenes and Rufus are muttering to each other in low tones. Saba watches Aemilia, who has not uttered a word the whole way across the city, run the palm of her hand across the rough wood of the table, lost in thought. Turning, she notices two pairs of eyes peering at her from behind the drapes: a rustle, a whisper, and they vanish.

Then the sound of uneven footsteps, and Antonus the Cripple is among them. He too is changed, thinks Saba at once. He is as unimpressive as she remembers, lame and greying and scarred: yet he is alert. There is a sharpness in his expression, and in his greeting. "Priestesses. You've brought the blessing and authority of your temple to my home. You are very welcome."

She nods in acknowledgment. "You're blessed for your hospitality. It's good to be here." Aemilia says nothing, dipping her head meekly.

As Saba and Antonus appraise each other, his wife enters the room behind him. She is an imposing woman, her heavy brows contracted in a look of guarded intensity. With her is an older man who is bearing a jug of wine.

This man, who must be a house-slave, says, "We're still waiting for one more, though I don't know whether she'll come. We may as well eat."

They seat themselves, and Saba finds that she has an appetite. She breaks a warm barley-loaf and reaches for a bowl of olives. Though there is nothing yet in her cup she already feels a little intoxicated. Tonight is a night for the impossible, for the unthinkable. She catches Antonus looking at her from across the table and meets his gaze with open curiosity. They are weighing one another. *Will you stand at my side, stranger, in this deed, in whatever we find beyond it?*

"Try the wine, won't you?" he says to her. "We make it ourselves."

"We make wine too, at the temple," she says, holding out her cup.

"I had some at the solstice. A little too much, truth be told."

"Antonus gets drunk on the *smell* of wine," says the slave, grinning at her as he pours out a generous measure. His eyes are the colour of the sea on a clear day. "My name is Felix. This is Junia."

"How should we to address you?" interjects Junia, leaning across the table. "Priestess? Prophetess? Or by your names?"

"Saba and Aemilia will do tonight, since we're not at the temple. Not *Prophetess*, that's a title reserved for our mother. Any oracles we make are under her authority."

"Did she teach you to see?" asks Myloxenes.

"She did. The flight of birds, the entrails, the smoke. Sometimes portents in the stars. We have learned about all of these since we were children."

"And did you pay attention in your lessons?" asks the slave Felix. "Can we believe your oracles?" He is partly in jest, eyes glittering, but the room waits for Saba's reply.

"Whether you believe or not, that isn't in our hands. We can only interpret the will of the gods as best we can, as our mother taught us."

"Forgive me if this is disrespectful – but how do we know if *she's* speaking the truth?"

"What about the oracles of a certain disgraced old man?" asks Rufus.

Aemilia, who has hardly yet touched a morsel of food, looks away unhappily. Saba takes a slow drink and remembers what the Augur once told her about the visitors who come to sit at the temple altar. *They will have questions, Saba, many of them. They might have complex enquiries about the nature and the will of the divine realm. About the pattern of events in their own lives, about calamity they have witnessed, about what is to come. Some of these questions will daunt you, but don't be afraid. Remember this: each person who comes to us here, in age or in youth, in poverty or in riches, in victory or distress, is as a naked child before the gods. They are not always asking what they are asking. Learn to see through to their hearts.*

After a while she says, "Nobody in any temple – not me, not the Augur – can claim more than human understanding. We are all small and senseless before the gods. And that's the heart of this. Isn't it? Our mother always taught us that the gods speak through the prophetess because she is nobody. That the gods can choose who they'll speak through, and city can choose whether it will hear."

"Whether the gods will speak at all," says Myloxenes.

"You've spent too many hours in that other temple, son of Athraxus." He flushes warmly. Saba is aware, somewhat to her surprise, of everybody in the room hanging closely upon her words. She had expected Antonus to take charge of the gathering. She sits very straight upon her seat and resolves not to be daunted. *You are here, are you not, Saba, to speak for the Augur? Only ask yourself what she would say.*

Words form like shapes in smoke. "I think that faith in prophecy comes from within and without. It seems to me that if any of us believe, it isn't just because we felt the earth shake, or heard Lennes, or listened to rumours. Or saw the writing at the feast. It is because we already had it in our hearts to see the end of this city."

Saba feels the truth of this resonate in the room. The faces around her show by turns confusion, shock, recognition.

"I think you have us," says Junia. "I think that's why we are here."

Why else, when the omens are yet so few and the price of heeding them so high? Why else when all of them could have turned before this moment and gone back to their ordinary lives.

"The earth shook?" ventures Myloxenes.

"I felt it too," says Antonus. He meets Saba's eye. "Whatever

185

our belief is made of, this is where it leads us. We believe that Lennes the Steward spoke the truth. Not just that he believed his own words to be true, but that his words came from the gods themselves."

"Our mother the Augur believes it," says Saba.

Rufus is leaning across the table, staring at Saba intently. He does not seem to have noticed the incessant, skittish tapping of his own feet. Junia's arms are folded, her brow furrowed.

"This is it, then," says a voice from the doorway. "We're living in ill-favoured times. If nothing is done to appease the gods, this city will burn. I believe it will happen soon."

They all look around. The diminutive woman who has spoken these dangerous words holds her cloak close to her body. Her face is painted to look like the Emperor's, his full mouth and golden skin, his powdered eyes. The effect is momentarily disquieting.

"*Hestia.*" Antonus rises to greet her. "These are the priestesses Saba and Aemilia, from the Augur's Temple. Myloxenes and Rufus, friends of this household. Hestia is a servant of the Emperor..."

"And an ally to your cause," says Hestia.

"How is my brother?" asks Antonus.

"He's still not sleeping. I gave him 'The Lament of Three Widows' and 'Blackbird at Dusk'. I think he would have sent for the Augur, but of course circumstances forbid it. He's with Athraxus now."

"Come in," says Junia. "Sit, eat."

Felix fetches a cloth and a bowl of water, and Hestia carefully wipes the paint from her face. She has round cheeks and dark eyes like berries. Saba wonders how it came to be that a person like this, who would ordinarily die a beggar, might have made a life for herself in the Emperor's service. Like the Augurs, Hestia has carved out a space to breathe and survive in.

"I remember you from a feast at the palace, when I was a little boy," says Rufus. "I saw you juggle flaming torches. Do you still do that?"

"My hands aren't so quick, these days," says Hestia. She lays them on the table; her wrists and knuckles look sore and swollen.

"Are you in pain?" asks Antonus.

"You're the same age as me. By now, everything hurts. As the old verse says, *the gods roll their dice, and we receive our misfortune...*"

"You're in the right company for that song, little sister," says Felix.

"I think the whole city will be singing it soon."

"How is it," blurts out Aemilia suddenly, "that we've displeased the heavens so badly?"

It is the first time that she has spoken all night. Everybody looks around at her, and she hangs her head. Seated beside her, Saba can feel her shaking.

"We haven't all displeased them," says Junia. She is looking at Antonus, who shifts self-consciously and kneads his bad leg. "There might still be something we can do. Isn't that what you said, child? It isn't too late."

Aemilia turns her hands in her lap. She looks close to tears. "Yes," says Saba firmly. "The Augur has seen the city's chance for deliverance. All that's left is what we have to do to bring this about."

Nobody wants to be the first to name the deed. Hestia lets out a thwarted little laugh. "Imagine! I have to go to Laonatus's chamber tomorrow and look him in the eye and play his favourite songs."

"If the Augur is right then the gods have singled out the Emperor," says Saba. "For whatever reason he's at the centre of their wrath."

"You think it will be enough?" Myloxenes seems stunned that their talk has already turned this way. "You think that... that the downfall of the Emperor will be enough to turn this prophesied disaster away from us all?"

Rufus, in nervous reflex, makes a gesture for him to lower his voice.

"Do you have a pigeon here, or a young goat?" Saba asks. "Before the night is done, I'll read the auspices for you."

Antonus looks at Felix, who nods. The slave has been listening with his hand resting on his chin, eyes narrowed. "And if they're favourable we will have the Emperor Antonus."

"Does it sound so very absurd?" Antonus asks the room at large.

"Of course not," says Saba.

"What about the people?" Felix asks her. "I don't mean to be insolent, priestess, but my master will need their favour as well. And that of the Emperor's courtiers, priests, philosophers, councillors and so on, unless we mean to kill them too."

"Then there is the matter of Laonatus's sons," says Hestia. "They are still young, but so was he, when he first sat on the throne."

"The wives and even the sons don't have to be our enemy in this," says Junia sharply. "Mandane and Cassandane came here as prisoners, they can have little love for this city."

Saba has a sudden image of the slaughter she never saw, the Augur's former priestesses stoned to death outside the city wall, and feels a fierce accord with Junia. Yes, let there be no more slaughter of women and children in service of men's ambition.

"The court is fickle," continues Hestia. "Many of them have no loyalty to Laonatus, not really. They will follow whoever rewards them. Others will need persuading, though I don't think we have time to bring them around before we act." She looks around the table. "And there are those who will persecute us to the last, Athraxus chief among them."

"The people are at the heart of it all, then," says Myloxenes. He has turned pale at the mention of his father's name. "Priests might hold the power, but the people outnumber them. If the people are ours, then so is the city, and the city is saved."

"That battle is fought in temples, not palaces," says Saba. *Some will turn to us,* The Augur had told her. *Those who have nowhere else to place their trust.* "It's like I told you: the first Augur was nobody. She has always been nobody, and so hers is the temple of the people."

For a moment Saba thinks that her words have conjured another city, forming into being before her the way the gods formed the created world from nothingness. This man Antonus upon the throne; wise judgements; plenty; ruins restored and new wine flowing. Songs composed in the streets. Athraxus laid low, the Augur's Temple fresh-painted and garlanded with flowers. And the Prophetess at the Emperor's right hand, the hope and consolation of the city.

In the pause which follows Felix peers into the empty wine jug, then rises to fetch more. Aemilia is staring out into the dark courtyard, vacant. Rufus and Junia it seems have both sat still for as long as they are able: the former paces the room, muttering to himself, while the latter peers around the drapes to see that her children are asleep.

"That's what is keeping the Augur alive, I suppose," says Myloxenes softly, to Saba. "The people's favour, such as it is. My father must be cautious."

"I think so. For now."

Her eyes meet his. She knows as well as he does what the savage hands of Athraxus might do to an undefended old woman. If the Emperor must die then it is certain that Athraxus must, too, in the aftermath. He does not look away from her, and Saba feels for a moment that there is nobody else in the room.

"So how does one kill an emperor?" The slave Felix has returned, apparently having taken a few cups of wine on his own in the kitchen. He pours more for Junia, then sets the full jug upon the table. His words slur a little. "I can think of a few stories, if we're in need of inspiration. There was the Emperor Caracus, who they stuck through the arse with a spear while he was on the latrine. Or the Emperor Ibron, whose throat was slit by his favourite concubine in the middle of the act. Or there's the legend of that foolish foreign king, who let a viper bite him on the balls because his treacherous courtiers swore that it would grant him immortality..."

"A viper," says Hestia, her face a white, serious oval. "There's something in that."

"Something silent," says Junia, sitting back down. "Something quick. We have the advantage of access to the Emperor's innermost chambers."

"Clearly," says Hestia, "If it came to a struggle, I couldn't overpower him."

"Then poison of some kind must be the way."

They have all been inching forward in their seats, Saba realises, leaning inward, their voices growing ever more hushed. The lamps stutter as a breeze blows through the room, carrying the scent of myrtle and of laurel-leaves in from the mountain. The aspirant Emperor himself is now attending to the wick of the nearest lamp, coaxing the flame gently back into life. His expression is hard to read.

Rufus, who has continued to lurk at the edge of the room, asks with an attempt at a level tone, "From where might one procure poison?"

"I'll fetch a flute, and charm some snakes up from out of the sea," offers Felix.

"We'd better be cautious," Saba warns. "Nobody should be drawn into this who can't be trusted."

"And besides," says Rufus, "there are fewer apothecaries in the city these days, for which we have my sister to thank."

"There's a plant..." whispers Aemilia. But she is too hesitant.

"Could we find a doctor or an apothecary who leans towards our cause?" interrupts Junia.

"Or who at least could be paid for his silence," puts in Myloxenes.

Rufus laughs. "Seeing as nobody else here is wealthy, I suppose you'd all be looking to me to pay for that? Do you think Mersia would have needed to marry Calix if we had that kind of money?"

"Couldn't you borrow money from Calix?" Myloxenes suggests. "Tell him it's for something else?"

"Because he holds me in such high regard..."

Out of the corner of her eye Saba sees Antonus, who has not joined in, touch Aemilia on the wrist in an encouraging gesture. "Go on, priestess," he says.

Eyes turn towards her. Aemilia's pale cheeks flush pink.

"There's a plant," she whispers, "which grows on the mountain. Wind-weed, we call it. Flowers like small white bells. Green berries. At the temple I boil them, make a draught so that the beasts will go quiet and still enough for the knife."

A pause. Saba feels a jolt of shock. The solution is perfect, savage and secretive.

"A measure strong enough to sedate a bull might be enough to stop a man from ever waking up," says Junia. A flicker crosses Antonus's face, and he turns away, towards the night beyond the archway.

Saba gathers herself. "We could brew it, Aemilia and I. It would be easy enough to gather the weed on the mountain without drawing any attention."

"How would it be delivered to me?" asks Hestia. "I shouldn't leave the palace again, not even under cover of night."

"The next council feast is at the full moon." Rufus has finally stopped pacing. He leans his hands against the table, then draws back again. "Me and Calix and Mersia will be invited. If you're performing for the occasion, I suppose it wouldn't be too hard to slip a bottle into your pocket..."

"And will he drink?" asks Hestia, turning to the priestesses. "If I put this draught into his cup will he drink it to the dregs, or dash it to the floor and grab me by the throat?"

"The taste is sweet and mild." The quieter the room becomes, the further Aemilia's voice drops. "I know which herbs to add, so that beasts swallow willingly. I don't like them to die with a bitter taste."

In the silence, Felix raises his cup to her. "Here's to that. If death came so sweetly to me, priestess, I would meet it willingly too."

VI

They slaughter a kid on a makeshift altar behind the villa, in sight of the mountain. Aemilia holds back the creature's head, strokes its silken ears, whispers reassurance. Its bleats echo thinly. Saba takes the knife from inside her robe and slices the throat in one assured movement. As dark blood spatters the stones the young animal screams and chokes. Junia lights a stick of incense and waves its smoke over the twitching body.

Saba beckons for light. Felix strikes a flint in the fire-pit nearby, and by the climbing glow of the flames she cuts a deep line down the goat's belly. Guts bulge dripping from the slit. She makes two more cuts, careful, precise, so that the innards are laid bare before her. The incense does not hide the stench of the bowels. Rufus, watching close by with Mylo, covers his nose with his cloak.

"Gods, receive our offering," intones Saba. "May this incense be sweet to you. May this life laid down be pleasing."

Antonus finds himself staring into the exposed innards. It all looks dark to him, a mound of shapeless, pulsing offal. The gods have written their will in these hidden places, wreathed it in flesh and in vapour. Split the stones and you might know their secrets. The world is rolled like a parchment, waiting to be read.

He feels a pang of wild impatience, perhaps an overflow of the emotion of the last hours. Why must the gods play games with us, like coy youths courting? Hiding their letters and tokens, whispering to us in the lamplight and then turning their backs.

The Augur's Temple teaches that the nature and will of the gods is hidden so that it might be found: but why must it be hidden at all?

Gods, lend us a little light to live by. We are about to undertake such fearful business on your behalf.

"What do you see, priestess?"

Saba is crouched on the ground beside the body, in the cloud of incense. She takes the warm, wet viscera from the belly, and spreads them in the dirt. "The organs of a healthy colour, well-positioned," she says, after a pause. "The lobes of the liver are well-formed, the heart is no bigger than my fist. The intestines are narrow, free of blockages. Here's the gallbladder, both kidneys..." She looks up at Antonus. "It's a good sacrifice. Whatever vow the gods have made, I think they intend to keep it."

She gathers up the carcass and the innards in sackcloth, and takes the bag over to the fire. When the contents are fed into the flames she bends and takes up a handful of ash from the edge of the pit. Approaching Antonus again she draws a dark line with her thumb across his forehead. The others, gathered around, are quiet.

"*Receive. For the gods are close enough to breathe on us.*"

He supposes that she must have said these words hundreds, perhaps thousands of times before. Tonight they seem sombre, and strangely tender. It is folly, of course. They are unlikely to come out of this with their lives. It is a scene from a comical play: this plan to have a jester poison an emperor with weeds, and supplant him with a cripple.

*

They do not leave at once, Saba and Aemilia and Hestia, though it is growing late and they cannot afford for their absences from temple and palace to last much longer. There is a heaviness in the air in need of release, like the weight of rain held by storm-clouds.

193

The eight of them are bound now to the same uncertain future. It is Felix who seems to know what to do, fetching his lyre from the house and toying with its strings until untidy strains of music fall among them.

The sounds are like the night beginning to breathe again. The fire blazes all the brighter, and then Junia has fetched her instrument too and a drum for Hestia, and somebody has brought out more wine and the children have woken and come sneaking outside. Nobody has the heart to send them back to their beds, so there is Adelfa dancing beside the fire-pit with her little brother, Antonia begging Mylo to tell her what mysterious matter has occupied them all evening.

Antonus watches his wife's face in the firelight as she listens to Hestia, trying to learn the words to a lively song, something about the wedding of six virgin sisters. They are laughing together. The priestess Saba is dancing too now, careless of her appearance, her bare feet nimble in the dirt. There is blood and black ash upon her robe, which she has hitched to her knees.

Leaning against a rock at the edge of the circle of light, he stretches his leg out stiffly. *Whatever vow the gods have made…* His heart rolls with the rhythm of Hestia's drum. It is her hand which will perform the deed, not his own, and yet this does not wash him of his guilt. He and Laonatus grew in the same womb, nine years apart; they share the same blood. They sat at their mother's feet together, while she was alive. After the fire Laonatus gave him this household and this land. Laonatus gave him Junia.

The image of his brother as they last met, his perfect body adrift in the water, the polished surface of his smile. That fevered picture of himself first conjured in the steam-filled cavern, the just, wise emperor whose name will survive the centuries, surfaces again. Antonus is about to vanish into this fantasy when he sees the priestess Aemilia seated on the ground close by. She too is watching the musicians and the dancers. Her hands twist in her long pale hair. She looks to him like a stranger in the world.

He limps across to her, and she looks up nervously at his approach. "Make sure Mylo and Rufus take you back across the city," he says.

"Saba will be with me."

"Even so."

Her eyes dart up the mountain, then down to her knees. "I never wanted to bear bad news," she says.

"I'm sure Lennes didn't, either. Nor the Augur. You didn't make those tidings, priestess. Prophets never do. You were brave to deliver them. At a time like this, truth is salt to preserve the city."

"It won't all be preserved," says Aemilia. She is silent for a long while, watching the children. Then she shivers as though she has felt a chill in the balmy air. "My people were lost in flames."

Her words catch him off-guard. A memory of acrid smoke crowding his mouth and nose and lungs. The blistering heat which scorched away his consciousness. The screams which might have been his own, or one of his sisters', or some nameless slave's. Waking in the darkness upon a bier hours later to find his body in blinding pain. Already cleansed and perfumed for the grave.

"Mine too," he says. She looks up at him again, wide-eyed. Antonus kneads his knuckles into the twisted muscle of his leg. He thinks of the salamander from Lennes' dream, crawling down into the city, fire upon its breath.

*

Saba casts off the weight of the night's solemn business. There is rarely music at the Augur's temple, but the villa is alive with it. And perhaps she has carried too much in the last days and weeks; perhaps there is a part of her that wants no part in what she has helped set in motion here. Her dancing is miraculous, as though her feet have no need to touch the ground. As though she moves, unburnt, upon hot coals.

After all, she is so young. Her spirit not tuned for mourning. Give me music, give me garlands and wine. Do not bring about our end, not yet. I haven't had my fill of sweetness in this world.

She glimpses Aemilia sitting alone at the edge of the light, and turns away. In this moment she does not want to carry anything or anyone. She thinks of Athraxus, bearing the Augur in his arms along the steep path down the mountainside. Doesn't a prophetess bear the whole city in this way? It seems strange to Saba that until so very recently she was ready to take up this burden without question.

My mother, are you thinking of me? She spins around, hands lifted to the stars. Sparks fly into blackness. *My mother*, and at once she is thinking of the Augur and of the woman who screamed to the desert sky all those years ago. Saba closes her eyes. She has never before felt her own body so alive, so vital with sensation. Her warm naked skin beneath her robe. Heat and light from the fire searing her eyelids. She can smell earth and burning flesh and the cedars on the mountain.

It seems to her that she is bound by nothing in this place. The Emperor may live or die, the city endure or fall, and she will be untouched. There is a path waiting for her, lit by the silver moon, towards another land through the rocks over the mountain.

Hot and giddy, she stops for breath. Struggles for a moment to find her bearings in the night away from the music and the fire. She sees Rufus carrying a fresh jug of wine out from the villa and asks him to pour her a cup, drinking to quench her thirst.

"Another?" he asks, and she nods. He watches her approvingly.

Junia, Hestia and the slave are still playing, a slower tune now.

The fire is still bright but burning lower. Saba notices that Antonus has moved across to talk to Aemilia.

"Mylo thinks I should bring my father to your temple," says Rufus.

"You can, if you want to. We'll make sacrifices and burn incense for him. But you know that the Augur herself won't be there."

"That must be hard, for you all."

Saba does not reply. She feels momentarily chastened: she has been dancing while the Augur is in chains.

"It didn't feel right to me, living in my father's house without my father. I imagine it's much the same."

"I'll see her freed," says Saba.

"In any case... I don't think it would help him. I'm not sure anything can help him now." This spoken without self-pity. Rufus looks away, and following his gaze Saba finds her eyes lighting upon Myloxenes, now surrounded by all three children, who are begging him to dance with them. Absently, Rufus says, "I never get tired of watching him."

A glimpse of understanding, in that moment, a tug of sadness and of joy. "Tell me, priestess, is there anything as beautiful in this whole rotten city?" Rufus laughs as though in jest, but grows suddenly sober as he glances back at her. "What do you see?"

Perhaps it is the lateness of the hour or the fire or the wine, or because her temper tends so naturally to openness, but she answers without hesitation.

One who is so loved, by so many, and utterly unspoilt by it.

*

When they all part ways at last, amid the darkness and the ashes, it is knowing that they will not meet again like this. Not in this world. In whatever life they are next gathered, they will all be changed. They take their leave soberly of one another, as nomads gathered at a desert well, departing each to their own journey. They bless each other by the names of their household gods.

This is a part of the order of things. This is a rite as old as anything our hands have built. For what is a city, after all, but a series of meetings and partings?

VII

Perhaps because Aemilia is afraid and in a hurry to be back at the temple; or because Saba lingers to smell the night-blooming jasmine by the side of the path, and Mylo waits for her. But the moment comes when they are alone.

A soldier passes by the colonnade, causing Rufus and Aemilia to turn into a side-street. Mylo and Saba drop further back to conceal themselves in the shadows. They crouch amid a cluster of trees, low in the long grasses. Their breathing is quiet as they watch the soldier stride past them, looking about him with careless attention, sword swinging at his side. When he is gone they do not move.

Saba can still taste ashes and wine. Close-to she sees that the sleeves of his robe are tattered and stained with ink. He smells clean. She remembers the night he came to the temple with sea-salt in his hair. Still she does not move, and neither does he.

"Will they wait for us, do you think?"

"They'll keep going. Aemilia won't like being out in the dark."

"But you're not afraid."

Saba shakes her head, and her heart is leaping.

"I was afraid when Lennes spoke out at the solstice," he says softly. "I was afraid when I heard what the Augur said at the Emperor's feast."

"Perhaps that's wise."

He looks out into the darkness over the city. Whole households sunk into sleep, oblivious. "How do you think it might happen? Will it be like the flood in the old story?"

"When the people were found feasting, you mean. Maybe." Saba heard this tale as a child, from the Augur, but never gave it much consideration. Is it truly better to be warned, before disaster comes upon a city? To spend desperate and unhappy final days in the struggle to avert it? Tempting to say, find me, death, in the midst of life. I do not know the hour, and so you will find me laughing, dancing, drinking my cup to its dregs.

Myloxenes plucks at a feathered tuft of grass with his fingertips. "Do you really think that it's possible for the gods to change their minds? Like they're merchants to be bartered with?"

"If gods can't be petitioned, we should never have built temples." Her mouth curls in a grin, but he is still serious.

"I have always struggled to believe... it seems strange to me that they pay such close attention to our affairs. That they care about us short-lived creatures, enough to crave our praise or hear our complaints. Isn't there anything grander in nature or the divine realm that should preoccupy them? But I know so little about these matters."

"And you have spent too much time in that other temple."

He glances at her from beneath his lashes, shy.

"Did Athraxus never tell you how the first man came to be? The gods breathed into him, their own breath. They haven't forgotten that, I don't think. Like a mother wouldn't forget the child that grew in her womb." Saba watches him consider this, and feels the truth, the certainty of it for herself. This is the cornerstone of all that she has ever hoped for.

"My father told me that the gods have long regretted begetting so weak and troublesome a race."

"That's not true."

For a while Myloxenes seems to consider this, and the night grows wide and quiet around them. "Listen," he says. "That's the ocean."

The far-off swaying of the waves. The ocean is enough to wash it all away for tonight: Rufus and Aemilia hurrying now through the city towards the temple, the Augur in her chains, the priestesses fretting in their beds, Athraxus and his threats. Saba's skin prickles pleasurably. "Will you show me where you swim?"

He turns to her, and he is at once surprised, and ready to meet her. His smile has a slow beginning, like a long-awaited springtime.

*

The sands are silver and the water is black. Mylo's cove is secluded from sight of the city, reached by a precarious path down the cliffside where the salt-grasses grow. They find their way over the rocks by the light of the moon. Saba has never stood at the ocean's edge by night before. She tastes the charged air. The water holds all the deep blackness of the universe. Its surface glitters with starlight.

Though the air is still, a wind is blowing out at sea, creating waves which crest and foam at the shoreline. Mylo waits a little way up the beach, watching as she takes off her sandals and throws them over her shoulder, hitching up her robe to walk ankle-deep into the water. He sits down on the sand to remove his own shoes, more carefully. His hands are trembling. Tonight, the possibility of something impossible, unlooked-for. He thinks of Rufus leaning over to kiss him in the smoke-filled chamber at Mersia's party. *It's the end of the world.*

He has always tried so hard to please. First his father, like trying to coax praise from the stone of the mountain; his mother, barely even awake to his presence; then Antonus, Junia and Felix, a far gentler audience. But even that is binding. Only in the embrace of this water, swallowed by the depths as though being born, or dying, has he ever felt free.

Now his future hangs suspended by a thread before him. Prophecy, peril and poison. Antonia, Adelfa; that debt of gratitude. The love of Rufus which he cannot return in kind. Saba is coming back from the ocean with her sandals in her hand, and he wonders if there is a place where none of this matters. Where there is no struggle or striving. Where fruit falls ripe from the trees, where crops grow without labour and the gods do not call for blood.

Saba stands a little way off, watching him. He takes off his tunic, his undergarment, and leaves them lying on the sand as he walks forward into the water. The sea is cool against his skin. He dips below the surface then rises again, brushing his hair from his face. Saba has taken off her robe. She stands before him on the sand, naked, perfect. A moon-goddess. He sinks lower in the water.

Saba walks in as deep as her waist and then dives without hesitating, pulling herself through the water with strong strokes. He wonders what her life in this city has been until now, what has occupied her thoughts and her days. What she wanted for herself, before Lennes the Steward dreamed his dreams.

She swims towards him and they tread water together in the darkness. Her bare leg brushes his, and they are almost entangled. A shock of longing. The next wave carries her away. The only noise is the sigh of the sea, the ragged rhythm of their breathing. A wave washes them close again. For a moment she has hold of his arm and has drawn his face close enough to touch hers, her sweet shivering breath, droplets upon her lips and eyelashes. He can feel the force of her life pulsing beneath her skin.

Suddenly they are aware of themselves, of a world that has yet to come to an end. The city sleeps atop the cliff. She lets go and they drift for a while, still close.

She is with him in the place that has always been his alone.

Her presence threads new colours through the night. The ocean is changed with her: the meaning of his being here is changed. For the first time in his life the freshness of the present blows in, scatters dust, calls out to him. Lay down dusty books filled with the dead, and run outside.

Mylo watches his past recede like a tide and then wash back towards him, illuminated, cleansed of its bitterness. She is the sea towards which every river runs.

They let the water carry them apart. Saba reaches the shallows first and he lets her go ahead of him, averting his eyes now as she finds her robe and wraps it over her wet skin. She lingers among the rocks as he pulls his tunic and sandals back on, but does not wait for him to draw level with her.

She looks back at him over her shoulder, sandals swinging from her hand as she heads alone up the path into the city. And he knows that he is seen, and weighed, and wanted.

VIII

Seven days and seven nights pass before Aemilia and Saba make it to the mountain in search of poison. In that time it does not feel right to leave the temple, not even for a short while. Their absence on the night of the gathering at the house of Antonus, it transpires, was cause for alarm among the priestesses.

"I told them Athraxus took you," says Eris, stone-faced. She folds her arms, standing easily taller than Saba. "Why else would you have left us? It was the only thing that made sense."

"You frightened them all needlessly," Saba scolds her. "We were seeing to the Augur's business. You should have known that."

"By the gods, sister, I can't know what nobody tells me."

Aemilia cannot know, since she has not been told, what delayed Saba's return that night. They do not look one another in the eye.

They each lie awake on their straw pallets, consumed by thoughts which go unshared. Saba is submerged in the memory of seawater, swept on a rising tide of new desires. Temple matters feel trivial and small.

Aemilia's world, meanwhile, is going dark. Cut loose now from the anchor of Saba's attention, no longer under the protection of the Augur, her timid heart quakes. Athraxus towers over her dreams, his eyes burning coals and his tongue a scorching flame. She knows that she cannot die bravely. Not executed for treason on the dusty slope outside the city; not perishing in that prophesied fire of destruction. If a bargain could be made with the god of the underlife, blood and worship exchanged for the promise of a body not subject to death, she would take it.

The white walls of the temple hem her in, and she feels for the first time what it is to be an animal awaiting slaughter. She no longer visits the goats in their pen, overcome by an understanding of their helplessness. This is what it is to be a creature without meaningful will. Barely more than clay in hands which throw and mould and shatter. What can be the purpose of gentleness, of small kindnesses, if power sits in hands like these?

So the priestess Aemilia stares into the darkness through the watches of the night when her turn comes to sit sentry at the temple gate. She wishes that everything could flow backwards. That choices made and words spoken would not give birth to consequences. That corpses would flip up again out of their graves laughing like children caught in a game.

*

"Aemilia."

Someone is shaking her shoulder. She flinches away.

"'*Milia.* Come on. It's time to go to the mountain."

Saba's face swims before her in the darkness, and she realises that she has fallen asleep during her watch. Full of shame, she turns away to tighten the cloth which covers her hair. "What about the others?"

"They're all sleeping. This won't take long, they don't have to know we're gone. I'd go alone, but you're the one who knows where it grows."

Saba lights a torch from the fire in the temple hall and they slip through the overgrown stone doorway onto the mossy rocks below the waterfall. They take off their sandals to cross the stream. By night the waterfall is a hissing torrent of cold spray. As the torchlight sweeps across the water it illuminates the carvings on the rocks beneath. To Aemilia they look like a scrawl, a nonsense scratched there by madwomen.

And from this follows the biggest, most frightening thought that has ever entered her head. *Perhaps this is all the Augurs have ever been.* Aemilia finds herself shivering as she follows Saba up the steep, uneven slope. Who is it, after all, that dares to declare knowledge of holy things? Who builds a temple and says here, here the gods will speak to us their secrets?

Perhaps none of the prophetesses ever heard what they thought they heard. Not Saba, not even our mother. Maybe the gods have been speaking all this time but we mistook the signs. The flight of the starling flock is meant to be read not left to right but right to left; it is a healthy liver tells of coming misfortune; it is not sage we are meant to burn, but asphodel. First the gods laughed, then they grew frustrated, now angry. This is why they mean to destroy the city: because since the beginning they have given of themselves, and they were never understood.

It is a secret and a hard way up the mountain, the waterfall path, which is why it is more usual for the Augur to go through the city and climb the gentler route towards the cedar grove. Saba is scrambling up one-handed, still holding the torch. By the time the ground levels, greenery springing up around them amid the boulders, Aemilia is dizzy and breathless.

They are sheltered from the worst of the wind on this side of the slope, and the flame of Saba's torch remains steady, surrounding them with jagged shadows. Aemilia tries to remember how this place appears in the daylight. She looks at Saba, whose back is now turned, and tries to remember how things were between them, not so long ago.

"This way," she says. "I think there's a patch on the ridge, around towards the sea."

She can tell that Saba is impatient with how slowly she is moving, but she cannot be any bolder. The cicadas are loud here and almond-trees grasp the rocks with clenched roots. When Aemilia has climbed up this way before it has been on hot afternoons with a basket swinging at her hip, sweat on her neck and knees, to gather kindling and herbs for the temple. It feels to her as though nothing this ordinary could ever happen again.

The moon moves across the sky as they ascend the steep path around the mountainside, finding their footing in the flickering reach of the torchlight. Aemilia and Saba have never been in each other's company for so long without speaking, not since they crossed the ocean in the belly of that boat. Between the boulders, and there is the far-off cedar grove, the place where the Augur goes at the solstice to hear the gods. And here: the ridge above the sea where the wind-weed grows.

They are quick, gathering pockets full of berries as the breeze plucks at their cloaks. There is a dizzying drop below the ridge where a pair of sea-eagles nests in the cliff. The city is spread before them, shrunk from this height, a few of its fires still lit. When they have finished the task still in silence they make their way back between the boulders, and perhaps they take a wrong turn or the torchlight itself guides them there, but without quite knowing how they find themselves standing before a gaping mouth in the earth.

Looking into its blackness Aemilia begins to shiver, and she realises that there has been a pain wedged like a bone in her gut ever since the Augur was taken. As though a promise has been broken.

"I found her here." Saba too is staring into the crack between the rocks. "After the solstice."

The smell of the air within the cleft is rank and overpowering. A rush of sulphurous vapour and Saba's torch is extinguished. Aemilia thinks she hears the darkness shift and breathe, like an unseen creature roused from sleep. The hairs on the back of her neck are standing on end.

"I went inside," says Saba. "Even though it's forbidden to everyone except the Augur."

Aemilia looks at her. Saba's eyes are shining in the moonlight. Is this a confession? A boast, a taunt?

"What did you see?" she whispers.

"The place where this realm meets the next. Do you want to go in?"

Aemilia recoils with a shudder, and Saba gives a soft laugh.

"I didn't think you would. You'll have to have to harden your face, 'Milia, if you're going to look towards what's coming. Whichever way this turns, we're for the underworld now."

*

At the villa, nobody is sleeping except the children. Mylo and Rufus came to break bread at dusk and still have not left. The latter is engaged in a hard-fought game of chequers with Felix, while the former paces the inner room distractedly. Antonus and Junia sit together on the wall behind her weaving-room. They have broken open a barrel of wine from their cellar, sealed there in the year that the twins were born.

They do not need to speak to one another. The wine tastes of cinnamon and of resin, of fourteen years spent in prosperity and peace. She has her hand laid lightly on his hip, above the twisted part of his leg. He turns his head towards her shoulder, to inhale the rich smell of her hair.

Mylo appears, silhouetted in the archway. "I should go to the temple," he says. He has said this every day, many times a day, since the night of their gathering.

"No, you shouldn't," says Junia. "Give them a little more time."

"They've had enough time…"

"Mylo," says Antonus quietly. "Let them do their part. One of us will go, soon. Believe me, we're being hasty enough in this."

The boy looks a little wild, his hair in disarray, circles beneath his eyes. None of us have slept, thinks Antonus, not in many nights. In the small hours the wind picks up and they move inside, bringing the remainder of the wine and lending their support to Rufus, who has now lost four games in a row.

Mylo is plied with wine until he finally consents to drink some and, to Antonus's relief, dozes off on the courtyard bench. Junia covers him with a cloak. They light the brazier. Cicadas chirrup and shadows dance along the wall.

"It's said," begins Felix, "that when men first asked for a king, the gods sent them a man who arrived among them on a pillar of cloud. To protect their city he killed a giant with a flat stone from the seashore…"

"Why do you get to tell all the stories?" Junia asks.

"I've got one," says Rufus. "There was once a slave of low character who became very skilful at dice, and all other kinds of games, because he frittered his days away in taverns instead of working for his master."

"Very funny."

"He met a sorry end when he fell into a gutter and was eaten by pigs."

"Who's there?" asks Junia suddenly. A rustle and scuff of footsteps. Somebody is moving around the outside of the villa in the dark. Junia, Rufus and Felix all rise instinctively to their feet, and Mylo sits up, groggy. Antonus grips the edge of the bench.

"They know!" hisses Rufus, his face transformed in an instant to a mask of fear. "*They already know, they've come for us!*"

"Sshhhh…"

"The dwarf must have betrayed us, or the priestesses…"

"Rufus!" calls a familiar voice, softly, from outside.

"*Mersia?*"

Junia and Felix fetch her into the courtyard. For her journey across the city in the dead of night she has draped herself in an embroidered cloak the colour of a ripe orange, with a dramatic hood that half-covers her mass of curled hair. She is wearing enormous earrings in the shape of peacocks. From the distasteful way she shakes her sandals as she walks, she has evidently stepped in some dung out in the yard.

"This was the last place I could think to look for you." She addresses her brother, not sparing a glance or a greeting for the others present. "The back of beyond. My slaves are so tired I had to leave them at the bottom of the hill."

"What are you *doing?*" asks Rufus, incredulous.

"I might ask you the same." Her eyes range to Mylo. "They're still talking about you in the city, Myloxenes. About how the High Priest's son has spoken for the Augur. And *this* man…" She cannot bring herself, it seems, to use Antonus's name. "My husband is right about that much, at least."

"And what do you say to these times, daughter of Lennes?" asks Antonus.

'I don't know what you mean. Nobody ever believes the Augur any more unless they are poor, or unfortunate, or in some other way ridiculous. Come." She holds out her hand, but Rufus does not take it.

"Have you come to keep me out of trouble?"

"Gods help me. This nonsense stops right now. What are you thinking of?"

"We didn't even do it yet!" Rufus blurts out. "You can't prove anything!"

Felix covers his eyes with his hand. Beneath her hood, Mersia's expression is shadowed, unreadable. There is a long pause.

"I don't know what's happening here," she says, very quietly, very clearly. At last she seems to be addressing them all. "I don't know what you're mixed up in, and I don't care. I only know, Rufus, you've spent too long carousing with this household — *with the Priestess's people*. Don't you know how that looks? Now come *on*."

'The gods honoured your father by making him their messenger," says Mylo. "Won't you honour them in return?"

'The gods should have chosen a stronger vessel. Our father's dead."

IX

The afternoon sun beats down upon the valley of ashes. Mersia and her daughter Calica, the remaining women of the house of Lennes, lead the way in funeral white. Their heads are downcast and their foreheads smeared with ash. Mersia sings the lament which her daughter echoes falteringly. *Death is before me today. The grave is open before me. I am to make a journey, I am to set sail for the land from which there is no return...*

Hired mourners bear the body. They wear sackcloth and walk stiffly. Others swing bronze bells and groan, covering their faces. There are many of them, since Lennes did not die a poor man; but behind them, the procession is thin. Rufus, heir to the deceased, moves as though in a dream. Calix carries his son. Antonus limps along at the rear. But where are all those men of the Emperor's court? Those tall palace gossips with their kohl-lined eyes, the generals into whose war purses Lennes would have counted out coins, the councillors and the magistrates whose endless meetings he would have sat in on, week after week, year after year? Only a handful are here.

And they look afraid. Mylo, the youngest among them, glances around at their sombre faces. The Emperor's third-favourite physician, a doddering old astronomer, a retired commander of the city guard. Forgettable men, all. They are not thinking about the Steward, about their friend, cold now after four days embalmed upon a bier in his home. They are wondering who might be watching. And sure enough Mylo thinks that he can see a tall, cloaked figure on the ridge above the valley, almost concealed among the rocks. The astronomer is sweating copiously. Athraxus will know their faces. He will have their names. He will know that these are the men who came to mourn Lennes, the blasphemer.

A priest of the Dark Temple is waiting at the pyre. His sweat has smudged the ash from his forehead. His robe is grey with dust. He ushers them forward, impatient to have the thing done, to be back to his doze in a shady corner of the temple courtyard.

The body is laid down. A cloth covers the face, clothing the features beneath. A blank landscape of mounds and troughs. The mourners are quiet now. Rufus bends to lift the cloth and looks into the face of his dead father. He pauses for a long moment, head bowed, then draws coins from his pocket. He kisses each one, then presses them into the dead man's eyes. *For the boatman, for the journey.*

They burn him with his sandals and his books, so that he might walk into the next world and find employment there. The priest pours libations onto the wood. He chants a prayer and lights the flame.

Who told us how to lay down our dead? In the savage age we used to sprinkle our dead in ochre, the colour of their lifeblood. Since the dead came to us in dreams, we knew that they lived beyond their bodies. We tucked into their hands the tools they would need for the other life, the life-under-the-world. Buried them in caves, surrounded by circles of stones.

The hidden nature of things is patterned like the visible world. The heavens, the earth, the under-life below. In those caves where we dwelt the walls had a slippery sheen of water, a membrane like the lining of a womb. It is in the shape of these walls that we began to feel with the palm of a hand and with fingertips in the darkness the contours of the spirit realm. An eye, a haunch, the protruding nubs of antlers. Creatures not like creatures upon the earth. We painted beasts in secret places, lines of limbs drawn in shadow, looming, vanishing with the flicker of a lamp.

Painted our palms. Pressed hands against the rock. An imprint reaching across the divide, into the place beyond.

Now when we bury the dead we cleanse ourselves afterwards with careful rituals. Who told us to dip our hands in spring-water, to scrub with hyssop and with rosemary? To blow out the lamp that we lit for the watching ritual, after the body has lain quiet for four days before the hearth, its spirit flown?

To die is to enter into doubt. Can the dead touch anything, once they no longer move within their bodies? What sort of land they walk we cannot know, or if they walk at all. They enter into unknowing. We shroud the faces of the dead and they are hidden from us. When we call for them or speak of their afterlife it is in the dark, as men fumble their way down the damp steps into the black heart of the Dark Temple. Breath misting, hands groping blindly along the wall.

We burn everything the dead have touched. Their caskets and their cloth wrappings, the tunics and undergarments they died in. Women who have embalmed the dead must keep themselves apart until their cleansing is complete.

Death spreads through everything. We learned this in the garden, with the change that crept into our hearts. Death began like a bleed, an insidious trickle and flow that grew and could not be staunched. Still in horror we try to scrub it from our bedsheets and our hands. This infection, this age-old stain. This conquering empire which lays to dust all in its path.

*

Mylo, close to Rufus now, lays a hand on his back. His friend turns towards him very slightly, but does not speak. The flames of the pyre sway sideways in a wind blowing through the valley of ashes. Mylo's eyes follow the stray sparks and he sees, with a jolt, a growing crowd of people gathering beyond the pyre.

At first it is not a crowd of any deliberate shape or purpose. He can see men young and old, women with their small children. He recognises the magistrate Estebus, from the baths, and the one-eyed water-seller from the market. A handful of the Augur's priestesses, Saba among them. An anxious clutch of courtier's wives, and Junia's favourite flower-girl. There are more, coming down from the city gate, and all seem surprised to find that they are not alone. They have come to watch the burial rites of the Steward, who not long ago prophesied their destruction.

The sound of their whispering grows louder, like wind in cedars.

The other mourners begin to notice. Mylo hears Mersia catch her breath, a surprised hand flying to her breast. The priest looks alarmed, and does not seem to know what to do. He takes a step back from the pyre. The crowd draws closer, and its murmuring becomes a tense, uneasy rumble. They are all watching the pyre, Mylo realises, as though expecting some kind of sign.

Then, from the heart of the crowd, a voice is raised above the others. "*Gods, take pity on us, and send another prophet!*"

Cries of distress, of agreement.

"*Stay your hands, and speak again!*"

"Our destruction will come from within and without!"

Fear ripples through the whole assembly. A woman in a red headscarf begins wailing. Two little boys huddle into their mother's legs. A tall man clenching his fists advances on the priest, bellowing at him as though he addresses the whole of the Dark Temple. "Listen to us, you order of crooks! We've emptied our purses for you, now give the gods whatever sacrifice they want!"

"And free the Augur!"

"*We want to live!*"

Someone flings a stone at the priest, who ducks and flees, cursing. The tall man and a handful of others break away to give chase. It dawns on Mylo that forces are shifting in the foundations of the city. *Hers is the temple of the people. Let's see where they turn.* Unthinking in his excitement he seizes Rufus's hand. "Saba was right! The people are on the Augur's side, and they'll side with Antonus too…"

Rufus is still staring white-faced into the flames. "I thought we could lay him to rest," he says indistinctly. He pulls away. "Today, just today. My father could never have imagined this."

Calix is shouting, sweeping his children up under his arms. Before Mylo can take hold of Rufus again, before he can reply, Mersia pulls her brother away. The figure on the ridge is descending now, and at his sign, twenty or so soldiers come running down from between the rocks. They are holding clubs and swords. A rolling dust-cloud rises in their wake.

Mylo finds himself caught up along with Antonus among the fleeing mourners. The old men flap around the edges of the chaos, panicked and uncomprehending. Mylo lets Antonus lean on his shoulder until they are clear of the fighting but then turns without explanation to push his way back towards the pyre, towards Saba, whom he can see standing her ground in the heart of the crowd. Saffron robe bright against her dark skin. Her eyes flash in the firelight as she turns towards Athraxus.

The High Priest must have known that there would be trouble, but his soldiers are too few. More people are flooding down from the city to sate their curiosity, having caught sight of the commotion in the valley. Some of them have been interrupted right in the midst of the day's business, still clutching their fishing-nets or cooking-pots or their purchases from the market. Some are laughing, pointing, entertained as though by a masked spectacle; but others run forward to join the fray.

The crowd now numbers in the hundreds. The pyre of Lennes the Steward sputters and sparks, while fishermen scuffle with soldiers and women wail laments for the imprisoned Augur. Some are pouring their own offerings onto the fire, or thrusting them into the hands of the Augur's priestesses, who look quite as stunned as Mylo feels. There are few here who would have been present at the solstice feast to hear Lennes speak, or at the Emperor's feast to see the writing on the wall. They have heard by some other means: the news has spread through the city like a little flame jumping at kindling.

And they have believed. Mylo's heart leaps. We are not just a handful of frightened conspirators, whispering to one another in the lamplight. We are many. The balance of the city still sits in the favour of Athraxus's temple, but Lennes does not lie here unheard or unheeded. His words were not wasted. Rufus ought to be comforted by that.

Are there enough here to see the Augur freed? To see Antonus secure on the Emperor's seat? Mylo's thoughts race. If all our plans fail and the gods will not be appeased, are there enough here to lead a retreat from the city before disaster comes? He imagines it for a moment, a numberless procession pouring out into the wilderness, shielding their faces against the wind that blows from the country beyond the distant mountains. *If all else fails...*

"Here, boy!" a painful grip upon his upper arm, and he is wrenched out of the daydream. "Did you have a hand in this?"

He sees clearly and realises that the commotion around him is in its final throes. Many in the crowd are being led forcibly away by soldiers, or have retreated back towards the city. An old woman has dug herself in near the base of the pyre and is crying noisily there, unheeded. A soldier slumps against a nearby rock, pressing his sleeve against a wound upon his leg. Lennes' body is all but burned away, and Mylo is the only person from the funeral procession still present.

"Do you hear me?" The shock of a blow across his head, and his ears are ringing. He raises a hand to his mouth and finds blood dripping onto his fingertips. *"Did you know about this? You and your cripple? You and that dead man's frivolous children? Have you been feeding this unrest?"*

He hangs from his father's hands, limp. Beyond the aftermath of the pyre and the dispersed crowd, over the city and the sea, the sun is sinking. The air is hot and thick in the orange light. He can feel the heaving of Athraxus's chest as the High Priest bears over him, and he is ready to close his eyes. Defeat washes into his heart like Aemilia's sweet poison. Many times, he has died this way.

"It was an unwise thing you did," says Saba's voice, clear, close at hand. "Locking up the Prophetess. You should have taken better advice."

Athraxus turns at once, snarling. Mylo is dropped to the ground in disgust. In the cloud of ash and dust he sees the priestess in her saffron robe, fists clenched, eyes bright. The High priest might flick her away with his finger and thumb: but he does not.

"You put her in prison, and you made her words forbidden. You made her important. Death did the same for Lennes the Steward."

"This was your doing, then. You and your priestesses stirred up these people and staged this farce. I've warned you before, what I'll do to them…"

The other priestesses are among those running back to the city. They are children, thinks Mylo, they are just children. "We didn't stir up anything," says Saba. "We came here to bury a prophet."

The word seems to stick in Athraxus's skin like a hornet sting. He rounds suddenly and viciously upon Mylo again. "Why are you still here? Run back and cry to your mother. You aren't worth spitting on."

*

Saba tails Athraxus as he makes to climb up towards the gate in the wake of his stumbling son. She can barely keep up with his long stride, but she grabs at the sleeve of his robe, insistent.

"What charge are you holding my mistress on? Under what law?"

"Oh, there are plenty of laws against someone like her."

"Will she stand trial before the magistrates?"

"You're not my adviser or my confidant. I don't have to tell you."

"Don't you understand what happened here today?" Saba tries to overtake him and block his path. "You'll free her before dark tonight or there'll be a riot at your gate. You'll see."

"Hark, another prophecy!"

"You'll let me in to see her. You'll let me take food to her and speak to her. Before midday tomorrow, or I'll—"

"You'll what, child?" He stops in his tracks and she almost trips over him. A red star blinks in the darkening sky above his head. He is laughing, and the sound is the creaking of the wheels which turn the whole blind pitiless universe.

She is small and silent and subject to whatever his hand might deliver. For the first time in her sixteen years, a chill reaches Saba at the very centre of herself.

They stand looking at one another on the wind-blown ridge. There are planets in the heavens now, smudges of green and cold blue. The priest throws his cloak about himself, and turns to go.

"I'll pray to the shadow-god." Saba barely knows what she is saying. "To the god of the underlife, I'll pray for your destruction."

He laughs again, but this time it is only a laugh. He is only a man.

"For a son of your temper!" he exclaims, seeming to surprise himself as much as her. His face twists and he spits out his words like rotten grapes. "My only son was born under a weak planet."

She is quick, Saba, in her dealings. She makes her choice. Douses her past and her future and all the close-woven plans of recent days, casts them off like a torn old cloak. What use are such things, on a night like this?

She runs to his side on the path leading back to the gate. There are people all around but they blur into the blue of the dusk. He is bruised and trembling. His hand brushes hers.

The shadows are long and the river flows dark alongside them. White wading-birds are resting in the reeds. There is still a crowd in the square but all seems muted by an eerie slowness and a quiet.

Some are nursing wounds, others searching out those they have misplaced in the chaos. Smoke hangs low among the carts.

On the bathhouse steps sits the old man with his cage of song-thrushes and he is whistling to them, poking his fingertips between the bars, but they have fallen silent.

*

He lights a candle in his chamber, as at a shrine. The shifting darkness pools in every corner and around the walls. At first he cannot look her in the eye, but she guides his face around, kisses the corner of his mouth where his father's fist drew blood. *You are beloved, you are whole, you are clean.* His hands slip the cloth of her robe from her shoulders.

She hears the sigh of her own released breath, feels his warm palms sliding down her shoulder-blades, into the dip of her back. Rests her head against his chest.

Perhaps here we find our rest. Here at last hands touch hands, skin meets skin, and we are known. There is no shroud. No more sacrifices, no more smoke. And knowing is possible.

DESTRUCTION

I

On the night that Lennes the Steward is sent on into the next world, a burning star is seen above the city. It is seen by the women of the slum beyond the old palace as they sweep their steps after sundown, looking up to follow the tail of fire as it streams across the heavens. It is seen by the priestesses of the Augur's Temple, who run to the top of the tower for a better look, and by the priests of the Dark Temple, who gather in their courtyard to stare into the sky. It is seen by the guards outside the palace, and by that ageing slave of the house of Antonus, who stops in his tracks, startled, on the path back from the tavern to the villa.

And it is seen by the Emperor himself, sleepless in his lavish rooms, wrapped in a silk robe with his astronomical charts spread before him. Every night since midsummer he has searched the skies for irregularities. He has had the shelves of the library scoured for relevant scrolls and tablets. He has consulted the whole array of devices in his collection: the water-clock, the gnomon, the system of spheres. The Emperor is well-versed in the study of the planets and stars.

This is no natural phenomenon. Signs like this, hurtling spheres of light trailed by showers of red sparks, are recorded but a few times in a century. Always they bring with them ill fortune. The Emperor rises to his feet below the arch of his observatory and steps out, trembling, into the garden. A fountain splashes, and the little bells hung in the trees shiver and chime in the night breeze. All is well here: but he cannot be calm.

He calls first for his philosophers, whom he orders to make an argument for the cause that every event from now until the end of time might be predicted using calculations from the movements of the planets and stars. They rise to the task as best they can, discretely rubbing their bleary eyes and concealing their yawns. But he is not convinced by their elegant proofs. He sends them away and calls next for his magicians, who entertain him for a short while with an illusion of cups and globes.

Nothing can quiet his mind. He has Little Laonatus woken and brought to him to play songs while he lies in his bed, wakeful. She knows how to read his mood and choose music to match it. She plucks at the strings of her harp and hums a melody that makes him think of days long-gone, of the mother he barely remembers, who used to stand over him and stroke his forehead until he drifted into sleep.

"What's the name of that song, Little?"

"*Maiden's Lament*, my master."

"Have you played it for me before?"

"Yes, my master. Last year, when you suffered with that sickness of the lungs. You said that it comforted you."

"It does again, tonight. Play on."

There is a lamp lit upon every surface in his chamber. She glances at him for a moment before resuming her music, dark eyes glittering.

*

He dreams of a rain of flaming stars which pours down from the night sky to ignite the city. He wakes, shaking and drenched in sweat, to find himself alone in his chamber. It is still the middle of the night. The Emperor howls like a child. When his attendants rush in to enquire what might be done for him, he makes a rash request, then paces the chamber, one hand pressed to his racing heart.

His will is always carried out quickly. They come for him within the hour, and lead him out of the palace towards the House of the Magistrates. He has not changed out of his night-robe, nor has anybody dared advise him to wrap a cloak over the thin silk. Titus, the chief magistrate, greets him with a deep bow, then shows him to the chamber where they have moved her.

"You see, my lord Emperor, the place is ventilated. There is air and light. She has a stool to sit on and a straw bed and a blanket. There's a pot so that she can relieve herself. I'll have my kitchen-slaves woken at once if you think that she ought to eat something."

"Bring us warm spiced wine and fruit and your best sweet-cakes," says the Emperor.

The barred window in the chamber is set high in the wall. When he enters, the guards closing and bolting the door behind him, he finds her staring upwards at the patch of night sky. She is seated on the floor, wrapped in a rough sacking cloak. They have taken away her head-wrap. Wisps of grey hair are plastered to her skull. She does not look around.

"You've got me to thank for this change. I gave the order for them to make you more comfortable."

She turns her head slightly. The skin about her mouth looks red and raw. "Thank you," she says hoarsely. "My master."

"This isn't a reprieve. You are still in the charge of the magistrates."

"I understand, my master."

The Emperor is holding a lamp. He leaves it on the sill, and then with a small hesitation steps closer to her. The Augur is looking at the wall, now. She places the palms of her hands upon the bare stone floor. She begins to mutter under her breath.

"What's that?" asks the Emperor sharply. Her hands make circles in the dust.

A knock at the door, and two slaves enter bearing platters of food and drink. Their heads are bent, their hands shaking. They have never served the Emperor before. They bow again and again, uncertain over whether to put the trays on the floor or on the sill. They settle on the latter, and make to move backwards out of the room.

"Go, my friends, go," say the Augur, loudly and clearly. "You're the wisest men in this city. Flee this house. Flee these walls. You may yet survive."

They hesitate, confused. The Emperor waves a hand and they are gone. He makes his way over to the sill and picks at a cake, before turning with a sullen expression. "Are you trying to provoke me? I should have you whipped. I might, if you keep on this way."

She says nothing. He looks at the door, which the slaves have locked behind them. "They are funny little things, aren't they? I'm glad that I only keep the handsomest in my household. Otherwise I couldn't bear to look at them all day."

Since she does not stand up, and still does not speak to him, he does what seems most natural. With a light touch he takes up a cup of steaming wine and a plate of cakes, and sits with them upon the floor. The Emperor begins to work his way through the choicest morsels. The lamp gutters on the sill, and after a while the Augur shuffles forward and takes a cake for herself from the edge of the plate.

Though he has feasted already that evening, he eats with abandon; she tears for herself a small careful piece, rolls the pastry around her sore gums. For a brief moment, at the taste of it, she closes her eyes.

"I need you to tell me something," says the Emperor.

The old woman allows herself one more moment with the cake. She takes another bite and feels it steady her. Remembering, perhaps, the ordinary pleasures which sweeten a long lifetime. The fig picked at its perfect ripeness. The stream which cools dusty, aching feet. That bold thrush which used to perch on the temple wall near the window of her chamber, singing in the golden hour before sunset.

"Why would the gods be angry?" he asks.

She opens her eyes.. He is sullen again, like a scolded child.

"I don't see why they should be. I always follow my priests' advice and make the right prayers and offerings. I've shown Athraxus great favour. I have kept the proper festivals. And aren't we prosperous? Has the beauty of this city ever been rivalled, has its strength ever been matched?"

He leans towards her, eyes flashing, warming now to his theme.

"Look at the delicacies which are served at my table, the fine silks which my wives wear, the height of my towers and colonnades, the number of ships in my fleet. Who can deny that we're in our prime? We are like the muscled youth who flings his friends easily into the dust of the training-yard. We are like the swift stallion who outstrips the herd. Who could look at my city and imagine this noonday is dusk?"

The Augur is moving her hands in the dirt again. "The smallest stone," she murmurs. "The littlest thing, in the city's balance."

"Don't speak to me in riddles."

"You think that you are ready to hear my words uncloaked?"

He laughs. "What an idea, that I'd be afraid to hear you or anybody speak."

"Upon my life, then, what the gods have made known to me. The gods are not blind to small lives. The gods are not deaf to small cries. They know what you cast into the fire, all those years ago, when your father and sisters and brother burned." Her voice is low, but the room so silent that not a syllable is lost. "They know what you cast into the fire, still."

It has been a long time since he was last lost for words. He grows suddenly pale, this golden man, ghostly in the lamplight. In another man this might have been a moment of turning. But the Augur says nothing. She waits.

"How do you know about these things?" whispers Laonatus.

"The gods have shown them to me."

"They pay such close attention!"

"A comfort to the weak, my master. A terror to the strong."

"Our *arrangement*, this is the agreement that we came to…I've fed them, I have brought their sacrifices, this is what they were hungry for…"

The Emperor is breathing hard. Beads of sweat breaking out on his forehead. He looks away, towards the high window, and for the space of a heartbeat it seems as though words of prophecy, boldly spoken, heard in fear and trembling, might be enough.

When he turns back towards her, he has changed. This is no mere surface calm. His whole being is altered: the colour has returned his face, and a smile lingers about his mouth, as though their whole exchange until now has been in jest. The confidence in his bearing is no less real than the horror of moments ago.

"But of course," he says, "you are disturbed in your mind. It's the effect of age, just like Athraxus says. I wonder whether we could find a medicine that would bring you relief? I will ask my physicians in the morning."

He yawns widely. "It is generous of me, to have thought of you in your distress. Isn't it?"

"Most generous, my master. I am grateful."

'To have interrupted my own rest so I could see to your wellbeing."

"I do not deserve such graciousness."

"Rest. Yes, I should..." He yawns again, and he is already folding his arms about himself, eyelids drooping. The Emperor continues to mumble for a while, stirring about for a comfortable position on the hard stone floor. He falls asleep, at last, in her lap.

II

She is up to her elbows in blood.

Aemilia wipes her forehead with a stained sleeve. It is not yet mid-morning, but already her hands are sore and her head is throbbing. In the last hour she has killed four goats, those beasts which trust her, which come running to the edge of their pen at the sight of her, bright-eyed. She has slit their throats, gutted them and stared blurredly at the entrails. Pronounced her reading of the auspices, tremulous, uncertain. Parcelled out the meat, flung the carcasses on the fire.

This has been going on all night. The gates of the temple, which usually see perhaps ten entrants in a day, have to be kept open. People push and jostle past one another in the line outside the sanctuary. Smoke belches into the sky as priestesses hurry to and fro across the courtyard, leading goats and carrying armfuls of herbs and firewood. Aemilia does not know whether she ought to put a halt to it all – send these supplicants back down the steps, return to them their coins and their little clay votives, silence their panicked prayers, close up the gate and let the priestesses collapse in exhaustion. She does not know what to do. The Augur is not here. Saba is nowhere to be found.

They had been together in the valley of ashes the previous afternoon. The last that Aemilia remembers is seeing Saba run off through that crowd, towards Athraxus. Some of the faces here today in the temple are familiar. They are still bloodied and bruised from yesterday's encounter with the Emperor's soldiers.

There are eggars and weavers and fishermen, harassed mothers with babies at their breasts: but as well a councillor here, a courtier there, trying to hide their faces under their hoods. They all smell of fear.

If Saba, too, has been taken. If she is rotting now in some cellar room at the Dark Temple. If Athraxus has his way. Aemilia's panic rattles around inside her ribcage.

"*Receive*," she whispers, again and again, until the words become meaningless sounds. "*For they are close enough to breathe . . .*"

"Priestess, can you tell us what's going on?"

"Priestess, take this bag of coins for me and for my family . . . pray that we'll be spared whatever is coming . . ."

She bears their pleas and their groans as though they are her own. A woman weeps before the altar with her forehead pressed to the floor and it is all Aemilia can do not to weep there with her. An old man presses the last of his life's savings into her hands and begs her to intercede for him. "One more blessing, to die at peace in my bed, surrounded by my sons. Not like this, with the faces of the gods turned from me. Not under a curse."

Give me no more gifts, she wants to say to them. Keep your fattened calves and bags of grain. My prayers mean even less than yours. When I listen for the heavens there is only silence.

"What do the entrails say? Do they agree with Lennes, and the writing on the wall? What are the gods saying us?"

"Priestess, last night I saw a flaming star . . ."

Aemilia saw it too. Dragged from her duties by sharp-eyed Liva, she ran up the steps to the top of the tower, leaned out of the window in the Augur's chamber to watch that strange light travelling across the heavens. Felt the back of her neck prickle, felt the cold hand of dread close more tightly around her heart.

When she pictures the gods now she imagines beings not in forms like men and women, but giants made of rock, made of mountain. In a rage their fists might crush nations, the stamping of their feet might displace all the water in the ocean. When they roar, cities might crumble to dust. There is no reasoning with them, no cajoling, no altering their will. They are implacable. The actions of a man can be connected to his character, can be predicted from his past: but the gods are not like this. Their anger, their favour, their love, their curses, blow out of nowhere like a sudden storm and then are gone.

And what is augury, but a denial of all this? A thin silk shawl to wear in a howling tempest. A little fishing-boat to set out into the vast and rolling chaos of the waves.

So do not ask when disaster is coming upon us. Do not ask what form it will take, or why we have been chosen for this fate. We all of us dream in the dark. If a fragment of what seems to be the truth is offered to you, then hear it and obey. Perhaps you will be saved. Perhaps not.

*

"Priestess. Priestess? It's me."

She blinks. She has taken money and mumbled blessings for the man sitting before her without looking up at him. He is wafting sage-smoke out of his face.

For a moment she stares at him stupidly. "Come," says Lennes' son. "I have a memorable face, don't I?"

"I know who you are."

Outside, a noisy quarrel has broken out. It is now afternoon, and there is still a large crowd waiting to enter the sanctuary. Aemilia is too spent to think of going to keep the peace. Rufus pricks up his ears like a hunted hare. "Did the whole city come to consult your temple today?" he asks.

"They won't gain anything from it. Our mother is still in chains."

"Don't tell me I'll gain nothing, I just gave you a bag of gold." She finds her head drooping, her eyes downcast. "Here, come on, don't do that!" Rufus shakes her as though trying to wake a stubborn sleeper. "Priestess," he says, with nervous urgency. "It's nearly time."

Aemilia understands why he is here, and gathers herself. She gestures to him to stay quiet as she rises unsteadily to her feet. He follows her out of the back entrance, through the passageway which leads to the store-room. She has him wait there for her, pacing between the heaped bags of grain, while she hurries up the staircase to the Augur's chamber.

Despite the heat of the day her teeth are chattering. She hugs her robe to her body and feels patches of sweat pool beneath her arms and on her back. She has hidden the bottle on the sill of the window beside the mat where the Augur sleeps. For a moment she pauses in the quiet of the familiar chamber, the crowd muffled in the courtyard below, and feels the absence of her mother and sister as an ache that will never heal.

Back in the store-room, Rufus uncorks it for a brief examination, wrinkling his nose and then slipping the bottle inside his robes. "Is that it, then?" he asks. She nods. "Well, I hope you mixed it up strong. This is a grim business."

He looks as sick with fear as she feels. Fleetingly she wonders whether they might reach an agreement here between them, to say that the wind-weed was never found, the mixture never made, the opportunity missed.

He seems to read her thoughts. "You don't say much, do you, priestess? And I always say too much. I suppose we're just different breeds of coward. Neither of us is right for this. We should have been born in a different time."

Aemilia remembers that he has just buried his father. She wants to give him a word of comfort, of consolation, but she cannot. "I don't think there is any such thing," she whispers.

"What?"

"A different time. A kinder age."

"I expect you're right. You know about these things, you prophetesses. Don't you? I hope so. I'm placing a lot of trust in your temple today." He touches his hand to the place beneath his robe where the poison sits. He makes to leave, but then turns back, frowning. "You know," he says, "the worst of all this isn't the fear of dying. Not yet, anyway. I suppose that will come. There are things you think you'll never lose, things you think are fixed on your horizon, like the mountain. Then you turn around one day and you can't see them any more. You have a friend who's been by your side half of your life, and then the day you need him most, he's nowhere to be found. He doesn't come and find you. So you're left to do the rest of your mourning with your lump of a brother-in-law and a sister who is pretending there's nothing wrong. Just like that, the ground crumbles away."

Aemilia knows in that moment what she is not yet ready to know. She pushes the thought back down into the darkness. "You haven't seen him?"

Rufus shakes his head. A small, unwitting bitterness twists the corner of his lip. "Not today. Not last night, either. He must have had more important things to attend to."

*

Run away with me, he whispers. *I'll wait for you by the colonnade, at the ancient gate.*

She laughs, despite herself. There has been a lot of laughter, this past day and night. What is laughter, but surprise? The intrusion of a new note into a familiar tune. The discovery of a survivor in the midst of a wreck.

Sweet boy. She smooths back the curls from his forehead. *Beautiful boy.We can't do that.*

We could.We can. He is in jest, and in earnest. His kiss is sweet as summer oranges. Imagine it, Saba. Fleeing the city, leaving the city in its painful throes, forgetting the city to live like those first people. The first man and the first woman, wrapped in furs, wrapped in each other, sleeping beneath the stars. No more emperors. No more temples. Brother and sister to the gods themselves.

She whispers in his ear that he is beautiful, and beloved. He hides his face in her neck, still shy. All her life she has heard that to be taken to a man's bed, wed or unwed, is a kind of death. For a priestess, a kind of sacrilege. Not so long ago the Emperor Laonatus had all the Augur's priestesses stoned to death, accused of losing their chastity. But though Saba searches for it within herself, she cannot feel defiled. Her skin is singing.

Everything she has ever imagined for herself is turned to air. Plans from before the dreams of Lennes the Steward, and from the time after. Saba, who has been a captive and a slave, is helpless for the first time in her life. She can only feel elation.

There is the matter of her body. She took the time, hours ago when it was still dark, to leave him sleeping as she washed herself in the courtyard fountain. Cleansing carefully her shoulders, arms, legs, between her thighs. Hands and breath unsteady. She has never conceived of her body in this way before. There are dangers. To live in a body that could conceive, that could betray you. She has heard whispers of the herbs which can prevent it.

Now Myloxenes has fallen into a doze again, his breathing soft and rhythmic. She kisses his closed eyelids. Lays her head against his chest, and prays as she listens to his heart. *Watch over us, you gods. Send your protection over us. Save us from what follows.*

She returns to the Augur's temple before sunset. Outside that dim little chamber it feels strange to find the city still standing.

The evening light stretches red over the rooftops. In the square and on the streets people are moving around her, on their way to the bathhouse or on their way home from the market. They seem to blow past in a blur, weightless as leaves on the wind.

It is only as she approaches the temple steps that it occurs to her she has been gone a full day and a night. There will need to be an explanation. Standing there alone looking up at the Augur's Temple, she feels the urge at once to laugh and to weep. She cannot tell anybody what has happened. Even if it were not forbidden, she would not be able to find the words. She has separated herself from her former home and life, as surely as if she were banished forever.

She lays a hand to her own cheek, and finds her face still glowing. Her heart hurts in its fullness. It is slowly, trippingly that she begins the long climb up to the temple, like one who has only just learnt to walk.

For you are changed now, Saba. From within and without.

III

A new morning, a new disturbance in the lower part of the city. It begins with a woman – or is it two women, or three? – who has had a dream. In the dream a great wave reared up out of the ocean and grabbed hold of the city like a greedy hand, wrenched it free from its foundations and pulled it down, down, a crumbling ruin, into the deep. Underwater the people of the city perished and its ancient fires were doused. The stones of the city scattered across the seabed. Drowned in the dark.

This woman – these women – runs out from her doorway, stands on the street corner, and proclaims her tale. Her husband cannot silence her. She grabs passers-by and begs them to listen. Her hair is unkempt and her manner is wild. A crowd gathers and grows as she shouts and gesticulates, and before long the crowd is shouting too, jostling one another, united in their fear. *The dreams of Lennes. The writing on the wall. The flaming star. And now this...*

The crowd is on the move. It gathers up women who are sweeping their front steps in the morning sunlight. It gathers up men on the way to their fishing-boats and market-stalls. It gathers up children casting stones in the dirt. Along its way the crowd finds a voice. *Our days here are numbered. Our lives here are ending. Take hold of your belongings, find your hidden coins, your warmest cloak. It's time we were gone.*

There are more here than those who came to bury Lennes in the valley of ashes, more than those who went to petition the Augur's priestesses the day before. The signs have come among them now, and even doubters must begin to wonder. Even those who care little for prophets or temples will heed their neighbours and their friends. There are those who mock, still, those who lean out of tavern windows chewing wild liquorice leaves, pointing and laughing; but the wind is not blowing their way.

By midday the procession through the city streets numbers in the hundreds. They have loaded up everything they own onto carts, pots and pans jangling, wooden stools and bundles of clothing balanced precariously. Horses snort and defecate on the cobbles, while dogs run yapping excitably through the maze of legs. The progress of this crowd through the streets towards the city gate attracts more attention, until it is impossible to move freely anywhere between the lower city and the square. And then, with a shock which ripples backwards from the vanguard to the children straggling at the rear, the whole procession draws to a halt.

The gate is closed. And not only closed, but guarded. Athraxus has learned from his miscalculation at the valley of ashes. There are enough soldiers here to put an end to any protest. For a moment anger thrills the people and it seems as though they will run towards the swords, as they did in the valley, reach to the ground and pick up stones. But all at once, with an audible groan and sigh, their courage dies like a dream at daybreak.

They stand confused, turning this way and that, looking for those who will lead them. Those at the forefront and the edges try to melt into the safety of the masses. Where are the women who began it? Where are the firebrands who will die for this cause? In their hearts the people begin to doubt themselves: and the realisation comes over them that the priests intended it this way. In the darkness in the halls of his temple Athraxus taught the whole city how to doubt, and so secured himself against dissent.

How can anything new come about, among a people who can know nothing? Who have been told to disregard the deceitful evidence of their eyes and ears and hearts? Before the guarded gate that day the people see how they have been taken in, and yet cannot overcome it. The darkness of that temple has a hold on them.

Since before the city stood, they have grasped at the scraps of divine favour thrown their way, fallen from higher tables. They have heard that their stews and their cloaks and all the love and the comfort that is theirs in the world must be thin things, by necessity. So what to believe now, in these days of dreams and prophecies and writing on the wall? How to trust these signs with clear eyes, when darkness is all the light they have been shown?

Slowly the soldiers disperse. Some among the crowd slink away, eyes averted, beckon for their children and lead their livestock back down the cobbled streets. Unwrap their burdens once more upon their beds and pause there in their inner rooms, unquiet. Others remain where they are, rocking forwards on their tired feet or sinking to the ground.

There is weeping. There is a wail of dull despair which rises up like incense to the sky.

IV

In the event of her return, accounting for herself matters less than Saba had feared. The temple has been consumed by chaos since Lennes' burial, and most of the priestesses have had far too much on their minds to notice her absence. They have been taking it in turns to sleep, and all of Aemilia's goats have been slaughtered. Though the courtyard is quieter now, smoke from all of those sacrifices still lingers. The white stones have a new skin of black ash. The place has the stunned air of having woken on the morning after a storm.

Only Aemilia's eyes accuse. Or so it seems to Saba: that her sister's blank-faced look is loaded with meaning. They say nothing to one another when they wake together on their straw mats, as they have done almost every morning for the last twelve years. They splash water onto their faces and put on fresh robes. Everything is in its place, and nothing is the same. Later, Saba takes to her vantage point on the wall beside the gate and watches what is taking place in the city below.

From the start of it her eyes are upon the armed men arraying before the gate, and she holds her breath, praying there will not be bloodshed. But the sad orderliness with which the crowd disbands is almost worse. Are they still waiting for another sign? As an eerie sound of crying rises from the square, Saba wills this grief to transform at the right time into bold action.

The priestesses of the Augur's Temple hear enough of the noise and disorder to have a sense of what has happened. They are all nervous as colts. Saba sends the younger girls to sweep the floors and clear up the kitchens. It is hard to know what else to do.

She summons what certainty she can. "We should expect more long nights up here, and more disorder down there," she tells Aemilia, Cassia and Liva, as they survey the empty sanctuary.

"They're turning towards us."

"What does that mean?" asks Liva. "If enough in the city come here and pray and make sacrifices, will the gods have mercy?"

"Who can know?" says Aemilia, very quietly, before Saba can reply.

"We should all get out," says Liva. "Before it's too late. I've been sleeping in my sandals. I'm ready."

"I packed my prettiest scarves," murmurs Cassia.

"Not yet. I'll tell you when it's time."

"Just don't take too long over it, Saba! Don't decide the moment's come when Athraxus has his knife at my throat."

"We should get Hestia what she needs," Saba says to Amelia, when the others have left. "As soon as we can, and try to end it all that way. It's the only instruction our mother left us with."

"It's already happened," says Aemilia. "While you were gone, Lennes' son was here. I passed it on to him."

That emptiness, that coldness in her face. Saba knows that she is not mistaken. She feels a momentary shadow fall across her heart: the premonition of a loss.

*

"Saba! Saba, come quickly!" The little priestess Amone is calling for her in a panicked voice. She makes towards the gate, already suspecting who she will find there. Sure enough, there he is, shoulders hunched inside his cloak and a face like a storm. His glower intensifies at her approach.

"I need to speak with you," says Athraxus.

He cannot know, she tells herself, *he cannot possibly know*. A dark vein is writhing on his forehead. She steadies herself. "What do you want?"

"You'll let me in, unless you'd rather I returned with soldiers."

She does not want him near the sanctuary, or the other priestesses. She takes him to the temple hall where they stand at a distance from one another, the long shadows of the pillars falling across the stone floor. His footsteps echo as he paces to one side, then the other. Saba wonders if he is listening for the voice of Lennes, still resounding here in the empty quiet, after all these weeks. Looking, perhaps, for a bloodstain upon the stone.

"Lies breed like fleas in the lower city ," he says shortly. "And they're twice as hard to kill. All those credulous slum-dwellers believing everything they hear. Gossips sitting around with nothing better to do. If they carry on this way they're going to put themselves in danger."

"How many did you arrest at the gate today?" asks Saba. "Will you have them executed?"

Athraxus runs his fingertips along the wooden tabletop, checking for dust. "You will remember that I told Lennes the Steward he had blasphemed the Emperor and the gods. Now we have a whole crowd of others like him. Their crime isn't diminished by being made a common thing."

Hold on, Saba wills the people of the city. Rufus son of Lennes might be carrying your deliverance in a bottle, hidden under his cloak.

"I know they've all come crying to this temple. Your coffers must be full. This has been your last day in the sun."

"That's a strange conclusion," says Saba.

It cannot be good, that he is here. Nothing that flows from Athraxus is ever good. But she thinks that there is a brittleness about him today. He must already be tired from having dealt with the morning's disturbance. She realises what he is doing, and feels a small spark of vindication. He has come here, on the attack, because he too feels the balance tipping back again. His loss is the Augur's gain.

Athraxus pauses in a patch of sunlight and stands silhouetted there, looking out into the courtyard.

"Now listen to me closely, priestess. Your mistress's fate is in your hands. You will come with me, and you will speak to her. You'll tell her to pour water on the flame of these rumours, which until now she has helped to fan. You will persuade her, as her trusted acolyte and successor, that it's for the good of the city, and the good of her temple, and for the preservation of her own life. There will be more trouble, and undoubtedly bloodshed, unless she ends it."

"Why, Athraxus," says Saba. "Are you losing your nerve?"

He moves very suddenly and very swiftly. Easy to forget, the force with which his ageing frame can bear down upon another body: the savagery of his fingers searching out weakness, seeking blood. Before she can flee or rise to resist him he has taken hold of her earlobe, wrenching her head to one side, pinching so hard that his fingernails meet through the flesh. Droplets of her own hot blood strike her cheek and she knows that her disgust for the father and her desire for the son are somehow bound together.

"Please stop,' says a trembling voice from behind the pillar. "High Priest. We'll go with you, we'll both go. We'll do what you want."

Aemilia has been listening from the shadows. Athraxus pauses and turns, just as he did at the solstice feast when Antonus spoke out for Lennes; just as he did in the valley of ashes, with Mylo in his grip. He does not let go of Saba. Her blood drips onto the stone.

"Who are you?"

"I'm nobody. Please, High Priest, let us speak with our mother."

*

"You didn't need to do that," Saba tells Aemilia as they walk close together, five paces before Athraxus, on the path through the

237

market square. "I know him. I had him. He's never bested me."

Aemilia does not reply. Saba checks the bloodied cloth she has been pressing to her own ear. "You shouldn't have been there at all. I needed you to stay and watch the others."

"You don't always get to decide," says Aemilia.

"I suppose you think we should do what he asks, then. Tell her to save her own skin."

"And I suppose you don't care any more what happens to her, or our temple, or this city."

Saba looks at her, shocked. Aemilia raises her eyes with a look of burning accusation, and Saba's stomach drops. *She knows.* Somehow she knows, and has taken it as a betrayal.

"Sister——" she stutters, but is lost. Then she feels the breath of Athraxus on her neck, the pressure of his hand.

"Save your talk. We're close." He steers them forcefully past the gardens behind the library, where breeze rustles the palms which grow along the riverbank. Courtiers in bright robes are out on a boat drifting past the palace, fanning themselves and gossiping under the shade of a canopy. A handful of children – the Emperor's sons, perhaps – run down through the reeds to trail their hands in the water. White wading-birds stretch their elegant wings.

The streets around the palace complex are strangely quiet for the middle of the afternoon. They're afraid, Saba realises: of the people, of an uprising. Of the omens themselves. A slave woman bearing a tall jug of water turns to stare at the priestesses as they pass, her eyes widening.

Into the forecourt of the House of the Magistrates. Athraxus still has his hands on their necks. Saba suspects that he would have preferred to have them leashed on ropes, or chained, like his dogs. Through the outer room, down a flight of steps, along a passageway. They accumulate guards as they go, uneasy-looking men who mutter to each other and to Athraxus, hands at their

238

belts. Groaning and shouting can be heard behind some of the doors in the underground passage. To Saba's relief they are pushed past each of these and around a corner, to the place where the Augur is being held.

"She needs four guards?" asks Saba scornfully. "She needs a door like this, padlocked and bolted? You're so afraid of an old woman?"

Athraxus signals to the guards, who begin to pull back the bolts. A cold flash of fear, suddenly. Since the Augur was taken, a part of Saba has believed that she need only hold her nerve for as long as her mistress is gone. That whatever chaos and disorder has befallen them, it will all be set right when she looks again into that lined, ancient face. But what if they have hurt her, broken her with beatings and starvation? What if she has succumbed to sickness in this dungeon? What if she looks at Saba and knows at once of that betrayal which would surely banish her forever from the temple, from the old woman's love?

The door opens. Saba shakes herself free from Athraxus's hand. "Let us go in on our own. Or we won't help you."

At her shoulder, she can feel Aemilia shaking. The chamber within is small and dim. There is an unmistakable smell of urine. A barred window near the ceiling. The door closes behind them and she wonders whether they have fallen into a trap – it would be easy to imprison them here now, too.

The Augur is sitting on the floor in the faint patch of light. Saba can see at once that she is thinner. That look she has always had, of being carved from solid rock, is diminished. They have taken away her head-wrap, and she is dressed only in sacking, sparse grey hair swept across her scalp. Aemilia, who is pale as chalk, at once begins to cry.

"There, child," says the Augur. "No need for that." Aemilia drops to the floor and wraps the old woman in a tight embrace. The Augur rocks her back and forth, glancing up at Saba as she does so. Saba lets out the breath she has been holding. The Augur's eyes, small and shrewd and hard, are unchanged. The skin about her mouth looks sore, and there are bruises on her cheek: but she seems calm, and present, and intact.

"I'm sorry, my mother. We didn't bring you any cakes."

"That's alright."

"Athraxus is in a flap."

"So I gather."

Silly, to imagine that even the Augur could know, just from a look. The knowing of another, even after a lifetime, is such a fragile thing. We part too often, and change too fast. Saba wants to sink to the ground too, to kiss the old woman tenderly on each cheek. But uncertainty holds her back.

"We didn't know what they had done to you." Aemilia is wiping her eyes on her sleeve.

"They didn't dare do anything. They need me. The people still listen when I speak."

"We've been sent here to silence you," says Saba.

The Augur laughs, resting her forehead in her hand. Aemilia looks distraught. "Mother. *Mother,* please, what more can you do now? What difference can it make, if you just do what they ask? The gods will do what they want, the people will believe whatever they choose, and you can be safe…"

"Dear child," says the Augur. "I do not fear my own destruction."

Saba looks away. "You think it will come to that."

"I patiently expect it."

That beloved face. Those wrinkled, unlovely, sun-beaten features. Saba already wants to be gone from here, from these omens of grief. Such a heavy sadness has never threatened to settle on her before. She wants more than anything to be with Mylo again, the rest of the world forgotten outside their chamber door.

"They won't have told you," she says, forcing herself back to the present moment, "but the people are turning your way."

"Is that so?"

"They've been flocking to our temple to make sacrifices. There was a riot at Lennes' burial——" She pauses, realising that the Augur may not even have known that Lennes is dead. Her mother's expression reveals little. "Athraxus brought soldiers, and there was fighting. This morning a crowd of people came to the gate, and tried to leave the city."

"Did any of them succeed?"

Saba shakes her head. "Athraxus saw to it, again."

Aemilia seems to be wilfully blocking out their words. Her head is resting on the Augur's shoulder, while the old woman fixes Saba with a piercing look.

"So tell me, priestess, how would you interpret these signs? How does the balance of the city lie?"

"It's tipping in our favour. The Emperor is leaning on Athraxus, but the people are losing faith in him. Their belief strengthens your power. Our power."

"Oh," says the Augur, almost exultantly, "there will be war in the streets, and soon!"

"I never asked you about the earth-tremor that I felt," Saba recalls, with a sting of urgency. "Before the solstice, before Lennes. That's what started all of this. Did you feel it when you were on the mountain? You never taught us about signs like that."

"Yes, I felt it. If I never taught you, it's because I never thought I'd see such an uncommon omen. Where these things appear in songs or tales, they signify that the end is near and coming fast."

"You should whisper." Aemilia glances over her shoulder at the door. "Please, Mother…"

The Augur barely disguises a smile. "My dove, everything that is whispered now will be shouted in the city square before long.

We are living in such times. Deeds done underground will see the daylight. Nothing will stay hidden…"

"Deeds?" asks Saba sharply. She does not know why, but her heart has just lurched in dread.

The Augur does not explain. She lays a hand on Aemilia's head, then says, "Tell me: that task I asked you to perform a while ago, did anything come of it?"

"It's been acted upon," says Saba. "It could bear fruit, and soon."

"If it goes wrong, for whatever reason, then you leave. You take the other priestesses and you lead them up the waterfall path over the mountain. Don't come back for me or anybody else, do you understand me? You're too young, you never carried this city. "

"*Please*, mother," says Aemilia again. "Just tell them that you misread the signs."

"And what then, dear child? Even if I believed in Athraxus's mercy, what use would it be, set against the gods' judgement? No, I will not be used by him. Since I came to this city I've spoken for its good, even when it hated me. I've counselled its Emperors as though they were my own sons, even when they turned from me. Fifty years, and I've never once been the puppet of any priest. Of any man." She sits on the floor in her sackcloth in the dirty patch of light, implacable, unbending. "For better or worse we are set upon our course together, now, this city and I."

V

"Mama," says a small voice. "Mama. I'm bleeding."

Junia stirs. There is no light in the room: it is not yet dawn. She reaches out and touches her daughter's tangled hair. "What's that, 'Tonia?"

"Blood, Mama. Help me."

A lurch in Junia's belly. The strain of an old, primal grief. She sits up in bed and, still blind in the darkness, takes Antonia's face between both hands. Her daughter's hair smells of rosemary and of sleep. Antonia is trembling. Junia kisses her on the forehead. "Come on, kitten. Let's get you clean."

Now is the time to tell her, is it not? To let her know what she has inherited with this blood? My dear daughter, do not walk the streets of this city alone, not even by daylight. The city is not yours. My dear child, when a man strikes you, do not provoke him to strike you again. Daughter, keep a bag of coins hidden in a secret place. This body is yours no longer.

Junia lights a lamp and pours out a bowl of water, takes her daughter to the inner room and helps her to wash. Fetches her a clean tunic, shows her how to bind a wadded cloth between her legs to catch the blood. Junia brews Antonia a cup of fennel tea, for the pain, then sits with an arm around her while the household sleeps. It is rare, for this sharp-clawed daughter to allow such a show of tenderness.

"Did you tell Adelfa?"

"She didn't wake up."

"I would take you to the Augur's Temple in the morning, dearest, and make a gift for your fertility. But it isn't safe. There was unrest in the city yesterday. We can pray to our own household gods, if you like, before we go back to bed."

"I'd like that." Antonia's thick, dark brows, identical to Junia's own, contract in thought. Junia is drawing a breath, preparing to whisper the necessary things beneath Antonia's hair, when she says, "Mama, is something bad going to happen to us? I know you've been trying to keep it from me. Felix told me that it's nothing to be worried about, but I don't believe him."

Junia strokes her hair. Says nothing, for a long while. To a child you would answer, *no, sweet one, there is no cause for you to fear. Whatever*

*comes I will shield you from it, I will lay my body over yours, and no harm
will ever reach you.* But Antonia is no longer a child.

"There is danger," she says at last. "It's true. There are things
at work in the city. I'll explain it all to you, someday soon. But
we're not waiting here to be cursed. There's a plan, 'Tonia, and if
it doesn't work, we'll be gone so fast you won't have time to be
afraid."

"But the guards..."

Junia thinks of her children fleeing with swords at their heels,
and turns cold.

"I'll break their necks," she says.

"They'll be afraid of you, mama."

Antonia does not seem entirely reassured, but she rests her head
against Junia's shoulder nonetheless. Lets out a low, sighing breath,
hands crossed over her belly. Her breathing becomes even and
slow, and after a few minutes Junia assumes she has fallen asleep.
Then Antonia says, "Can me and Mylo be married soon?"

*

Junia sits upon the end of the bed as an overcast dawn reaches
the horizon outside. She binds her long hair to the back of her
head, the better to flee unhindered, and wonders how it might be
done. There is no question of climbing the sheer eastern face of the
mountain, which overshadows their home. If a guard or two were
to be silenced, could the city wall be scaled by moonlight, with a
rope and a strong measure of daring?

Not with little Eryx in tow. Not with Antonus. I should have
got the children out sooner, she thinks grimly. At the first sign of
trouble. I should have been more awake.

And all at once, today beckons, and there are chickens to feed
and dough to knead and wool to dye. Antonia's betrothal to plan.

How strange, that the future simply persists in this way, like a flame still alight long after the lamp has burned dry.

When Antonus awakes he turns over and says to her at once, "One more day. The council feast is tomorrow."

She nods. He sits up, swinging his bad leg out to the side of the bed. He looks as though he has hardly slept.

"Is there news?" he asks. "I thought I heard you get up last night. Anything from Mylo, from Rufus? The priestesses? Do we know if everything is in place?"

"Nothing, from any of them. But that could be a good thing. We'll hear when it's done."

Antonus is resting his face in his hands, as though already wearied by the day's toil. "Will I be written into history as my brother's killer?" he asks.

"Don't talk that way."

"That man in the Dark Temple has kept himself lean and hungry as a wolf in winter. And how have I spent my years? Making wine and feeding chickens. If I'm remembered at all, if I'm ever carved in stone, it will be thanks to the worst act of my life."

Junia lets him singe his fingertips upon this thought until it burns out. She leans over to him, laying a hand against the back of his neck. "Antonia began her bleeding last night," she says to him, quietly. "She's ready to be betrothed. We should talk to Mylo."

He turns around, surprise and delight shining for a moment through the clouds upon his face. Junia moves her fingers through the greying hair at the back of his head.

"When you are Emperor," she says, "your daughters and your son will have such marriage-feasts."

"Junia…"

He does not want the gods to hear her, and think them boastful. She kisses him lightly. "Go outside today, old man. See the sky. Think about vineyards, and fruit trees, and chickens."

*

The birds fall quiet in the oppressive heat of the afternoon. A cloud is gathering over the mountain, a mass of ochre dust which slowly expands to hang above the city. Dogs slink indoors, their tails tucked between their legs. Shadows creep outward from the towers and the colonnade. The drapes and banners billow fitfully.

The thickness of the air stirs up a rare rainstorm. Heavy drops strike the dust. The dice-players on the bathhouse steps look upwards, puzzled. Children trawling the sea-shallows for fish stop and hold out their hands. The gossips in the marketplace exclaim and pull their shawls over their heads. No, they are not mistaken. The rain falls harder and with rising horror they see that it is staining their robes the colour of blood.

They cry out and clutch at one another's hands. They crowd into the entrance of the bathhouse, trying to take shelter, but in the meantime those inside are pushing their way out to see what is happening. Stallholders in the marketplace abandon their wares and run for cover. Old councilmen fresh from the baths, naked but for the loincloths around their waists, walk barefoot into the square and stretch out their hands in terrible wonder.

Discoloured puddles are forming in the dirt. In the lower city, gutters run red. A ragged little boy splashing his feet, oblivious, is snatched away by his mother. Those women who dreamed their dreams pause in their doorways to remember themselves.

They and those who believed them believe once again. This is the promised end, the prophesied wrath. And this time, with the proof of it raining down upon their heads, they will not be so easily turned. The fear of the hand of the gods is greater with them now than the reach of the dark priest. Doors fly open, and a shout goes up in the streets. *The curse is come! Death is come upon us!*

They are making this time for the palace, for the seat of the

Emperor himself. The rain falls harder, until it is no longer merely rain but fragments of something hard, ice perhaps, or stone, pelting through the straw rooftops of the lower city. Palm trees are flattened. An old man leaving a public latrine is struck on the head and falls down at once, never to get up again.

A procession of the Emperor's courtiers, those tall preening men with their painted eyes, comes out of the palace to find red stains falling upon their white robes from the sky. They look upwards, baffled. Then they see the crowd which is running towards them, mouths open, fists raised.

The people have no weapons but their hands and the stones they pick up. The courtiers flee, robes streaming behind them like wings, into the reeds beside the river. Not all of them are fast enough. A few fall into the hands of the crowd, who set upon them with desperate cries. Bodies stampede to and fro in a crush like frightened cattle. Cloaks are torn and blood spills into the dirt.

By the time the crowd reaches the palace steps, the rain has begun to ease. But nobody notices. They are wild now with the heady scent of their freedom. As the clouds clear and the soldiers descend upon them they pound the door with their fists, scream until they are hoarse.

A curse on the Emperor, a curse on the lying High Priest! The concourse of maggots, the two-headed beast that has brought our city to this!

*

All of this he has seen before. He has been a free man and he has been a slave. He has stood outside so many cities, and looked inward. He never intended to find himself dwelling in this city in its last days. He never meant to stay so long. Sleepless through the past nights he has dwelt on what it is to be a poet, a prophet, a priest, in such a time.

Now he watches the people storm the doors of the palace, the people who are silent in history, and its entire substance. They first told stories among themselves in the garden, and who can imagine what tales those were? Stories from before the exile, before death came into the world. All lost now in the forgetting which followed. (And Felix has forgotten too: has remained here, year after year, though he never meant to stay.) Fragments of a broken vessel folded into a cloth and hidden away.

This is the true power of the priests: to say, *your story is not your own. Your story is ours to portion out as we please, to be sold back to you at a price. You may not speak unmediated in the ears of the gods, nor hear them speak in return. You can have no relation to your own life that has not been paid for in blood at our altar.* And what choice are the people left with? Hungry and thirsty for their lives, will they not turn to the men who have made these promises?

Pay your bronze and your silver coins into the hands of the priests. Pay with your sweat and you may draw near enough to feel the heel of the gods upon your neck.

So say the priests of the Dark Temple. So say the powers which are ruling in this world.

*

The soldiers beat the people into silence. They throw some into prison, to strike fear into the rest. They slit the throat of a woman who has tried to scale the city gate. The sky above the city simmers in a crimson sunset. The High Priest Athraxus stands on the palace steps and watches all this. He throws his cloak across his shoulder, and goes back inside.

He decrees that from this day on there will be a guard set at every part of the city wall, day and night. Only a blasphemer, only one who hates the Emperor and the gods, would try to flee.

This rain is a warning to the people. Defy the priests who make supplication for you, believe these rumours born in madness, and you will bleed.

The people hear him and they despair. The Emperor is hidden within the palace walls. If the Augur is speaking, if she is giving guidance from her prison, they do not hear of it. The priestesses left behind in her temple must be too young and too afraid.

In our desperation we cry out, and beg the gods to show themselves in these evil days. To raise up more prophets among us.

May our mothers read the flight of birds, our fathers dream of things to come. Send visions to our sons. Set your burning words upon our daughters' tongues.

VI

Red rain stains the stones of the Augur's Temple the colour of dusk. Saba sits cross-legged between the pillars of the temple hall and looks up into the tumbling clouds. A strange calm settles upon her. Her nose fills with the smell of rain-struck dust.

What does a city smell like in its decline? She thinks that she knows, now. Like indolence. Like fruit past its ripeness in a bowl. Like bodies burning in the pit outside the walls. Like old ways forgotten. Like feasting in the halls while there is famine in the streets. Like an old woman shut in a stone cell with a full chamber-pot.

In the streets below, the unmistakable sounds of fighting. Saba closes her eyes. The end is before her.

And for some reason she thinks of the day when, as a little girl only a few years at the temple, she saw a parade in the city. She remembers noticing two richly dressed women sat silent and veiled upon a bier as they were borne in colourful procession through the streets. From her vantage at the side of the street she had watched them, those two mute unmoving figures amid the drummers and the dancers with their bright streamers. A man walking beside the bier declaimed in a loud voice that here were Mandane and Cassandane, the Emperor's wives, who had borne him sons and never a daughter to shame him.

She had asked her mother the Augur, "Why must those women wear veils?"

"Look at them with a prophet's eye, my daughter. They're not veiled – they are shrouded. Their husband's chamber in that palace is their tomb."

"What does that mean, Mother?"

Even to Saba's young eyes the Augur had seemed hesitant, in answering this. She had seemed sad.

"Saba, do you know that we were made late? After the creation of the world was done, after the gods had pulled the canvas of the sky in around the earth and set their creatures in the heavens and the deep, they crafted men from dust and breath. But men complained of their desires and brought petition to the gods beneath the spreading cedar-trees. So it was granted that if the men took a handful of clay from the riverbank and spilled their seed into it, this clay would take form and life. The gods did not know us, and we hardly knew ourselves.

"The men learnt in time that if they put more of their seed into the clay of our bodies, more life would grow. Our bodies were like jars to hold perfume, to hold olive-oil. We carried sons and these sons climbed out from inside us into the cold air, screaming, slippery with our blood. Since the memory of coming into the cold was so terrible to these sons, they came to despise us, and to despise their own wives when they were grown.

"This is the hate that has been with us since the beginning. We were not the gift they had wanted. Their flesh still burned and we could not extinguish them. For this reason they were further angered. Since ancient days their hands and their hearts have turned against us."

Saba had listened, and though she did not understand much of this, she felt older.

Her mother the Augur told her, "Since the beginning our bodies were the books where they wrote songs, the theatres where they staged their tragedies and comedies, the stones from which they built their dwellings. As emperor's faces are immortalised in marble, so their bloodlines, their legacies were carved from the smooth surface of our bodies.

"Our mother's voices were swallowed in their graves so we had no memory, save those few scraps they whispered beneath our hair. Our feet left no marks upon the earth. We had no names and no deeds. We had no cities and no nations. In the places we were born we were strangers without inheritance.

"This is all that is passed down to us: we know how to bleed. Because our mothers bled time after time when they were violated, when they were struck down, in the agonies of birth, our bodies know. The day comes when they begin to bleed of their own accord, in readiness.

"It was this way, my daughter, for all of us, until the coming of the Augurs. And that is why you must rejoice in the honour of belonging to this temple, and never to any man."

The Augur had bent down and beckoned her close. "Years ago, the High Priest Athraxus told the Emperor what the gods are hungry for. So he had fires lit in the catacombs, in the foundations of this city, where he keeps his contract with their appetites. These deeds are the stones the city stands on. So it is whispered between women as they comb through their wet hair at the baths, so it is muttered in the marketplace where grandmothers sit on the steps and chew willow-root.

"What is that sound, they say, *what is that weeping in the night? Why, it is Mandane, crying for her daughters, taken from her arms with their first breath. Gone before she could put them to her breast, fed to the hungry flames. And Cassandane cannot comfort her."*

*

"Saba. Sister." A hand on her shoulder. She opens her eyes and there is Liva, pale and trembling. The rain has stopped and the night is nearing. "Will you come? I need to show you something." Saba gathers her cloak about her and follows the younger priestess through the empty hall, past the flickering hearth-fire and under the shadows of the pillars. She realises that they are making for the crack in the rock of the mountain behind the temple, for the gorge where the shrine lies under the water. "Liva, what is it?"

"I came out here during the rainfall. I wanted to see if the stream had changed too, or if it still flowed clear. And I found..." She beckons Saba after her, and they climb between the rocks, taking off their sandals to tread upon the soft moss on the other side. In the twilight it is already apparent that something is amiss. The familiar rush and splash of the waterfall is muted to a slow trickle.

"It should be flowing faster, shouldn't it?" says Liva breathlessly. "The water always rises when it rains."

The pool in the gorge has all but disappeared. The rocks of the submerged shrine are now exposed, as though the ground itself grew thirsty and drank the sacred water. In horror and disbelief, Saba picks her way across to where the ancient symbols are marked out, their shapes warped now in the shallow, reddish flow that remains. The carvings seem to loom before Saba's eyes, suddenly suggestive not of comfort and the long lineage of Augurs, but of an unnamed and present menace. The stones are strangely hot beneath her feet.

"I don't dare imagine what this might mean," whispers Liva.

Saba does not answer her. "Who else knows? You didn't tell the others, did you?"

Liva turns to her, wide-eyed, and Saba's heart sinks at the prospect of facing twenty panicking girls. She knows with clarity that she does not want to be here tonight. Behind them, the dripping waterfall stains the mountainside.

*

The future persists. Dawn still comes. The morning after the rain Saba wakes again to find her lover with her.

She hears a humming on the air, as though someone has struck up a song nearby. Wrapped in a robe she slips through the empty library. The day outside is dull, though the sun has risen.

The market square is too quiet, and there is no sign of singers or musicians anywhere. Still the air seems to vibrate in Saba's ears. The water in the river is too low and too dark. A dog runs past at the bottom of the steps, barking at nothing. Her eye is caught by a flock of birds flying in a pattern like an arrow over the rooftops. They loop, then fly back across their own path, ready to begin again. Her stomach drops as she watches them dive.

She wonders if they are watching too, those priestesses of the Augur's Temple. Aemilia, eyes raw for want of sleep, rising from the floor in the sanctuary. The Augur herself, looking up through the window of her prison. What might it all mean, Prophetess, this pattern? Are the gods writing their will onto the parchment of the sky?

She could not bear to stay at the temple, to sit with the wakeful priestesses in the hall and speculate endlessly about the meaning of it all. To offer them some false kind of comfort. She knows this is neglectful; she knows she is letting them down.

Since the night of Lennes' burial Saba has made no attempt to interpret the signs. She feels the loss of it now, that lifetime in the temple, when it seemed she always knew what was to come. I am only sixteen years in the world, she thinks, and already I have had three great loves: the mothers who made me; the Augur and Aemilia; and this boy, Myloxenes. My heart will break like the banks of a river. The love of each feels like the betrayal of the others.

What would she say, my mother the Augur, if she knew what I had done? Nowhere in any of her tales did she say that it could be this way between a man and a woman. As though the rent fibres in the fabric of the world were being knit together again. Hands and hearts turned aright. I have given my whole self and lost nothing. If only we had time, this boy and I, we might build a whole new city from the ruins.

But our hours are already running short. Where shall we go together? Where should we love each other, except this city? She returns to his bed and kisses him awake. He smiles up at her, honeyed with sleep. *Your family,* she says, meaning Antonus and the others. *You should be with them.*

Wildflower, he says. *Dearest one, I want to be with you.*

She is only sixteen. Hardly begun to drink from the cup of her years, and she is tasting her first grief. She wraps her body around his and her ears hum with the coming judgement of the gods.

And he says, between kisses, *I will make you my wife.* And she does not say, *sweet boy, beloved boy, in another world, perhaps. In another life.*

VII

It is time at last: tonight he is one of the Emperor's men. His robe is silk and blue as summer sky. He lays the palms of his hands to the fabric, smoothing out each last crease, seeing that it hangs elegantly from his shoulders. It is the most expensive garment he has ever worn: he is glad his father did not live to see him spend so much gold on such a thing.

Rufus can hardly steady his hands. Before a silvered glass he tries to oil his bright curls and lighten them with powder. He always takes this same care before a feast, but there is something different about the ceremony tonight. A touch of rouge to the pale cheeks. Lacquer to the nails. A dark line drawn a little shakily to the corner of each eye. Spice and oil of cedar massaged into his skin: and he has the horrible thought that he is embalming his own body for the funeral-bier.

Gold bracelets upon each wrist. Trying to put on his many rings, he drops a handful to the floor and kneels to retrieve them, cursing. He realises that his whole body is shaking, and grips at the stones with his hands like a man aboard a sinking ship. *I was not made for this,* he breathes to the empty room. *I was not made for this.*

His father's house is dark and empty, but he finds it more bearable to be here than with Calix and Mersia. Besides, it seems right to finish here the task which Lennes started. Still on his knees, he checks the inside of his sleeve for the small bottle that he has sewn in there. "Father," he says aloud, "I expect I'll be with you again soon."

He cannot see to the end of the night. Whoever dreamed of such a thing, to have an amateur like himself take on this role in the closing act of the play? Any other actor would have made more of it. He is bound to fumble his lines, to trip over his costume or otherwise stain the dignity of the whole undertaking.

And after that, who knows. *What is rotten will be devoured. What shines will be extinguished. What is decaying must burn.* In whatever manner it comes, death might not be far from him now. Rufus has never especially thought of himself as someone who could die; he is young, and unserious. A lover of beauty. He covers his mouth with a cloth when he must walk past the slaughterhouse, or when the wind is blowing in from the valley of ashes.

To die is to enter into doubt. He cannot be sure that he will see his father in the country beyond, or know his face. There are stories of a cup of forgetting which must be drunk upon passing over. Perhaps it is better that way, to enter the under-life unburdened by the remembrance of sunlight, of dancing, of wine. Of beloved faces left behind.

*

Heads turn to take in this new man of the Emperor's council, the city's next steward. He reads suspicion in a few faces: he is still, after all, the son of the madman Lennes. But there are friends here too, ready to greet him. Already he is known as a far more profligate man than his father: they are hoping that his hold on the city's purse-strings will be looser. His choice of dress tonight was more than vanity. Let these nobles and councillors see a man who will eat and drink as one of them.

There is no note in this gathering of alarm, of solemnity. If these men have been chastened by the events of the last days and weeks, it is in their interests not to show it. If anything, their talk is louder, their laughter brasher than usual. They are eating boar-tongue tarts and quail's eggs dipped in sauce. Rufus knows that only the previous day, five of their number were injured in a riot outside the palace. It is in a chamber along the hall that the writing appeared upon the wall. There is no trouble in the city, say the sideways-glancing eyes of every man, so long as we are feasting here in our finest robes. Nothing beyond these doors is real.

The room feels too hot and too close. Men seem to loom in front of him from out of the crowd like rocks in a sea-mist, wine on their breath. He hardly hears their greetings, or his own responses. Snatches of conversation reach him as though from a great distance.

"...matter of the funds for my wife's father's villa..."

"Do send your sister my compliments, won't you? The most exquisite oysters..."

His eyes dart about: and there are the Emperor and his High Priest, sat together upon the dais. The Emperor is wrapped in a cloud of gold, hands twisting together where they protrude from his blue-trimmed sleeves. His painted face looks oddly rigid. Athraxus is leaning over to whisper in his ear.

Scanning the edges of the room, Rufus collides with his brother-in-law, who mockingly offers him a plate of stuffed figs. He shakes his head stiffly.

"What's the matter, wastrel, concerned for appearances? Don't worry, nobody expects us to mourn for long."

"You finished *your* mourning before he was even dead."

"Your father was unpopular in life and disgraced in death. Don't play righteous, brother, it doesn't suit you." Calix raises the goblet in his other hand and drinks deeply. "I've been thanking the gods I don't have to put up with Mersia tonight, the last thing I need is you whining in my ear."

Rufus feels himself beginning to shake again. *Hold your tongue, hold your tongue, remember why you are here.* "Won't there be musicians?" he asks.

"What?"

"Tonight. I was hoping for entertainment."

"They say the Emperor's not in the mood for it. Here, tell me something." Calix is standing too close. His face is flushed. "I hear you still haven't broken it off with Athraxus's son. Is it because you're sleeping with him, or are you in thrall to the Augur now, too?"

"It's not your business who I go to bed with."

"It's my business if the rot runs any deeper in your family. Brother."

"Has Mersia been telling tales on me?"

"Oh, she doesn't do that. But she might if I knocked some out of her."

The room seems to spin. Rufus wipes his forehead on his sleeve, and he knows that he is failing to hold himself together. He takes a handful of figs from the plate and crams them into his mouth. When Calix is hailed from the other side by the councillor Altecus, Rufus takes the opportunity to slip away.

He brings up the contents of his stomach in a vase outside the council chamber, knees smarting on the hard stone. He has sweated through his beautiful robe. History, he thinks, is full of conspirators: how did any of them hold their nerve for more than an hour at a time?

Rising unsteadily to his feet, he walks a little way down the passage, staying in the shadows. He looks over his shoulder before pushing open the heavy door of the Emperor's feasting-hall. The soft sound of trickling water. Sleeping birds nest amid the vines. And there on the wall – though undoubtedly many attempts have been made to scrub them away – those pale words. *From within and without.*

"Friend."

Before he can think too hard about what he is doing he bends down and kisses her cheek in greeting. As he does so he clasps her hand, delivering into her palm the little bottle from inside his sleeve. He kisses her other cheek, and holds her for a moment in the embrace before rising to his feet. She nods to him; they part, and neither looks back.

*

The figure who has followed Rufus across the council chamber pauses in the passage, concealing himself in an alcove. He is not stealthy, but he does not need to be. It happens right before his eyes, that strange meeting, and he knows beyond a doubt that something is amiss.

A moment of weighing as he draws back into his hiding place. He risks staining his own name too, by association. But will it not be all the more rewarded, to have chosen loyalty to the Emperor above loyalty to kin? He touches the mark of the Dark Temple cult, where it is burned into the skin of his shoulder. He anticipates being brought into the Emperor's innermost circle.

By the time he glances again into the passageway, Rufus and the dwarf have both vanished. What was whispered between them, what secrets shared, what sedition set in motion, he does not know. But within minutes it is in the High Priest's ear.

And he is quick, Athraxus, in his dealings.

VIII

"Is he here?" asks Mylo. "Is he alright?"

"Yes, he made it back." Junia takes his cloak as he hurries to remove it, then points him through to the inner room. "It's in Hestia's hands now. Where have you been?"

Mylo avoids her question, rushing straight through to Rufus, who is sat at the table with Antonus and Felix. He looks white-faced and shaken, but otherwise unhurt. Knowing what the task must have cost him, Mylo feels a pang of guilt for not having called to see him at the house of Lennes, before he left for the palace. The day simply seems to have melted away. Even now he is only half here, his thoughts following Saba on her path back to the temple.

"We've called you away from more important business," says Rufus waspishly.

"I'm sorry. I was at the library. I didn't realise the sun had gone down." He wants to embrace his friend, to tell him what courage he has shown. But the moment for a show of relief, if there was one, has already passed.

"*At the library*," mutters Rufus.

"It will probably be morning before we hear any news, either way," says Antonus. His face is contracted, as it often is when the pain in his leg is especially bad. He is bent over the table like a hunchback, grey hair dishevelled, shadows beneath his eyes. No man could look less like an Emperor ascendant.

Junia, who has followed Mylo back into the room, lays a hand on Antonus's shoulder. "So we wait on Hestia."

"Gods go with you, little one," says Felix. "You may save us all."

Mylo cannot wait with them, as an honest man and an honest friend would. It is not long before Rufus has fallen into a doze, tucked onto the reclining-couch in the corner. Antonus is silent and grim. They are all of them too preoccupied to look again at Mylo, to notice the flush in his cheeks, to question again his absence today and on the night of Lennes' burial. They don't know that he has abandoned his books, as well as his friends. The world has already ended, and another is born in its place.

He goes to the courtyard for air, and stands in the archway looking up at the stars above the mountain. He thinks of all the times he has gone to the sea to try and drown his massing thoughts, and then again of Saba. The saltwater on her eyelashes, her body against his in the dark. How she undoes in him every curse of the Dark Temple. *Beautiful boy. Weighed and wanted. Seen and known.*

How she brings light to what is buried in him. Mylo turns back from the archway and runs his hand along the wall, finding what is hidden behind a loose brick in the inner room: the shrine of the household gods. He cannot remember which they are, but it hardly matters.

I do not know your names, but you know mine. I cannot see your faces, but you see into the heart of all things. I have no offering tonight. I am a man upon the earth, and my hands are empty. I come here in the hope of seeing your mercy...

"Here. It's not much." Junia's voice calls him back from his reverie. She is offering him a small cup of oil. He takes it from her and pours it onto the shrine, then stands back.

She brushes his hair from his forehead, as she used to when he was small, and he tries to smile at her. Junia is looking closely at him, and he shies back from her searching gaze. Surely it must show. Surely passion must light his skin's whole surface with its glow, like the moon in the water.

"What are you thinking, with such a serious look?" asks Junia.

"About the morning, my mother, and who we'll be by then."

"You'll be who you've always been, dearest boy. Our scholar. Our son."

The weight of all he has not told them, of all that he could lose, whichever way things turn, falls upon him. He thinks, there are three things I love in this life: my family in this household, my mother in the prison of her chamber, and the priestess Saba. The ground is about to break beneath us. I cannot hold them all in these two hands.

"Mylo," says Junia, "there's something I have been meaning to talk to you about. We've hoped for it for a while now, Antonus and I. You must have some idea."

Now, Junia, now? As we peer over the brink of the fall of this city, you choose to talk of such matters, as though we are taking wine together in the calm of a summer evening? Reading his expression, she adds, "Humour an old woman, won't you? This is what will get me through to the morning."

She means more than this: she means, too, that if we are to be saved at all we must carry on stubbornly weaving pattern from the thread of our lives. We keep making our lives even from their

261

unravelling, as the gods first formed the world out of chaos. Mylo aches to give her back some small portion of the comfort she has given him across the years.

"Antonia is ready to be betrothed," Junia says. "We're hoping that you will agree to take her as your wife."

*

It is coming now, that chaos, hurrying through the city's dark streets on swift feet towards their door. A woman in a cloak, its hood covering her unpinned mass of copper hair. No gold, no jewels, no paint upon her face. Her cheeks are streaked with dried tears and a bruise is forming around her swollen eye. Not one among her many friends would have known her.

She has left behind a household shaken by her repudiation of the coward who is her husband, by his defence with his fists of his own wounded pride. She has left behind a lifetime of carefully exercised control, of strategy and craft. If the city stands another thousand years this cannot be put back together. As she passes the soldiers who now guard the city walls, she thinks of her father, and her children.

She is making for the house of Lennes, but finds it dark and empty. Myloxenes' quarters at the library are similarly abandoned. Time is not on her side: her husband will soon find out she is gone. Athraxus might already have sent his soldiers ahead of her. Breathless she runs through the moonlit vineyard towards the house of Antonus, the last place she can think to look.

She hurries close, and there is Myloxenes, talking with the wife of Antonus in the courtyard. Rufus must be here, if he is not he has already been captured. She stumbles into their midst, weeping again, words already spilling from her tongue.

You have been betrayed. Fear for your lives.

IX

Night, and all the torches are alight. The High Priest Athraxus and the Emperor Laonatus make their way together from the palace to the House of the Magistrates. They do not speak. The priest has his hands clasped behind his back, his long red robe trailing on the ground behind him. The Emperor is still in ceremonial gold. His painted eyes stare ahead into the darkness, and there is a look about him... if he were not the man upon the highest seat in the city, had he not this very night escaped death by a lucky chance, you might call him desolate.

The chief magistrate comes out to meet them. "My masters. I've had her moved, as you requested. Is there anything else you need from me?"

"Thank you, Titus, and no."

"No guards to accompany you?"

"We have nothing more to fear from her. We will speak with her alone."

They are led along the passageway to the chamber of judgement, where sentence is passed upon convicted criminals. A large fire is burning hot in the grate there, though the night is a warm one. The rows of stone benches and the seats upon the dais are empty. In the centre of the room, blindfold and gagged and bound to a stool with thick ropes, is the Augur.

The two men regard her. The priest turns to the Emperor. "Are you prepared, my lord?"

Laonatus blinks. He is very still. "I am."

Athraxus pulls the chamber door closed behind them, and then moves to the middle of the room. He unties the old woman's blindfold. She truly looks despicable, he thinks: a shrivelled hag with her wisps of grey hair, her reptilian skin, her small, bloodshot eyes. She does not even have the grace to flinch back from him. She stares, baleful, and he spits in her face for her weakness.

Laonatus stands back. Athraxus takes hold of the ropes across the Augur's chest and pulls her closer to him. The stool screeches on the stone floor. He is breathing hard. "Your charges. Sedition. Conspiracy. Treason. Betrayal. Blasphemy. False prophecy."

She makes no sound: no muffled attempt at speech, no struggling against her gag. He strikes her hard across the cheek with the flat of his hand and sees a red mark raised there at once. "Sedition! You incited rumours and unrest in this city through your puppet Lennes the Steward and through your trickery at the Emperor's dedication feast. You wrote those words upon the wall, or paid some slave to write them for you. Your priestesses have been whispering in the ears of the people. You have been breaking up the ground in order to plant an uprising. You were first imprisoned here on this charge. What do you say?"

No reply: he strikes her again, this time with his fist. The old woman's nose makes an ugly crunching noise as it breaks. Blood dribbles down into her gag. He recalls Lennes the Steward spitting blood and loose teeth out of his mouth. Athraxus is beginning to sweat in the heat of the fire. He removes his red robe and lays it on one of the benches. The Emperor, who has done nothing but stand to the side and watch the Augur, blinks slowly. The paint around his eyes has begun to smudge and run.

"Conspiracy. Not an hour ago we apprehended an assassin within the walls of the palace. She wasn't acting alone. But in the end it hardly matters whose hands delivered the poison: this was your doing, through and through. You have corrupted the minds of the weak to do your bidding. Confess to this and the manner of their deaths might be more merciful."

The flicker of an expression, for the first time. The Augur's eyes dart from left to right. She juts her chin forward and makes a muffled noise, perhaps asking for the removal of her gag, but he does not acquiesce. Athraxus takes hold of the ropes across her chest and pulls her yet closer, tilting back to the stool so that her face is inches from his. "*Treason*," he breathes. Her eyes move sideways again, this time towards Laonatus, who is silhouetted against the fire. She is breathing unevenly, wincing as blood bubbles in her nostrils. "You were sworn to the service of your emperor. Your temple exists only to serve his throne. But you wanted his power for yourself, didn't you? *Didn't you?*" He shakes her and watches her head roll queasily upon her shoulders. "You've coveted power since the day you arrived in this city. You have been a friend to the Emperor the way a crocodile is friend to a child on the riverbank."

"And I have been such a fool," says Laonatus.

He is still stood, unmoving, before the fire. He raises his hands to rub his eyes. Far below, somewhere in the bowels of the magistrates' house, someone is howling.

"Do not believe it. If it weren't for your greatness of spirit, my lord Emperor, her deception would never have worked. If you hadn't so wisely, so diligently sought her guidance over the course of your life…" Athraxus grasps a handful of the Augur's thin hair, and pulls her head back. "…you couldn't have been so despicably betrayed."

The Emperor's chest rises and falls rapidly. For the first time, he steps closer to the seat. His golden eyes are huge in the firelight. He looks at the choking, bloodied Augur, and then at Athraxus. He says, "Tell me again."

"Since she crawled out of the gutters of this city and placed herself in the highest seat of that temple, her appetite and ambitions have known no bounds. She has invoked the names of gods who never spoke for her hearing. She has brought their names down upon you like hammers upon stone. Who gave you your first education, my lord Emperor, and encouraged your interests, and taught you how to understand the world?"

"She did."

265

"Who directed your hand as you played the game of warfare? Who called on the heavens to foresee the strategies that would give you an advantage? Who oversaw your advances and retreats, your victories and losses?"

"She did, Athraxus."

"Who claimed the gods' authority for advice given about trade, about investment, famine, construction, the drawing up of edicts and laws? Who invoked the gods' guidance over matters of justice, appointments to positions of influence, and the way we kept our festivals? She has called her words their own. Her own plans, her own wishes — she has brought them to bear by these treacherous means. This is how she has blasphemed the Emperor and the gods." His voice swells and echoes through the chamber, so that he seems to surround the patch of firelight on all sides. "She has ruled this city in all but name."

"I see it," breathes Laonatus. His eyes well with tears.

"Of course you do, my lord Emperor. Why else would you have started to reject her influence in your later years? She has felt her hold loosening."

"I began to reject her influence. I began to see what she was."

"And so she has been driven to these desperate measures, to the spreading of insurrection, even to your murder."

The Emperor shivers with a horror that is almost pure pleasure.

"We know you," says Athraxus. "*Prophetess*. We see you. And what are any of you, but liars? Wasn't your temple built on false foundations, back at the beginning? *What are the names of the gods?*"

"*Their names are not ours to utter,*" replies the Emperor at once.

Athraxus rips a handful of the Augur's hair from her head. "*Shall we see the faces of the gods?*"

"*Their faces are hidden from us.*"

The priest tears out another handful of her hair. It flutters down like seed from a sycamore tree. She is struggling now, rocking the stool to and fro upon its legs, contorting her face to try and free it of the gag. Tauntingly, Athraxus covers her ears with his hands. "*Shall we hear the voices of the gods?*"

"*They do not speak for our hearing.*"

"So it is. What will you do with her?"

The Emperor is quiet. He takes another step closer, and regards the Augur with his head tilted slightly to one side. There is a certain pity in his gaze. "Let me speak to her," he says.

Athraxus obeys, lowering the stool back to the floor, unpicking the knotted cloth from her mouth. He is watching the Emperor's face with close attention. The Augur's lips and teeth are stained with her own dried blood. She seems to be trying to speak, but no sound escapes her throat. She coughs, her whole body wracked with it, and croaks again.

The Emperor seems faintly disgusted with this display. Then, from nowhere, he lets out a laugh. "Isn't she absurd? How funny, all this trouble over a creature like this. What do you say, old woman? Grandmother? Are you going to make a prophecy for us?"

The Augur gapes, but she cannot make a sound. Laonatus steps forward, and with an air of childish curiosity reaches out to lay his hands over her eyes. Robbed now of her sight the old women becomes still. Laonatus smiles his beatific smile. "I was blind for a time," he says. "But I see you now as you are."

He moves back from her, and makes towards the fireplace. He pulls out a long iron poker which has been resting on the hearth. The pointed end glows white-hot. The Emperor tests its weight in his hand. Turns and plunges it with sudden savage strength into the Augur's eye.

Why did the gods create us?

This secret is hidden in darkness.
This riddle robs our days of their peace.
This wound pierces the deepest places of our hearts.

DESOLATION

I

"Junia," he says. "I can't run."

A moment alone with her, in the disarray of their fleeing household in the night. Mersia has gone. Felix is running to and fro from the kitchen, bundling food into sacks, aided by Antonia. Rufus is in the doorway with Eryx, swinging him by both arms and chatting to him with a false, calming cheerfulness. Mylo is helping a desperate Adelfa coax her cat from a crack in the wall.

Junia pauses in the act of rolling her daughters' tunics into a bundle. Her long hair, which has come unbound, hides her face. Antonus touches her gently on the wrist. "We all know it. What are you going to do, scale the wall? Outrun the soldiers? You'll barely stand a chance as it is, let alone if I'm with you."

"We'll hide in the city for tonight. We'll go to Renna."

"Her husband's with the council. You don't know what he'll do."

"The lower city, then. There are plenty of people there who believe the Augur. They'll hide us."

"You can't stay in the city, Junia. I won't have it."

"Then what should we do?" She turns to him, eyes flashing fiercely. "This isn't all about you, Antonus. They'll be looking for us. They'll be coming for us, before dawn. If we were going to flee the city we should have done it weeks ago. Now we'll have to hope that the people rise up against the Emperor before…"

"Before the end comes."

The face of Lennes the Steward comes to his mind. The way he trembled as though the fearful sights he spoke of were unfolding before him. Antonus has believed the Augur for many days: but he has not gone so far as to imagine a world in which Lennes' words come to pass. The gods are not appeased, and so their anger must fall upon the city. *What is rotten will be devoured. What shines will be extinguished. What is decaying must burn.*

There is no time to mourn the death of that other world, the one which sprung tentatively into being the night Aemilia first came to call, and died less than an hour ago with the arrival of Mersia's message. Antonus the merciful, Antonus the just, sitting on a golden throne. Power held in his right hand. What a laughable thought. That future perished in the fire long ago.

He wonders if he is in his brother's thoughts tonight. Laonatus will feel the betrayal like a blade in his heart. He will give the order for my execution, thinks Antonus, and then watch with tears in his eyes. He will turn away so tenderly as my children are tied into sacks weighted with stones, and sunk into the sea.

*

No time to bid farewell to the villa, to each beloved stone. There is the place beside the hearth where Antonia and Adelfa lay in their cradle. There, Eryx took his first steps. This is the worn surface where Felix kneaded loaves, this is where Junia would sit and sing to the strings of her instrument when the stars came out. All her bright cloths are still hung swaying in the night breeze. *Happiness is a bird of rare beauty.* Antonus pockets his household gods and blows out the last lamp.

What will happen to their home now? Who will walk these rooms, who will sleep in these beds? The stones, thinks Antonus, they will remember us. Whatever comes to pass here they will hold on to the warmth of our firelight, the sound of our songs, since the fullness of our lives has overflowed here. We are woven into the cloth of this place.

The cicadas are chirruping. They leave the chickens sleeping in their coop ("Can't we take them with us?" begs Adelfa) and set off down the hill through the vineyard. They have nurtured these vines together for eighteen years. Sprinkled water onto their roots on hot days. Stripped back the dead branches to make way for new growth. Harvested the fruit, poured it into the presses. And it was Laonatus – how strange, still, to think of it! – Laonatus who gave us this gift. How tightly they are bound together in your life, Antonus, the blessing and the curse.

Their progress down the hill is painfully slow. Felix draws the small cart which bears their bundles of belongings, and Mylo carries Eryx on his shoulders. Adelfa clutches her struggling cat. Antonus clenches his teeth as he drags his bad leg over uneven ground. He catches Junia looking sideways at him, and knows that he does not have to say it aloud: whatever happens, take the children to safety. I am old. I have already lived through one disaster, which is surely one man's share.

Safety can mean nothing more at this moment than being gone through the gate of the city. Whatever waits outside those bounds must be met another day. Antonus feels the dawning of a fateful calm. I cannot run out on the plain either, he thinks, nor climb the distant mountains, nor labour for bread, nor protect my children.

They make it as far as the colonnade, where noise from the city beyond causes them to pause, cautious. By the light of the moon it is possible to see movement somewhere in the region of the square. Many voices are rising in contention. Then, the blink and flare of torches.

"Mama," whispers Adelfa, "why have we stopped?"

Rufus, close to Mylo's shoulder, is ashen with fear. "Do you think they're coming for us? Are they sending out soldiers?"

'I don't think so." Junia is watching the scene, tense. "We should get a closer look. We need to know what's happening. I'll go quickly, I'll cover my face."

"I'll go too," says Felix at once.

Antonia takes a tight hold of Antonus's hand. His fierce daughter is trying to conceal her trembling. "Junia…" he begins, but he cannot offer to take her place. His leg will not carry him. He has never felt more helpless.

"Stay here. If you hear anyone coming, find cover. Don't go back to the house. They'll search for us there first."

*

Felix and Junia stay close together in the torch-lit crowd, alert to one another's movements. Neither of them was present at the Augur's feast or at the Emperor's. But they feel now what it is to be in a city on the brink of ruin. There is a fever in the people here tonight.

Far ahead on the bathhouse steps, a figure is shouting, but his words are indistinct, drowned by the rumble of the crowd and the pulsing beat of a drum. It is the High Priest. Junia turns around, shawl held to her mouth, and sees the faces around her contort with anger. The people are not here tonight to hear Athraxus, but to silence him. Some of them bear scars from the valley of ashes, from the soldiers at the gate, from the day of the rain. Their mingled protests grow louder until they converge to a furious roar.

"*Open the gate!*" bellows a woman's voice somewhere close at hand, and the cry is taken up by those around her.

"*Open the gate!*"

"*Let us go!*"

And then, astonishingly, from some anonymous quarter of the

crowd: *"Death to the tyrant Emperor! Death to the shadow-god's priest!"*

The drumbeat cuts off abruptly. Junia's heart leaps to her throat and then her body is jolted violently sideways. The crowd sways and howls like a forest in a high wind. Soldiers have pushed in among them to strike down all those who have given voice. Junia grabs for Felix and for a moment she has only the corner of his cloak to cling to, shipwrecked in the sea of jostling bodies.

People are screaming and fleeing in all directions: but Felix takes hold of Junia's arm, steadying her and then pulling her forward through the chaos. He seems hypnotised by something he has spotted up ahead.

An acrid taste on the air. A smell like the ancient entrails of the earth. In the corner of Junia's vision sparks fly towards the stars. Spit, flare, swallowed by the dark.

The priest has disappeared. There is a gibbet on the steps. The figure which hangs from it is no bigger than a child. Her are feet swaying high above the ground, in the vast empty air.

II

What does death smell like, when it comes to the city? Priestesses, you know. Since you came to the temple you have dealt in death. You dream your dreams in its shadow. Your hands are never clean. The business of the gods is always bound close to the business of death.

Tonight the gods are about their business. From the wall of the Augur's Temple the priestesses look on, as the gods themselves must watch the distant world of men from their own realm. As the crowd in the square parts to reveal the little body suspended on high for all to see, Saba closes her eyes. Silently intones, for Hestia, a lament. *The grave is open before me. I am to make a journey...*

When she opens her eyes again, she finds herself looking looks into Aemilia's white, sombre face. The other priestesses are close by, huddled together in their distress. Some of them have brought their small bundles of belongings down into the courtyard, ready to flee. They are waiting for her to give them the order.

She tries to gather herself. The picture of the new city she glimpsed that night at the house of Antonus has just been whipped away like smoke on the wind. *I must have read the auspices wrong,* she thinks numbly. *I could have sworn it was a good sacrifice. Whatever vow the gods have made...* Yes, she could have sworn the gods held Antonus in their favour.

Was there more you could have done? If your eyes and your heart hadn't been turned elsewhere, could tonight have seen the Augur's hopes come to pass? She feels Aemilia's gaze on her, and wonders if her sister is thinking the same thing. In the square below, soldiers have moved in among the crowd. Screams cut into the night.

Saba casts off everything that might have been, and finds her voice. "Listen to me now. The city's lost. I need you to take the others—"

"Our mother," Aemilia interrupts harshly. The noise from the square is growing louder.

"We'll take her with us," Saba insists, "I'll find her..."

But Aemilia's face is still like stone. "Will you? Sister, can you promise me? Can I believe your promises now?"

Saba flinches back as though slapped. She has never heard Aemilia speak like this before.

"You broke the oath you swore to the temple. If you go into the city now, you'll be searching for *him*."

The sharp words catch Saba by the heart, and she finds herself at the brink of tears. She covers her mouth with her hand. She hears Aemilia as though from a great distance.

"We don't know what's happened to them. Myloxenes, and Antonus, and the others. They might already be dead."

274

Saba turns away. In front of the palace the crowd swells and seethes like a pot about to boil. And what is that sound? Is it coming from the city, that insistent, troubled ringing? She thinks, the sky is being torn apart, the gods themselves will come thundering from out of the clouds.

With a great effort she brings herself back to what is required of her. Behind Aemilia, the priestesses are waiting for her word. Concealing the break in her voice she calls their names and beckons them closer.

"Cassia, Eris, Liva! Listen to me. It's time. I need you to lead the others through the shrine-under-the-water, the steep way up the mountain. Climb as high as you can before daylight, then take cover and wait for us there."

"Where will you be?" demands Eris. "Aren't you coming with us?"

Saba glances at Aemilia. "We're going to find our mother. We're going to free her and bring her out."

The priestesses are looking at one another. They exchange whispers. Cassia looks around at the others, arms folded tightly across her bundle of possessions, then blurts out, "Saba, we don't want to go up the mountain. Not where the water disappeared." Her eyes have grown round as coins. "The gods don't want us going there anymore. That way isn't safe."

"The gods are closer on the mountain, aren't they?" puts in Eris. "In the grove and in the cavern. We think maybe they're here now, in our realm, and they're coming for the city."

"And there's another omen today." Liva is quiet and serious. "Can't you hear it? The mountain is singing."

*

The sky above the city is full of darkness. From their hiding place

275

in the ruin of a house near the lower city, Antonus, Junia, Mylo and the others watch for a dawn which does not come. Eryx is sleeping, thumb in his mouth, head resting on his mother's shoulder. Rufus is sat against the wall, head in his hands. With every renewed sound of footsteps or of shouting from outside, Adelfa begins to shake and cry.

To Mylo, huddled by the window with Felix and Antonia, each passing minute is unbearable. He does not know what has become of the priestesses, whether even now their temple is being torn to the ground. Perhaps they have met Hestia's fate. It is impossible to tell from here what is happening in the upper city: it could be that Athraxus has brought the whole crowd under his heel.

Mylo wonders if Saba is still alive to fear for him, as he fears for her. In his mind she is at once immortal, a being no mere man might destroy – and fragile, slight as a lantern-flame. After all, when it comes to it, she stands barely as high as his father's shoulder. His trembling hands twist together. And then there is his mother, probably still supine, oblivious in her dim perfumed chamber. He is dumb and helpless as a child, cowering while they perish.

He is about to stand to his feet, to announce action – any action – over the agony of waiting, when a violent tremor shakes the ground. Instinctively he seizes Antonia in both of his arms and dives for the doorway. The roof of the small dwelling is sliding sideways. Adelfa is screaming, Felix cursing at the top of his lungs. Mylo has a momentary impression of Antonia's body pinned beneath his, quivering, alert. Stones clatter past them as the road slants and cracks. A wall collapses close at hand and a palm tree sways, torn up by its roots.

Even after the ground falls still, Mylo is frozen with shock. Antonia recovers first, shaking him until he releases her then crawling back through the rubble, calling for her parents. He is relieved to hear both of their voices answer.

"Are we all here? Is anybody hurt?"

"You'll have to help me..." Felix and Junia between them lift the beam which has fallen and wedged Antonus to the wall. He feels about for his staff and rises with a grimace. Panicked yells and screams fill the air from the surrounding houses. There are grazes on Adelfa's arms and face. Another low, deep rumble threatens in the ground.

"Look!" Rufus, covered from head to foot in dust, raises a hand and points over Mylo's head towards the mountain.

"All the gods above," breathes Felix.

The darkness in the sky has a shape. It is rising now in a column like a towering pine tree from the top of the mountain, spewing out ash and ochre-coloured earth. There is some noise of ringing or whistling on the air, rising in pitch now, punctuated by deep notes of thunder. In the unnatural dark the people of the city crawl from their ruins to stare into the sky.

Junia encloses Adelfa in her arms. "What in the world- "

"We need to get out," says Felix. Mylo has never seen him afraid of anything before. The slave clutches at his chest as though ready to rend his clothes. "I've seen this before. We need to get out *now*."

Footsteps hurry past them. "*The gate!*" someone cries. "*The gate's broken open!*" The sound of strangled cheering rises out of the wreckage. Within moments there is a rush of people through the rubble-strewn street, women hiking up their long tunics, men sheltering their heads beneath their arms, children wailing with dust in their hair.

Many of them carry nothing. They have no time to salvage their belongings, such is their desperation to be gone. They are stripped bare of everything but their lives. The smoke in the sky has revealed who they are, as smoke and other signs reveal so many things. Words of gods and hearts of men. A shock like lightning shakes Mylo's bones.

He turns to Antonus, to the patient face which has welcomed and heard and counselled him since he was a small boy. The older man is covered in dirt and dust, his whole body contorted with pain. His stick shakes beneath him, a grim-faced Antonia supporting him on his other side. Antonus seems to know, before Mylo speaks, what he is about to say – and extends a hand, resting it for a moment on Mylo's head, as though in blessing. As though in release.

"My mother, she has nobody…"

"I know, boy. Go to her."

Mylo kisses him swiftly on the cheek. No time for any other goodbyes, if that is indeed what this is. The sky is falling and he is running, running through the wreckage towards his father's house.

III

He cannot pass the wall near the old palace, since the surrounding buildings have been felled and scattered by the quake. There are jagged stones everywhere, thick tree trunks criss-crossing the path. Beyond the old palace gardens the low river seems to bubble and boil. He tries to climb a section of the wall which still looks solid, but slices his hand on a broken brick. He withdraws cursing, clutching his bleeding hand to his chest, and sets off at a lurching run towards the square. From there perhaps he can follow the river down past the library and the palace complex.

He weaves his way through a herd of panicked cattle, turned loose in the chaos. In his mind's eye he is picturing Laeyla's chamber. Will the shuttered windows and hanging drapes keep the smoke at bay, or choke her faster? Nearing the square he catches sight of a woman who is tenderly cradling a child too still to be sleeping. He is about to fall down beside her – for what purpose he does not know – when a man grabs his arm.

"Here, friend, are you coming to the Dark Temple?"

There are a group of them, filthy and sweating in the heat. They are shaking with a strange exhilaration. It is hard to tell beneath the dust whether they are young or old, renegades from the lower city slum or noblemen he might have once sat beside at a feast.

"What-?"

They tug at the sleeves of his robe. All around these men are accosting others, urging them back into the city even as they flee for their lives. There are women with them too, laughing, dancing on light feet as though they are celebrating the solstice festival, not caught in the midst of a great calamity.

"Haven't you heard? This judgment, it isn't for us. It can't harm us. The gods are here among us."

"We're going to string up the High Priest by his neck."

"We're going to dance on the ruins of his temple. There won't be a stone left standing!"

Mylo does not know whether they are holy or mad. He tries to push past them, his thoughts still with Laeyla, but then over the heads of the broiling crowd he catches sight of something on the far side of the square.

The library is on fire. Slowly, the sight holding him in horror, he finds himself drifting towards it. Great gouts and plumes of smoke, a noise like dogs feeding on a carcass. The flames snap and snarl and growl. A flare, and there go the scrolls on the high shelves, the records of emperors past, the precious pages over which he has laboured through many long nights.

All of his work. The hours given to it, the meticulous care, the problems puzzled over, the small satisfying revelations. Years of his life. The little room with his desk and his piles of notes, the place where he now knows he first went in search of love and home. The bed where he lay with Saba. Mylo realises that he is weeping. Standing in the firelit chaos of the square, ash and debris falling all about him, weeping for his books.

He comes to himself. Backing away, still bleeding, still bent with grief, he fights through the thick smoke towards the river. A soldier is beating a woman with his belt while she screams and cries for him to stop. Two dead men lie atop each other on the ground next to her. So much within his sight that is pitiful, and time only to care for one life.

Lights are lit within the palace. Inexplicably there seems to be nobody either coming or going at its gate. Downriver, breathless now and gasping in the heavy cloud of ash, he is relieved to see the house of Athraxus still standing. It does not seem to have attracted the ire of the crowd: they have assumed that the High Priest will be at his temple. Mylo hopes fervently that they are right, that they will mete out what Athraxus deserves, out of his hands, out of his sight.

The dogs are not chained to the wall and the slaves have gone. The ground trembles as he makes his way inside, and he braces himself against the walls of the passageway. Two of his father's vases fall from their alcoves and smash upon the floor.

"Mother!" he calls. "*Mother!*" But there is no reply.

Then from the corner of his eye he catches a movement in one of the adjoining rooms. He stumbles to the doorway. A cloaked figure is crouching in the corner. Two of his father's dogs lie motionless upon the floor, as though sleeping. How can they be sleeping through all of this noise? The figure in the corner lets out a snarl. It is Athraxus. His hood is drawn up and his eyes are wild beneath it. Scattered in front of him are objects of value and import: his High Priest's seal and ceremonial knife, some small faceless idols from the temple, the gold-inlaid bowls he had inherited from his own father. He seems to have come up short, somehow, in the midst of wrapping these things in cloths and packing them into a bag. At Mylo's appearance he has become quite rigid, except for the flickering of a vein in his temple. He looks as though he has had a fit.

"You've been crying again," says Athraxus. "Haven't you, boy? The stain of it is on your face." He licks his teeth twice, in rapid succession. "Soft boy. Spoilt boy."

Mylo realises that there is blood pooling on the floor beneath the immobile dogs. Their throats have been cut. There is blood on the blade of the knife. So there is mercy then, he thinks dimly, even in Athraxus. He takes a step forward but his father snarls again and flinches into the wall, a cornered, savage thing.

"I'll take what's mine," says Athraxus, and he begins frantically rummaging about the floor, as though searching for something particular among his belongings. Whatever it is he cannot seem to find it. He throws the bag aside in frustration. "Have you seen my son?" he asks with sudden intensity, his hood falling back from his face as he looks up at Mylo. "He keeps running away. I'll beat him when he returns." A string of saliva is hanging from the side of his mouth.

"I know him. I've seen him. He won't be coming back."

"To his father's house? He'll be made to. That cripple, he will answer…"

Mylo moves back towards the doorway. His knees are weak and he cannot stay any longer. "You have lost the city," he says to the man upon the ground. "Burn, if you like, or run away. You have no power here any more."

The house is shaking again. He feels his way along the wall to the drapes which mark the entrance to his mother's chamber. Everything is dark. He cannot see her but he can smell her, the thickness of her perfume and her sweat, even beneath all the dust and smoke. His hands guide him to her bed, and he crawls there on his knees, coughing. He hears a murmur. He finds her face and then her hand, pressing it in his own until he feels a response. He laughs in relief. He rests his head against her breast, feels its rise and fall. Breathing life, breathing courage into him again.

"Laeyla," he says. "Mother. It's time."

*

Never before, since the day that the first woman calling herself Augur lit a fire on the rocky outcrop above the city, has the temple been abandoned. Tears roll down Saba's face, to be brushed roughly away on the back of her hand. That torch, that flame, handed to her from a long line of foremothers. It is on her watch that the fire will finally burn out.

A heavy thing to bear. To be the link that shatters and breaks the chain. The little girl who first walked up the steps to this temple, who stood awed beneath the shadow of its stones and applied herself so eagerly to the acquiring of its wisdom, could never have foreseen such a fate.

The priestesses straggle down the steps. Some of the other girls are weeping too. Saba has been stern with them, has had them lay down the little treasures they would have brought along. She has allowed only provisions, sandals and cloaks. They did not want to go over the mountain, but suddenly the path through the city looks just as treacherous. The chaos in the streets has spread; the square and the road in front of the gate are heaving now with torchlight and noise.

She wonders what has become of Athraxus in all this, and feels a surge of jubilation. The High Priest made one last mistake, in thinking that the death of a conspirator would quiet the crowds. Instead he has set his own end in motion. Saba hopes he is fleeing even now through the back streets, bare feet bloodied, cloak in rags, the hunt at his heels. Oh Athraxus, she thinks, you ought to have asked my counsel.

If this is destruction from within, then the rest must follow. Yes, Saba, grieve for the hope that failed, grieve for Hestia and all who will meet their end tonight: but rejoice in this. The city is waking up. This time there will be no retreat, no surrender to the old powers. The day of judgement is here at last.

If the crowd can force open the gate, the priestesses can escape along with them. People are surging through the upper city, met by a line of soldiers. Firelight illuminates the flash of swords, and Saba knows that they ought not to have gone this way, ought instead to have risked coming face-to-face with the furious gods on the mountain. From above it had looked possible to navigate a path through the square and towards the House of the Magistrates, but down here this feels like nonsense. The familiar streets have been transformed to an underworld realm.

It is too late. They have already reached the bottom of the steps, and are enveloped by chaos. A press of frantic bodies squirms on every side. Saba loses her view. The priestesses are scattered like a brood of chicks. Liva clings to Saba's arm, and someone else seizes a handful of her cloak. With quiet clarity beneath the tumult she thinks, I have failed again.

Some in the crowd are trying to run away, fleeing towards the alleyways and back to the lower city. But others are beyond such fear of men. They scramble towards the soldiers wielding sticks and stones. They fling themselves at the impregnable city wall like caged tigers. The singing of the mountain, the high-pitched whistling in the air, is unmistakable now: and the people's cry seems in harmony with this terrible music. *Let us go! Let us go!*

The foundations shiver. Saba cries Aemilia's name, the names of the priestesses. The press of bodies is suffocating, and the air itself seems suddenly thickened, hot. Saba presses her sleeve to her mouth and grasps at Liva's hand. Then the earth shakes as though a giant below their feet has woken and come unchained.

The carts in the marketplace overturn. People slide this way and that, clinging to each other. Soldiers drop their swords to take cover. Tiles skitter down the bathhouse roof and stone walls crumble. Clay jars shatter with a crash. A line splits the square from one side to the other, a thin crack in the ground which hisses with vapour.

Saba has flung herself to the ground, her body shielding Liva's. There is a moment of cavernous quiet. And then, amid the rubble, an eerie sound of laughter. A few faces light up around her as people raise their heads, flushed and ecstatic. Their eyes look black, like those of dancers at the solstice. A seething, febrile energy is coming over the square. They have smelled it, thinks Saba. Not just their freedom, but their deliverance. The fall of the former order.

A child squats in a ditch, wailing. Nearby a woman weeps over a man who will not wake. Many are rising to their feet, bloodstained, covered in dust. The air smells like the sulphurous cavern on the mountain. Saba sees blue lightning crack the clouds overhead. Sparks leap among the people like a blessing.

A roar of noise begins to swell again, triumphal this time, as the soldiers scramble to regroup. She tries to pull Liva back, still desperately straining around for a glimpse of the others. Time seems to loosen, losing its- shape, and the crowds look endless as a sea. She could search forever and never find her priestesses. Lights extinguished by the quake are flaring again at the palace, and Saba wonders if the Emperor, still surrounded on all sides by his whispering, fluttering advisers, might send reinforcements to the gate. He may not yet know that the battle is lost.

Could it be that the Emperor and all his household and his council and his priests will flee too, tonight? That the whole foundation upon which the city is built has been cracked to its heart? Men begin to throw loose rocks at the statues in the entrance to the library, jeering as the stone heads of former Emperors crack and crumble. Then somebody is running inside with a torch held aloft in each hand, and moments later the fire has caught, an orange glow filling the high windows as centuries of scrolls and charts and maps and ledgers give up their secrets to the flames.

And then Saba sees him, though the world is in ashes around her. Silhouetted against the flames of the burning library. He is close enough to call for. If she cried out his name, now, into the desolate city square, he would turn.

Beloved boy. In another life.

IV

A dizzying blow to the side of her head brings Aemilia to the ground. The crowd roars and the fire inside the library climbs higher. There is blood on the ground, and Aemilia realises that it is her own. She tastes it on her lips. She watches the soldiers wielding swords and clubs cut down those in their path. There is the pretty priestess Cassia, the songbird, her head sliced cleanly from her shoulders.

The earth is still shaking and there are bodies all around. Aemilia finds that she can crawl. Across the stones, through the forest of legs, beneath the choking cloud of smoke. It smells like sulphur. It smells like the vapour from inside the fissure in the mountain. Hot blood trickles down her neck and soaks her robe. She has feared for so long, feared pain, feared change and loss, and now it is finally come she feels a hollow sort of calm. As though she has been scraped out of her own body, like an oyster from its shell.

Drapes and flags are burning on the colonnade. People are flooding upwards from the lower city, their lives and households bundled in their arms and loaded onto carts. A toothless man with silver hair throws his staff into the path of a soldier's horse and the animal buckles, throwing its rider. The crowd swarms the fallen man, stones in their fists.

Somehow Aemilia finds her feet again. She follows the length of a wall, hardly knowing what direction she is moving in. She sees boats, heavy-laden, moving out onto the water far below. Bodies jostling at the edge of the harbour, arms outstretched, screaming.

All of this has happened before. All of this will happen again, in another city, in another age. Aemilia closes her eyes. She feels as though she is about to fall from a very great height.

When she opens her eyes again it is to see a family of nobles fleeing before her with their retinue of slaves, all in their nightclothes, their dogs dragged behind on chains and their children protesting. They have tried to bring all of their wealth along with them: their gold candlesticks and jade trinkets, ivory combs and silvered mirrors and silk cushions. Their ornamental songbirds in wrought cages. The slaves struggle under the weight of it all. Aemilia staggers onward and men are running left and right now with the looted wealth of the households of the upper city.

And there before her is the House of the Magistrates, with its doors torn down and its walls charred black. Prisoners shuffle blinking into the night, their ankles still shackled. A crowd is already inside, torches held aloft, shouting for the Augur.

Aemilia is suddenly swifter and stronger than any of them. Something flares in the emptiness of her chest, a fire she did not light, a word she never thought to speak. It sears and scorches her. It compels her forward as though another creature has clawed inside her skin. She pushes her way through the mass of people, through the pool of torchlight into the darkness beyond. Runs down the flight of stone steps, along the passageway to the cell at the very end.

The door, like the others, has been broken open. But the prisoner still sits inside. The glow of the burning city at the barred window casts a red light upon her. The Augur is sat unmoving upon the floor. Her robes are filthy rags. The straggling grey hair has been shorn from her head. She has no eyes.

Aemilia falls to her knees, sobbing. She is faintly aware of the old woman moving towards her, of the fingertips which feel for the contours of her face. Blood is crusted down the Augur's cheeks. Where her eyes were, there are scorched, gaping pits. Flesh soft and red like a peach when the stone is torn from the centre.

Her voice is low, and hoarse, and kind.

"Oh, my dear. You have lost everything, haven't you? That means you are ready to be an instrument of the gods."

V

So tear it all down, Prophetess. Take your rage and your grief at all that you have lost in your lifetime and turn it to a fierce strength. Turn it towards the stones of that other temple, and tear them to the ground.

A word has come to you. Cry out to the people, and tell them what they have lost. Tell them what has been stolen from them. Tell them that in the beginning there were men in darkened tents who conspired to own for them the secrets of their hearts. Tell them that ever since, these secrets have been sold back to them at a price, that the source of their lives has been hidden from them, shrouded in smoke and drowned in blood. Tell them that the heart of this city has been sick and ailing, since the beginning.

Tell them how the priests of this temple – see them now, as they flee! – have fed upon their very flesh. Tell them how these priests covered the lamp of the truth until its light no longer shone upon the city, and every street and household was in darkness. Tell them how these priests have feasted on their offerings and become drunk on the libation-wine. Tell them how these priests have made crooked what was straight and made impenetrable what was once simple. Tell them how these priests have laid such burdens on them, until their backs were broken and bent and they crawled like beasts.

Tell them that the gods never belonged to this temple. Tell them that the gods never sold their truth to any man for a payment of blood. Tell them that the gods, who walked among us once, have never knelt in any throne-room of this world or kissed the ring of any emperor.

Tell them that now is the time of unveiling. Now is the time of lifting the priestly robes to show the maggots and worms which crawl within. Now is the time to stop burning incense and smell the stench of rotting death. Tear down the stones, tear down the walls. The floor of this temple has never been swept. The bones of rats and sacrifices lie knee-deep. The dark belly of this temple has never been lit. The prisoners there are sunk into a pit of silence and of shame.

Give the darkness its name. Open your mouth, now, and name it. Such an assault it cannot long survive. This is how we find our lives again, by speaking. This is how power comes back to our hands.

*

We will know again the names of all the gods. They will speak again for our hearing. Call upon them, now, for they are not far from any of us. We came from their hands in the beginning. We do the work of their hands now.

We must tell new stories. Those we have told until now are not sufficient. We will wander in the wilderness until we are made known to ourselves, in the hard light of the desert day. We will know again our own stories, which until now have been incomplete, half-forgotten, diluted with untruth. On the tide of our telling, empires will be washed away.

So tear it all down. Lay waste to the temple of darkness. Have the people lend their hands and their strength to the destruction, since they must build whatever will rise in its place. Teach them how to dance in the ashes and the ruin.

Teach them how to speak: teach them to say, *ours now are the hands that will build the altars. Ours the ears to hear the breathing of divine breath. Our eyes will watch for signs, the flight of birds, the paths of stars, the entrails of slain beasts.*

A new city and a new age. We the people are the prophets and the priests.

VI

Saba, why is your heart singing, even as the walls crumble and the earth breaks open, even as tears wet your cheeks and your friends are lost to you? Is there nothing that will extinguish it? Your heart is rising, it is responding to the music from the mountain. You have prayed for this. In your anger. In your hope. In your chains, in the belly of that boat. Rejoice, heart, for the gods have heard.

The square is emptying of the living as the people of the city flood towards the gate. At last after all her searching Saba has gathered the surviving priestesses under her arms, wept with them. Aemilia is not among them. On its outcrop high above them their temple has been swallowed in the cloud of ash. The heat is becoming unbearable. Nobody can remain to bury the dead.

Saba holds on to Liva and fierce Eris and little Amone, bent like an old woman with grief. They are moving against the crowd. She says to her priestesses, *flee, flee.* But they say, *no, our sister. We are with you.* The hands of the other girls clutch at her cloak. When the ground shakes again Saba takes them all beneath her arms as though this might shield them, as though this might save them.

They are making for the upper city, for their mother the Augur in the House of the Magistrates, when the wave comes. Saba looks down towards the ocean and sees a wall of darkness moving in from the horizon. The sound of screaming from the harbour. Boats snap like split kindling. What remains of the lower city is enveloped in the wave, a hiss of hot steam as fires are doused. The water washes as high as the colonnade, and then out again, wreckage spiralling in its wake.

"Sister, look, look!"

Fire and water, make us clean. Saba's eyes are drawn from the sea to the black column rising from the mountain, and then to the rooftops below. Everywhere else people are in motion, crawling like ants over the rubble. But around the Dark Temple, or what is left of it, a crowd is gathered. Even from this distance Saba can recognise the figure who is stood atop the heap of stones.

*

The temple has been torn down. Its stones are scattered and scorched. The crowd is wild-eyed, euphoric, the skin of their hands bloody with their blasphemous labour. They seem stunned at themselves. The bowels of the temple lie exposed, that most secret sanctuary now laid bare for every eye to see. It is nothing. No more fearful than a rubbish dump. There are bones underfoot, a smell of grease and burnt flesh. The slaves of the temple, the blind girls in their chains, crawl among the scattered stones. They keen and tremble. They do not know how to run.

"Your Prophetess says, dance!" cries the priestess Aemilia. Her hair hangs in white tangles like weeds, caked in blood from a wound on the side of her head. "Dance in the ruins of the Dark Temple!" She is laughing. Ash dances all about her. She tilts back her head in unearthly ecstasy to catch a falling flake upon her tongue.

As Saba and the other priestesses move in among the stones, the people begin to laugh too, stamping their feet, howling to the sky. Somebody begins to beat a rhythm on the bottom of a tin pan. The people sway and weave between the fires they have lit.

"*Aemilia!*" cries Saba, her throat thick with dust. "*Aemilia!*"

She fights her way through the dancers. Aemilia turns and looks down at her as though peering through a cloud of mist. Saba stretches out a hand. "Aemilia... you're bleeding..."

Atop the stones Aemilia does not move. She seems to be struggling to remember Saba's face. Saba scrambles up towards her, tries to seize at her arm. "What happened here? Where's Athraxus?"

"Gone. Gone."

"And where's..."

"We tore down the temple." Aemilia is breathing hard and fast. She is exhilarated, wrecked. Ash settles in her hair. "The gods spoke to us."

"You madwoman." Saba takes hold of her hands, and then, choked, kisses the bloodied palms. She wants to cling to Aemilia and clasp her close, but her sister seems rigid, entranced. "I thought you were dead."

"It's over now. The Augurs, we've done our part. They're going to raise up new prophets."

Saba brushes the tangled hair back from Aemilia's forehead, then holds her face between her hands. "You're hurt. Come down now, dear one. Come with me."

"The priests ran away. They're finished."

Saba folds Aemilia into her arms as the mountain overshadowing them spews out black smoke. She does not let go, and after a moment she feels the body in her embrace begin to loosen, to draw breath. Aemilia makes a noise like a surfacing swimmer, and buries her face in Saba's neck.

Joy pierces Saba through the heart. She tightens her hold as they sink together towards the ground. "Our mother," she says, in Aemilia's ear.

The sound of a thunderous cracking, as though the firmament is being split in two. She feels Aemilia's body shudder. A terrible whisper amid the noise.

"Oh Saba. They put out her eyes."

*

The Augur is sat on the far side of the rubble, where Aemilia left her, facing the mountain. She is wrapped in Aemilia's cloak. When the priestesses gather around her she lifts her head. Her face lights briefly at the sound of their voices. One of the younger girls is carrying a skin filled with water. Saba tears a strip of cloth from her cloak and dampens it, tries to dab at the dried blood around the Augur's wounds. The old woman shakes and whimpers with renewed pain. Signs wordlessly for her to stop.

She will not stand up again. Like a boulder she has rolled to the place where she will remain, take root, gather moss. She already seems at one with the surrounding stones. Her head is bowed, resting upon her chest. Saba crouches beside her. The Augur's breathing is laboured, growing ever more so as the ash-cloud thickens. The wounds where her eyes were leak yellow water.

The dancers have fled now, and the priestesses are beginning to wail in mourning for their mother. Saba turns to Aemilia, who is at her shoulder.

"Go. Take them to the gate. She shouldn't be alone, not until..."

Fierce tears cut tracks through the dirt on Aemilia's cheeks. "I'll stay with you!"

"No. Lead them out, 'Milia. I'll follow after." Their temple is finished: Aemilia under no obligation, now, to obey her. But her face tightens, and she nods. Saba understands her. *This last time, sister.*

She leans close, whispers something to the Augur which Saba does not hear. The priestesses cover their mouths with their hands, coughing, shoulders heaving with the effort of each breath. If they stay any longer they will suffocate.

"I'll follow after," says Saba again.

VII

There is lightning in the clouds.

He fell, on the way to the gate, in the rush of people fighting to get out of the city. One moment Junia at his arm, stick in his hand – the next, his feet snatched from under him. Eryx screaming over Felix's shoulder. Antonia trying to fight her way back to him, too small, not strong enough. Horses blocking his fallen form from view, sandals trampling, the ground shaking beneath. Even when the crowd has thinned he cannot rise. There is nothing to grasp hold of, so Antonus lies flat on his back, breathing in gasps. Ash lands in his open mouth.

For once he is aware of no pain. Fingers of lightning reach across the sky, and behind them is a terrible red glow. Everything smells of sulphur. He wonders if the gate is within crawling distance, and tries to roll himself over, grunting with the effort. There is ash in his lungs. Now all he can see is the ground, strewn with rubble and with the dropped belongings of the fled. A whole dead chicken, fallen from a split bag. Somebody's unfastened cloak. A broken plaster bust. The absurd thought comes that he is merely another of these objects, discarded on the road out of the city, hardly fit for use in the world beyond.

They will be crossing the plain now outside the city. He hopes that they are running, every last one of them, their carts rattling

293

behind them and their children borne in their arms. He hopes that Junia and his children are at the heart of that vast crowd, surrounded on all sides, unable to think of turning back for him. He hopes that Adelfa still has hold of her cat. He hopes that Mylo finds them, tonight perhaps, beside one of the hundred fires lit in the wilderness.

The stars will be out. The hare, the drowned man, the drawn sword. The weeping widow. He imagines Mylo and Junia embracing in the smoke and the dark. He hopes that Felix has taken enough herbs and spices in his pack. *Make them something sustaining, my dear friend. They have a long road ahead.*

A goat skitters through the wreckage, bleating plaintively, as the mountain hisses and rumbles. A handful of stragglers runs past, but though he cries out, they do not hear him. He heaves himself forward a little way. His leg catches on a rock and he is forced to stop, wincing.

After the mountain has spoken there comes an eerie quiet. Antonus wonders whether he is the last man alive in the city. It is only him now and the bodies of the fallen. The burned and the hanged and the drowned.

He closes his eyes. And the thought that comes to him is the face of Laonatus. Was he among the fleeing? Not likely. Laonatus does not like to get his feet too dusty. And besides, how would he choose what to take along? Which scrolls, which maps, which instruments and curios? Most importantly, which robes would he wear? No, the whole thing would seem a distasteful chore to the Emperor. Better perhaps to have a slave bring a lyre to his chamber and sing him songs until the end of the world abates. Perhaps he, Antonus, is not the last living soul left here after all.

As if in answer to this thought he hears again the sound of approaching footsteps, a solitary set this time, heavy and uneven. "Here!" calls Antonus, as loudly as he can. His mouth is bone-dry.

"Here, friend, help me!" He cannot twist himself around to get a better look. But before he knows it, there are hands at the neck of his robe, pulling him upright. His rescuer is strong but far too rough, and Antonus howls as his leg is twisted agonisingly to one side.

Breath in his face. He recognises Arthraxus by his smell. Like the mouth of a grave. Antonus smells the approach of death, and his heart falters. Above the mountain flames flare in the darkened sky. By their light the face of the High Priest is shown twisted and terrible.

"Take me with you. Athraxus," begs Antonus. "Please." The lips lift in a snarl. He is like a wolf in a trap, ready to draw blood before his end. Not even the dead have lost as much today as Athraxus. "Please! By the mercy of the gods!"

"There are no gods left."

The sky is raining black ash and pumice stone. Athraxus has a knife in his hand, a relic of his temple: the only possession he has seen fit to save from the city. Its blade is already stained with blood. Antonus tries a final plea. "Won't you at least tell me, where's Laonatus? Is he alive?"

"The Emperor is in his feasting-hall." Athraxus is panting. The tip of the knife stings Antonus between his ribs. His eyes are clouded, but for a moment they clear. "You. You are the thief who stole my son."

"Stole? Athraxus—"

"My only son, to shame me. A scheme to mock my authority before the city."

Saliva hangs from the corner of the High Priest's mouth. Astonished at this turn, Antonus hears himself let out a helpless laugh. "You don't understand. All I did was take pity on a lonely child."

"Then you die for that."

Antonus is still laughing in disbelief as the knife goes in, laughing at the superfluity of the savage act, which comes even as flames leap down the mountainside towards the city. He holds Athraxus by the neck to keep from falling. They are locked together in this strange embrace as the mountain expels its fire.

VIII

The Emperor is on his throne. Around him are those loyal among his counsellors and generals, his courtiers and philosophers, the men who have stayed steady amid the Augur's lies. A sea of silk and gold and painted eyes. There is no reason to be afraid.

They have music. The notes of pipes and lyres drown the screams and crashes outside. His favourite fool is gone, and this makes him melancholy. But look: here are those acrobats who so charmed him at his dedication feast. Here is the poet who will recite a handful of old favourites. The Emperor settles back in his seat and motions for the musicians to play on.

He is calm at last. He has been so worried, through so many wakeful nights. He can hardly now remember the cause. It ought not to be the way of things, that an Emperor should battle with troubled thoughts in the darkness. It seems to him now that the cause of his trouble was always the old woman, who preyed on his mind and goaded him into anxiety.

There has never been a city like this city. Its beauty has never been rivalled and its strength has never been matched. He knows that he has made every offering the gods required. His wives, who so often begged and pleaded against the sacrifice, never understood this. Now they are fled with the other cowards and the blasphemers, and his sons with them. Theirs will be eternal darkness.

He wishes Athraxus were here, at the hour of his triumph. The priest left to see to some business of his own. No matter:

tomorrow, they will talk together. They will walk in the palace gardens and speak of every matter of the city. Perhaps Athraxus will be able to advise him as to weightier things, too, the reading and observation and enquiries of thought which are the Emperor's pastimes. He likes to keep close those who are companions to his mind. Yes, Athraxus will be friend and brother to him now.

*

They told him, *the plot was for your brother to supplant you. We know this because the fool Hestia had her poison supplied by Rufus, son of Lennes, who is the lover of Myloxenes, who lives in the house of the Cripple.* The Emperor took to his rooms when he heard this news, emerging to watch Hestia hanged. Her death brought him satisfaction but did not dull the ache in his chest. *Antonus. Antonus.*

He had wanted to sleep, but no sleep would come. When the palace walls began to crumble he called for his nobles and sent word to the kitchens. His instructions were lengthy and detailed: he would have calves' feet broiled in wine, a favourite of his father's; oysters from the palace pond; a whole suckling pig, basted in honey; spiced lampreys; peacock; veal tongue; peppered eggs; platters of fruit, of course, and sugared ice. Though many of the palace slaves had already fled (cowards, blasphemers) the rest laboured through the night. As they brought up wine from the cellar the ground tilted this way and that, sending the barrels rolling in every direction, as though possessing a life of their own.

Now the Emperor and his nobles toast with full goblets and redden their lips with wine. When the food is brought out to them they clap their hands. Look, look at the delicacies which are served at the Emperor's table. Their cheeks are reddened with pleasure and with the heat of the fire. Between their talk they stuff their gaping mouths.

They are beginning on the ices when the roof caves in above them, crushed beneath descending tonnes of liquid rock.

IX

The gods once pulled up the walls of the world from out of chaos. There was only sea, but they brought forth land. There was endless blackness, but they pitched the tent of the sky and lit fires there to be the sun and stars. They pushed their thumbs into the ground to form valleys and mountains. They planted seeds and watched it all grow green.

They formed fish for the depths of the ocean and birds for the air. They formed livestock and running deer and wild wolves. These creatures flourished and multiplied. And then from dust and from blood and breath the gods made men.

*

Know this: whatever the gods make is theirs to unmake. The sea boils as though monsters are waking in the deep. A flood of fire and darkness covers the land. Rock flows in red rivers from the mountaintop. Rock creeps and weaves like a lizard, inflating as it goes, flattening trees and overflowing walls. Rock flows like honey, like water. The created substance of the world has come undone.

X

Saba sits beside the Augur on the ground. Rivers of flaming rock are flowing down the mountainside towards them. Flashes of lightning illuminate the column of black smoke above the mountain. The city in its final moments is beautiful, and the Augur is beautiful too, her unseeing face lifted to the light. Her cheeks are flushed as though with youthful excitement. At last she looks over the precipice into the realm she has sought all her life. Hot wind stirs her sparse hair.

"I'll tell you what I see," says Saba to the old woman, the pines and cedars bending and cracking, the sea rising up, the sky full of tumbling red cloud.

She reaches for the Augur's hand and feels fingers close blindly upon hers. *I have been your consolation, and you have been mine.*

They are already covered in the rain of ash and dust. Already grey with it, the two of them, side-by-side like two stone figures carved this way, fixed this way for millennia to come.

EPILOGUE

Beyond the city on the great bare plain they hear the thunder and watch the ash-cloud descend. The people run as though fire is at their heels, though it spills eastward, towards the sea. The wheels of their carts catch on sharp rocks. The old and the young are slow and must be harried onward. Sheep bleat and bulls toss their horns. There is no leader at the fore; the people flee only out of instinct, a flock which billows outward then collects again for safety's sake. The ground is still unsteady. Many of the wounded fall and are left behind.

Dawn barely brings light. By this time a loose party has gathered at the front of the column of those few who have left the city before. Soldiers, travelling tradesmen, foreigners and slaves. They argue amongst themselves and point to the western horizon. The blue ghost of a mountain range rises from out of the plain. There might be shelter there, and water. For those who will scale the heights, a chance to look out at the surrounding terrain.

The view of the mountains is deceptive. However many miles the people trudge, away from the ash-cloud and the smoke, they seem to get no closer. When nightfall comes they make camp in the wilderness. They have no shelters so spread their cloaks upon the dirt. The stars are hidden. Their fires sputter uncertainly. They huddle close and throw stones at the wild dogs which slink around the edges of the light.

All of those thousands, scattered across the plain like new constellations. Even their animals and their children are quiet,

301

now. The people douse their fires and lay their heads on the rocks that are their pillows. They are too numb to weep.

*

She will not see him again. Junia knows this, knew it even as her children ran to and fro in the crowd, calling for their father. Let their hope die in its own time. She felt the ground shake with the weight of the fire that fell from the mountain, and knew that he had not survived it. She lies now with her body curled around the sleeping shape of her son, her daughters at her back. She is dimly aware that Felix sits watch over them in the darkness, head resting in his hands.

On the second day the ash-cloud carries on the wind and engulfs them. It becomes impossible to see more than an arm's length ahead, and the little coalition at the fore calls a halt to the whole column. The people huddle with their friends and kin and whisper fearfully. The ash makes every face corpse-grey. They do not have water for washing.

Somehow in this grave stillness Rufus, who has been searching with this purpose all night, returns to Junia and Felix with his sister in tow. Mersia is ragged and filthy and furious, her anger having no fixed object, except perhaps the mountain itself. Her children are with her and the slave Haran but not her husband. To Junia's surprise Mersia has bread and fruit and jars of pickled fish in her bags, as well as silks and jewels. They eat well that night, feeling strength return to their tired bodies.

By day Junia and Felix walk shoulder-to-shoulder. He pulls the little cart and she carries their packs. At dusk on the fourth day he leaves them for a while and returns triumphant, clutching two dead quail by the feet. With what weapon he has hunted them Junia has no clue, but she is unspeakably grateful.

She thinks, I am not left desolate. Together they pluck and gut the birds, and she thinks, you and I, we are not so desolate as many who are here. The city when it stood was never ours.

Antonus is like a deep well in the ground which she must not fall into. As she knows him to be dead, she knows Mylo to be alive, out here somewhere among the survivors of the city. She awaits their encounter with an ache in her chest. *"Mama,"* whispers Antonia, after Eryx and Adelfa have fallen asleep. *"Where is Father? Where is Mylo?"* Junia presses her face into her daughter's hair. She is not yet ready to turn her thoughts towards what is ahead. To unwrap her arms from around her children and imagine what life might now be theirs.

The mountains are beginning to look at last as though they are within reach. The wind changes and the ash-cloud blows away towards the south. There is some talk among the people of going back to the city to see what remains, though none seem willing to lead the way. As the terrain becomes greener, others turn away from the column to find their own path, heading for towns and cities along the coast where distant kin might welcome them. It will be a dangerous road away from the protective ranks of the crowd; bandits, wild animals.

The people come to a lake amid the foothills and run towards it with hoarse cries of relief. All afternoon they make a crowded encampment on its banks, bathing and filling their flasks, their sheep and goats grazing amid the sparse greenery. Men wade deep, searching for fish. Junia walks a mile or so away from the camp to set snares for rabbits in the gorse bushes, and pauses there in the quiet, her senses sharp. A blackbird is singing. Little white anemones between the rocks are in bloom. Just a few days' journey from the rain of darkness and the consuming fire, nothing here knows that the world has ended. She finds her body bending and squats upon the ground like a woman in labour, wracked by violent sobs.

Who will we be? Where will we lay our heads? And there he is all of a sudden, as she walks back into the encampment, crouched beside a woman whom Junia supposes to be his mother, feeding her broth from a spoon. They must have been at the very tail end of the column, limping along with the old and the sick. Mylo's mother is pink-faced, wrapped in blankets. He catches sight of Junia and rises to his feet, eyes widening.

He reads her grief in her face. They embrace without saying a word. She holds on to him and allows herself to breathe deeply, loosening the pain in her chest. She draws back and takes his face in her hands, examining him for signs of injury. For the first time she allows the door into another life to open a little way. Because he is here, there will be the thought, in time, of another home.

Because he is here, and he and Antonia will one day be wed, and weddings are not matters for the wilderness. Where there are weddings there must be wine, and honey-cakes, and garlands of fresh flowers. If there has been a wedding there must then be a home, even if this is only a tent to be pitched for a season. Not too many years after a wedding there will be children and children must be fed. So there must be a place to plant crops or graze livestock, to fish or sell wares.

Press these seeds into the ground, Junia, and cover them with earth. First there will be a season of dying, when the wind will blow cold through your cloak. But Myloxenes is here, that miraculous boy to whom your husband gave his heart. And so you may hope.

*

He is glad to camp with them. When the time comes to move on from the side of the lake, he takes up much of the baggage that was in the cart and helps Laeyla aboard instead. Mylo walks beside Rufus, but does not tell him or any of the others that he saw Aemilia, two days outside the city. She had been with her priestesses, consumed by their care, the group of them straggling at the end of the column. Some of them had no sandals. When he ran to her she had looked at him as though at a stranger.

Saba? Saba? She had shaken her head. He had heard himself babbling, *isn't she with you? Didn't she run?* Aemilia's features crumpling. Shaking her head, again, again, even as he tried to take her by the hands. He wanted to howl but instead was struck mute. The priestess glanced back to the ruin of the city and then pulled away from him.

So he has looked for Saba and not found her. Swallowed down his grief which is new and bitter every day. Because he never told Rufus or Junia or the others what passed between himself and Saba, he cannot tell them now. Everything that happened in the city happened in another life. When he sleeps, she waits for him in his dreams.

It is enough, in any case, to grieve for Antonus. His tenderness towards the dead man's family is almost as raw as the grief itself. All day he carries little Eryx on his shoulders. He carves a set of stones to play chequers with Adelfa, and saves scraps for the cat. He finds himself sitting with Antonia as they watch the fire, walking by her side to search for water before nightfall comes. *Do you remember,* she says, trailing a stick through the undergrowth, *the way my father would call each of the chickens by name when he went out to feed them in the morning? Do you remember how he'd respond to a question, so slowly, as though everything depended on the answer?* And she seems taller to him now, and more sober, and fiercer than ever.

These are his comforts: that his duty will one day be his joy. That his friends are with him, and his mother also. He holds these comforts close, since the wind blows so cold here in the wilderness. At night now there is weeping in the camp. Supplies run short and the children are hungry. It is a terrible thing to be a people without a city.

Where will we now find our rest? This question is asked every day among the people. It is very well to flee from a disaster, but it is another thing to have a destination. The crowd has thinned, but still they number many thousands. They can hardly come to the gate of some city and knock there, plead, *will you let us live among you?* There are too many of them. If they are not to be a people of the wilderness they must divide and depart from one another.

In this way the memory of their former home will be lost. The banners and the colonnades, the frescoes in the Emperor's palace, the boats in the harbour, the library, the old man with his songbirds on the bathhouse steps. In years to come who will still tell stories of such things? There will be no-one left who says with certainty, there was once a city between the mountain and the sea.

By the light of a new day they climb the slopes towards the blue mountains. A temporary camp is made in the valley while the youthful and the strong continue as scouts to the first peak. They clamber breathless over rocks and call to one another of what they see. The light is pale and the air is thin. From the height of the peak the world lies spread before them.

The priestess Aemilia finds a sheltered place amid the boulders. Waits there for a time, wrapped in a shawl. Deep in her doubts. For the people, what future? For you, daughter? Will you now speak for your own life? Striking a flint she sets light to some small quantity of sage. Watches the rising of the smoke, the shapes it makes as it is carried on the wind.

*

Thirsty after the long climb Mylo and Felix sit together in the shade of a cedar-tree. All the world looks brown from up here, except for the sea which sparkles blue in the distance. The two of them perch on a rock like grandfathers with nowhere to be, and bat their hands at the flies.

"Don't shout about it," says the old slave, "but I still have something left from Antonus's garden." He takes out a cucumber wrapped in a cloth. They eat slowly, appreciatively, sucking each piece dry of its moisture. Around them men are arguing, exclaiming, pointing out rivers and little settlements. Signs of life.

For the first time since leaving it behind they have a view of their city. The mountain is still smoking, and beyond it what looks like a monstrous heap of ash. A thick black ooze covers the landscape, cracks still glowing fiery red.

"A man shouldn't look too long at such a sight," says Felix quietly.

Mylo shivers. There is something about the totality of that ruin. As though darkness from under the earth reared up and swallowed the city whole. His eyes sting. "There will be no returning, I suppose."

"I don't suppose so. No."

He turns to Felix. "You've lived through ruin before. Haven't you?"

"I've been telling you stories your whole life. All of this has happened before. This is the course of every city."

"And that's a comfort?"

Felix does not reply. Mylo feels something crumple in his chest. He covers his mouth with his hand. Far away the ruins of the city are smoking. "Felix," he whispers, "do you think it's possible, that somebody... that somebody, even in the final hours of that disaster, might have found a way..."

"Dear boy. He wouldn't want you to pain yourself by hoping for him."

"No, I know. But someone young, I mean. Someone fast, and clever, and brave. Someone favoured by the gods."

307

Felix looks away, the light of the morning sun brightening his eyes. He is smiling slightly.

*

So here is a new story. Let us picture her: she is alone on the plain outside the city, but she is unafraid. She has nothing in her hands and her heart is light. She has waited for this all her life.

Behind her the city lies buried. As she looks back at it over her shoulder she sees the moon going down over the ruins. It seems to her that she already sees the progress of greenery which sends out shoots through the blanket of ash, creepers taking possession of the columns. The years and the rain wear down the tops of the towers which crumble into the sea. And then the sea is receding as suns come and go across the sky, flowers blooming in the earth that the fire once scorched black. The earth breathes and sighs and settles, holding the ruins of the city and the bones of the dead there in the darkness. Waiting to be found one day, in centuries to come, woken from its sleep.

She turns back to her path and sets her face to the horizon. Shakes the dust from her feet.